The
Starving Saints

The
Starving
Saints

A Novel

CAITLIN STARLING

HARPER Voyager
An Imprint of HarperCollins*Publishers*

✠ ✠ ✠

HarperCollins books may be purchased for educational, business, or sales promotional use. For information, please email the Special Markets Department at SPsales@harpercollins.com.

FIRST EDITION

Designed by Patrick Barry

Library of Congress Cataloging-in-Publication Data has been applied for.

ISBN 978-0-06-341881-3

$PrintCode

For David,
you knew this one was special right from the start

The
Starving Saints

N FIFTEEN DAYS, there will be no food in Aymar Castle.

She has done the arithmetic forward and back. They have been down to strangled rations for weeks now, and there have been mistakes. Thefts. Impulsive, desperate gorgings. Even if every soul in Aymar Castle keeps to their allotted portion—and Phosyne does not think that is likely—every soul in Aymar Castle will run out of food in fifteen days.

And though Phosyne is one of the few outside the Priory who can work sums, everybody else is bound to realize this soon.

They are packed in one atop the other; a castle meant to hold at most three hundred for any length of time now shelters three times that. Every nook and cranny is full to bursting of terrified farmers and a pitiful handful of overwrought knights. They've been living in this unbearable press for almost six months now. It's a testament to Ser Leodegardis's leadership that they've lasted this long, that the siege outside their walls has not broken them, that plague has not crashed down heavy on their heads. But time is inexorable, as is the human stomach.

Relief has not come. They do not know if it will.

Fifteen days.

Phosyne counts out her own stores, meant to last her another three. She doesn't eat much, so they might last her a little longer, except she has two little mouths to feed that the quartermaster doesn't know about. Her companions slink along the walls and ceiling, all long, sleek bodies and dark scales, looking for a crevice to slip through. Ornuo stole a chicken a month and a half ago, but Phosyne has since stopped up her few windows. No chance of that happening again. (She does not know the depths of their hungers and desperations, nor even their real nature. She worries that they will begin to nibble on her toes as she sleeps.)

She tosses out a bit of ox hide she can't bring herself to stomach yet, and Pneio snaps it from the air, then retreats beneath her desk to gnaw at it. His brother darts after him. They tussle.

For herself, she takes nothing, instead locking the strips of tough dried meat and gristle back inside the heavy box she's reassigned for the purpose. Later, she'll eat later, after she's made some progress. Progress is the only reason she's been afforded the rations she has been, the only reason she is allowed to live alone despite the pack of bodies throughout the rest of the keep. Progress earns her the candles she burns down to nubs in the close darkness of her stoppered tower.

Progress has not been forthcoming, as of late.

Her stomach cramps in irritation as she mounts the steps up to the loft above her main floor. When she moved in, this room was one of the most unpleasant in the castle: damp, fetid, filled with moss and fungus thanks to the cooling influence of the rain cistern below the floor. Now it is dry and warm, yet another impossibility she tries to keep hidden. It's the sort of thing the Priory would take issue with. Eventually, somebody will notice, word will spread. Nothing lasts forever without changing.

Or breaking.

She settles on the sill of the one window that still lets in a shaft of light, through a dull pane of glass she's secured into a mass of wood and mud and pitch. Outside, it's early evening; the sun is setting atop the keep walls, and beyond them, she can just make out the line of contravallation, the wall their enemy has built to keep them in, should they ever risk leaving the castle's safety. That wall sits between them and fields, fields that have either been torched or taken over by the thousands of soldiers and laborers that surround them. In six months, they have built a thriving town. They squat on the land and take its bounty for their own.

Her last experiment was too bold, she can see that now. Transporting food that she cannot see, through so much stone and across so many bodies? Impossible. But she is getting desperate, just like the rest.

Her other attempts were more reasonable, yet no less doomed. She has failed to speed the germination of seeds for the castle gardens. She has caused only blight when she has attempted to divide and propagate summer squash and sprigs of herbs. Her only success so far has been a process by which fouled water can be made clean again; invaluable, necessary, but not enough.

Phosyne's head pounds, and she curls up into a tight little ball. Her fingers itch. Her whole body itches, really, with the lice and fleas that have grown rampant in the last few months, but her fingers itch for action. Desperate action. If she opens the little glass pane, and lets Ornuo and Pneio out—

They will not go out to foreign lands and bring her back a feast. They'll only stalk starving babes in the crib. Foul creatures, unknown to any bestiary she has consulted, affectionate but untrustworthy.

Something bangs against her door.

It happens again, and she must concede it's not an accidental collision. She is beginning to panic that they are here to take her food in punishment for her failures, or that somebody has seen Ornuo and Pneio, when she hears the rhythm to it. It's not somebody come to hurt her. It's somebody come to ask for help.

She leaves her window perch. She goes down the central spiral of stairs, into the main space of her workroom, with its astrolabes and charts and stuffed curiosities. She ducks below the corkindrill that is suspended from the floor of the loft and creeps toward the door, where the knocking is now accompanied by polite shouts. Her door is barred with a haphazard mix of materials and locks, and she is relieved to see it hold.

Phosyne goes to the series of pipes that feeds through a hole in the wall beside the door. The gap was originally designed to deter attackers, but she is no good with a spear or a sword, so instead, the pipes, with a little window at the end. Inside, a series of mirrors. She can see the whole hall from the safety of a little podium a good five feet to the left of the door.

The king stands just outside her rooms.

She shoves the glass-capped pipe away, then grabs it again, cursing, and peers once more. Yes, it is the king, still in velvet finery even after all these months, a little thinner in the cheeks but not by much. He stands at ease, flanked by guards but not wearing armor himself. He trusts the walls to defend him, and he has not come to kill her.

Silly; the king would never kill her. He has people for that.

So she measures the people: two soldiers, looking furtive and nervous but no more so than usual. Probably not here to kill her either, but the absence of Ser Leodegardis makes her uneasy. She only glancingly knows the king. Leodegardis, responsible for this castle in particular, is responsible for her as well. But a king cannot be denied; she needs to open the door, or else there will be even more trouble.

"Coming! Please wait!" she cries; the pipes should carry her words out of the room. And then she sets about unlocking locks and shifting planks of wood. Her serpents dive beneath rugs, hiding among her piles of texts and tools, more mess in the maelstrom of her room.

She pulls open the door, but doesn't move out of the way, bowing where she stands. "Your Majesty," she says to his fine leather shoes.

"My madwoman," he greets, and his rich voice is pinched thin. (*Not yours*, she thinks.) "Do you have another miracle for me?"

"Not yet," she says, wincing. It's been nearly a month since she solved Aymar's water problem. In any other circumstances, her work would have been enough to earn her safety and acclaim for years, if not a lifetime. Here, now, it is nowhere near enough.

She sees his shadow shift, feels him lean beyond her, peering into her workspace. "May I observe, Phosyne?"

No. No, he may not. But she can't refuse a king, and she's never been skilled at polite dances. So she grimaces and backs up a few steps, finally straightening, hands tugging at the roughspun fabric of her robes. She looks for all the world like a nun, except that where a nun keeps her skull fastidiously close-shaven, her head now shows nearly a year's worth of shaggy, dark growth, untended and unminded. Her clothing has been leeched of color in several places by experiments gone wrong. She is far thinner than even the privations of the siege demand.

He follows her in with a wave of his hand. His escort remains outside and closes the door after him.

Phosyne has never been alone with a king before. She can't tell if she's suffocating under the weight of his presence, or if she's shocked that he is, in fact, still just a man.

A very tired man, who goes to the stool by one of her workbenches and sits down heavily. He's picked the more familiar array of her tools to look at, vessels grudgingly loaned to her by the Priory mixed in with her own more-chipped and haphazard implements. He must notice the mess of it all, even in the gloom, but he seems to look right through it. His gaze doesn't stop on the half-sketched frescoes on her walls, attempts at understanding pigment and form. He does not speak.

Phosyne flinches anyway.

"No progress," she mutters, eyes averted. "I thought I had something, but—but not yet."

He sighs. "The quartermaster tells me—"

"Fifteen days," she accedes. "I know."

"You have done the impossible for me once," he says. "Surely it cannot be so hard to do it again?"

Unfortunately, she is fairly sure her first miracle was pure luck. She still doesn't know where the process came to her from. A dream? A half-remembered theorem from her days at the Priory? But if so, the Priory itself would have solved the problem long ago.

Though—

"Has Prioress Jacynde had any luck?" she asks. "Any progress at all? If I knew where their work stood, I might be able to build on it." And though the prioress would sneer with disgust if Phosyne came to her directly, even in this time of greatest need, she would not do the same to a *king*.

"No," the king says, dashing her hopes. "None at all. They claim it cannot be done. That matter cannot be transformed, that something cannot be brought forth from nothing."

Phosyne chews her chapped lip to keep herself from arguing. Or, worse yet, agreeing.

She's still not sure where she stands on the concept.

They are silent for several moments, long enough that Phosyne spies a shifting shadow beneath her other desk—Pneio nosing out from his hiding place. She moves, half a step, to shuffle him back out of sight.

And then he hides himself, and not because of her.

Because of shouting.

It's muffled by her stoppered windows, but it's getting louder, and the king raises his head with a haunted, hunted look. Phosyne stares back at him for just a moment, then turns and races up the steps to the loft, crouching to peer out her tiny plate of glass. She expects plumes of dust, jagged wreckage along the walls, the signs of an attack they have been half expecting for weeks now. But the walls are whole, and beyond them, the enemy all but lounges. No assault. No threat from without.

So Phosyne looks within.

A scrum, boiling quickly into a mob, crowds against the short walls that surround the kitchen garden down in the yard.

She sees a flash of metal. It is not a sword.

Not yet.

It's sun on armor, the blinding reflection of a knight's breastplate, and the only knights who go about in metal armor inside the walls are the king's knights. The woman (for the side of her head is shaved, and the remaining dark hair hangs in a braid to her shoulders) has climbed on top of the garden wall, and she bellows for order. The wind steals her words away, but not the sound, and Phosyne is transfixed.

The mob should be afraid. It's not.

It's angry.

Somebody throws a stone.

Shouts become screams as the knight draws her sword and descends into the mob.

From here, Phosyne cannot make out details, can't see if hands are severed, necks are cut, or if there are only threats and shoves and intimidation. She sees at least three people fall to the ground. She sees other guards wade in, along with the familiar fair head of Ser Leodegardis. Somebody is dragged, kicking and thrashing, out of the maelstrom. The soil grows dark.

The king is by her side, frowning at her makeshift shutters. "What is it?"

"A riot," Phosyne breathes, eyes wide. And then they grow wider because she sees now who was at the center of the mob, as he is pulled from the crowd, hurried back through the garden, into the kitchen. "They had the quartermaster. They were going to tear him to pieces."

The king snarls and thrusts Phosyne out of the way, crouching to peer through the glass. The screams are quieting now, and so the action must be too. Only a minute more passes before the king pulls away, running a hand through his hair, tugging his beard.

"Ser Voyne has it in hand," he grinds out. But he does not sound happy. Unrest will kill them far quicker than starvation.

Phosyne will have to revise her numbers.

"I need my miracle."

Her shaking worsens. "It can't be done. I can't promise that. Food—food is not as easy as water, and water was not easy either. We need something else, another solution. I'm sorry, I can't—"

"You can," he says. "You will." He regards her closely, then the room at large. It is a far cry from the orderly cleanliness of a Priory workshop. She's not surprised at his grimace.

She thinks that perhaps now he'll agree, that he won't believe she can do it either. For the wrong reasons, but if it gets her relief—

"I have clearly been too generous, allowing you to work unobserved, at your own pace. Your success with the water seems to have been born of luck, not labor. Leodegardis had me convinced of your unique point of view, of the necessity of thinking more flexibly, but I think now that Prioress Jacynde had the measure of you. You need a firm hand."

No.

No, she does not want anybody else in here. There have been miracles, yes, but disasters, too, and she cannot keep disasters hidden if—if—

"Ser Voyne will be your minder," the king says, and Phosyne looks back down at the tall, broad slab of a woman, all muscles and flashing blade, blazing eyes that Phosyne can feel, even from this height.

"A minder will not help me," she says, hunching over herself protectively.

"Ser Voyne will be your minder, and you will find me my miracle. You will feed my people. You will buy us more time. And you will remember that you are here on my sufferance."

2

ER VOYNE, STILL sweat-soaked and itching for a proper fight in the wake of the riot, listens as the rest of the king's fellows debate the merits of killing their own.

It will free up food for other mouths, the pragmatists say. (They do not say that flesh is flesh, but Voyne sees hunger in their eyes.) The fearful and the faithful say that law and order must be kept, no matter the cost; in the closed system the castle became six months ago, there is no room for chaos. But the loyalists, they cry that there must be as many hands to bear arms as possible when at last the relief comes, when the siege is broken, when they can take back the fields.

This is when Voyne moves forward in her seat, and the room quiets.

"I would agree, except that treasonous hands had best not hold swords," she says. That earns nods and soft murmurs of assent; after all, she is a war hero. She was at Carcabonne, has seen terrors. She should know.

Does know, she reminds herself, when her confidence falters under the weight of eyes on her, eyes that see her fine armor and her seat at the king's right hand. They're listening to her, but perhaps they shouldn't. Perhaps she's lost the taste; she hasn't seen any terrors lately.

The king doesn't let her get close.

She feels his eyes on her most of all, and so Voyne doesn't add the more damning rebuttal to the loyalists' argument that is burning a hole in her breast: that there has been no sign of a relief force, and the chance of them ever leaving these stone walls is so small she can no longer see it.

There will be no taking back the fields, with treasonous hands or not.

Today's riot is just the beginning.

They were not meant to be pinned down in Aymar, though of course it was constructed for just such a possibility, a strong spur castle on a ridge manned by Ser Leodegardis, his brothers, his household. A garrison of not inconsiderable strength, managed and provisioned well. But even Aymar has its limitations, and feeding so many refugees and knights and servants for six months was never going to be possible, and that is before they consider that the king is here in residence with them with his own sizable retinue. The farms beyond the walls have all been torched and squatted on and turned to shit, and the kitchen gardens, while extensive, have now been picked bare of even the autumn-bearing crops, far too soon. The stores have sustained them this far, but only due to a miscalculation, because they'd all hoped they would be gone long before now.

Relief was supposed to arrive a month ago.

Instead, they are stalemated. They have fended off rounds of attacks from Etrebia, but they have destroyed few of their rams and towers, only fought back hard enough to make them bide their time out of range. Etrebia's men are entrenched and willing to wait for resupply. Aymar's inhabitants are prepared only to starve.

Voyne sees all of this, and is furious, and wants nothing more than to ride out herself and force her way through to victory. Instead, she puts down riots and sits at her liege's side, spoiling for a fight she must not start.

"We need to send another messenger," Ser Leodegardis says from the king's other side, fists clenching on the table as he resists the urge to bury his head in his hands. He, too, feels the weight, but he bears it better. "Before our strength begins to fail. The descent—"

"Is too treacherous," his cousin, Ser Galleren, snaps. "Why do you think the relief has not come? Every single person we have sent down the cliffside has either died or been captured."

"One more messenger is one less mouth to feed," Denisot, the chamberlain, points out. "We lose nothing by trying. A faint chance of hope is better than none at all. And hope may stave off another riot."

King Cardimir closes his eyes, pinches at the bridge of his nose. "We must provision any messenger we send. We can't even give them a knife."

Prioress Jacynde does not flinch, not even when all heads turn to look at her. Her engineers are even now hard at work, trying to manufacture their salvation in exchange for nearly all the iron in Aymar. Every hinge, every pot, and even a fair number of weapons and plows, the dregs that would have been given to the refugees to arm them in an assault. All handed over, melted down, into a new tool that they hope will buy them more time.

Time to starve.

"We must consider," Jacynde says, "that our messengers *have* gotten through."

Silence.

Voyne clenches her jaw. Tight.

Cardimir does not move.

"Prioress," Leodegardis warns.

"If we refuse to consider all options, we will miss opportunities," Prioress Jacynde says. "If our messengers have gotten through, and if relief has not come, then we must assume we are too great a risk to rescue."

The silence cracks, explodes, and there is shouting. Cardimir and Leodegardis share a look, and Voyne considers getting to her feet, joining the fray, with words if not with fists. That need to act boils in her blood. It would feel so good.

It would do no good at all.

The prioress is right, after all. Even if no messenger has gotten through, word must have reached the capital city of Glocain and the princes by now. There should be a relief force.

There is not.

There may never be.

Their army has always been proud, and skilled, and well-funded. They have laid siege, and this is a perversion of the way of things.

They know every way that a siege may be won or lost, and yet they have not been able to break their attackers' lines.

Voyne has marched across every mile of the king's land. She has led armies to great victories and called for desperate retreats. She knows that, realistically, there may be no winning move here.

And she knows, too, that whatever happens here is not her responsibility. She does not wear the mantle of a strategist anymore, or even a leader. She is a knight of the king's guard. It was not her job to prevent this.

But that doesn't reduce the weight Voyne feels on her shoulders and chest every waking moment, as hunger gnaws at her belly—though not as harshly as it does for others. She is well fed. She sits at the king's right hand, or near enough, and that comes with perks.

The king reaches for his honeyed wine. He drinks deep. And then he passes the cup to Leodegardis, who sips, and to Voyne, who stares.

"Drink," he says. "One last comfort, before the horror."

And she takes the cup and drinks.

AFTER, WHEN THE room is quiet and all but empty, she and Ser Leodegardis sit alone in the chamber, heads bowed together over a map. The physical aches and pains of the day have at last made themselves known. She has shed her armor and sent her page away again, and rubs at her aching shoulder through her gambeson.

There is so much to be done, and so little. The chaos and physicality of the riot provided the smallest break in the unending stretch of days endured, and now she is having trouble fitting back into her shell.

"Send me out," she says, the first time either of them has spoken since the sun set.

"You know I can't do that," he says. "Least of all because I have no actual authority over you. His Majesty—"

"His Majesty has kept me useless on a leash for two years," she interrupts, not looking up from the map, the routes more or less accessible to a clever climber marked out along the topography of the cliff they sit on. She tries not to sound bitter, only practical. She knew (*knows*) how to be practical. "I am ornamental, not useful."

"You were useful today. You stopped the riot quickly, without death."

"But with much frustrated rage," she points out. "If I remain, that rage may turn to hatred. If you send me away, you may buy peace for another week."

"Are you a coward, then?"

Voyne flinches, recoils, finally looks up at him. "Excuse me?"

"You'd abandon your king."

"I would risk my life to save him."

"But you wouldn't die by his side."

Leodegardis holds her gaze in challenge. They are close in age, a difference of no more than three or four years. They have known each other since they were teenagers, perfecting their work with the blade, strengthening their bodies and learning tactics, learning languages. They were heroes together, for a time, planting their flags on conquered battlefields, making legends of themselves. Now they stare each other down across a vast gulf that grew when they weren't looking.

In another life, Voyne could have been him. Tasked with the protection of the border, entrusted with a castle, with a span of fields and towns, with the lives and well-being of hundreds, thousands. They both won their king's favor on the battlefield, earned his trust. They should be equals.

Instead, she is a glorified lapdog. Within besieged walls, she is worthless.

She turns away, finally, bowing her head. "I was mistaken," she said, throat thick. "But please—please promise me, that if my actions today threaten your control here, that you will remember my offer."

Leodegardis doesn't promise, but he also doesn't foreswear her. "Go rest," he says instead, offering a tired smile. "It's almost time for evening service, I think. Perhaps the Lady will grant you some comfort."

A good suggestion, and kindly meant. She clasps his shoulder, then leaves him to his nightmares. They all feel it, the weight of death bearing down on Aymar, but he *is* Aymar. They are all about to die, and she is about to fail, but he is about to crumble.

She winds her way through the keep and to the chapel tower. Jacynde's nuns are indeed hard at work, ready to guide the few parishioners who are here to observe the setting sun. Voyne, grateful, lets the familiar words and hymns wash over her. It isn't the balm it used to be, back when she was young and idealistic and fervent in her belief that the world could ever be orderly, could ever make sense, but it still soothes her jagged edges. It is a relief, to be reminded that she isn't alone, is never alone. The Constant Lady always has a hand upon the world.

After, she makes her way up uneven staircases long-since memorized, twists and turns as familiar as the halls she played in as a child. Few rushlights burn, but there is midsummer moonlight streaming through windows, more than enough to guide her by. She steps aside to let a serving girl pass, then takes the final turning to reach what used to be Leodegardis's room, now given over to Cardimir, to Voyne, to their servants. A little household for the king, shut up in a keep and starving quietly, only a little slower than all the rest.

She slips inside, and is surprised to see Cardimir waiting for her.

He sits by the hearth, where there's no fire thanks to how warm and sticky the air is. "Come," he says, voice pitched so as not to wake the servants who have already bedded down in their partitioned section of the room. Voyne goes to him, kneels before him in greeting. He touches her shoulder absently, the one that hurts, the one that is scarred from an arrow she took for him years ago.

"I had forgotten," he murmurs, "the power of your presence."

"You saw the riot?" she asks.

"Through the strangest vantage point," he says. "What do you know of Leodegardis's madwoman?"

"The heretic?" she asks. "Very little. Only that she arrived a few months before we did." It hadn't felt important to learn more, no matter Leodegardis's odd affection for the woman.

But the entrance to her tower room is not so far away. Voyne has seen the woman a few times, drawn and furtive and skulking. Her eyes drift in that direction.

"I have charged her with finding a way to restock the quartermaster's stores," he says. "Now that our other options have run out."

Voyne averts her eyes so that she does not stare in horrified disbelief.

"My liege?" Her mistrust colors her words more than she wants it to, but it's been a long day. A long day of nearly killing desperate, hungry people. She understands, of course. It's tempting, to hope for an impossible solution, but she had thought her king was better than that. More reasonable.

But it's also a distraction. They can't afford distractions.

"I have asked her for a miracle," Cardimir says.

Voyne bows her head, mastering herself with the reflex of long practice. "I see," she says. "And what provisions does she demand for such a thing?" If it's not much, if it's only a way to keep the woman occupied, perhaps it's not so bad.

There is so little to do but wait for death now.

"Very little," he says. Her shoulders ease. "But I want her to have more. I want her to have you."

Voyne's head jerks up. She stares, unable to stop herself. "Me."

"I need you to watch her," he adds. "Encourage her. She is . . . disorganized. I would see her supported. Given oversight."

"So that she can conjure food from nothing?" she asks, brow pinching. She searches her king's face for some scrap of sense. She finds it. He is confident and calm.

That's a hundred times worse than misguided faith.

"What is a second miracle after a first?" he asks with an indulgent smile that makes Voyne feel small, childlike. She hates that smile, and if she were not so worn down, so stunned, she would bristle at it. Instead, she just shakes her head, helpless, not understanding. He takes pity on her. "She is to be thanked for fixing our water issue last month," Cardimir says.

Voyne's world lurches into a new alignment. She frowns. "But the Priory—"

"Agreed to take responsibility, in case there was a problem. And in case it worked. Nobody would have trusted the cisterns if they knew a heretic was responsible for clearing them." He waves a hand. "She is . . . a wild thing. One of Jacynde's order, originally, but strayed. Jacynde hates her, but Leodegardis is adamant in his patronage, and she has paid her way admirably so far."

That gives her pause.

Because the water issue of last month was also an impossible solution to an impossible problem. Aymar's location was strong, but its strength had nearly been their undoing. Built on a rocky outcropping, the castle's only source of water was rain and a single well in the lower yard. The rains had stopped months ago as summer rolled in. The cisterns had begun to dry out, so they'd hauled water up and out, up and out, before the well could dry, too.

With that water, so desperately needed, had come pestilence. It had begun slowly, a few children beginning to vomit, low fevers rolling through, and in their meetings, they had steeled themselves for the sorts of illness that spread among the closely packed. They let the Priory step in, begin segregating the ill, treating them, fumigating the castle with cloying incense.

They had known, at least, that it couldn't be the water. Water pulled from stone was clean. The cisterns were capped and guarded. It couldn't be the water.

But it was.

As the well's level had dropped, the water had turned foul, and they had spread that foulness to every cistern. At first, the water had tasted normal, had looked clear, but eventually the buckets they hauled up stank of shit. There was no other water.

And then, a miracle. Jacynde's nuns had created a powder that, when mixed with the water, caused the water to heave and shudder and shine with wondrous colors, before finally turning clear and odorless again. Leodegardis had ordered his household to test the cleared water themselves, and when they did not sicken further, when they grew hale once more, the cisterns were cleared.

Voyne reflects that she has not actually tasted the cleared cistern water; there is another tank, one that captured rain before the summer began to dry, that lives just below the madwoman's room. It delivers clean water via a pipe into the kitchen, and Cardimir drinks from it exclusively, as does she.

Just in case.

Knowing now that it was not the Priory that solved their woes, but this strange, gaunt wraith of a woman who has somehow bewitched her king, Voyne is glad for their caution.

She scrubs at her face, sitting back on her heels. "What of the Priory's new invention?" she asks, testing out the new landscape beneath her. "Do we also have this madwoman to thank for taking our iron from us?"

Leaving us ill-armed to repel an attack? she does not add.

"That was Jacynde's order," the king assures, and the world slows its spin, settling into its new configuration with a groan. It's only a little off-kilter. "But I do not doubt she could have derived something similar. And until Etrebia strikes again, we have far more need of food. You know this, Ser Voyne."

"I do, my liege," she says, then takes a deep breath. Tries to be grateful for the clean water, hopeful for *miracles*. It does not sit well in her practical breast, which burns instead for a blade, a battle plan.

This will have to suffice.

"What will you have me do?" she asks.

"Her name is Phosyne," Cardimir tells her. "I want you to go to her tomorrow. Do not let her out of your sight, and do not let her remain idle. Reassure me that she is working as hard as she can. We have only enough time for results."

She wants to say no, wants instead to ask *him* to send her away as a messenger. It would be a better use of her skills. But if he is right, if this Phosyne has worked one miracle already and only needs help to produce another—

She can trade one escort for another. A king is not so different from a madwoman.

"Yes, my liege," she says.

3

YMAR CASTLE DOES not quiet with the setting of the sun. Soon, moans of hunger will echo through the halls, and even now people are restless. Few are sleeping, though there is little to do for those not on guard duty, no candles to see by. Some attend the evening Priory service. More sit and talk in window niches, looking nervously toward the walls, half expecting another night assault, though Etrebia has not moved in a fortnight. They argue about trivial things enlarged by the growling of their stomachs. They search for scraps of food in the empty dirt.

Treila prowls.

There is an art to catching rats. It is not one she learned in childhood, but she has become quite proficient. So proficient, in fact, that what little money changes hands inside these walls eventually makes its way to her, in exchange for one, three, five cooling bodies. Most think that rat-catching requires bait, and that would be the easiest option by far, but this is not the first time Treila has faced down starvation and survived it. She knows how to entice when she has nothing left to give.

Or, more accurately, how to spot something a rat would want and set a trap to waylay it.

They're clever creatures, rats; they avoided or even foiled her first attempts, years ago, when she was too desperate, too ashamed, to be clever herself. Now, though, she has snared another one with nothing more than some rags and a long-empty turnip box, and she dashes its skull against the floor before it squeals too loudly.

Half an hour later, Treila has found a buyer: a young mother with three small babes. It will hardly take the edge off, but it's something, and she has the coin to pay. For her, Treila presents a veneer of calm concern; this is not a mercenary transaction but a kindness. A mother is more likely to pay for kindness.

Treila does not feel guilt as she slinks back into the keep, down the stairs, into the small space that was once her workroom, where she stitched gloves and other fine leathers for Leodegardis's knights. Others used it too, of course, when there was handwork to be done; but even then it was cramped and poorly lit, and now it's half-clogged with items made useless by their communal captivity. Empty barrels, empty flour sacks, empty looms.

She keeps her cache of food and money here, tucked safe so nobody can take it away from her again. She has been careful, careful for so many years, and since the gates closed six months ago, she has never once hoped for knights to ride in dragging salvation behind. She knows better than to depend on them. They were too late to save a single inhabitant of Carcabonne, even as they fought bitterly for the rocks that formed its walls.

Even before rations were cut, then cut again, she has not eaten her full allotment; she has hoarded and protected, and now her cache is fat and rich.

She has food for at least another month.

Which gives her one more month to save herself, so long as the castle continues to stand. So long as desperate people do not attack from within.

How changed her life has become, how different she is from the coddled, moneyed girl she was raised as. No fine slippers for her, no delicate undergarments. Her soft skin is long-since toughened, her nose grown blind to both the stench of refuse and the gentle waft of perfume.

It's past midnight when she returns to her assigned sleeping area, if the murmurations of the nuns in the east tower are anything to go by (and they are—the nuns keep fastidious time even with their steadily dwindling supply of timekeeping candles). Though no one person enforces the division of space, nobody would think to go elsewhere. There are rules, spoken and unspoken, of how each role within Aymar relates to another.

Treila obeys them, even as she can see the fiction of them. Nothing physical makes the king more worthy of a cooler, more private sleeping space—just the loyalty of his guard, his servants, and his subjects. And that, she must concede, is power.

The castle has finally settled, all sleeping save for the night guard and two boys, playing at dice by the window. She joins them, ready to act younger than she is as she always does with them. It puts them more at ease, to think of her as a big sister and not another adult. They are freer with their chatter.

The room reeks of bodies, all of Ser Leodegardis's household staff tucked in together to make room elsewhere for the farmers and the court. They keep their voices to whispers as they play.

"And then Ser Voyne," breathes Simmonet, sandy-haired, son of one of the washerwomen, "came out of the keep, her armor shining, and she drew her sword."

Treila's shoulders tense. She catches her lip between her teeth, the better to keep herself from an angry snarl.

"No," Edouart counters, "no, she couldn't have. Da says nobody died, and if a knight draws her sword, she's going to use it."

"But I *saw* her."

They both look to Treila as she reaches out for the dice. They pass them to her, hoping she'll break their stalemate.

She rolls. It's good. She wins the pot of pebbles, then redistributes half across the varied flags of the floor that count as specific wagers. "Depends on the knight, doesn't it?" she whispers, instead of what she wants to say: *This knight will spill as much blood as she pleases.*

"And Ser Voyne is so *good*," Simmonet proclaims, because he knows nothing, loud enough that the sleepers nearby stir, send glares their way. He flinches, bows his head, continues in a whisper. "Kind and strong—I saw her spar with Ser Leodegardis last week. And she led the charge at Carcabonne."

Treila says nothing, casts her dice again, and this time loses. She passes them to Edouart, just as she pushes aside the fleeting memory of Ser Voyne as she'd been just *after* Carcabonne, bruised and bloodied, recovering in Treila's father's home. To remember would be foolish.

Edouart looks uncomfortable as he takes the dice. But he doesn't speak until he's lost, too, and they've gone around a full turn. "Nobody died," he says at last, "but there were a lot of people hurt."

"Then they shouldn't have stolen food," Simmonet returns.

"Genovefe had her nose cracked. I don't think she stole anything."

"But she was there at the riot, right? So . . ."

He is having trouble reconciling reality with his beliefs. She feels a pang of sympathy, followed swiftly by annoyance that he hasn't crashed headlong into exactly this dilemma twenty times by now. He's nearly ten. He should know better. He's not going to see eleven.

But he is trying to be strong and good, the way they describe boys in stories. She can see Edouart is wary of him, and she's glad; it's the strong and good ones who cause the most damage, in her experience.

"I overheard," Simmonet says, trying to change the subject to something that will earn him more approval and engagement, "that they're going to pick another messenger soon."

Treila perks up at that for just a moment, then recoils. She would make a fine messenger, but she knows the previous messengers have all sat with King Cardimir and his council before leaving, and Treila cannot risk that.

No, better to stay until a safer opportunity presents itself, or she is desperate enough to take the risk. After all, it's been five years, and Treila is good at playing a role; maybe Ser Voyne won't recognize her.

She hasn't recognized her so far.

"Treila, would you go? Over the wall?" Simmonet asks, scooting closer.

"No, she wouldn't," Edouart says, and Treila keeps her expression steady, not scowling like she wants to. What does he know of her? Nothing. Nobody here knows anything of her. "They all die," he adds.

She cants her head, surprised.

Simmonet stares. "What do you mean, die?" he asks.

"If they don't die," Edouart replies, shrugging and casting his dice again, "then why don't they come back? With help?"

Treila nods, slowly, thoughtful. He's right, of course; she figured out long ago the messengers were likely dying, but she hasn't heard anybody else voice as much until now. Morale is truly cracking, then. The riot was just the beginning.

Things are going to get ugly. She can feel it.

"It's a hard climb," she says. "But I would risk it," she lies.

Edouart looks at her dubiously, like she's mad. Simmonet stares in awe. "Yeah," he says. "Me too."

They play for maybe twenty minutes more, silent now except for the clatter of dice, and then she leaves them, so that they may finally admit their exhaustion, yawn, crawl off to bed.

She lies on her little pallet and tries to sleep, but sleep refuses to come. It's a learned frustration; she should know how to sleep like the dead when she has the chance, and instead she knows how to survive on so little sleep she might as well be dead. She lies there, motionless, for as long as she can stand it, but her mind is on fire, thinking of the riot, of the dwindling number of rats, of the dead messengers. The buzzing of summer insects fills the room and adds to the chorus in her mind.

And then she's up and headed down the stairs again, toward her workroom, because maybe, maybe, the coolness down there and the thick stone will shield her enough, the touch of her fingers to her heap of food will still her soul.

It doesn't, of course. She's still restless. She hides the cache once more and paces around the tight confines of the not-really-a-room, wondering how long before somebody finds her, raises questions she doesn't want to answer.

Nobody appears. Treila eventually sits, legs tired from a long day, scrubbing at her face. It's not a space amenable to sleep; there's not much floorspace and the windows are nearly level with the ground outside, there only for air and a bit of light. But its depth makes it quiet and cool. Perhaps she should move down here, stack up a barrel or two to make a nook, except that would draw attention to her cache. Not safe in the long run.

But a little rest . . .

She lies down on the floor, curled up tightly to fit between a loom and a heap of sacking.

Her brain settles, just a little, just enough, and soon she's drifting on the edge of sleep. Flickers of forest greenery and split wood spark across her mind, eager for her to dream again, dream of home and shame and rage.

She smells water.

And that is new, and unexpected, and it rouses her just a little. She opens her eyes. She rises onto her hands and knees. She inhales, deeply.

She smells growing things, algae and muck, and damp stone, and shit: the same smells that rise from the well. But the well is several hundred yards away, through so much stone. This is something else. Something different.

Treila presses her palm to one of the flagstones. It does not budge. But the one up and to the left of it does, just a little, rocking in its seat, and the one beyond that a little more. Treila crawls to where the floor meets the wall, shoving detritus out of the way, and wedges her fingertips into the mortar, wiggling just a little.

It crumbles. The smell thickens.

By dawn, when she's forced to retreat and dress for work, she's made a little hole, barely large enough for even a small rat to squeeze through.

But it is something.

It is salvation.

4

HOSYNE PRODS THE rotted lump of flesh with one slender piece of bone, fashioned into a polished pick. It is a small bit of flesh, received in her rations three weeks ago. She thinks it was ox, at one point. Now it is furred and pitted, oozing a riot of colors that combine into an unpleasant, sticky black. It took a lot to get it there, as it came to her well-dried, not fresh at all, in a controlled rot instead of an active one like this. But now it is exactly where she wants it, the pinnacle of putrescence. Perhaps putrescence can be reversed into fecundity; the two concepts are clearly related, after all.

She prods the flesh again. The lump shudders, the puddle of ichor around it spreading another hairsbreadth. Its stench lessens, just a little, and so Phosyne leans in, spears another little grass seed with the tip of the bone, gently nudges it into place. Encouragement. A pattern for it to follow. New life, please; the rapid growth of seedlings, woven now into flesh.

The sun is on the verge of setting, just the slightest shift in light through her tiny window. She sees the furred layer of tissue move a little, ripple slightly, and then the pits of it are winking, opening, closing, respiring, and she holds her breath. She squints. Rubs her eyes.

Mutters a string of syllables that might be curses, and then rocks back on her heels.

The sun is setting, and the shifting of the light is throwing shadows. The damn thing didn't shudder at all; it's only her exhausted eyes, her desperation to satisfy the king. She sets down her tools and stands.

So that's a day wasted. She makes a note on parchment she may eventually need to boil and chew herself, though it has five layers of ink on it now, written in different colors and different directions. She can still read all five layers, if she gets enough light on it, but she thinks another iteration will finally obscure the first.

Perhaps she will take to writing in the bound volume of copied alchemical texts and treatises she has accumulated over the last several years. But it pains her to imagine writing over even the parts she has memorized: *true and shining, certain and most true, that high and low are in truth the same in each direction . . .*

There has been no sign of Ser Voyne, at least, and Phosyne has entertained the hope that, perhaps, the king has thought better of his threat. Perhaps the knight is more needed elsewhere. Exhausted, she stretches out on the threadbare rug on the floor, presses one ear to it so she can hear the liquid sloshing of the cistern below, as somebody in the kitchens opens the valve and siphons off a little of the remaining rain.

Pneio and Ornuo hop down from where they were perched on top of her corkindrill and circle her, then come close enough for her to stroke. They nip at her fingertips. She thinks it is meant playfully. She thinks that if they wanted to eat her, they wouldn't hesitate to sever a finger.

Strange creatures, these boys, like nothing she has ever seen or read about. They appeared in her chambers some four months ago, and she couldn't explain to save her life where they came from. She had been working on something—she can't remember what, not anymore, and thinks it must not have been that important—and there had been cracking, a whiff of sulfur on the air, and though she has no hearth or chimney in her rooms, she had felt a blazing heat.

Then one of her bookshelves had crashed to the floor, and Ornuo had looked up at her from on top of it, blinking wide, golden eyes.

She'd been terrified for weeks, of course. Terrified she had caused some great calamity. Terrified she would be found out and hanged. But the two slippery creatures had stuck close to her and caused no more mischief than a pair of tomcats. Aside from the incident with the chicken, they had brought her, ultimately, only comfort.

"Have you decided to tell me what you are?" she asks Ornuo as he flops onto his side and presses his spine into her ribs. He wears a coy expression, and bares his teeth just a little so that she might rub one finger along them. The sound he makes is like embers crackling. "Or at least listen to reason? Provide me with a miracle?"

He lashes her with his tail, instead, then nips at her chin, and she clambers to her feet, too exhausted to serve as a chew toy.

She's up only a few seconds ahead of the rapping on her chamber door. Her odd companions dart into their hiding spots.

Of course; it would be too much to ask, to be forgotten once more. She groans and drags filthy hands down her face, wondering if she can pretend not to have heard. Perhaps to already be asleep. The moment she opens that door, she will be lost. No more time to work unobserved, and she is no closer to her miracle. The king will not be happy, because the king doesn't understand that if she is *watched*, if she is *intruded upon*, then the chances of her succeeding are even lower.

Still, perhaps Ser Voyne won't stay long. Even a knight must sleep.

She hides the rotted flesh away beneath a dark earthenware bowl and hopes the lingering odor can be mistaken for something else, scrubs her hands on her apron, and goes to the door. She doesn't bother peering out through her mirrors, because the knock comes again, and it is firm and considered. Phosyne hears no movement of metal over metal, however.

She opens the door.

Her minder looks down at her, from her vantage nearly a foot above Phosyne. She's a broad woman, tall and made of muscle, and even in the absence of her steel plate, she is remarkably, intimidatingly solid. Phosyne instinctively takes a step back. Her eyes drop to the floor, one hand scratching at her scalp. "Well," she says, instead of any introduction, "come in."

She turns and goes upstairs, hoping the knight will not follow.

She's not so lucky. Ser Voyne keeps her distance, but follows, and when Phosyne hazards a glance back, disdain is written clear across her handsome brow. She's likely looking at the mess of the workshop, what little is visible in the gloom, and judging it lacking.

"His Majesty would have me summon food," Phosyne says, as lightly as she can, as if that will set the knight at ease, "but I have not cracked that mystery yet, I'm afraid. How familiar are you with miracles?"

Ser Voyne does not respond. Phosyne reaches the box made of roughhewn wood that stores her few belongings. She pulls her apron off and shoves it, still dirty, into the pile. She tries to remember how to be polite. How to give the illusion of subservience even if she has no intention to actually obey.

"Because," Phosyne continues, "miracles tend to happen when least observed, in my experience. So if you have some handwork, perhaps, or some—some polishing to do, that will serve you best, I think." Her voice is a little shrill, but she can't quite master it. "Serve *us* best."

Voyne is at the window now, reaching out to trail fingers over the jumble of items that block it up. Testing. Evaluating. Phosyne tries not to scowl.

"Do not think to give me orders."

"I suppose I'm not His Majesty, no," Phosyne concedes.

Ser Voyne doesn't like that. She pulls away from the window and levels a cool stare at Phosyne, then retreats back down to the main floor. "Tell me what you have so far. What you've spent your day do-ing." She has years of experience with that commanding tone she's using, enough that it makes the skin along Phosyne's spine prickle and tugs her toward the stairs.

When she realizes she's coming to heel, she digs in and crosses her arms, refusing to go any farther. She feels, acutely, how close her bones are to the surface of her skin. How much more fragile she is than the other woman.

"What I have is nothing," Phosyne says. "So far. I've just wrapped up one experiment, and it will take time to devise the next one."

"Tell me what you have ruled out."

Phosyne doesn't want to; it will be a waste of time. Voyne won't be able to understand, will likely respond with anger when she can't. This is why Phosyne left the Priory—or, if not why (that was a matter of faith), then an early sign that it would one day come to pass. She appreciates how thorough her sisters can be, with their careful measurements, their detailed logs, their mechanical precision, but she is thorough in a different mode, one that defies easy ordering. Concepts are linked, though not always in ways words can capture. They resonate in a way undeniable to her senses, as real as anything she has seen or heard or smelled, but impossible to truly describe. And the proof of her process is this: it all works in the end.

So she says nothing. Ser Leodegardis may trust her enough to keep her housed and fed, but Ser Voyne—

"What is this?"

Oh, no. She has found the dish. Phosyne's heart sinks as she lifts it up, then wrinkles her nose at the stench.

"Research," Phosyne says, before she can think to lie and say, *Oh, I must have forgotten it.* Better, in hindsight, to be thought flighty than willfully . . . whatever she is.

Ser Voyne stares at the rotted meat. "No. No, this is madness," she says. "This is not research. I have seen the nuns at their calculations. This is *filth*. How, exactly, did you expect food to appear? Out of nothing?"

"Not *nothing*," Phosyne scoffs, coming closer, gesticulating with one clenching hand. "Out of a pattern. The meat is in a process, now, yes? It is rotting. There is growth in it, and decay, both. I thought that if I introduced seeds, that might steer the process more firmly toward growth—"

"Of mold."

"—of *meat*, to allow regeneration, production of pure, clean flesh. The flesh itself was once fed by the grass plants that produced the seeds. I need only remind it of what it once was. Or that was the idea, anyway. It hasn't worked. I'll try something else."

Ser Voyne stares another moment at the lump, then covers it again, drags one gloved hand over her face. Then her eyes, blazing with indignation, rise to Phosyne. "And this is logic, to you? This is work worth pursuing?"

Phosyne wrings the fabric of her robe, hands clenching as she looks between the workstation and the knight. Her face is hot with shame and affront. "It wasn't my first theory," she concedes. "Or even the tenth. But the rest, though they seemed more plausible, didn't bear fruit. So to speak."

Ser Voyne laughs, as if startled, and spins on her heel. She goes to the door. Relief kindles in Phosyne's chest as the taller woman throws the door open, makes to leave.

But then she turns back and pulls it shut behind her again, leaning against it with arms crossed over her broad chest. "Please tell me," Ser Voyne says, choosing each word with care, "that you're making fun of me. That you hope your mockery drives me away."

"I wouldn't do that."

"This is your work. Truly."

Phosyne straightens her spine. "Yes."

"Then you are a fool and a waste of resources."

That sends a bolt of panic through her. She does not eat much, but she must still eat; she must have her space; she has done all that she can. "I cleaned the water, didn't I?" Phosyne protests.

"And how did you do that?"

"What?"

"Your method. Your research. Prioress Jacynde is still trying to untangle it, figure out how to produce your powder. She says you will give her no recipe."

"She couldn't make it, even with one."

"*How?*" Ser Voyne demands.

"I . . ." Her words fail her. She looks around. A demonstration, she could do a demonstration. But even as she thinks it, she can see how Ser Voyne will look at her, as she mixes powdered rat feces in with dried sweet william to form the substrate of the clarifier. And that does not even encompass the whispering of poetry.

"You are wasting my time. *Our* time," Ser Voyne spits.

"Then allow me to waste it in private, and not to trouble you any longer," Phosyne snaps. She advances a step, as if to push Ser Voyne out the doorway.

It is the wrong move. The older woman's eyes flare with haughty anger. "You have been spoiled. I don't know how you bewitched Ser Leodegardis, why he keeps you like a pet dove, but if you cannot work—"

"I work very well, thank you! I have only been asked to do the impossible!"

"—Then I will *put* you to work."

They are close, closer than Phosyne meant for them to get, and her rib cage aches with how fast she is breathing, how hard her blood pulses in her veins. She hasn't been so close to another person in months, maybe years, and for all her fury, she can't look away from Ser Voyne's blazing eyes. They're a piercing shade of hazel, and they are so bright with answering fervor. Her whole imposing presence, her coiled, barely leashed threat, is making it impossible to think.

And then the ground shifts below their feet.

Behind her, furniture judders against the wall, the floor. Phosyne pulls away, spins on her heel, but Voyne is already ahead of her, pounding back up the stairs, over to the window. She pushes hard against the glass pane, then starts disassembling everything blocking it up.

"Stop!" Phosyne shouts.

"I need to see what's happening," Voyne bites out, and there comes another crash, this one more sound than movement. The shadows that are Pneio and Ornuo dart out from their hiding places, find new ones. Scraps of wood hit the floor, roll down the stairs, and Phosyne presses herself against the wall as she climbs.

By the time she gets there, Voyne has stopped halfway in her dismantling. There's no need to keep going; the shouting from below, the torchlight on the walls, the continued slam of stone against stone gives them the answer:

They are under attack.

5

HERE IS A sick poetry in it; Voyne has spent the whole day making excuses to avoid coming to the madwoman's tower, pretending that she was in some way helping the defense of Aymar, and instead attack comes when she is trapped here in this foul, fetid little chamber. It's as if Etrebia has sensed her dereliction (which is not fair; to be here is duty too, even if it's farcical).

She watches through the gaps in Phosyne's window as another blow strikes the outer wall. The sun is low enough now that she cannot see the extent of the damage, but the steady rhythm of the assault tells her what she needs to know. This is not some light sortie. They mean to attempt the castle once more.

She can't stay here.

"Take shelter," she says, pulling away from the window and longing for her armor. She seizes Phosyne by the elbow, steers her toward the stairs. The witch resists, of course, but Voyne is stronger and more certain. "Down in the lowest levels, with the others."

"But—my research—" she stammers out, and Voyne wants to shake her.

Your research is a joke, she nearly says, but this is an emergency, and she is built for action. "Your research will not matter if you are dead," she says instead as they reach the main floor of Phosyne's squalid chamber. "Take some of it with you, if you must, but you are going to take shelter, and you are going to wait for my return."

And the woman has the gall to try to climb back up to the window.

Now she shifts her hold to Phosyne's collar and drags her to the door. "You may not be able to see sense," Voyne hisses, "but I will be cursed if I let you throw away your life."

She ignores Phosyne's wailing all the way down the stairs. Past her liege's room, down to the lowest level, where terrified farmers and servants are already massing. She shoves Phosyne into the press of them. "Keep her here," she demands of an older woman whom she thinks she recognizes from the kitchen. And then she allows herself to stop caring, and plunges out into the yard.

A flash of golden hair passes by her, half-recognized and then gone in another breath; some serving girl, guiding younger boys to safety, making her job easier.

This is no Carcabonne. Not the battle for its release, nor the state she found its halls in. But the fear, the fear is so thick in the air she can taste it. Little blood slicks the stones of Aymar, but more will soon, if salvation does not come.

And yet she is exhilarated all the same. The waiting is over. The moment is here.

Constant Lady preserve her, but she should have her armor now. Even if it weighed her down as she did exactly what she is doing now, herding the frightened innocent to some semblance of shelter. At least she would feel more herself. At least people would know to look to her for aid.

But perhaps there is a mercy here—without her armor, she is much less obviously the queller of the riot. Some, no doubt, fear her less when she doesn't gleam. And despite her silent pleas, there is no Constant Lady here. There are only people, as there always have been. Voyne must be their intercessor.

The yard empties, the panic contained within the walls farthest from the bombardment. She doesn't think all of the enemy's strikes are hitting home; if they are, the walls are holding well. Adrenaline filters out the collisions that are too soft, too distant, not relevant. That still leaves several that hit, one after the other, that crumble an interior wall into the lower bailey yard. Smaller chunks skitter and fly to all corners. It's not safe to remain.

This is the held breath before the battle. She would do well to make use of it.

She retreats inside, into the press of too much humanity. Too many people. Even with some in the great hall, even with others in various towers, there are too many people to move. She can't spot any of the attendants who are trained to help the knights into their plate; she will have to arm herself. She can barely reach the stairs and climb up. If any of these walls collapse, there will be mass death.

Perhaps that is why she finds her king two floors up, in their converted quarters, where she goes to fetch her armor.

That does not explain why he stands by the window.

She feels unaccountably naked as she goes to his side, but he doesn't seem to care. He's staring out.

"My liege," she says. "We must get you somewhere safer."

He doesn't look at her. He is twisting pinches of his beard into tight spirals. "This is the moment, Voyne," he says instead. "Look. See what our iron has bought. This may be the moment of our ransom."

The Priory.

She crouches down so that she can see out the window below him. Out on the far wall, she can see figures working in shadows, the torches doused to deny Etrebia anything to aim by as night falls in earnest. But she can make out enough: the nuns help work small catapults, each of the Priory's design. They are not, strictly speaking, a martial order, but their designs have always been of use in times of war. Those catapults, she knows, are stronger than their footprint should rightly allow, and around their rotational bases they bear notations she has heard called *radians* that allow precise calibration, aiming, destruction. From here, she can barely see the nuns at work, their shorn heads wrapped in black fabric hastily donned to hide them in the night. They observe the turning of the machines. They load them with what Voyne can only hope is their precious new invention.

(*But what if,* her treacherous mind whispers, *that invention is as laughable as Phosyne's rotting meat?*)

The catapults release in a wave; she hears the *thunk* as they reach full extension. She can't see what they lob out across the field, but when they strike the siege engines below, they explode into bright, multicolored flames that spread fast. She can see the silhouettes of the Etrebians trying to douse the flames, but they're pushed back.

And then the siege engines begin to buckle.

"Bless the Constant Lady," Voyne whispers, awestruck.

They stay there, the two of them, her king standing above her, Voyne crouched by his feet. They watch. One by one, every siege engine that is struck by these Priory-derived incendiaries collapses in the flames. And the nuns are skilled at their mathematics, their geometries; they know how to aim, and aim fast.

When the catapults fall silent, Voyne can only assume they have exhausted their munitions. But it has been enough.

The attack on the gates never comes.

Etrebia has been held at bay.

Tears burn Voyne's eyes. There is no hope of any repeat performance, not without resupply, but the Priory has done the impossible. She can only hope that it breaks Etrebia's will; that in the morning, they will look out and see the camp pulling up stakes, retreating. It is what she would do. Take the measure of their new opponent, and return again when ready.

"My gambles do work," her king says, and she feels his hand settle briefly on her scalp. Her skin crawls, but she remains still, because—he is right. He must be right. "Now I only wait on you to help me feed our people."

She tries not to let her relief sour. Hopefully, there will be no need of his madwoman; they can discuss in the morning.

For now, there is work to be done; in the absence of impacts and the crumbling of stone, she can hear crying. Screaming. People have been hurt, likely killed. "I must go to them," she says. She half expects him to stop her, but he lets her go. Down the stairs once more, down to the yard, where Ser Leodegardis, Ser Galleren, all the rest, have gone to work.

Torches flare to life. There is far more destruction than she anticipated. Stone to move, wounded to tend to. But it could have been far worse, and her brain feels cooler as she gets to work. As she does what she was built to do.

They have been working side by side, hand in hand, for no more than fifteen minutes when Voyne sees movement to her left. Quick and fleeting, nothing more than a shadow. Something falling, she thinks, though it makes no noise.

"Is that Phosyne?" Leodegardis says, startled. Voyne's blood runs cold, then hot, and she shakes her head.

"Leave her." She doesn't have time to care about the madwoman, her bizarre "logic" or her heresy.

"She's running," somebody else says, and Voyne snarls and pulls away from their efforts. Damn the witch's chaotic nature. And damn Cardimir for making Phosyne her problem. There, in the gloom, a flash of movement, Phosyne's pale face; her dark robes blend into the shadows. She *is* running, and full tilt.

"Go," Leodegardis murmurs, and she can't tell if he's entreating her to rush after his pet, or warning her that she must follow Cardimir's orders, even when they are foolish.

The sooner she has penned Phosyne up, the sooner she can attend to those who *really* need her.

She follows.

Phosyne's path is erratic, twisting, turning. It's as if she's chasing something unseen. But no matter her desperation, she is unpracticed and underfed, and Voyne gains on her. Just as they reach the smithy yard, Voyne falls upon her, tackling her into the dirt.

"Let go!" the witch cries, but Voyne only holds her more tightly. She is bird-boned beneath her, barely anything of substance, but she thrashes and squirms like a trapped stoat.

"Stop resisting," Ser Voyne commands, and it only makes Phosyne thrash harder. Fabric tears, loud and organic and more human than crashing stone.

Something collides with the charcoal pile three feet away, sending black chunks skittering in a hundred directions in the dark. Voyne hunkers down reflexively, head ducked, so that her face is pressed to Phosyne's throat. But there are no more missiles coming over the wall; she can't make sense of the collision, given half a second to think. Below her, Phosyne goes limp, gasping for breath. Voyne can feel her pulse against her cheek, fluttering wildly.

And then she smells smoke.

She sits bolt upright and there is a glowing spot, orange and hot, spreading quickly.

"Oh, no," Phosyne whispers beneath her, half a whine.

Voyne has a hand on her briefly, on her throat as if to keep her from wriggling free. But that isn't the best use of her. "*Fuck*," she snarls, and then she's up and off Phosyne, snatching up a shovel from where it leans nearby, stabbing it into the pile.

Fire in the fuel could mean conflagration. That there's no more iron to smelt barely registers as she scatters the pile, searching for the ember.

Behind her, Phosyne wails, drags herself to the pile for some un-knowable mad reason. Voyne is digging too slowly. The bright burn-ing spot is the size of a fist, fingers about to unfurl. The heat is already almost too much to bear, and it will only grow. "Get back!" Voyne barks, even as Phosyne plunges her hands in.

She will burn. There's nothing for it—she has no shovel, she will burn.

And she does. Phosyne falls back, clutching air. Her hands are burned, no doubt, curled in as the flesh melts and bubbles. It looks for all the world like she is clutching something, some slip of shadow, but that can only be Voyne's overtaxed mind.

It doesn't matter. Voyne shouts, instead, for help. In an instant, Leodegardis is there, Galleren is there, they are scattering the ignited coals, kicking dirt over them, stamping them out. That leaves Voyne to return to Phosyne's side, furious.

Phosyne is on her belly in the dirt now, hugging herself. But she is not sobbing with pain.

She lifts her head, and looks back at Voyne, defiant.

Snarling, Voyne seizes her by the hair, barely long enough to al-low rapacious fingers.

Phosyne gasps in pain and her arms twitch. Again, it looks as if she holds something slender, like a cat, but there is nothing there. Another bit of her madness? Does she hallucinate, too? Or does the witch force the world out of its order? Spit in the Constant Lady's face?

"Do not *dare* move, witch," Voyne growls into her ear.

Phosyne tries to hunch, but Voyne drags her head back; she has no patience left to let Phosyne hide.

"I apologize," the madwoman gasps out. "I didn't mean—let me go. I'll go back to my tower, the attack is over, I will go back to my work, please—"

And Voyne is out of patience. She slams Phosyne into the wall of the smithy.

"Give me one reason why I should not have you brought before my liege for nearly finishing Etrebia's work," she says, low and even into Phosyne's ear. There is none. None at all. Whether Etrebia retreats or remains in the morning, Voyne will be quit of this insipid creature.

But the glow of the explosions of Etrebia's siegecraft, the glow of the charcoal pile, is in Phosyne's eyes as she says, triumphant, "I have an idea for a miracle."

6

HEN THE NEXT dawn comes, Etrebia remains encamped. Treila is not surprised; she has long given up on miracles. But Edouart and Simmonet are distraught. They thought their salvation was at hand, when the news spread through the tight press of bodies sheltering in the lowest levels of the keep. She'd taken them with her into her workroom, if only so she could get there quickly, make sure her little gap was safe, and had been kept up far past the end of the bombardment by their hopeful whispers.

They cry themselves to sleep each night, now that they know the truth: victory does not mean freedom, and they are all still starving.

Some died in the bombardment. There is a funeral the next day. Treila thinks that, had nobody died at all, the inhabitants at Aymar might have collapsed in on themselves in frustrated, aimless agony. Death provides catharsis. She knows that her own father's murder gave her focus, in those first terrible days.

It was all she could see, as she scraped for bits of food, for makeshift shelter: her father on his knees before King Cardimir, her father's neck bared to Ser Voyne's sword. Her father's young wife, so recently wed, begging for mercy. Her father silent, all his obscenities exhausted before dawn, when he was dragged from his bed, from his chambers, from his title. No longer Lord de Batrolin: the king had declared him a traitor, and so her entire world had been redefined.

A lesser girl would have been consumed by that grief, even as she and her stepmother and her father's closest servants were thrust from the house, marched off the land and into the wilderness. A softer girl would have wept, and refused to walk, and starved.

Instead, she had taken the rage beneath the grief and used it to keep her going. The servants left, or died; her stepmother disappeared the first night, likely running back to the king to beg mercy once more. And Treila had kept walking.

Aymar has nowhere to go, though. Soon the grief will pass and the stomachs of its wretched inhabitants will remind them how much they can still suffer. It will ease things, briefly, having fewer mouths to feed, though not nearly long enough. Each mouth already eats so little.

Treila does not attend the funeral. She does not attend many services. Half of it is her squandered faith, trampled in the dirt five years ago and never quite recovered; the Constant Lady does not have a saint for her, no Vengeful Saint or Starving Saint. No true balm for her bitterness, no witness and no succor.

The other half is pragmatic wariness. She knows how quickly a single beesting can multiply to hundreds, courtesy of her desperate attempt to tear a wild hive open to get at the honey within. They stung her bleeding and raw. She had nearly died.

She'd fled, then collapsed in a meadow where, swollen and still starving, she'd dreamed of the Constant Lady. Each stinger throbbed where it rested in her skin, and the too-perfect Lady had looked down at her, face immobile. No benediction, no offer of salvation— just silent judgment, and then She'd turned and walked away.

It seems absurd to think that a visitation, when a fevered nightmare makes far more sense. But Treila still has never shaken that feeling of abandonment, of censure. And if the Priory knew about that day, about how she'd violated the hive, how she'd been struck down in retribution, she imagines they wouldn't want her, either.

So she takes their blessing on her tongue each day as they walk the castle walls, because everybody else does it, because she does not want to stand out. But otherwise, she keeps her distance.

Instead, Treila works to clear the hole at the base of the wall. She pulls out loose stones one by one and discards them among the rubble. It takes far longer than the length of the funeral, of course. She works for days. Sometimes, it is busy enough that she is lost in the bustle, but people are moving around less and less. They are hunkering down, preparing for their own individual sieges. And by a day after the bombardment, word has gotten out; the scanty rations the quartermaster gives out each morning will still be gone in two weeks. Maybe less.

Boots are being hoarded for boiling.

And people are watching. Prying. The guards are now looking inward instead of outward half the time, afraid of another riot, and every idle farmer watches for any alteration in patterns of behavior. Everything is a potential threat, even Treila with her rocks.

So when she can't excuse her ramblings in the day, she does it at night. The rats help, or their scant corpses; she makes a deal with the quartermaster, finally, to bring him what she catches. She can see anger in his eyes when she offers, because he could have used her months ago, but he has no room to fight her.

She brings a rat; she deposits a stone. She isn't paid a single coin, but she is earning her escape, so she accepts it.

A messenger *is* selected; Simmonet was right that they were looking, and Treila was right that they are realists, and will not believe in quick salvation, no matter the staying of Etrebia's weapons. This time, they send the houndsmaster. And then, once he is over the wall, they slaughter his ten remaining dogs.

They're careful about it, of course. They learned the hard way, when they slaughtered the first batch, nearly two thirds of the pack, months ago to reduce the number of mouths to feed. Half the residents of the castle would be horrified if they knew, and the other half would rush the great hall, screaming for the meat. So Ser Leodegardis does it himself, because nobody would expect it of him, and he does it quickly. Treila watches from her perch in the rafters of the kennel as he takes each one behind a half-height wall, crouches, and slits its throat.

It is a subtle thing, the way the kennel quiets. It takes a few days for the word to spread, and by then everybody's gotten a small portion of fresh meat, so they're already satiated, already complicit.

The horses are next, Treila figures. The hay is all but gone, the grass in the yard long turned to mud by all the refugees. With no food, the horses will starve soon enough, so better to take the meat; but without horses, they will have no way to sortie with the enemy.

They will be giving up their last chances of anything but a close fight. They will be choosing to outlast on their stomachs alone.

But it's not really a choice.

Hopefully she'll be long gone by then.

On the fourth day, she's cleared a gap that might be big enough to fit through, and she sits back on her heels, staring at the hole. Her fingers ache. Her heart pounds. She thinks of sliding through that gap, down and out, and then—

And then what?

She came to Aymar for a reason, and if she leaves, she will be abandoning it.

She sits down fully now, and closes her eyes, and pictures Ser Voyne. Not holding the blade to her father's throat, but before that. Before, when she was recovering from her injuries from the glorious rescue of Carcabonne, when she was a guest in Treila's father's house. Beautiful, strong, brave Ser Voyne, intimidating and beloved by all who have so much as heard her name.

Treila's mouth tastes sour at the thought.

She remembers Ser Voyne's hands on her hips, nudging her into a cleaner stance, a practice sword heavy in Treila's hands as she struggled to focus. The memory's five years gone, but not faded in the slightest. Treila can still feel Ser Voyne's breath ghosting on the back of her neck, and how her own body responded with awkward, coltish want and alertness. She remembers sparring, and though Voyne had nearly a decade of age and experience on her, half a foot and a substantial weight in muscle, Treila had won more than once. She'd been clever, and fast, and she'd laughed and fancied herself in love, even though her teacher hadn't noticed, not once, and—

And then King Cardimir had arrived, jealous and volatile, and everything had gone wrong. The memory stops its shadow play there, because Treila has lived long enough in that pit, and has woven the anger of it into herself. She doesn't need to remember her father's head on the executioner's block, Ser Voyne's gleaming sword poised above his neck. She doesn't need to picture the woods the rest of her household had fled into. She doesn't need to remember starving.

She's going to do enough of that again, and soon.

So while she'd love to stay and find some way, despite the constant watchers, despite the constant strain, to get Ser Voyne alone, to ask her, *Don't you know me?*, to wrap her calloused fingers—no longer those of a young, promising lady—around that bitch's throat . . .

She leans down. Scents the air. Opens her eyes and looks at the hole, and then sets about shucking her clothing.

Treila moves quickly, keenly aware that there is no door anymore separating her little workroom from the rest of the keep; all wood was requisitioned and inventoried for firewood back near the beginning, when the nights were still chilly. It sits in one of the smaller towers along the east wall of the castle, for when they need it, no thought given to how much privacy is now at a premium.

She sheds her boots, her cap, her kirtle, her smock, her smalls. She strips down to nothing but her skin, then sets about bundling all that fabric into something small and compact. She can't afford the bulk of it lying on her body, if she's going to fit into that hole. She hesitates a moment before tying it closed with some of the last of her waxed thread, thinking she should add her stores, her trinkets, but this is not likely to lead to an escape immediately. Surely there will be more excavations.

And if she can get out, she can get back in. Probably.

She ties up the bundle and comes to crouch by the gap, considering the best way in. Feet first, and she can keep an eye on this room as she goes, but if it is anything less than straight, she will be at a disadvantage. So headfirst it is, despite the flutter of panic in her breast at going straight down into the unknown. She gets onto her belly. She pushes the bundle in ahead of her, then squirms in after it.

She manages to fit her shoulders through the gap, and for once their stringy narrowness is a help to her as she wriggles and twists, inching a little farther into what she can now tell is not just a hole, but a tunnel. There is no other side, not within immediate reach, but she feels that same fetid, damp air moving on her skin.

She has never been so glad to smell shit.

Her heart quickens, and she claws her way forward, past gritty gravel and onto solid stone. Her hips catch on the entry for just a moment, and then she is through, entirely encased in cold stone against her naked flesh. She pushes the bundle of her clothing another half foot ahead of her, then follows it, moving slowly, her knees scraping hard against the rock. It's not smoothed for human passage; this is not a manmade tunnel. It has not been dug out, only found.

Another foot. Another. She is going down, just slightly, but she can feel the blood beginning to pool in her head. She starts to worry. Should she have gone in feet first? Should she have brought a light, somehow? She can see nothing now, her body blocking what little light comes from the cellar behind her, and she feels her way forward instead. Inch over inch, but the stone is closing in again, and her breaths are coming faster.

A rope. She should have brought rope. Foolish, foolish girl, to plunge ahead without any thought but rescue. Her breathing fills the narrow gap, and her spine presses into the rock above her. Her head thickens, her hands scrabble beneath her, she feels like she is falling.

She feels like she is dying.

She can't even curl in on herself, and when she tries to retreat, her toes can't find the way. It's not as simple as crawling backward, it's not like trying to climb out from beneath a table in a game of hide-and-seek, and the feeling of space behind her, when she finds it again, is terrifying. She can't see where she is going, forward or back. It's a single passageway, she has passed no turnings, and yet she is suddenly so confused. She is lost. She is closed in on all sides and simultaneously alone in an empty, vast space.

But no, no, that's not true, and she knows better. She *knows* better. She has come through so much, and a little rocky grave is not for her, and when she stretches out one leg, she feels the incline that leads her back up and she knows she can push herself along that way. When she stretches out one arm, she finds a drop-off, but not too steep, not so steep she needs a rope.

She is in a tube. She can retreat. She can advance.

She advances.

Still, she should have brought a light, she thinks, as she passes from the tight confines of the tube into something more open, just a little, where she could gather herself and turn around, go back headfirst. She clutches the bundle of her clothing to her chest and tries to think, one hand on the path home so she will not lose it. A cooling breeze comes from below and to her left, soothes her sweaty brow, helps her put her thoughts in order. If she goes back, there's a chance she can steal a rushlight, but she will have no way to keep it lit through that tunnel, and no way to light it once she's through. The same for any candle, though there's a better chance, if she can find a glass housing to put around it. The nuns will have them, surely, though obtaining one from them seems unlikely. The madwoman's tower, then? Perhaps, but now the king's lapdog is her guard dog instead. So no, there is no chance of light.

Which leaves one decision only: Can she go forward in blackness—or will she die if she tries?

There is no guarantee that this path leads to safety, or anywhere at all. But the breeze from below is not only in her imagination. The wind must come from somewhere, mustn't it? If she goes slowly, if she leaves things behind her to mark her path, if she turns back the *moment* there is a branch she may not remember later—she can do this. She can go by touch and instinct. She is a slippery thing of darkness, an eel in girl's skin, and she is brave.

She loses all sense of time as she inches forward, down, following the whisper of air. She leaves one stocking first, then the other. Her cap. Her girdle. Her smalls. She does not find any branch, not really, a few gullies that are only the depth of her shin and then stop. Her stomach grumbles, and she thinks of food, and how she should go back, loot her cache, bring food with her, but what if she edges forward just another step, squirms through one more gap barely large enough for her to pass, what if she—

And then there is light.

Light.

Not daylight, but the thin blue of night, and she has not been down here so long at all. She makes out the shadows of footholds, descending a steeper section. She sees a ledge below her, drops her dress down first, then follows after.

She emerges into a room.

No; not a room. This was not made by human hands. It's a grotto, an underground stream, and she can hear the water moving now.

The stink of human waste presses in, and she knows she has found the water that feeds the well. She falls to her knees and wants to kiss it, but knows better.

But the light . . .

The light is coming from the water, and Treila frowns down at it. Then she lifts her head and peers around, and sees no crack in the stone, no way for moonlight to filter in. Confused, she rocks back on her heels. She looks up and down the length of the faintly glowing water, looking for how it enters, how it exits.

She can't see anything. The water passes through gaps that are so minuscule she cannot see them, or perhaps just appears, as if by magic, through the stone. The water will not help her.

She makes herself stand, makes herself feel for the breeze.

There.

It's coming from a narrow fissure in the wall, barely visible. It might have been impossible to find without the thin light that throws strange shadows on every surface. Treila approaches, slides her fingers into it, but it's not wide enough even to admit her hand. She presses her face to it, nose and lips in the gap, and breathes, breathes the first fresh air she's had in months (because she does not count the air in the lower yard, not even if she can see birds flying above, because she cannot *leave*).

But she can't leave through here, either.

"Are you lost?" the crack breathes against her lips.

ER VOYNE TAKES to sleeping in Phosyne's room, across the doorway. She is a better block than the old haphazard stacks of detritus. Nobody comes in, and nobody goes out.

Phosyne is very glad that only Pneio left her tower during the bombardment, and that she was able to haul him back without Voyne's notice. Her best guess is that Voyne cannot see the little beasts, for she doesn't comment on them, even when Phosyne can clearly see them dart between hiding places. They are like smoke.

Their heat, though, Voyne has noticed.

"Unblock the windows," Voyne demands, the morning after the bombardment.

"No," Phosyne says, scrambling for some excuse.

"A person needs sunlight," Voyne says. "Fresh air. A break from this infernal heat and stench."

Phosyne positions herself in front of one of the filled windows. "My work requires the dark."

Voyne's jaw tenses, twitches. It's clear that she is itching for relief. For a summons to do as she did the night before. She is not a creature made for standing guard, but for action. Phosyne hates to see her caged like this, but it isn't up to her.

She waits to see if Voyne will lunge.

Bruises make a patchwork of Phosyne's dry, pale skin, lurid and uneven as if her body lacks the resources to soothe them. She feels the ache of each one, even as her mind is afire.

"Leave the windows," she says. "Let me work."

"Your miracle," Voyne says.

Her miracle. Her *idea* for a miracle. "I have much to study," she says, desires coming into conjunction for a blissful, hopeful moment. "I need supplies. Can you get them for me?"

She requisitions twenty candles from the priory. It earns her an hour's privacy, and Voyne an hour's walk.

The next several days are spent deep in work. Her hands dance over the candles, purest beeswax, clarified and cast by exacting standard. She burns them down, one after the other, observing, reading, waiting for the next shift in perspective, the next advancement.

She revisits the memory of the bombardment. The press of bodies, her terror over Pneio and Ornuo free to wander, the moans of the frightened and injured. The flash of racing shadow that she'd had no choice but to chase, out into the strange silence after the attack. She'd smelled such odors that night, bodily and chemical, some traces of what the Priory had done.

Salvation, Voyne called it, when Phosyne had enough presence of mind to finally ask. *Intercession*. The Priory, too, plays with fire these days.

There are innumerable references to fire in the books she has accumulated since she first became aware of the unseen world that seems to lie parallel to their own, within reach for those who know to search for it. They are worn and dirty things missing pages, passed from hand to hand, filled with knowledge that in her Priory days she would have mocked as fanciful, imaginative forays into nothingness. She knows better now. Some of the books, she thinks, are correct, though she can't figure out how to utilize the knowledge within; other parts are wrong, but there is some truth to them anyway.

Her teachers in the Priory would have demanded proof. Measurement, replicable observation, a mechanism of action. And she understands the appeal. Certainty feels safe. But certainty is also limiting. Certainty did not purify Aymar's water.

These texts, with their parables, their fictions, their outlandish claims, are exactly the opposite. And yet with enough study, she has teased meaning from them. She has made tangible changes to the world. She must keep searching for the next revelation.

One of her fragments, a haphazard translation of the works of somebody only credited as "the weeping philosopher"—a man who died of œdema some six hundred years ago at least—describes the soul as measured in fire and water. Water, for soft growing things; fire, for the element that transcends death. An everliving flame, not constant, but shifting in its parts, some extinguishing, some springing up to life. There is something there, she thinks.

Occasionally, Voyne is called away. It's never for long, but Ser Leodegardis occasionally sends for her. The king, less often. Phosyne can see how each summons tears at her. She longs to leave, but hates to abandon her post.

Three days after the attack, Voyne is summoned just after dawn. As the door closes, Phosyne feels herself unwind. It is too much, living under such strict and hateful observation, even when Voyne stays out of her way and allows inspiration to guide her. Alone, Phosyne leans against her worktable and closes her eyes.

Her stomach cramps and ripples. Terrible, wretched body; it reminds her, ceaselessly, that to pursue the fire distracts her from the ultimate goal of food.

They are the same, she tells her belly. *Hush.*

Before she can feed herself some scrap, there comes a soft knock. Not the king's. Not Voyne's. She holds still, hoping that silence will make whoever it is disappear. She doesn't want to look through her spyglass.

Sweat beads upon her brow. *Is it getting hotter in here?*

The door opens. There is nothing to stop anybody's entrance with Voyne gone. Suddenly afraid, Phosyne looks up.

Prioress Jacynde stands there, in her raiment. It's the simpler version, for working days, but it is still cleaner and more elaborate than anything Phosyne has worn recently. How she can still starch her robes, Phosyne could not say.

"Phosyne," Jacynde greets. The name sits ill on her lips; she still remembers calling her Sefridis, and Sefridis was obedient and useful and small. Well, Phosyne is still small, she supposes. That part hasn't changed.

"Your Radiance," Phosyne replies.

"I have come to see for myself what you do with my candles," Jacynde says, looking doubtfully at Phosyne's workspace. Her nose wrinkles with distaste. "You certainly do take liberties with your independence."

No clean cell for Phosyne anymore, no orderly calculations, no tending to the beehives. Not even a steady pattern of wake and sleep; Phosyne often works through the night, especially when Voyne sleeps.

She must have some visceral memory of cloistered life, and yet it evades her. How did it feel, cleaning her cell? How did it feel, to be in community, to have faith? Surely any sane person would remember. Surely that cannot evaporate so fast.

But it has. All that is left are the things worn so deep into her that they are no longer feelings, but axioms. There are physical habits tied to this woman's voice, habits that are hard to resist: ways of standing, ways of holding or avoiding gaze. Shame bubbles out of a pocket Phosyne thought long-since sealed. Her scalp itches.

She wishes, briefly, that her heart would itch instead. She thinks it was easier, when she believed.

One of the Priory candles is lit. The flame shifts in the gloom. Barely enough to work by; a waste, no doubt, to Jacynde's eyes, because she cannot see what Phosyne has been observing.

"Congratulations," Phosyne says, when the silence stretches, "on your success against Etrebia."

Jacynde just looks exhausted.

"What were they?" Phosyne presses, though she doesn't expect a true answer.

It's not how she is supposed to talk to Jacynde. Training dictates deference. Even as a laywoman, she should be appeasing, receptive, attentive in a submissive form. Instead, she can't help but speak to Jacynde as if they are equals.

The storm upon Jacynde's brow shows just how poorly that is received. But Phosyne cannot stop herself.

At some point, she lost the knack.

She will never taste honey again, Phosyne remembers with a pang.

This woman has forbidden it, and even if she had not—Phosyne cannot imagine allowing herself to be welcome in service. Not after their break.

"Green vitriol," Jacynde says, finally, "partially. Some of the sisters have been working with Theophrane in his smithy, which I understand you nearly destroyed."

Phosyne flushes and looks away. "It might have been a spark from your incendiaries," she says, because there's no way to explain Pneio. No way she could have caused a spark without him.

"There was no spark until they struck home on the enemy line," Jacynde replies, dryly. "But then, I don't expect you to understand the complexities."

"No? And yet I cleaned the water," she says, before she can hold her tongue.

Acknowledge me, she thinks. *See what I can do. Be intrigued. Desire what I can teach you.*

Jacynde never will.

The water is clean, and Jacynde cannot explain it. Their bellies are empty, and Jacynde cannot fill them. Phosyne understands, then: Jacynde is insulted. Deeply insulted, that Phosyne can do what she cannot. The water, she had hope of solving one day. But the food—

If Phosyne can do it, it will not be by the Priory's alchemy, and it will be, incontrovertibly, magic.

It will be the domain of the Constant Lady, if they are lucky. If they are not, it will be something beyond.

How can Phosyne ever claim to be capable of such a thing?

I'm not, she wants to say. *The king has decreed, but that can't make it so.* And yet even as she cringes away from the theological consequences of what she hopes to achieve, she also longs for it. Hears a siren call, a whispering that there are rules to this world the Priory has no ability to understand, rules that nonetheless exist.

How can the Priory reject understanding the world, just because it follows an unfamiliar order?

Jacynde, unimpressed, says only, "You should make the most of what I've given you. There will be no more."

And then she is gone.

In the silence after Jacynde's departure, Phosyne gazes at the dancing candle flame. It consumes the wax beneath it, transforms it into heat, the way the body transforms food into warmth and movement. But stomachs cannot break down the wax. She will burn her meager stores away soon.

A nun of the Priory can summon fire from iron. There, then gone, explosive and powerful, eating away at a new kind of food. What did it consume? Perhaps that is the new angle she has needed, the next conjunction of ideas.

Jacynde's visit has been illuminating. She has been looking at the problem all wrong. The king has asked for food from nothing; she will find a way to let them have nothing as food.

It will begin with the candle.

Her mind is full of hymns. The fire cants as she hums them nearly below hearing. Green vitriol, sulfuric acid, the gasses that caught fire and melted Etrebia's engines of war. She will wait no more for fire from the heavens.

She needs more supplies.

8

IVE DAYS AFTER the bombardment, Ser Leodegardis
sends a runner to fetch Ser Voyne for Priory service. It's
a welcome relief. Phosyne has now added stinking sulfur to the mix of her experiments. Voyne's only balm is
that Phosyne is running low on candles, and when they are gone—
well, then the Priory will give her no more, her work will stop by
force, and Voyne can argue to be freed.

Another day or two. She need only bear the madwoman's inanities
a little longer. Then she will be able to sit at the table once more with
the other knights and strategize: How will they take what the Lady
has granted them, and win salvation?

Phosyne still has not told her how the fire started, the night of
the bombardment. She will not tell her anything about her miraculous idea. Voyne leaves her to her dark and stinking cell, guards now
posted at her door to stop her from any other smoldering wanders.
Outside, she breathes the clean and slightly cooler air, and tries not
to look at the scars from Etrebia's assault. There are so few strong
hands to put things back to rights.

The chapel hums with the buzzing of bees, the air filled with
winged bodies passing in and out of the arched, open windows. They,
unlike everybody else in this castle, can pass freely over the walls and
to more fruitful fields, but they always return home, filling the rows
of painted boxes with honey. It's a shame that they work too slowly
to feed the hundreds of mouths that wait.

Voyne kneels beside her liege on pillows once cased in velvet,
now only sacks of worn-away nap. She is so grateful to be near him,

and far away from Phosyne, that when Prioress Jacynde leads voices raised in hymns, hers is strongest among them.

And what a balm those hymns are: predictable words, in predictable order, about how to find solace in an unpredictable world. The hymns preach order, measurement, constancy, when all the world is yet lost in chaos. To build a bed, a house, a nation is to create an anchor, something to hold on to.

When Voyne was a little girl, the engineers in service to the Constant Lady had not yet solved the problem of comb-building. They had not divined the correct proportions that would persuade a hive to build only within movable frames, instead of filling every nook and cranny with waxy lattices. They'd used skeps still, lovingly-woven baskets that the bees would fill all the way to bursting—and then, each fall, the skeps would be destroyed in the harvest, and the bees with them. Honey had been far more precious, more rare. She'd tasted it only on feast days, but she'd gorged herself then, on honey cakes and mead and sweet comb crushed between her teeth. Now, she parts her lips and Prioress Jacynde places just a dot of honey on her tongue, a benediction.

It is, of course, sweet, but more than that, it brings with it flavors floral and vegetal, freshness she now longs for with her whole soul. This is not last year's honey; they must have begun to process some of the frames of honeycomb. It's too early for it, but perhaps they were so full they had to be drained.

Or perhaps it's because the quartermaster has more need of it than holy rites.

The offering given and received, Ser Voyne anticipates the end of the service, and a moment to talk alone with her liege, but instead, there is a rustle of fabric as two nuns enter from the lower chamber, bearing up a body between them. *Another funeral*, Ser Voyne realizes, and looks around, but nobody else appears surprised.

They all know, she realizes. It is only she who is out of the loop.

The dead body is that of an older man, his features already drawn well before death; the lines creasing his skin are deep furrows, and there aren't many that suggest laughter. Beneath his skin are only hollows, empty spaces, where his flesh has withered down to nothing. She thinks, horribly, it might be the first starvation death, until she sees the abbreviation of the leg, just above the knee. One of the people rescued from the rubble, she realizes.

She had thought the funerals concluded. She had thought they had known the measure of their loss.

One last soul taken by Etrebia's hand, before the rest of them begin to succumb to privation. Somehow, this is worse. Worse than the mass funeral she had been summoned to on the first day after the attack; she'd stood guard for that one, watching the crowd as they regained their fervor, their commitment. It had been beautiful, glorious, terrible; she could see every mouth lapping up the balm they were given, the righteous reactivity of a people acutely wounded, not slowly eroding. She'd known already, though. There was no sign of Etrebia's retreat. There was no change, despite a miracle.

She'd suffered, that day. A brilliant crash from the exaltation of the night's victory down into the muck and mire of entrapment, of Phosyne's madness, of the resumption of the ordinary.

Is that why today's funeral is so quiet? So ill-attended?

She watches as Jacynde anoints the dead man's brow with honey (*food for somebody else; how dare they waste it?*), arranges the limbs into a death repose, leans close and closes her own eyes, as if in sadness.

"Death is the natural result of life," Jacynde says, and her voice rings out through the room. "One follows the other, inevitable as the sun rises and sets. But though the setting sun cools the air and wakens the beasts of the night, death instead is a singular rupture. Death does not come all at once; it leaves many of us in the sunlight behind, to grapple with a loss that comes seemingly out of order. Our own rhythms distract us from the procession."

Voyne and the others echo assent, understanding, though Voyne does not entirely feel it.

There are few people in the chapel outside of the king's retinue and Ser Leodegardis's household. The most pious, perhaps, or direct relations. Nothing like the first funeral; if there could have been a feast, there would have been.

But people sensibly keep their distance from death, when it lurks just outside their door.

"This man, Jecobe de Avienten, has left us seemingly out of order. A single death, too late to join his fellows. But his death was a natural thing. His life has ended, his death has begun. And so we honor and respect that change, that brave venture into the unknown."

Brave, Voyne thinks, and almost laughs. *Brave,* truly? She thinks of his family, who has likely watched him suffer, then realizes, bitterly, that chances are good that he has no family at all. Otherwise the empty pews make no sense.

And what of the people who will come next? When starvation comes, it is the isolated who are taken first. Men like Jecobe. That he died in the attack was, perhaps, a mercy.

This is a bellwether.

The rest of the funeral is unobjectionable. The service that follows is reassuringly, predictably standard, and if not for the body on the slab, the bees dancing over its cold flesh and suckling at the honey on its brow, Voyne could almost feel okay again.

When it's over, King Cardimir still kneels, head lowered in prayer for the salvation of the keep, as he does every week. Around her, Prioress Jacynde's nuns launch into motion, a carefully orchestrated dance, just like the bees they tend to. They avoid the body and busy themselves with the processional that follows the service. Their dedication and order is a far cry from Phosyne's scrambling madness. The thought galls Voyne, enough to make her stand, knees creaking. She thinks to ask something of Jacynde, some advice, some clarity—or at least to confirm her suspicions, that there is nothing useful in Phosyne, after all.

Perhaps it wasn't true that the Priory had taken the credit for cleaning the water to still fears; perhaps they'd planted the thought that it was Phosyne who had done it out of kindness, to allow her blighted mind some privacy instead of allowing her to be cast out into the general population, where she surely could not manage.

But before she can reach Jacynde, the icon of the Constant Lady rises into the air, four nuns taking their positions to bear her gilded palanquin. The poles sit heavy on their slender shoulders, and two of them falter, swaying slightly, their heads no doubt rushing from lack of food and the heat of midday. But they rally, urged on by the thick perfume of the box. It's old now, a bit stale, but still strong, soaked into the preserved flowers that are heaped around the statue itself. Only the Lady's elongated, stylized face peers out from its desiccated bower, pure white around the jaw and hairline, fading to the brilliant goldenrod of crushed dandelions on Her cheeks and lips. Her eyes are wide open, the irises concentric rings of red and blue and green, and Her lips curve into a beatific smile.

Despite the circumstances, the Priory has kept Her immaculate. The dried flowers are a much better option than none at all, and the horsehair wig that tops the statue has been kept combed and carefully braided. The clockwork that allows Her to lift one hand in benediction still moves when the nun at the back turns the crank tucked out of sight. The small skep that rests in the Lady's lap hums with activity, bees climbing out and wriggling inside, but no honey leaks from it. It is a blazing beacon of order in a world threatening to abandon it, and Ser Voyne finds herself kneeling again before it, shivering.

She should probably focus her attentions and her prayers on one of the saints. It is said they intercede more readily, and the Constant Lady has now soaked in their collective adoration for two hours, while the saints have watched on from their smaller litters, less elaborately decorated. She should be prostrating herself before the Warding Saint, to beg for the continued strength of their walls, or pressing a kiss to the silvered lips of the Absolving Saint, confessing to her impulsive demand to be allowed to ride for help. She has no need of the Loving Saint, but even he would be a better option, more human, more likely to do more than observe.

But Ser Voyne wants nothing more than for her world to make sense again, so she gazes up at the Lady's ringed eyes, and prays.

Time, however, will not wait for her prayers, and the Lady's gracious girls are on a tight schedule. The candles have burned down to the noontime mark, and the day is hot, the sun blinding. They begin their procession, leaving Ser Voyne on her knees behind. They bear the icons out of the tower and onto the walls of the upper bailey. They will walk the whole perimeter of the castle today, just as they have every day before, and will every day after. Then they will go down to the yard, down among the tents and the starving children, and they will minister as they are able. Help to mend broken things, give the smallest touch of honey to the tongues of all who will kneel before them.

They leave the body behind.

Jacynde remains as well. She drifts to the body's side once more, and Voyne joins her.

"Are there others?" she asks, when it is only the four of them left in the room: Cardimir, Leodegardis, Jacynde, herself. "That were so badly injured in the attack?"

She wishes she already knew. She *should* already know.

"No, just the one," Jacynde says. "He likely would have died soon anyway; he was too weak to recover." She's more practical, in private, than she is in her sermons. Voyne appreciates it. She sidles closer. Thinks to speak of Phosyne. If she asks questions, and the king can hear them, can hear what madness is passing under this roof—

She doesn't get the chance.

"Ser Leodegardis," Prioress Jacynde says, and Voyne comes back to herself and sees that Jacynde is holding out a knife, hilt first.

The keeper of Aymar takes it with only the slightest hesitation. His fingers wrap tight as he approaches the body.

She rushes to his side before she can think better of it. "Leo—"

"Step aside, Ser Voyne," he says, and his voice is so strained it nearly breaks. "This must be done."

"What—"

But he has taken the man's arm, is stretching it along his side on the platform, fitting the blade to his wrist. He is going to cut the dead man's hands off.

"Look away, if it distresses you so," he murmurs.

He begins to cut.

"No," Voyne says, then, as her overheated brain begins to make sense of this, louder, "*No*." She grabs Leodegardis's hand, and his lips twist in anger.

"Ser Voyne," her king warns. "You are harder than this. Steel yourself, please."

"You can't. You can't send him to the quartermaster," she says, looking between them, to Jacynde, desperate. "Things aren't so bad yet. We have *time*."

"Not much of it," Prioress Jacynde says. "And meat spoils."

Leodegardis shrugs off her hold.

The blade meets bone. Aymar's keeper grimaces, shifts his grip, guides the point of the blade into the joint space. This man has been dead for long enough that he is no longer rigid, and so his blood is sluggish and clotted, but it still seeps out, dark red, almost brown.

The hand falls away from the body. The cross section of the wrist does not look so different from that of livestock. Voyne closes her eyes against it, and, unbidden, remembers the taste of flesh.

There have been times, before, where there was no other option. Leodegardis knows as well as she does; they have been pinned down in bleak winters, in blighted fields. They have done what they needed to survive. They have made pacts with their fellow knights, *If my body should fail before yours, you must take my flesh into your own, you must get out.* But that was different. That was done with eyes wide open, among equals. Here, now—

"You cannot do this," she repeats, even as she hears Leodegardis begin to saw at one of the feet. *It's easier to consume a man when you've forgotten what he was,* her experience whispers. No feet, no hands, no head, and the body is not a man anymore, just a package of flesh. Deliverance. Salvation. It will buy them a little more time. But— "Not while we still have horses."

"A horse on the hoof will keep longer," Leodegardis argues, voice flat.

"*Stop,*" she begs, and looks to her king.

Her king looks back, unmoved.

"My people," he says, "must eat. They do not need to know. Nobody else needs to know but us."

He, she knows, has never had to make this choice. Perhaps that is why he can be so confident. To him this is all theoretical. And he won't be the one eating human meat.

"In times of extremis," Jacynde adds, voice even, "we must use what we are given by the saints. And this is what is given."

"And the other dead?" she snaps. "What is different today? What has changed so much in three days?" What is she missing?

Leodegardis grimaces. "The meat had already begun to spoil," he says, softly. "And too many were already thinking about the bodies. Here, in this instance, we have privacy."

"We'd hide it from them." When she has been driven to this desecration, she walked into it knowingly. This deception, this paternalistic, horrific management—

"For their own good," Leodegardis says. "If they do not know, then they need never blame themselves."

He is right, of course. But she cannot accept this butchery. "If we do this, we cross a line," she says. "We cannot go back. We have time, still. The Priory has come through for us. Etrebia's siege engines are broken. Will we not ride out to break their line? Will we not *try*?"

Her liege's lips curl in a snarl, an expression she hasn't seen on him since the siege first set in and proved it could not be broken. "Ser Voyne, master yourself. We do not have the strength to fight. This is not the time to be precious." He looks so arrogant, in this moment, chin lifted, tongue virginal to the taste of human meat. "Give me a miracle, and I will relent," he proclaims. "But I see no miracle."

"The woman is ungovernable!" Voyne cries. "You cannot rely on her. You can't ask me to—"

"I can ask you to do anything I please," he cuts her off. "She gave us clean water. She *will* give us food. Until then, I will do as I see fit." He looks down at the body of Jecobe de Avienten, touches the cut stump of his wrist.

"You screech so loudly of what we should and should not do. We should not eat him, hm? Then what if we give it to your charge instead?" Cardimir asks. "Not so bad as eating, but it could still give us food one day. It could be the link to our miracle. Would that mollify your nerves, girl?"

Girl strikes her deeper even than the thought of Phosyne fumbling about with a man's remains. Cardimir has never spoken to her this way, and she bristles. "And what would she do with it, Your Majesty? Let it rot and try to make it dance with grass seeds?"

"I must agree with Ser Voyne," the prioress admits. "To be consigned to meat is terrible. To be *wasted* would be more so."

"And have you given me a solution?" the king snaps, rounding on her, his fury growing. "Either of you, will you give me a solution? No? If you tell me she is mad and cannot give me my miracle, then I will trust you. But if that is so, then this man's flesh goes to feed my people. He is a sacrifice. *This* is a sacrifice. You must know what we have done, but they have no need to. It buys us time. Stand *back*, Ser Voyne."

Helplessly trained, Ser Voyne steps back. She sinks to one knee. She stares up at her king, and wishes she were anywhere else at all.

9

RE YOU LOST?"

Treila screams. She falls back, staring wild-eyed at the whispering fissure, but she sees no movement, no indication of life. She hauls herself back up onto the ledge, clutches her dress to her front, never looking away.

But there is nothing. Nothing but the water, the breeze. She needs to go. She needs to squirm back through the gap in the stone, back into Aymar, back into her slow, slow death.

"Don't leave," the gap whispers. "Not yet. You are so tired."

"Shut up!" Treila cries, feeling for the edges of the hole, pushing her clothing inside. The milky blue light of the trickle of a stream is dim, but the unnatural color scrapes at her eyes, making them sting and water. Or perhaps those are the fumes, whatever fumes she's inhaling that are making her hear—this. This impossibility.

This useless impossibility, because even if that voice belongs to a person, and that person does not itch to kill every soul in Aymar castle, there is still no way to get through the stone.

Whoever, whatever the voice belongs to does not speak again.

Her chest aches with the fierceness of her gasping breaths, but slowly, in the silence, she calms herself. Her fingers shake against the rock, but soon it is with exhaustion, not fear. She looks at the stream again, considers a drink before she remembers how terribly it had hurt, when she'd sipped at the foul water before the Priory had clarified it. She doesn't need that again.

With one last cautious look at the whispering crack, Treila forces herself back into the earth. She stretches out on her belly and begins to climb.

As she ascends, she finds each scrap of clothing she left behind save for one; a single stocking, the first thing she had abandoned to mark her way. But there's nowhere it could have gone; she makes it from the second stocking to the entrance back into the keep in barely more than two minutes, her path entirely illuminated by the daylight that seems to have arrived too early.

But there is no stocking. She frowns at her bare foot once she is dressed again, then shoves it into her shoe.

She was down there longer than intended; there's a good chance she is missed. She hurriedly covers the gap and moves her chair in front of it, grabs up work, sits. Fiddles with thread and needle.

It's a way to get her breath back and to think, and if anybody comes in search of her, it gives her a ready excuse; she wanted to use this first light of day, while the air is still cool, to get a little piecework done.

Nobody comes in search of her.

The day grows warmer, and sooner than she expected, she hears the bells of the Priory ring out. She forces herself up then, and her body protests. Her joints ache. Her head spins. She pitches forward, catches herself on the wall just beside where her cache hides. She needs sleep, but won't get it until night; the heat and her chores will make sure of that.

First things first. She hurries up the steps and out into the yard, notably behind her fellow servants. When she takes her place at the back of the line, Denisot, the chamberlain, has already taken his blessing. He shoots her a glare for her tardiness.

Treila fists her hands in her skirts so that he won't notice how raw and scraped her fingers are.

The high noon sun glints off the metals that decorate the Constant Lady and Her saints, flashing into Treila's eyes, making them water, making her head pound harder still. She thinks she might crack, break into pieces. If she did, might she be narrow enough to get through that gap?

As things stand, there's no point in going back. Even if the voice was only in her head, she doesn't have the tools or strength to widen out that passage.

The realization is sobering.

Her turn comes at last. When she kneels, she nearly falls. Her pulse thunders in her ears. She knows this feeling, and she curses it even as she braces herself, plants her hands against her thighs, tilts her head up and closes her eyes with her lips slightly parted. She doesn't want to see the pity of the nun who dips her thin glass rod into the dish of honey, spins it. The nun knows, too, that Treila is starving, but doesn't know that this was avoidable. That if she'd eaten a little more before going into that tunnel, she wouldn't be so tragically feeble now.

But that one sweet dab of comfort doesn't grace her tongue. Treila opens an eye, then both, and closes her mouth because the nun isn't even looking at her.

Instead, she's looking at the king, come sweeping down the steps at the entrance of the chapel, flanked by Ser Leodegardis and Prioress Jacynde. Behind them is a woman, set apart, face gone pale with . . . shock? Devastation, surely. She has the look about her, every furrow deepened, eyes staring after the other three.

Treila recognizes her instantly.

It's Ser Voyne, more broken than Treila has ever seen her, and twin shocks of fear and delight rock her back onto her heels.

There is murmuring all around her, and nobody is looking. Treila quietly joins the crowd. She can't stand the thought of waiting for a meaningless touch of honey to her tongue, not when *this* is playing out before her.

It's not much. It's subtle. But Treila has watched Ser Voyne for months now, whenever their paths cross, and she has seen Ser Voyne at the king's heels like a favored dog. They have never walked so far apart, let alone with Ser Voyne looking so hurt, so devastated. So vulnerable, without her armor.

It clears Treila's head in an instant. Makes her mouth water.

Treila cannot take vengeance on a king; even she is not so bold and desperate to believe that. But she notes now with interest how very little the king marks his chosen lapdog, how that lapdog's carefully controlled countenance is broken now, pained, frustrated. Betrayed. Treila knows *that* feeling too well to miss it here.

She has waited months and months, months longer than she thought, and until this very moment she didn't know what she was waiting for. A moment to slip some poisoned nectar into her drink? A night when Ser Voyne sat alone, distracted, her throat bare to a quick knife from an unexpected corner?

But this is far more poetic, and it is almost worth the roaring pit of her stomach, the terror of the cavern below the castle.

She will break Ser Voyne's spirit, the same way hers was broken.

It will only take the slightest push.

Ser Voyne lingers a moment longer, and then she turns, not to the keep where she has been holed up for the last week, but to the great hall, to the walled-off sod of the kitchen garden. To the scene of last week's riot, but Treila doesn't think that's what's on her mind.

She trails after, head down. Pulled inexorably toward her, and feeling, for just a moment, like the girl who adored the great Ser Voyne, who thought something special was quickening between them. She knows better now, but this close, the old habits stir back to life.

Behind her, the nuns lift their burdens; they will take the icons around the walls, then down again to the lower bailey, more succor for the innocents. Treila quickens her pace, and follows Voyne into the garden, close enough on her heels that the guards don't question it.

Voyne slows as she takes in the rows of feeble plants. There's not enough rain to keep them fed, not enough water to go around, and many have been harvested too soon to provide some limited sustenance. What remains is not encouraging. Voyne's expression darkens, and Treila thinks she hears her breathing hitch, as if with repressed sobs.

But the knight doesn't cry. She sits on a low bench, stares down at her hands.

Treila considers her approach. She has avoided being alone with Ser Voyne for this long out of caution, and she isn't sure she's ready to announce herself. But a woman like Ser Voyne, cautious though she is, is also used to having a certain amount of power. Impunity. She knows more of the servants by name than most, Treila will concede, but not all. Those who do not serve her directly are simply acts of nature. A soothing rain, a warm day. A breeze.

Treila tries not to think of the breeze below the earth, or the heat of the day sapping what little strength she has. She needs to eat.

She needs this more.

"Ser knight," Treila murmurs, voice pitched in such a way that it could belong to anyone. "May I get you something?"

It's been many months since she needed this deference, but she learned it well by necessity. It slips over her like the leather of the gloves she makes. That Ser Voyne wears now on her hands. Treila recognizes her own work.

Voyne's head jerks up; she must have thought she was alone, or followed only incidentally. But she doesn't turn. Treila's read on the situation appears correct.

"No," Ser Voyne says at last. "What is there to get?"

"Water," Treila suggests.

Ser Voyne laughs, and it is dark and bitter, and Treila wonders if she knows something Treila does not.

She will take her water from the kitchens tonight, then, not the cisterns.

"I apologize," the knight says, when she has control of herself once more. "It's been a long few days." Weeks. Months.

"I have a little extra food," Treila says, risking some exposure for a greater reward: Voyne's vulnerability. It breaks over her like ocean surf. Treila can see her shoulders tighten, then unclench, and Ser Voyne sags where she sits.

"I am not in need," she says, guilt and shame weighing her down. "Keep that for yourself."

She does not threaten to take it away and redistribute it. Treila feels a pang for the woman she once thought Ser Voyne to be, who Ser Voyne seems to play at being even now.

There is silence, then, and Treila ponders her next move. She wants Ser Voyne weak, reliant, and she has gotten there so swiftly, but the next steps are treacherous. Should Treila reveal her identity, and hope that there is guilt there, too? Or should she stretch this out, encourage Voyne to come back to this spot, meet her here again and hope that they can have another anonymous exchange? Given time, Treila can pry apart this woman's armor, make her desperate, and then leave her betrayed, broken on the rocks.

The king would allow it. The king has already begun to cut her loose.

But before Treila can decide, Ser Voyne makes a move she was not expecting.

"What I am about to say," Ser Voyne addresses to the air, "cannot be told to anybody else. Do you understand me?" She doesn't turn to look at Treila, and that is the measure of how desperate she is, how broken.

Lying is easy. "Of course, ser knight," she breathes, coming to sit behind her on the bench. Their hips brush, just slightly, and the contact steals Treila's breath away. She can *hear* the older woman breathing. Can hear the shaking in her chest. She is going to freely offer up another dagger to point at her breast, and Treila is so eager she could cry.

Ser Voyne is silent at first, marshaling her will or slowly letting go of her propriety. And then she places her head into her hands. "Food is dwindling. Rations are scant. You know that, or you wouldn't have offered me some of your portion."

Treila nods. "I know." A pause. "We all know."

Ser Voyne nods, not surprised. "We have two options left, if we are to last until rescue comes," she murmurs.

Two options. Treila frowns, thinking. One is simple: humans are made of flesh just as much as dogs are, and the deaths will begin soon enough. But the other, she can't imagine.

"And *is* rescue on the way?" Treila asks, mind working.

"I don't know," Voyne confesses, heartbreak weighing down her words. "It should be, but it should also have arrived by now. And because it has not . . ."

Her voice breaks completely.

Because it has not, we must assume it is not coming. That it will never come, no matter how many messengers we send over the wall.

Treila hesitates only a moment, then reaches behind her, places one slight hand on Voyne's gloved knuckles. The knight flinches, but doesn't turn to look. She needs the anonymity if she is to speak. Treila hides a smile. "Ser knight," she says, "I know that you would defend me until the end. All of us. Tell me, what has you so distressed?"

Voyne draws in a shuddering breath. "They will either begin to feed us the dead," she says, "or they will feed us heresy."

Heresy. Treila rolls the word around in her mouth, even as she makes the appropriate noises of shock, distress. To eat the dead is terrible, of course.

But she has done it before. She assumed it would come to that, sooner or later. "I don't understand," she says.

"I am glad of that," Voyne says, and Treila bites down a sharp laugh. The knight's hand has turned over beneath hers, is clasping her fingers gently. "But flesh is flesh. I don't think they will announce when the change happens, but it will happen. I am sorry."

"But isn't that heresy itself? To—to do that?" She minces around it as if she is not intimately familiar with the taste of human meat.

As if she is not, in a dark part of herself, looking forward to it—if only because she knows it will not break her.

"There are worse things," Ser Voyne breathes, "than that."

"What?" Treila pushes. "What can be worse than what we are driven to, when all else is lost? Doesn't it all become the same, then?"

But Ser Voyne does not answer, not immediately, and Treila feels her hand tense against her fingers. Ser Voyne turns, finally, to see who she has been speaking with. Treila freezes, considers, then turns her head as well. She pushes her blonde curls out of the way, tucks them behind one ear, twisted by a scar from a knife. She knows her cheek is visible now, the line of her nose. The patrician arc of her brow.

Treila hears her sharp intake of breath. She forces herself not to smile.

"Do I know you?" Ser Voyne asks.

And finally, Treila looks up. She meets the troubled gaze of the woman who took everything from her without a lick of hesitation or regret. She shapes her expression into one of fear, of sadness.

She sees the spark of recognition.

The confusion.

And for a moment, she is caught. Caught by how she thrills to Ser Voyne's attention after all these years, and caught, too, by the pain glinting in those familiar eyes.

But she can't stay. Staying would be too kind. Treila untangles their hands and flees, knowing Ser Voyne cannot follow, because the leash is, as ever, tight around her throat.

10

HOSYNE THINKS SHE might be dying.

Her face is flushed, and her skin feels tight with dehydration, but she's pissed into her bucket six times today, and the fumes are only a little stronger than usual. Water does not help, not any longer than it takes to swallow it, and when she rests, head pillowed on her arms atop her workbench, she smells the sickly sweet stench of rotting fruit, though she hasn't eaten fruit in months. Her head pounds. Ser Voyne is staring at her, watchful and exhausted, and Phosyne can't put one thought in front of the other long enough to figure out where her latest experiments have once more gone wrong.

The sulfur bought her a few steps forward. Even Ser Voyne was forced to admit that a candle that could burn unceasing without consuming the wax beneath it was a miracle. But it is not the correct miracle. Phosyne has managed the impossible once again, but cannot bridge the gap between the fire and her belly.

She has squandered what little time they all have left. They need food. She is desperate for it, and cannot for the life of her see the path forward. All she has left is longing. A prayer on her lips for sustenance.

"Eat," Ser Voyne says, and Phosyne looks up, startled, to find the broader woman towering over her. She has put a plate in front of her. Phosyne frowns at it. A scrap of meat, as usual, but there is honey, too, a bit of leaking comb.

She hasn't been allowed honey since she left the Priory. Jacynde's people know not to give it to her, and it is hardly given out in rations.

She looks up at Ser Voyne, confused.

"Eat," the knight repeats, this time with a little more force. "Or I will pry your lips apart and force it down your throat."

"The honey," Phosyne tries, then falters. "I can't."

"You can, and you will, if you don't want your body to shut down."

Phosyne looks back at the plate, at the honey and the meat, the meat she has been living off of, slaughtered cattle and chickens and everything else the farmers brought with them, when they could not bring their crops. Too early in the season, when Etrebia had swept in and forced them off the land. Aymar's gardens could only produce so much. She has not had fruit in months.

It clicks. She has only had meat.

"I have seen men die like this," Ser Voyne confirms.

Phosyne can hear the weight in her voice; she has been withdrawn, the last day. Something happened when she was called to attend worship the morning before. Many somethings, perhaps. Phosyne was vaguely aware of a change, but something about the honeycomb Voyne has presented her with makes it all slide, briefly and brilliantly, into focus.

Voyne is distraught. Pulled in too many directions at once. Angry at Phosyne, of course, always, but also desperate.

"I thought," Phosyne says, slowly, "that you might not mind my death."

Voyne scowls. "You are mine to care for," she says, too quickly.

There are so many things bound up with those words, *to care for.* Phosyne sees them like threads, winding tight around Voyne, biting into her exposed skin. She really needs her armor, Phosyne thinks. She doesn't know how to exist without it.

Ser Voyne's care only comes from duty, and anger that Phosyne might die instead of producing something *useful*, but it still makes her flush with shame.

Phosyne doesn't speak, doesn't move. The room's thick heat is blanketing, smothering. Her mind wants to drift again, and perhaps Voyne's drifts, too.

"I've failed too many people," Voyne says, the words clumsy on her lips. "While thinking I was serving. Yesterday, I thought I saw a ghost. A starved ghost who would have fed me if she could."

It is like there is a wound in her breast, wet and weeping, and Phosyne can see it pulsing.

And then Voyne turns cold again.

"Eat the honey," she says, and pushes the plate toward Phosyne once more.

Phosyne's heart aches, and she picks up the comb with delicate hands. She wants to keep a little, just a little, for her research, but its sticky sweetness coats her fingers, and she knows, then, that she will eat all of it. All of it wasted, ultimately. What does it matter if Voyne forces her to live a few days longer, if she loses an avenue to saving them all?

But perhaps she should be realistic: see that it will be wasted no matter what. There is no way out. Her unseen world has only let them starve for longer. Maybe she's only mad. Maybe the method of purifying water will eventually be explained and defined, repeated, wrestled out of the numinous, inhuman unknown and into the Priory's understanding.

Maybe it's better if she takes the Lady's blessing on her tongue, the sweet honey made from the pollen of wildflowers beyond Aymar's walls, brought back past an encircling army that could not stop a bee's flight even if it cared to do so. Maybe it's better if she tries prayer for the first time in almost a year.

We are hungry, she begs wordlessly, eye sockets aching with tears her body isn't sure it can shed, *and we are lonely, and we are desperate.*

Save us, because I'm not sure I can.

She lifts the comb to her lips. She closes her eyes. She prepares to bite.

And then the saints arrive.

II

HE BLAST OF trumpets steals Voyne's attention away from Phosyne, her blood running cold, then boiling hot, as she thunders up the stairs to the little glass plate that Phosyne has insisted on reseating. She grips the sill hard as she leans forward, peers out of the gloom into the bright light of midday. Her eyes refuse to adjust at first, and the glass is uneven.

But she can see movement, shapes, the glint of sun off metal. The garrison is rallying. Has Etrebia made another move at last, recovered so quickly from the routing of their siege engines?

No; the patterns of movement are all wrong. All focus is not on the walls, but inside them. As Voyne's eyes adjust, she makes out a broad circle of uncovered soil down in the lower bailey, ringed by a thick press of bodies.

Something is *inside*.

"Stay here," she snaps as she races back down the stairs, dodging *something* that waits at the landing that she is certain wasn't there before. But she doesn't have time to think. "Eat the honey. That's an order, witch."

Phosyne's hands drip, sticky and golden, and she nods. Then Voyne is in the hall, and the door is shut behind her, and she doesn't have to think about the madwoman or her own tender, anxious heart anymore.

The king's chambers are empty. So are the rooms below, and so, even, is the wall of the upper bailey, because *everybody* is crowded in the lower yard staring at whatever is just inside the gate. She has her sword in hand before she's tramping down the stairs, and she is on the verge of barking orders, demanding knowledge.

Then she sees Leodegardis and Cardimir standing halfway down to the yard, staring with open wonder. Sitting ducks to any attack. She makes for them, staggers to a halt, panting at their sides.

They don't look at her.

Her eyes flash over the crowd, trying to see what everybody else is staring at. Her gaze catches on a head of blonde curls. *Treila de Batrolin*, her ghost from the garden. Her heart threatens to strangle her, but she doesn't have time for a haunting, not now, not here. No time to think of those she's already failed.

She tears her gaze away, and then, at last, she sees them.

Four strangers stand inside the gates.

"Who let them in?" she demands, unable to look at her king as she addresses him.

"I don't know," he replies, voice filled with wonder. It should be filled with fear.

"Etrebian? Come to parlay?"

"I don't think so." That is Leodegardis. He, at least, sounds cautious. "Nobody told me of riders approaching." Well, they were not riders. There is no sign of horses. "And the gates? Who gave the order to raise the gates?"

"I don't know," the king says, and Leodegardis does not offer anything else.

There is a murmur, a rustling, and then the crowd below them shifts, opening a path leading straight toward them.

Voyne steps in front of her king, sword drawn, as they approach. They move in steady procession with a flowing grace, so different from the haggard lurching that colors every moment inside of Aymar now. They do not stop, and nobody moves to stop them.

They draw close enough that Voyne can, at last, make out the detail of them.

They look like . . . saints.

Voyne isn't the first to think that; there's no other explanation for why the lower yard is hushed, prostrate, everyone with their heads bowed, their shoulders trembling, as the party makes its way through their masses.

At the front of the little group is a tall, slender woman, all angles and hard lines. She is draped in layer upon layer of fabric, flowers pinned to the stole that falls over her shoulders, but the skin that Voyne can see is pure white except for where dandelion-gold stains her flesh over her cheeks and nose and lips. Her pale hair is a thick mass of braids, carefully arranged, not a strand out of place. There is no dust of the road on her, no weariness, no *wariness*.

"A ploy," Voyne makes herself say, unable to look away. "This is a ploy. They have sent people here in—in costume—"

But her words sound hollow, even to her ear.

In her chest, something blooms. Something tremulous and terrifying. Hope, out of season. Impossible hope.

Another miracle for the pile.

The pale woman's three companions have that same unearthly cant to them. One, a young man, looks across the crowd with an ecstatic smile of welcome. One watches with furrowed brow, silvered lips pursed in a moue of empathetic pain. One is clad in armor that, Voyne thinks briefly, incongruously, does not quite make sense. The buckles are in the wrong places. The metal reflects the sun strangely. But in another moment she does not care, because the woman with the golden face is turning toward her.

Her irises are rings of color, red and blue and green. Ser Voyne goes completely still. She has never seen anybody with eyes like that, except for the painted image of the Constant Lady, and that, more than anything else, is what brings her to her knees.

Tears sting at her eyes. She can feel a scream building in her chest, desperate and overwhelmed and exhausted, and she feels the same passion rippling through the crowd.

The Lady smiles, leans down, touches Voyne's face. Her hands are delicate, nails clean, and She smells only of flowers. Flowers, sun-drenched meadows, proper summers without starvation and death and hopelessness, and Ser Voyne weeps now, openly. The Lady won't let her look away.

12

REILA SEES VOYNE fall.

The whole crowd sees it. The yard is packed with every single person in the castle, all drawn out from their tents and their holes and their miseries, all watching the procession that approaches the king. Every single one sees Voyne step forward. And every single one sees her fall.

They also see the blonde-haired, painted woman touch the top of Ser Voyne's head in benediction, then turn to the king, who does not kneel, but holds out a hand.

The crowd breathes. Inhale, swell, exhale, wither. The fear they have clutched hand in hand with hope is released. Treila can *feel* the charge of expectation that dances from shoulder to shoulder, lip to lip.

She steps forward, unable to help herself.

Ser Voyne is crying, wholly focused on the painted woman, unaware of everything else around her. It's greater than the pain she wore when she at last recognized Treila's face. It is bigger than Treila, than their sordid history, than guilt over a single death. And why shouldn't it be? Ser Voyne looks at this woman and sees salvation for all of Aymar.

Treila's struck with the laughable feeling that they've taken away something that is *hers*, and that's her signal to get the fuck out of there and clear her head.

She retreats into the crowd.

The first ring of people she pushes through is silent, but beyond that, there are whispers, growing to stronger murmurs. She hears talk of food. Of rescue. There is giddiness. Not just hope, but giddiness, no wariness at all. She wants to punch somebody, shake them until they see sense again. Captivity has honed her mistrust of every other soul in the world to a fine point. What has it done to theirs?

She can't stand it. Any of it. This sudden happy ending makes no sense.

Treila reaches the nearest tower and finds it unguarded. Whoever is meant to be here has joined the thrumming mass. She slips inside, up and around the stairs, out onto the wall. Without soldiers blocking the way, it's the quickest path back to the upper bailey, and from there to her workshop. But her workshop has no answers. It only has a hole to a dead-end cave that whispered to her in her starved brain.

The chapel is closer. She does not want to go there, doesn't want to hear the hum of bees, risk a sting, but it's the only place she can think to go for answers. After all, those four people were painted to look like the icons. There must be some connection.

It's weak, but then she's feeling unsteady all around.

Halfway to the chapel, she finds Edouart perched on the rampart, staring down at the yard. His fist is pressed against his teeth. He is gnawing on his own flesh. Then he glances over, sees her, and his eyes turn desperate.

He doesn't say anything, though.

She comes to stand by him anyway. When she sneaks a look herself, she can only make out Ser Voyne's retreating back, trailing after her liege and the strange party, ushering them into the great hall.

"Is it over, then?" Edouart asks. He doesn't sound happy. He doesn't sound hopeful.

Clever boy. Always cautious, this one. She could've stood to have been more like him, back when it would have mattered. "I don't see how it can be," she says. "It's just four people."

"Simmonet said they were the saints, come to life. Come to rescue us."

"Where are their swords?" she asks. "Food? No, if anything, they're a ploy. A way to get somebody inside the gates."

He looks like he's about to cry. "I think they're here to judge us. They'll help us only if we deserve it. And if not . . ."

Anxious boy.

"Well," she says, "if not, there's not much to be done about it. But nobody down there seems worried."

He nods. Bites his knuckles again. Treila offers him a tight smile that he doesn't see, then keeps walking; she doesn't know what to believe herself, after all. And regardless of his fears, he believes too much.

The chapel is empty, save for the bees. Her back tenses as she spots the first one, then ten, then a hundred. Treila has only stepped foot in here three times in the last six months, and every time she has been accompanied by every other servant in the keep, and many of the refugees. Without human bodies massed within, the room feels all wrong. Feels like something out of place.

She keeps her distance from the hives. Outside, the sun is beginning to set, and she figures that must mean the bees are coming home for the night. Taking shelter. It should be safe, to walk among them, but she can't. Not when she can still remember how her flesh had swollen, how her skin had wept. Her stomach had been empty, her veins on fire.

Treila keeps to the walls instead. She presses a hand to one, and feels it warm beneath her fingertips. Solid. Real.

Then she hears footsteps, fast and angry, and she retreats, slips behind one of the pillars of the hall and presses herself flat to it, sinking into the growing shadows.

"—Your Radiance," says a nun, voice thin as she struggles to keep up with the prioress ahead of her, "I am sure His Majesty meant no disrespect—"

"Do not make apologies for him!"

Oh, the prioress is angry. Treila tastes it on her tongue. She is *furious*, and that makes Treila stand to attention.

"They are desperate," the prioress says. "Of course they are desperate. We all are. I cannot blame them for that, but Ser Voyne, Ser Leodegardis"—she does not say the king, is too afraid to speak treason even here—"they refuse the barest inch of caution. What does it cost them, to simply treat them as unknown envoys, sequester them for a night, *question* them as to their intentions? And instead, they accept every request, in public, in broad view of—eugh!"

Metal clatters on the floor. One of the Priory's fine instruments of worship, no doubt.

"Your Radiance, you must admit, the circumstances of their appearance . . . what are we here for, if not to believe?"

The prioress does not immediately respond. She also stops pacing, her footsteps falling silent.

"We have reached the limits of our resistance, Your Radiance," the nun continues. "You said yourself, we have run out of time. And if this is the moment of our greatest need—"

"Silence a moment, Sister," the prioress says, and draws an unsteady breath.

Treila dissects every word, every pause, every outburst, because she needs to know if this is territorial anger, or something more. If the prioress only objects to not being consulted, that is one thing. But if the prioress does not, for even a moment, suspect those painted strangers of being what they appear to be, then Treila's fears are well-founded. The rest of the castle has gone mad.

And Treila needs to get out, as fast as she can.

It doesn't matter that her brief attempt at destroying Ser Voyne has been interrupted. What matters is her own hide. If even the prioress, who surely believes in the Constant Lady with some honest piece of her heart, is as wary as Treila feels, then Treila cannot count on miraculous salvation.

"I have never in all my years," the prioress says at last, voice grudging, pained, "seen any indication that the Lady or Her attendants give a single shit what happens to Her worshippers. And I can't believe She would choose to start here, now, with us."

The faceless nun is silent, stunned.

A bee hums beside her ear, and Treila jerks aside. There is nothing left for her here; she slips out of the chapel, in search of a way out.

13

ER VOYNE IS nowhere to be found, and Phosyne is left to her own devices. She can find no joy in it. Her body still shakes. Her head still hurts. She should eat the honey Voyne has left her, but every time she tries, her body rebels. The floral aroma goes to her head and she nearly vomits.

So she doesn't eat the honey. Instead, she watches out her window, and tries to think.

When thinking doesn't work, she sneaks out.

It's not hard. Her guards are missing, and the room directly below her is empty. It's easy, from there, to pick one of the lesser-used staircases and creep down and out into the yard. It's early evening now, the air dancing with the steady pulse of glowing flies, and there is hushed laughter in the air. *Laughter.* Phosyne tastes hope on her lips, but it transmutes to something far more sour, and she presses herself up against a stone wall and holds her breath.

Something is wrong. She doesn't quite know what, but she saw the tableau down in the yard at noon. She thinks she saw Voyne fall to her knees.

That, and the lack of her guards—those recent, desperate additions—it adds up to either greater fear, or the removal of fear. Neither make sense.

The great hall glows with firelight, and she creeps closer to peer in through one of the many small windows. She is not alone, but there are only a few others peering in; not the crowd she would have expected. Good behavior, for what should have rightly been a mob.

Inside must be stifling, even though she can see no more than ten bodies within, crowded around a table. She sees the king, in his fin-ery, and Ser Leodegardis, in his stoic remove. Prioress Jacynde is not there. Ser Voyne is, stone still with some form of shock, and Phosyne doesn't like that look on her brow.

It looks broken.

The chamberlain is there, too, and the marshal, and the four guests. And those four guests . . .

She knows them. She knows them, because she cleaned their icons for years, knelt at their feet, offered up praise and processed the honey from the hives painted in their colors. The Warding Saint, so similar to Ser Voyne in appearance, but richly ornamented; the Absolving Saint, all silvered and earnest, head bent to listen to every whispered word; the Loving Saint, one hand curled below his chin, fine fingers sliding back and forth against his jawline, enticement and comfort both; and the Constant Lady, sitting statue-straight in Her chair, only a breath away from looking up and seeing Phosyne staring.

Her heart gives an unexpected pang of recognition, of longing.

A young boy tends to the fire, then runs to fetch food from the kitchens. And there *is* food, a whole spread of it, not just dried meat. Phosyne thinks she smells verdancy, then shakes it off; she's too far away.

But she does *see* green.

There are vegetables on those plates. Her mouth waters; her stom-ach cramps. She knows exactly how everything on that table would taste in her mouth, and her mind shrieks at her to force her way inside, to gorge herself. It had been easier to starve when there was so little to eat, and so little that appealed. But these vegetables are plump and fresh, not dried and stored through the winter, somehow uneaten until this very moment at the height of summer.

Fresh ones, not grown in the castle gardens, because those have all been picked clean. Nothing to flower, nothing to fruit.

They're from somewhere else.

When? How? Perhaps Phosyne missed the moments the gates were raised, but for somebody to have reached them at all without cries of death out on the walls—no, she's missing something.

Phosyne's rotting breath fills her nose, and is acrid enough to make her duck down, take shelter, instead of staring like a desperate fool. Her stomach riots, but her higher faculties resume control. *Green* means outside. These strange visitors, then, have come from outside and have brought offerings. So many offerings that the tables looked ready to groan.

A miracle. Food, and the hand of what appears to be the Constant Lady.

And yet, no sign of the Priory.

For just a moment, she thinks to run to Jacynde and ask if she, too, can feel the wrongness. If that's why she keeps her distance. Of course, that presumes she can *run*, and that Jacynde's creatures would let her near.

Still, she makes herself stand up. Makes herself leave all that bounty, and staggers to the walls for a closer look at the world beyond.

In the eight months she has lived in Aymar castle, even before the siege, she has rarely wandered. Her room is her sanctuary. She knows almost nobody in the castle household, let alone the refugees or the king's contingent. There's nobody she can go to, except perhaps for Ser Voyne and Ser Leodegardis, to ask what is happening.

But when she reaches the gatehouse, the shadows wrap around her, and she goes unseen as she listens in.

Three guards in armor sit around a pitted table, all perched on wobbling stools.

"Georgie didn't do it," the redhead is saying, throwing down worn cards on the table. "And I didn't do it. And I don't know that anybody could've done it without somebody noticing, that winch can't be moved on its own—"

"But they're here," says the one with the coiled dark hair. "Somebody must've. If a door's not open, no one's getting in. And if they *can* get in, then we're all fucked, because Etrebia could just march right up here and—"

"We'd skewer 'em before they got close," says the angry one, and their fury seems to bleed through the rock and into Phosyne's cheek, and she is panting, and—

She realizes, suddenly, that even if the shadows abandoned her, they would not see her; she is pressed against the stone wall on the *outside* of the gatehouse.

She doesn't know how she can see them, hear them, and suddenly she can't anymore. But that is for tomorrow, or the next day, after she deals with the more obvious terror:

Nobody opened the gates.

Nobody opened the gates, and yet there are four strangers within Aymar's walls, gentle and kind and beautiful, and they are allowed to move about under their own power. They are *guests*. This makes no sense. Phosyne has been kept up in her tower, and Ser Leodegardis *knows* her. He saw her walk into this castle under her own power. The gates were open, then.

But they are closed now, and surrounded by a heavy earthen wall manned by enemy soldiers, and how, *how* could anybody make it all the way along the path that leads from the plain beyond up to the gates of Aymar without anybody on either side noticing?

They are not natural. They are not people in costume, or people at all. Phosyne knows that with a galling certainty that makes her head spin, the same certainty that tells her what the guards inside the room look and feel like. She pushes herself up off the ground (When did she kneel? When did she fall?) and nearly vomits, but keeps whatever bile is left to her down. She staggers back toward the upper bailey, the safety of her tower, the comfort of the wicked creatures that reside in her workspace.

But that thought brings her up short, too. She slows. Leans hard against an inner crenelation, hopes nobody with a bow sees her weaving shadow.

Pneio and Ornuo appeared, as if from nowhere. The gates did not open, but suddenly she was den mother to two creatures she has never seen before, never read of. They came to her from *somewhere*, just as her theories about the purification of water, just as the technique by which she can light a candle and have it burn without using up its fuel.

Her stomach sours far beyond its physical pangs.

These saints are here by her hand, and she doesn't know how she did it.

14

HE GREAT HALL is hot enough that Voyne sweats cease-lessly. It seems she is all made of salt and tears today, soggy and close to spilling open.

She doesn't remember the last few hours in more than flashes. She knows she has not left the strangers alone, nor her king. They have all remained together, cloistered, even as the hall was surrounded by desperate petitioners. She knows that Prior-ess Jacynde did not come to join them, even though Ser Leodegardis has sent off at least five runners. Now, though, the hall is quiet, and beyond the walls, people have dragged themselves off to bed, driven there, perhaps, by guards—but Ser Voyne couldn't say for certain.

She has been too focused on the food.

Somebody must be preparing it, for it appears on the long table they sit around, over and over again. She does not remember the saints and their Lady bringing baskets or bushels with them, but there is more than dried, stringy meat on their plates. There are red fruits, cherries and currants and strawberries, all ripe and burst-ing, all *fresh*. More sweet comb than the Priory's hives could have produced is scattered between every serving dish. There are tender leaves, and crisp cucumbers, and early squashes, roasted to perfec-tion. Voyne can't help herself. She picks up one of the pea pods be-tween her fingers, squeezes, stares at the smooth green pearl that emerges.

She places it in her mouth, chews, and nearly cries once more for how her tongue is coated with fresh vegetal brightness.

Voyne thinks she could eat forever, fingers stained red with juice, but then she glances at the window and it is night. Where did the time go? It takes every inch of her willpower to drag her focus back to her king, who sits beside her, beard stained red as well.

He is speaking about his childhood.

Stories tumble out of him, and Ser Voyne remembers, now, how they have passed the afternoon: not in counsel but in these fountains of stories. Her head aches. What has she told them? She thinks not much; her throat is not sore from speaking. But she remembers scraps of Leodegardis's tales, about how it felt to be granted Aymar to protect. The importance of careful governance, of the reciprocal relationship between lord and subject. How he is so glad to have a chance to feed his starving people, how he thought he had failed them. She listens, now, as Cardimir talks about his wife, dead three years, and his sons, almost full-grown. He is speaking not as a king, but as a man; where is his propriety?

"And you, Ser Voyne?" asks the Constant Lady, at last turning Her gaze on Voyne. "Will you gift to us a piece of your past?"

If Voyne doesn't think (and it is so *hard* to think right now), she can see not just the Constant Lady with Her curtain of golden hair, but Treila, too. She can feel the rage and silence of Carcabonne, the warmth of Treila de Batrolin's household, the glittering period between betrayal and judgment, before Voyne knew who to blame for the suffering and deaths of so many. And then she thinks she will weep again, pinned by old mistakes, fierce regrets, confusion, desperation.

When did she become so weak?

Perhaps it is only natural, in the presence of divinity. Weakness as holy offering, radical devotion. Her king cannot see her falter, but the Lady accepts it. Drinks it in. It is okay to fall apart, when there are long white fingers to catch her.

She doesn't need the attentions of the Lady; she needs the Absolving Saint to come and kiss her brow and ease the guilt and pain in her, recognize her, see her for who she is.

The Lady notes her silence. Her brow softens, but Her eyes seem to sharpen, to cutting glass. "Surely, you have triumphs?" She presses.

It's a gentle nudge, from the blood she remembers on her hands with guilt to that she remembers with pride. Yes, she has had her conquests, too.

"Many," she agrees. She doesn't know where to start. She looks to Leodegardis, to her king, and they gaze back with gentle expectation. Neither moves to offer her direction.

And then, at the far end of the hall, the doors open. Memories fall away, and she and Leodegardis are on their feet reflexively. Voyne reaches for her weapon, only to realize it isn't on her hip. When did she remove it? Where did she place it? How could she not notice, when she has spent so many years carrying its weight, that her gait is slightly but irrevocably altered?

But it's only Prioress Jacynde in the doorway; it would be blasphemy to draw a sword. Blasphemy doubled by their holy audience. The worry about her sword drops away as she and Leodegardis make their bows.

Jacynde does not look pleased.

She has brought with her two of her nuns, their shorn heads covered by cloth knotted at the napes of their necks, the knots stuck through with heavy ornaments. They are wearing full robes, which Voyne realizes she has not seen them do except for the three high holy days they have passed in captivity. Jacynde herself is in full regalia, embroidered stole draped over her shoulders, layer upon layer of gauzy silk hiding all the lines of her body. Her face is painted, in seeming echo of the faces of the saints.

Voyne registers, dimly, that this looks like armor. Perhaps it is the martial set of Jacynde's jaw.

Jacynde's attendants hold two small skeps. Not live ones; they do not hum with life. Not offerings, then, but—

"Your Highness," Prioress Jacynde says, and the sharpness of her voice stops Voyne's thoughts, reorients them once more toward defense. "May I speak with you?"

Behind Voyne, Cardimir stands as well. "Come and sit at my table, Prioress," he says, and Voyne can hear the threat in it.

Where *is* her sword?

Jacynde ignores the king's warning, his invitation, and does not break stride as she sweeps down upon the saints.

"I don't know who you are," Prioress Jacynde says, standing within a breath of the Constant Lady, "but you are not welcome here."

"Prioress," the king warns. "These people are my guests."

The Constant Lady does not flinch, nor cower, nor offer appeasement. She blinks, placidly. "Jacynde de Montsansen," she pronounces, and the prioress's rageful countenance stills, dulls. "I do not begrudge you your doubts. But please, let me help you. Let me bring food to your table, as you have begged me so often these last weeks."

Jacynde's face contorts. Her lips part. Her girls shift where they stand, stealing glances at each other, at the saints arrayed behind the Constant Lady.

"And from where comes this food?" Jacynde asks, gesturing at the dishes arrayed across the table, the fruit, the greens. "Whose fields? Whose hands? This," she says, stalking forward and grabbing up slender stems of asparagus, tender and pliant, "is gone some three months now. And there will be no currants in this abundance for another month on."

The prioress has a point, Ser Voyne realizes with a lurch, like the shock of a cool breeze piercing the heady haze inside the hall. She knows this. She *knew* this. When the Constant Lady came through the gates (*through* the gates? a knowing part of her whispers), there were no stores with them, no traveling companions, and though the Constant Lady is no mortal woman, surely, *surely*, the divine must either be far less solid, or far more understandable.

If Prioress Jacynde told her otherwise, Ser Voyne would believe it. She is not a student of metaphysics, of faith. Perhaps she is wrong. But Jacynde is afraid, and so Voyne remembers to be afraid.

This is a war. The chances that an unknown, unexpected kindness is safe and good are so minuscule she could laugh.

Voyne is lethargic from the food, the heat, but she rises to her feet all the same. Her gaze darts across the room, takes in all the details again. These strangers with their paints, their luminous eyes, their fine clothing. Their appearances, so close to the icons that are walked around the walls each day. How have they sat here, for hours upon hours, and talked of *nothing* of substance?

No plans for escape. No explanations. Not even hope, not really—only distractions.

The food curdles in her belly.

Jacynde tosses the asparagus on to the floor, steps back in disgust. The few servants and her attendants look between it and her, and Voyne can see the hunger in their eyes. But then Jacynde is rounding once more on the Lady, and Voyne moves to stand behind her king, as if she can offer protection.

"Whatever you are, you are not Her," Jacynde snaps. "Where is your *order*?"

Order. The Priory's machines, their careful measurements and engineering, all at the behest of the Constant Lady. Constant, because She is the reason the world works as it should, in predictable ways. For a moment, Voyne feels a spike of doubt. This Lady who has brought them food—She is something wilder. A riotous wood in place of a manicured garden.

But what else *could* She be? Because She is certainly not human.

The king snorts, derisive. Jacynde's attention shoots to him, then back, as if she cannot risk taking her eyes off of the Lady.

The Lady only gazes back at her, perfect yellow-painted lips frowning, hurt. A perfect pantomime. "Does it frighten you so much, that you might have been wrong?" the Lady asks.

Jacynde makes a shocked, choking sound.

"That you may have worshipped wrong all these years, imposed so many strictures upon when and how you may ask for help? I have always been here for you, Jacynde de Montsansen. But sometimes it is so hard to hear you, through all your machines. Come. Sit with me. I will take your anger into myself and give you back only bounty."

Murmurings, from the two nuns, desperate, confused, hungry. They step as if to go to her, but Jacynde spreads her arms out, forming herself into a wall. Her anger is fracturing, though. Voyne can see it. Can see devastation, can *feel* it, echoing through her with so much familiarity. Voyne knows what it is to doubt, to realize that the lens through which you have viewed the world and built your life is only one possibility.

But then Jacynde's expression hardens. "My faith does not waver," she spits. "And you are not that which I serve."

The Lady's lips curve in a perfect painted frown as She picks up a goblet of wine and holds out one fine hand. The Loving Saint rises and gives Her a piece of weeping honeycomb. He has pulled it from one of the skeps, taken from Jacynde's girls and now buzzing with life. She has a flash of memory: a comb dripping gold onto Phosyne's hands. *Phosyne.* Voyne should be with her. Watching her. And then the thought is gone, and it is all Voyne can do to keep her eyes trained on the Lady as honey slides down Her pale skin, drips into the wine.

"That can be righted. Kneel, sweet child," the Constant Lady says, raising Her eyes to Prioress Jacynde. Jacynde moves as if to look away, then stops, caught. Voyne knows what she sees, those impossible rings of color. But unlike Voyne, she remains standing. She backs away. She turns as if to flee.

The Warding Saint rises from his seat and seizes one arm. The Absolving Saint takes the other. They hold her gently, so gently, their fingers barely pressing into her arms. Jacynde doesn't fight, but weeps.

The Lady raises the cup to her lips.

Jacynde drinks. Her eyelids flutter.

This isn't right.

Cold burns down through Voyne's spine, snapping hard against the heat of the room. Her fingers close over Cardimir's knife. It isn't a sword, but it will do. She bares her teeth and lunges for the Constant Lady.

The Warding Saint steps in between them. Voyne's blow lands on armor that rings strangely in the sudden silence of the hall, and the blade skips, jumps, cuts into the exposed divot of the inside of the saint's elbow. A roar rips from the Warding Saint's placid face, and then he catches her by the jaw, and stares into her eyes.

And Ser Voyne is on her knees again, and it is the Constant Lady bending over her.

She hears the buzzing of bees inside her skull as the Constant Lady gazes into her eyes. The spiraling colors seem to dance, and Voyne strains upward, lips parted, thoughts all in disarray. Did she really lunge with the knife? There is no knife in her fingers. She does not smell blood. The Warding Saint still sits at the table, speaking with the king.

Jacynde is prone upon the floor, and her nuns have joined the feast.

The Constant Lady strokes Voyne's cheek, and Voyne trembles at Her touch. "Be still," She murmurs. "Breathe. Breathe for me, Ser Voyne."

The righteous fury bleeds from her so swiftly she doesn't notice its passing, and she is filled, instead, with yearning. Her lungs work to a steady beat. Inhale. Exhale. The Lady smells of honey.

"What a beautiful creature," the Lady says. "Honed to such a sharp edge. So loyal. So brave. So ready to leap into the fray." Yes, Voyne thinks, and then frowns as she recalls the weight of a blade in her hand. Recently. So recently she can still feel the vibration of a blow up to her shoulder, the faint echo of collision. But she doesn't remember lifting a blade.

"Your king is not as good to you as he should be, perhaps. Does he not know what he has in you? The passion. The strength. You would break yourself open against every weapon Etrebia could bring to bear on you, and still push forward. You'd spear yourself on the blade and keep walking, until you could wring the life from their necks. Wouldn't you?"

"Yes," Ser Voyne says, and she can see it. Taste it. She wants to be outside of the walls, riding down hard against the enemy. She wants to push them back. She wants to free them all.

But there is a leash around her neck, and she can't go beyond the wall. Voyne cannot stop the animal whine that builds in her throat at the thought, but the Lady is there to soothe her, press cool lips to her brow.

"He wastes you. I can see how you strain."

"Yes," she gasps.

"I would cultivate you," the Lady breathes into her skin. "Only say that you will be my champion, and I will loose you upon the world."

Something twists in the back of Ser Voyne's head. Something

howls. But this is all Ser Voyne has wanted for five years now, and she tilts her head up. She doesn't look at Leodegardis, or her king, or anybody else in the room.

She looks up at her Lady, at Treila de Batrolin, at the rising sun, and smiles. "It would be my honor," she says.

Her Lady rewards her with a kiss. Voyne tastes honey on Her lips.

15

HE NIGHT COOLS around Phosyne as she rocks on the wall of Aymar castle.

She has called the Constant Lady and Her saints. She has done the impossible. The divine does not walk upon the earth like humans, like dogs, like creeping bugs. If it were that simple, there would be no wars, no disorder in the world. And yet her prayer, her desperation . . .

Perhaps it was only coincidence. Perhaps it is the Priory that has done something unprecedented. But she knows that can't be true; she knew it when she saw Jacynde absent from that room. Knew it even when she spoke with Jacynde the other day, when she realized that any success of hers would be something beyond what mortals were meant for.

Magic. Intercession. A summoning.

Will it even matter that she has called their Lady?

A miracle so profound may be indistinguishable from horror. Phosyne certainly feels horrified.

Every step away from her faith and toward an understanding of the unseen world has done a little more damage. First, she was no longer so fascinated by the exactitude of the bee space's measurements that she couldn't see the alchemy in how honey was formed, or in the transformation from egg to larva to winged beauty. From there she pursued her heretical texts, ignored all guidance, all advice, broke with the Priory and abandoned her nun's name and chose to call herself Phosyne. To that point, it was all theoretical, but then she cleaned the water, and that . . . that began to break the order of things. Her pursuits are anathema to the divine structure of the world, even if Phosyne believes them to be more true. Her sisters might even now be waiting for her in her tower room, and she has only escaped them and the flame by the barest margin.

And yet there is nowhere else for her to return to. It is the little world she has made herself, a refuge from all the rest.

Feeling like she is walking toward death, she makes herself stand up. Her knees wobble. She pitches forward, and uses the momentum to keep on toward her tower.

Each step is harder than the last, though. The weakness she felt earlier in the day is back a hundred-fold, fed on her guilt and shame. She reaches the upper bailey without falling, but it is a near thing. She weaves in the darkness, closes her eyes, and when she opens them again, she is at the base of one of the towers. Not hers, but close.

She stares at the spiraling steps.

Up seems impossible, but down is easier. She stumbles down the steps, into a pocket of darkness. Her head is spinning. Her knees are weak. If she just sits a little, rests, she can put herself back together again. She needs to construct an argument that will sway Ser Voyne and all the rest, and she doesn't think *I may have summoned them from someplace dangerous* will get her the results she wants.

She sinks to her knees, then keeps going, helpless to stop herself. One breath she is upright, and the next she is laid out, aching, skin tight over her bones. The stone below her is cool, at least, and drains some of the heat away, but she cannot move, and she cannot *think*, and oh, this is bad.

Walking this much was a bad decision. She didn't have the strength for it. She hasn't walked so far since chasing after Pneio, and she has only eaten less and less.

She lies there for a long time, hoping that the strength will come back to her. It doesn't. She should call out for help, but she doesn't want to explain what she's doing down here. Instead, she imagines her little pallet and wonders, if she dreams about resting there, if she'll wake up there when she opens her eyes again.

Unlikely.

She forces her eyes open again a few minutes later; she's fairly certain she heard footsteps, though she doesn't know how long ago. A girl with blonde, curling hair peers down at her. She can't be more than twenty, but Phosyne sees something in her eyes that makes her twitch and roll away with a weak moan.

"You're Ser Leodegardis's madwoman, aren't you?" the girl asks.

Yes, she supposes she is.

The girl leans in again, her face too close for comfort. Then her nose wrinkles. "Stay there," she says, and then she is gone.

Phosyne doesn't particularly want to follow orders, but she can't get her legs to work again. She's tired. She's so *tired*, the panic having stolen every last drop of her waning strength.

She half expects the girl to come back with Ser Voyne, or not at all, but when she returns (how much later? Five minutes? Five hours? Phosyne can't be certain), she is carrying a little pouch. She crouches down beside Phosyne and from that pouch pulls—

Dried fruit.

Phosyne's mouth would water, if she weren't such a dried-out husk herself.

"You realize you're dying, right?" the girl says.

Phosyne manages a weak smile. "Aren't we all?" she whispers hoarsely.

The girl quirks a brow. "Fruit will help. I've been there before." Echoes of Ser Voyne. How many in this castle have come close enough to death to learn from it? That means something, Phosyne thinks, but can't discern *what*.

Maybe just bad luck.

"Please," she says, when the girl doesn't move to put the wrinkled fruit between her lips. "I don't know if I can get up."

The girl looks her over, appraising. "You can," she declares. "For a little while longer, anyway. Probably doesn't feel like it, though."

There's an undercurrent of something sharp in her words. *Cruelty*, Phosyne realizes. "Please," she says again, more forcefully this time. "Or—or send for Ser Voyne. She will want to know where I am."

"She's a little distracted with our visitors," the girl says, smiling. It doesn't look like a real smile.

Then again, much of the room doesn't look like a real room. The darkness is emptiness, and if Phosyne doesn't concentrate very hard, she thinks she'll fall through the floor. She pays attention to its solidity. It's very hard. Her back hurts.

The girl waggles the fruit. "I've only got a little of this left," she says. "So in return, I want something from you."

"Oh," Phosyne says. Blinks owlishly up at her.

"Glad to see you understand," the girl says, that not-smile still on her lips. "They say you're a heretic. Is that true?"

Phosyne winces. "More or less." She's thinking of Pneio and Ornuo and their new guests. Yes, that probably counts as heresy. Then again, if she can summon whole people now, she really should be able to summon food. Fill this little room with cabbages.

No, better to focus on not falling through the floor.

"Focus, please," the girl says, but she doesn't mean about the floor. Phosyne squints up at her. "I want a way out."

"I'm afraid," Phosyne replies, "that I'm fresh out of miracles."

The girl looks at the fruit, then takes a bite herself.

Phosyne groans.

"A way out," she repeats, hoping the girl has more of an idea than *that*.

From the way her brow pinches, she does. "There's a way *down*," the girl says after a brief silence. "To where the well fills. But there's—" She falters. Reorients. "I can feel a breeze, but it's coming through a very narrow crack."

"I'm told picks work well on stone."

That not-smile is back, wider this time. "But we melted down all the iron," she says.

Ah. So they did. *Thank you, Prioress Jacynde*, Phosyne thinks. No iron. No iron makes this harder. Makes . . .

A thought almost sticks in her mind, an idea, something that makes her deeply uncomfortable. But then it's gone again.

"I don't know," she says, closing her eyes tightly. She doesn't want to see the girl finish off that bit of fruit. "Stone is . . . I can't say with any certainty what to do. I know a little about water. That's all." She needs to offer up something, though, if she's going to get back up to her tower. Maybe, if she gets that far, she can confess to Ser Voyne, and then the knight will slit her throat and go to fix this whole mess.

That thought is far more comforting than it should be.

She tries to wet her cracked lips; it doesn't work. But she does open her eyes, looking at the faint suggestion of shapes above her, stone pressed against stone. Stone below her, too. It's very solid, but she knows she could fall through it, if she isn't careful. That must mean there's space there, even if she can't see it.

"You give up?" the girl asks.

"No," she says, surprising herself, but her mind is already working. Space inside the stone, so if it could be reconfigured—but how?—wind can pass through it, water can pass through it—stone becomes rubble, becomes gravel, becomes pebbles, becomes sand—

They have no iron, but they have water and air and, Phosyne thinks, flame. *Flame.*

"I need more information," Phosyne says, slowly, "but I would presume its . . . dark down there?"

"More or less," the girl says.

Strange. No time to consider it, though. "I can give you a candle," Phosyne says, looking back to the girl's face. "It will burn without ceasing. The wax won't run out."

"It's a tight squeeze," the girl says, but Phosyne can see a little light behind her eyes, eagerness, desire. Oh, yes, this might be enough to get a few nibbles. "How easily is it snuffed out?"

"It isn't," Phosyne says, lips twisting in a return not-smile. "Only water works."

"Good," the girl says. "Oh, very good. Here," she says, and presses the bit of fruit to Phosyne's lips at last.

She tries to chew it. It's hard. It'll take a bit of time, but she can just hold it in her mouth, let it soften, ooze. Her throat is so dry, though. She's not sure she can swallow.

The girl takes out another bit of fruit, pops it into her mouth. Phosyne can't help her pained whine, to see it disappear. But the girl holds up one finger, chews, and does not swallow. She just chews and chews and chews, and then she bends down and presses her lips to

Phosyne's. Phosyne's jaw drops open in shock, and the girl's tongue is there, pressing the sweet mush into her mouth, liquid with saliva.

Phosyne nearly chokes, but instead manages to swallow.

"Better?" the girl asks, sitting up. Her eyes sparkle in the dim light.

"Better," Phosyne whispers, weakly.

"Good." She pulls another few bits of fruit from the pouch, but doesn't chew them, thankfully. Instead, she presses them into Phosyne's palm. "Take your time getting up," she says. "But try not to fall asleep, not until you've eaten it all. Can you get out of your tower again, once Ser Voyne has you back?"

"Probably not," Phosyne says with a grimace.

The girl considers, then nods. "Right. Well, she's not there now. Tell me where the candle is."

"No," she says, and tries to sit up. The girl moves to stop her, but Phosyne manages to get upright. Her head spins. "No, it's not safe to go in there on your own. Help me up. Help me up and I'll give you the candle, show you how to light it." And Pneio and Ornuo wouldn't have an opportunity to slip out and wreak further havoc.

The girl doesn't like this option (her scowl is not at all hidden), but she grudgingly wraps an arm beneath Phosyne's shoulders and heaves upward. For all her poise, it's immediately clear that she, too, is weakened. They get to their feet but it's a near thing, both of them holding tight to the other's clothing.

Walking is harder, but they manage. The only real problem is the stairs, which are too narrow to climb abreast. The girl winds up behind her, pushing, hands firm on Phosyne's lower back. The world tilts wildly. They climb.

When at last they reach the king's chambers, they can hear soft voices inside, and the girl pulls Phosyne hard against the stone wall. Then she stops, and Phosyne realizes she must not know where the entrance to her tower is.

Phosyne steers them through the shadows to the little door that leads up and up and—there are no guards, no sign of Ser Voyne—into her fetid rooms.

They really do stink. It's embarrassing. The girl behind her is trying to be stoic, but she twitches with the first tremors of vomit.

Phosyne pulls away and staggers to her workbench, where the candle is still burning. It's the second one she's made; the other is upended in a cup of water, because the moment she takes it out, it starts to burn again. This one is a little more polite. When snuffed, it stays snuffed.

She holds it up. "Here, watch carefully," she says. The flame trembles because her arm is trembling. She sits down on her stool before she can fall.

The girl waits in the doorway, watching. The door, at least, is closed behind her.

Phosyne upends the candle. It continues to burn. Wax does not drip from it. The girl's eyes go wide; apparently she didn't really believe Phosyne until this moment.

Phosyne looks at the inverted flame that does not dance *up*, that ignores the rules of the world, and then she dips it in the cup of water. The flame disappears without smoke.

As she pulls it out, she finds she's feeling better, a little firmer, a little more real, because the girl is staring with naked want now, want and interest that Voyne hasn't matched even while watching the same impossible demonstration. "To light it again is a little tricky. You can't light it from another flame, or it will be just a candle. It will melt, it will gutter. Instead—" And here she rolls the words around in her mouth, hesitating just shy of revealing her secret. It will likely make the girl afraid.

Still, it's how the flame is kindled. "Instead, it needs blood. Possibly my blood. I don't know yet; Ser Voyne won't let me test it on her."

The girl's face transforms, eyes widening, lips parting in a *real* smile, and Phosyne files that away for later. For now, she picks up a little lancet, pricks the tips of her forefinger and thumb right through the existing scabs.

"It also needs a little sulfur." Her blood is sluggish, but as she rubs her fingers together, it spreads out, slickens. She takes a pinch of the foul-smelling yellow powder from a little jar and it soaks up the blood hungrily. "And a note. Can you sing?"

"A little."

"How well do you know your hymns?"

"A little."

Phosyne casts her a curious, appraising look, then shrugs. "The opening note of 'On Breath,'" she says. "Can you sing it for me?"

Nothing.

Phosyne turns back to the candle, sings it herself. It's a clear note, high, higher than feels *right* for this, but it does work. She feels the change in her fingers, where the bloody slurry shifts, realigns. She pinches the wick of the candle.

As she pulls her fingers up and off, it flares to life.

The girl is staring now. Phosyne picks up the candle and holds it out to her with her non-bloodied hand. "Take this down, look more closely at everything, and maybe you'll find a way out you missed. If not, find a way to get to me again. I'll keep thinking."

Cautiously, the girl creeps closer and takes the candle from her. She cradles it in her hands. Tests the flame, then hisses and pulls back; it's hot, of course. Real flame. But it continues to burn even as the girl tests it, waving the wax back and forth. No guttering, no faltering.

Phosyne sifts some of the sulfur into another, empty jar. She holds it out. "Take this, so you can douse that as needed and get it lit again."

"Thank you," the girl says, slipping the jar into a pocket with nimble fingers. "I assume I'm not supposed to tell anybody?"

"It doesn't matter," Phosyne says. She grabs one of the bits of fruit, pops it in her mouth, chews. She closes her eyes in bliss. She moans a little. "But you seem like the type who'd like to hide that. The candle. You don't want them seeing the flame, seeing where you are."

"No, not really," the girl agrees. Phosyne hears her move, but not toward the door. She feels warmth, a little ways from her back, and then hears the hiss of the flame extinguishing once more. "I'm Treila," the girl says, directly behind her.

"Phosyne." Strange, to tell somebody else her name. She hasn't done that in a long time. It makes her feel a little more solid, or maybe that's the fruit. She opens her eyes, leans back, looks up at the shadowy young woman.

"You should eat the honey," Treila says, and points to the chunk of comb, now covered in dust and detritus.

"I'll think about it," she says, but doesn't mean it. It'll serve better as an ingredient, anyway. "Stay away from the *guests*," she adds.

"I'm no fool," Treila says, hiding the doused candle, retreating to the door. "Why do you think I want to get out?"

Phosyne has to concede she has a point.

16

HE CASTLE IS unnaturally quiet. Treila has no trouble slipping down the steps, through the king's quarters, and over to the staircase that leads down to her little workroom. Her mind is loud enough to make up the difference, however, humming with a hundred different thoughts. The impossible candle in her hand, the rotted fruit smell of Phosyne's breath, the renewed possibilities of that hole in the ground.

And she can still feel Ser Voyne's hand on hers the day before. The sweeping *rush* of being so close, finally, to what she's dreamed of for years.

She can also see Ser Voyne's face in the yard just a few hours ago, transported and transfigured and—

Very far away from her.

She missed her chance to really drive the knife home. Take the guilt she'd seen in Ser Voyne's eyes and pluck at the taut harpstring of it until, finally, Ser Voyne fell at *her* feet and begged for forgiveness. She would have been so beautifully devastated when Treila refused. But the rhythm of the castle is changing drastically, and Treila isn't sure how it will shake out, except that Voyne is too central to how their closed world runs; with these intruders, she will be in her element again. She won't have space for doubt and regret.

If Treila's lucky, she won't care about leaving Voyne to her fate, either.

There's no point in wasting time. Whoever these guests are, however they got into Aymar, they're not a way out. At least not one that Treila can take advantage of. They've shifted the balance so abruptly that Treila hates them by reflex. *Saints*, she thinks, and wants to laugh, because there is no such thing as saints. If there were, she wouldn't be trapped here.

Really, she's right back where she started, but she can see more clearly now. She's got a light for her darkness.

Treila crouches where Phosyne had lain not half an hour before, and sucks at her lower lip, staring at her fingers. Just little pricks; Phosyne's had barely bled (though Treila thinks that has more to do with why she'd been lying half-dead on her workshop floor than any calculation of how deep to pierce her skin). Treila has suffered worse. She'd bled more from scraped knees when Ser Voyne—

She pricks her fingers, and the pain seizes her attention, drags it back to the present. She dips her fingers into the little pot of reeking sulfur, then swallows down sludgy saliva and hums the opening note to "On Breath," wavering and embarrassed, and pinches her bloody fingers to the wick.

Heat springs to life between them, and Treila snatches her hand back, stunned.

It works.

It fucking *works*.

A candle is not a pick is not a door, but it is *real*, and it shouldn't be, and Treila can't look away.

She stays there, kneeling on the cold stone, for several minutes, staring until she sees that light burned into the inside of her eyelids. Then, and only then, does she remember what she's here to do.

She wriggles out of her clothing once more, but this time remembers to pack food in the bundle she makes of it. Nothing to do about the water, though. She will have to move quickly.

The light should help with that.

She lowers onto her belly on the cold floor, picks up the candle once more, and places it as far inside the gap as she can. Then she clasps the bundle between her calves, and wriggles her way in after it.

The candle burns without protest. It illuminates jagged stone, fractures in the earth that she hadn't noticed with just her fingers before. It both comforts her and makes her skin crawl; the earth feels so much closer and *heavier*, now that she can see it. In a brief fit of panic, she tries to blow the candle out—and it refuses.

So Treila squeezes her eyes shut, and continues forward by touch.

You're acting like a child, she scolds herself, but it's easier in the dark. There aren't any turns, anyway, and without sight, the walls that press in on her feel only like boundaries, not like the tons of rock above her. They are simply lines she cannot cross, not because of man-built walls but because there simply *is* nothing on the other side.

She wriggles forward, legs grasping tight to her bundle, a rat in a nest. With only one hand free, she drags herself along, loses track of herself in the dark. She makes the trickiest turn without issue, barely noticing it. She's through almost before she realizes it, reaching for the ground and finding nothing beneath her. She pitches forward, drops the candle, eyes snapping open. Carefully, Treila rights herself and drags the bundle up her body. She clutches it to her chest and picks her way down to the ledge below.

The chamber is exactly as she left it, though the golden glow of the candle where it has come to a precarious stop clashes with the faint luminescence of the stream. Treila can only see the blue light at the far end of the little cave, where the candlelight begins to fail. Otherwise, it is erased by more aggressive yellow. She lowers herself down to the narrow bank, righting her candle as she passes.

She dresses this time. Single stocking, smalls, boots, chemise, kirtle, apron, even cap. It cuts the chill, and she has been below the earth long enough to appreciate the barrier, now. Her skin is goose-flesh all over, scraped and raw, and she realizes, as she puts herself back together, that her heart is racing.

Her gaze fixes on the crack.

It is innocuous, in the light. A little line of darkness. There's no obvious path forward; no spidering accessory cracks, no widening a little ways up that she missed in her panic. But Treila takes her time, even turns her back on it to scan the far wall for a matching exit; perhaps the air flows in and out down *here*, and the breeze she feels back in her workroom is only an echo.

But no. There is only the one crack. Wherever the water goes from here, Treila cannot find it.

So she approaches the crack.

It doesn't whisper to her. It remains only stone, even as Treila reaches behind her, fumbles, grabs up the unmelting wax and manages to singe the pad of her palm for the trouble. She brings the candle to the crack, and hopes that her desperate madwoman's heresy can reveal a way forward.

It's still too narrow to admit her whole hand, but the candle is as slender as a finger, and she feeds it into the darkness. A little farther in, she sees the passage widen again. And then she has reached the limit of the candle. She draws it back and tries to think. If she can find the tools, she can break this thin ridge of stone and get through, but she told Phosyne the truth: she doesn't think any pick has survived the Priory's requisitions, and what remains (swords, armor, arrowheads) will not be strong enough for this.

So much for the flame revealing anything useful.

Frustrated, she turns back to the tunnel that will return her to the castle, but one glance of the flame off the close walls has her heart hammering again. She dunks the candle in the stream. The cavern plunges into its almost-darkness, and now she is lit only by the steady, unnatural glow of the water. Her fear ebbs.

She rubs the heels of her hands against her eyes and lets out a creaking laugh. Her confidence wavers, threatens to crack beneath the absurdity of her situation, the desperation.

Moved, perhaps, by whimsy, she sets the candle down and turns back to the gap. She rests her head against the stone. "I *am* lost," she confesses, to herself, laughing again. "So many roads to walk down, and all of them lead nowhere."

The air shifts around her. Her eyes shut. She waits.

"I've missed you," the crack breathes against her lips.

This time she does not scream.

She stands entirely still. Her lips curl just a fraction. This might just be her mind, fracturing at last from the strain bowing her shoulders, but she doesn't think so. Above the smell of damp earth and stone, she can smell a metallic tang, too, like the inside of the smithy. It cuts through the lingering stink of shit, replaces it entirely as she breathes deep.

If this is not just a desperate imagining, then perhaps it is a new road.

"And who are you?" she asks, now trembling with eagerness. With a flash of desire. Down here, in the crowded dark, she feels like *herself*, truly herself, so close to how she'd felt when she'd dangled that fruit in front of Phosyne but oh, so much sweeter than that.

It's time to escape, but not to give up.

"A friend." The voice is growing firmer, louder. It's still just a whisper, but it sounds young. Boyish, perhaps. Pleased. She fights the urge to light the candle again, press it into the gap to get a look at the speaker's face.

"A friend? And how do you know that?"

"Because I'd like to help you," the voice—the boy—replies. "If you're lost, I can help. I know where you are."

A thought occurs to her. Her brow furrows as she flattens herself against the gap, standing straighter. "Are you a sapper? Sent by Etrebia to find a way into our water? Did you foul it yourself?"

He laughs, delighted. "Look down," he says.

She does. She sees only the faint glow of the water, running into the crack. Into the . . .

Oh. The well shaft is between her and the encamped army. From here, the water flows out toward the cliff edge. There is no way the enemy could reach here, *would* reach here without spilling up into Aymar itself first.

Fear twists in her at last. He cannot be Etrebian, and he cannot be *here*, because there's nowhere for somebody to come from.

"You see," he murmurs, still pleased. "Oh, you are clever. I like you. What is your name?"

Treila is a common name, and she's never lied about it. She's too possessive of her own identity, even transformed as it's become. But fear makes her hesitate. She's too cautious to answer straight out, no matter how harmless the question seems. She turns the question around, barbs out. "Tell me yours, first."

He laughs again. He doesn't answer. "I'll just call you *clever*, then," he says instead. "Are you frightened? You sound a little frightened. You don't need to be."

Treila doesn't speak.

"I know the way out," he says. "To freedom, and green grass, and the bounty of summer. I can give it to you."

Her stomach cramps with longing. She closes her eyes and imagines it, fleeing once more into the woods, but this time in a better time of year, with more skills at hand. She would stay close, she thinks. Watch the castle from afar. Wait to see if it falls, or if Ser Voyne emerges, scarred but ready to be pursued once more. She can reset the calendar, try again.

Or maybe leave. Walk away. She suspects she could find a home in Etrebia's camp. If they lose, she could follow them across the border. If not, she has some knowledge their leaders might find valuable, and perhaps one day she'd sit in her childhood home once more. Be the traitor they accused her father of being.

"What are you dreaming of?" the boy asks.

Home, she almost says.

"Your breath sounds melancholy," he adds. "Do you long for it so much, then?"

"If you're going to do it, then do it," she snaps in challenge, suddenly too raw, too delicate to be pushed further.

He hums, but offers nothing else.

He also doesn't retreat. She can feel him, through the narrow gap. Patient. Waiting. She thinks of Phosyne on the floor of her workshop. "Or tell me what you ask for in return."

"That's more fair, don't you think?" he asks.

"It is the way the world works," she concedes.

"A touch."

Treila blinks, confused, unable to form any response, question or otherwise.

A soft sound comes from the crack—not a word, not a breath, something closer to a hand against rock.

"Just a touch?" she asks.

"To start with." She swears she can hear a smile. She doesn't hear a threat, though she imagines one anyway. *To start with* is an open door. She doesn't want an unbounded bargain. Too many things can slip in.

She looks down, steps back just enough to measure the height of the gap again. Thinks over what she knows. Here, now, she has no further options; a candle gives her nothing. Above, the world is swiftly contracting, and the rules have changed so much Treila will not know where to step safely for much longer. What can she give Phosyne to produce another answer? What else does she have to bargain with, herself?

She doesn't suspect she'll find the woman half-dead again anytime soon, anyway. She's more likely to find a corpse.

Just a touch. She thinks of the green world beyond this dark hole, and comes once more to the gap. She hears a boyish intake of breath. She closes her eyes.

She slides one finger into the stone. She waits to feel skin, or scruff, or fabric.

Instead, she feels *teeth*. Wet lips closing around her. A tongue curling around her joint, sliding along her nail.

Treila shouts and draws back, stumbles, nearly falls. She loses a strip of flesh in the process. Blood oozes from the open welt as she clutches her hand to her chest.

"Come back," the voice entreats. "Come back, or the deal won't be satisfied."

"You said a touch!" she cries, shocked, horrified, confused.

"I'm hungry," the voice whines, louder now, loud enough that it echoes around the little cavern.

Treila can't stop her bark of a laugh. "Join the club."

"You understand," he counters. "You know what it is to starve." And she does, but she has never—would never—

Except she has. Just not like this. Not so openly, so baldly, and she remembers Voyne in the garden, disgusted and overwrought. Nausea rises in her.

"Can you even free me?" she asks.

"Oh, yes. Just satisfy my hunger."

"I have food," she says, swallowing the bile down.

"I don't want your food," he says. "*This* is the price of freedom: one finger. You can even choose it."

She shudders.

When contrasted against her stores, though, it's not so heavy a price. Strange. Unthinkable, almost. But not heavy, and for a moment, she even thinks to pay it. That only lasts as long as it takes her to ask, "What kind of man wants a girl's finger?"

He only laughs in reply.

No kind of man, she realizes. Not even a starving man would ask for a *finger.*

With shaking hands, she grabs up the pillar of wax again, finds the little jar of powder. She fumbles for the pin she left in the hem of her skirt, pricks her fingers and dips them, whistles out the note.

"What are you doing, clever?" the voice asks. He sounds curious, not afraid. Treila doubts, but pinches the wick anyway.

The flame springs to life once more, and she jams it into the crack. Nothing looks back at her. No teeth, no lips, no tongue. Not even an eye, peering out at her, watching.

"You'd hide from me?" she hisses.

There is no response. The scent of metal is gone. And Treila, for the first time since she doused the candle, feels like she's alone again.

Perhaps Phosyne's bargain was worth something after all.

Treila leaves the candle burning, stuck between two stones just before the crack, and she retreats back into the castle by touch.

17

ORNING COMES WITH the blare of trumpets.

Phosyne wakes, sprawled face down among her books and the rags that make up her pallet, two warm, sinuous bodies draped across her back and legs. Ornuo and Pneio are heavy when they want to be, which seems to coincide with when she most wants to throw them across the room. Groaning, stiff and exhausted and *hungry* like she can't remember being (really hungry, not just starving, because she understands now that the two are quite distinct), she wriggles out from beneath them and hauls herself over to the window.

It feels like yesterday all over again. The yard is full of bodies, people watching with upturned faces as salvation is once more dangled in front of them. The saints (visitors, guests, *impossible creatures*) stand in the lower yard. The king and his attendants this time remain in the upper yard, but Ser Voyne is not among them.

No, she stands in the lower yard. She is not wearing armor, so it takes Phosyne longer to spot her, but there she is, half-shorn head turned to the woman who looks like the Constant Lady, gaze unwavering.

Phosyne chews her lip. Peels up a patch of dried skin, swallows it down. It only makes her stomach growl harder.

The trumpets blast again, and this time the noise sends the boys skittering below her blankets, huffing grumpily. Phosyne hesitates just a moment, then pushes on the glass, wriggles it free so that she can breathe a little fresh air and, just barely, make out the words below.

She can't hear the king himself, of course, but his criers repeat his words at the tops of their lungs.

"*We have been delivered,*" the criers shout. "*Our prayers have been answered. Our saviors bring with them good food and good wine, and tonight we will dine as one people, in gratitude.*"

Nothing is said of the army that still (Phosyne checks) masses outside the gates. Nothing is said of how they will leave this place. But at the mention of a feast, Phosyne watches the crowd ripple.

They are falling to their knees. Her own have gone weak as well.

"*Every person in Aymar will eat and drink their fill tonight,*" the king continues through his speakers. He doesn't seem to notice that there are no wagons of provisions below him, behind him, or anywhere at all inside the walls. Do they mean to bring them up from beyond the enemy lines? Or will they do what Phosyne was tasked with, and conjure sustenance from nothing? "*There will be no rations, and no divisions among us. Rest, today, and make ready for the revels of the evening.*"

A cheer goes up. Nobody sees what Phosyne sees, that this is wrong in so many ways. And it isn't even the promises of salvation, or the sudden appearance of the saints who now turn to their swarming petitioners, or the mass of bodies that bows to touch the hems of their robes, while Ser Voyne stays glued to the Constant Lady's side.

It's the simple fact that the king should not be the one making this announcement. That is the Priory's task, to be the intermediary between the numinous and the mundane. They should be organizing this adulation, rewarding patience with honey on the tongue.

But there are no nuns in the yard. Even Jacynde is nowhere to be seen. Just like the night before.

That's because she knows this is your fault. Phosyne groans and closes the window. *She knows something is wrong, and she knows who is to blame.*

Still, nobody dragged her from the tower in the middle of the night. That sits wrong in her gut, even as she feels relief. Ser Leodegardis will, of course, stand by his liege, and might even attempt to protect her, even if he doesn't believe the saints are who they claim to be. But he's no fool. If Jacynde has doubts (and she must, or she would have been out in the yard)—and if she has realized that the only other source of dubious miracles in these walls is Phosyne (which she did months ago)—then she would have demanded Phosyne, and Leodegardis would have at least come to question her.

That nobody has so much as knocked since Treila returned her to her little pen is concerning.

She stumbles down her steps, braced against the wall, and tries once more to recall how she summoned Ornuo and Pneio. Why can't she remember? She *does* remember the terror of it, and the subsequent delight, as they curled into her lap and nuzzled at her jaw, companionship when she didn't know she had been aching for it for so long. But the actual invocations? It's a blank spot in her memory. Food, perhaps, will unlock what she couldn't remember last night, but her thoughts remain sluggish, recalcitrant.

The fruit was not enough to revive her fully, and her continuing, gnawing hunger demands she sate it, so she eats two pieces of tough beef, and another strip of meat she doesn't recognize the flavor of. As she chews the last, she has a flash of brambles beneath her feet, nose low to the ground, a hundred different scents, and then the bright clarion call of a horn.

She swallows. It goes away.

Frowning, she looks for more of the fruit Treila paid her, but finds none. Either she ate it all last night (hopefully), or the boys decided to eat it (likely). Then she remembers the honey again, but when she turns to it, she finds it . . .

Well, it doesn't even look like comb anymore.

Phosyne scowls at the puddle of muck. It looks like *rot*, but that is impossible. Honey in the comb doesn't turn; the bees have made sure of that. Her gaze slides to Ornuo, who has twined around her ankles and gazes up at her with wide, ruby eyes.

"What have you done this time?" she groans, then hops on one foot to extricate herself.

He lets her, merciful beast, only to sit up on his hind legs and snap the jerky she tosses him from the air with powerful jaws. His brother joins him, and when a bit of hide lands between them, they tussle for it. *Just beasts*, she tells herself, watching them. They are only beasts, like cats or hounds, and that they came from nothing should not be so damning. Her ideas come from nothing, after all, and they have given her pure water.

The door to her tower moves in its frame.

The boys stop fighting, and instead flatten themselves to the ground, backing up to take refuge in their hiding spots. Normally, they would have thrown themselves under the table by now; Phosyne's skin turns to gooseflesh as she edges closer to the door.

She should have rebuilt the barricade, or at least reset the locks.

"Ser Voyne?" she calls, hoping it is only that, but Ser Voyne would have thrown the door open, stalked inside, demanded answers. And Treila, though Phosyne barely knows her, would have simply entered as well—of that, she is unsettlingly sure.

The door does not move again.

She goes to her spyglass and peeks through to the hall. Nobody is visible in the limited scope. Just empty stone.

It makes no sense. But this is an opportunity: her workbench is long enough to span the doorway, and Phosyne can block it all up once more. For the first time since Ser Voyne was assigned as her *minder*, she can have real privacy again. There's a threat outside, and she can truly take shelter, and give herself the time to think and remember.

But why would somebody knock, and then leave so quickly? Phosyne's teeth chew at her lower lip, and then she opens the door a crack, just to get a better look. A wider vantage.

There's nobody there.

Phosyne looks back into her room, sees the rot and filth, smells it anew. She shudders, feeling disgust for the first time. The ownerless knock hangs in the air around her, a temptation, a question. Search for the answer, or retreat back into her moldering hovel, trying to unravel why her invocations would be worth listening to?

She steps out onto the stairs. She closes the door tight behind her. She rests her head against the wood.

Soft footsteps pad down the stairs.

Phosyne follows.

It's very similar to how she chases down her ideas. They come out of nowhere, in sudden flashes, and she is helpless to do anything but pursue them. Something similar, she thinks, happened before Ornuo and Pneio arrived. She had been stringing up her corkindrill, face-to-face with the beast's sharp teeth, and she had leaned in, put her head inside the jaws, and—

"Sefridis!"

Phosyne staggers to a halt, and realizes she's gone all the way down to the ground floor, where the garrison should be stationed.

Like last night, it's empty, except for the person who called her name.

Her old name.

It's one of the nuns, thin-faced and desperate. She looks *hunted*, and Phosyne instinctively looks past her for a threat. She sees none. The room is empty. The woman tugs on her sleeve, and Phosyne looks at her again, mouth open with a question.

"You must come with me," the nun demands. "You must help."

"Prioress Jacynde?" Phosyne ventures, though this feels wrong. Her old name, and a direct plea for help? Jacynde would never do either. And this nun, she is young, younger than Phosyne by at least five or ten years. Little more than a child.

Phosyne doesn't recognize her face.

The little nun nods. "Yes, the Prioress, she's—but you must see for yourself."

She should say no. She owes the Priory, if not Jacynde, for so much of her education, her life until just recently. And yet if she is responsible for the impossible food the night before, the coming feast, the appearance of the Constant Lady . . .

"Where is she?" Phosyne asks. "Is she—is she with the visitors?"

The little nun wrings her hands. She is the very image of pathos. "She was," the nun says. And then terror seems to clot her throat, if the whites of her eyes are anything to go by.

"Of course, I'll help as I can," she says, blood turning to ice.

The nun nods, relief making her tongue her lips a moment, and then she turns and is off, racing for the chapel.

Phosyne follows.

The yard is still full of people, though Phosyne cannot see the king, nor the saints, nor Ser Voyne. They have to weave through the crowd, and Phosyne hears them weeping, praying, cheering. The crush of hopeful bodies is almost too much, and twice, Phosyne nearly loses track of the little nun.

But when they reach the chapel tower, the crowd doesn't thin; it abruptly stops.

It makes no sense. There should be a crush of parishioners here, too; if the faithful can't touch the hem of the saints' robes, they should be on their knees inside, thanking the icons instead. And yet there is nobody.

Her guide is the only sister she sees as they slip into the chapel, though Phosyne cannot see the whole wide room. Now, at midday, the open walls only let in sharp shafts of light and a dim glow; otherwise, the rest of the room is cool and shadowed. But at this time of day, there should be at least ten women here, engaged in various devotional tasks, or sitting with the faithful. Tending the timekeeping candles that burn despite the availability of the sun for measuring each hour, the better to calibrate each measurement. Instead, Phosyne can only make out the shadowed form of somebody standing at the far end of the hall, their posture too martial to be praying.

She doesn't have time to look closer. The girl's hand tugs on her sleeve again, and Phosyne turns to follow.

They wind up the stairs that lead to the observatory platform above the chapel proper, and are almost to the door when the nun stops. She bows her head, and Phosyne expects she's praying, but then she asks, "Did you do this?"

Phosyne can't stop her panicked smile.

"We were tasked to find food," the nun continues, without looking back. "Impossible task, of course, and yet—and yet there's food here now, and when we were tasked to clean the water, impossible task, you delivered us."

If Phosyne speaks, she's going to blurt out her guilt. The temptation is too great. She doesn't like the weight of secrets on her, wants *help* to solve this problem, wants absolution. Phosyne makes a weak, strangled sound, animal in its tone.

"No, it doesn't matter," the nun says, presses her hands to her eyes, then beckons for Phosyne to go ahead of her. "She's up there.

She wouldn't talk to me, but maybe she'll talk to you. I just . . . this all feels wrong. Is it blasphemy, for this all to feel wrong?"

Phosyne wishes she remembered this girl. Wishes, too, that she remembered that oceanic feeling of faith she knows she must have had. Worship was her *life* for twenty years; shouldn't it feel more real to her now than an old, unraveling dream? If it did, maybe she could offer some comfort.

Instead, she slips past the nun and eases open the door.

The wind fights her. The insubstantial breeze down in the yard is stronger up here, where the walls can't stop it, where it's maddening instead of useful. She can't move the door more than an inch until the wind abruptly changes directions, catches the door from the other side, and throws it open. Phosyne stumbles out into the midday sun.

Jacynde *is* there, just as the nun said she would be. Phosyne stares at her prostrate form, then looks behind her. The door stands open, but her escort is gone. She feels unmoored, and sways on her feet as she forces herself to look at the prioress again.

She will have to confess, she tells herself. She couldn't tell that poor girl, no, because what would it have changed? But if she can help Jacynde now, and then tell her what she knows, perhaps Jacynde will have some better idea of where to start. And if not, Phosyne might at least beg some honey to help get her mind working better. If she shows contrition and obedience, maybe Jacynde will take pity on her, given the strange circumstances.

The thought makes her grimace, but she still twitches her robes into some semblance of order and walks away from the shelter of the stairway tower.

Around her are the astrolabes, the telescopes, the tools of measurement that make order out of the world. Jacynde is not using any of them. She is kneeling, head uncovered, staring at nothing. She is inanimate, and Phosyne does remember enough to be afraid. Jacynde is so rarely still.

"Your Radiance," Phosyne says. It comes out as more of a croak.

Jacynde's shoulders shudder.

Phosyne circles around so she can see the prioress's face. She expects to see . . . pain. Pain, and desperation, and the wreckage of a crisis of faith. If Phosyne concentrates, she can imagine it: a lifetime spent as the intercessor to the Lady and Her saints, only to be caught unprepared and unbelieving when the Lady and Her saints actually appeared. Maybe that, instead of doubt or suspicion, is the reason why she has retreated here. Maybe faith, when brought to life, is too much when you are drowned in it your whole life. The sustaining liquor of it suddenly made solid.

And Jacynde doesn't look comfortable, no, but she doesn't look like she's drowning either. She looks . . .

Blank.

There are old tear tracks on her cheek, cutting through layers of paint. Sweat, too, once beaded on her brow, blurring the edges, warping the design. But now her skin looks dry and red. She has been sitting out in this heat for Phosyne cannot guess how long. Too long.

Phosyne reaches out, then stops, hands only an inch or two away from Jacynde's shoulders. The prioress frowns, but not *at* her. Perhaps only at the way she blocks out the light, casting shadow over the woman's face.

Jacynde's lips part, and Phosyne smells blood. It doesn't run out past the prioress's lips, but it clings to the margins of her teeth, lines her gums. And behind that, Phosyne sees—

Nothing. Her tongue is gone. Cut out at the root.

Bile rises in her throat, and Phosyne falls back onto her ass, staring.

As she stares, she catches movement, a pulsing. A faint buzzing.

A bee crawls along Jacynde's hard palette, along her teeth, and out onto her upper lip. It lingers there a moment, flicking its wings to dry them of pink-tinged saliva, and then it alights and disappears into the wide heavens.

That breaks through Phosyne's shock, and in another moment, she's dragging Jacynde against her skinny chest. The prioress is so heavy, in all her robes, but Phosyne urges herself to move. She uses every scrap of strength left in her and hauls Jacynde back toward the stairs. Jacynde is dead weight in her arms, her only response a thin, high whine.

"Who did this to you?" Phosyne asks, shaking, knowing already that the answer is *her*. Not the Lady, but Phosyne herself, somehow summoning salvation. It is *wrong*, has always been wrong, and if Phosyne still felt the slightest bit of control over the situation, that's gone now. Gone, along with the prioress's *tongue*, and oh, Phosyne thinks she is going to be sick.

She crawls instead, pulling them both into the shadow of the tower.

"I'm sorry," she whispers as they collapse together down the spiraling stairs. "I'm sorry, I don't know what I did."

Jacynde only moans in response, and does not flinch as her hip strikes the edge of a stair.

The little nun finds them where the stairs open up onto the chapel, and clasps her hands over her mouth to stifle a cry of horror. She goes to her knees, staring into Jacynde's unblinking eyes. "Is she—is she—"

"Not yet," Phosyne says, head falling back against the stone. It is cool, and the tower is dark, and she has that same feeling she did the night before, that she could very well simply slip through the floor and into somewhere else. "But she needs water, badly." She almost asks if the girl can help carry Jacynde all the way back to her tower, but the thought of Jacynde in her territory is a bridge she cannot cross. "Get her somewhere cool and dark and quiet, get her water, stay with her. Do you understand?"

"Yes," the nun agrees, and though she is likely as weak as Phosyne is, she does a better job of hauling up the limp body of the prioress. "What happened? All I know is that she went to see the—the king and his guests last night, and when she returned, she went up to the observatory. And nobody else thought to check on her."

"Where *is* everybody else?" Phosyne asks.

"Preparing for the feast," she whispers, and she sounds broken.

Phosyne closes her eyes, trying to think, to understand.

When she opens them again, she's alone.

She's still in the stairwell. The *same* stairwell, too, because from where she sits, slumped, she can see the pillars of the chapel, hear the humming of the bees. She must have fallen asleep, then, and the girl has correctly taken Jacynde to safety instead of trying to help her. Slowly, stiffly, Phosyne stands up, expecting her head to spin.

It doesn't.

She's still hungry, of course. Still confused and frightened, too. But her body is no weaker than it was when she climbed these stairs. It's almost as if it never happened at all, save for Jacynde's paint that is still smeared on her fingertips.

And the martial shadow across the chapel is still there, too.

It looks familiar.

Warily, Phosyne steps into the chapel. She half expects to be swarmed by the bees that buzz through the chamber, chased out as a heretic, but they ignore her, tracing out their usual patterns, heading inexorably out past the castle walls instead of turning in. They know there is no nectar to find here.

Phosyne is halfway across the floor by the time she realizes the shadow is Ser Voyne.

Ser Voyne stands alone. There is no king for her to guard, nor the Lady, and her gaze slips over Phosyne, as if Phosyne doesn't exist, let alone require her minding. Phosyne wants to stop and look and evaluate, but if she stops, she's going to drop back to the floor. So she keeps walking, comes so close she can see the color of Ser Voyne's eyes.

They're brown.

"Ser Voyne," she says, barely above a whisper.

Those brown eyes blink, placidly.

"Can you hear me?" Phosyne asks. Ser Voyne does not move from her post. She does not even flick a glance at her, and Phosyne's heart sinks.

This is bad. Voyne should be lunging into action, snatching Phosyne and throwing her once more into a wall, demanding what she thinks she is doing outside of her tower, not working on their miracle. Or she should at least be sneering in irritation, waving Phosyne's madness away like a fly. She does neither. She does nothing. And it is galling, that after a week of hating this woman's presence, that her inattention . . . hurts, even more than it unnerves her. Maybe that's why she seizes the knight's arm, hauls her back into the shadowed niche of the chapel.

That *does* get a response. Ser Voyne looks at her at last as Phosyne crowds her against the wall. She doesn't have the strength to shove her, not like Voyne did to her out by the smithy, but Phosyne feels the echo all the same. She waits for Voyne to fight back. She may be feeling stronger, but the knight is still six inches taller and nearly twice as broad.

And Ser Voyne squirms, but . . . that's it.

It's like she doesn't know what to do. How to lash out. She looks *confused*, brow pinching, lips parting. The glaze of her eyes sharpens, and for just a moment, Phosyne sees panic.

"*Ser Voyne,*" she demands in response. "Listen to me."

Where the command in her voice comes from, she cannot say. Maybe just desperation.

Wherever it hails from, it works. Ser Voyne goes still, but her eyes remain sharp, her brow pinched.

In the brown of her iris, there's a ring of color that doesn't belong. It's hard-edged, like it was inked with a paintbrush.

Phosyne cannot fix this on her own. She knows that. She knew it enough to consider begging forgiveness of Jacynde, who would have her jailed at the slightest opportunity. But Jacynde can't help her, and the feast is tonight, and she needs *somebody* on her side to tell her what to do, what question to solve first. Ser Voyne is supposed to be on her side, even if that hasn't ever worked out for her before.

She reaches up and touches Ser Voyne's cheek.

"Can you hear me?" she asks.

Ser Voyne nods shakily. Her skin twitches beneath Phosyne's touch. Where Jacynde was hot, Voyne is cold. Her eyelids spasm. She's having trouble focusing, thinking.

Phosyne can relate.

"You are to look after me. Do you remember that?"

Ser Voyne nods, slowly, the movement ungainly and wrong. But she does not look away. She is listening. She's *remembering*, with great force of will. Her body has begun to tremble.

Phosyne leans into her. Drags her hands along the muscles of her arms, corded and tense. There's anger there. *Good.* She should be angry. If she could see the mess they're in, she would be raging, and she would be beautiful in her rage.

"I'm out of my tower," Phosyne points out. "I'm not supposed to be. The last time I got out, you nearly killed me. You were so *angry*, because together, we're supposed to be saving this castle, and I never do what you ask."

That gets a snarl out of the bigger woman, and then suddenly, it's not Voyne pressed into the wall, it's Phosyne. Her head cracks against the stone and she bucks, trying to get the knight's weight off her. It doesn't work.

Ser Voyne's fist closes around her throat. Her thumb and forefinger press into the points of Phosyne's jaw, and she gasps, head falling back against the wall. She's supposed to be afraid, she *knows* that, but this whole mess is so confusing and turned on its head that Phosyne isn't really surprised to realize she's enjoying this. That her body *sings* when Ser Voyne squeezes a little tighter, and panic blooms in her chest.

"That's it," she gasps out. "You hate me. Remember?"

Ser Voyne squeezes harder. Phosyne can barely breathe. But on the gasp she does manage, she smells—

Blood.

And she remembers Jacynde's empty, bloody mouth, the pieces clicking into place as she realizes why Ser Voyne was standing below the observatory. The eagerness in her flips to pure terror in an instant, and she begins to thrash. The stone is no longer cold against her back, it's hot with the heat of her body, and she scrabbles against it, eyes closing, lips parting in a silent, airless scream—

And then she's outside of the chapel, on the narrow walkway that rings the tower. There is a wall in front of her. She hears sobbing coming through it. Voyne's sobbing. Somehow she's fallen through the stone and come out whole the other side—and Voyne cannot follow.

Phosyne doesn't look. She just runs.

18

REILA SLEEPS ONLY fitfully. The heat of the summer makes her sweat and thrash in her sleep. Her workroom would be cooler, but she's woken from enough nightmares of teeth against her flesh as it is; she doesn't need to be any closer.

She almost sleeps through the king's proclamation, but Simmonet drags her from her pallet at the first blast of the trumpets. She stares blankly while she's summoned to an impossible feast, pats Simmonet's back as he begins to weep with relief.

All wrong. This is all wrong. She needs to get out, and to get out, she needs to find the madwoman. *Now.*

But by the time she gets up to the tower, it's empty. Phosyne isn't even lying dead up in the loft. There's nobody in the room at all. She considers ransacking it, taking everything that might even slightly be of use, but aside from the candle still submerged in the bucket of murky water, Treila sees absolutely nothing useful. Rotted meat, ratty blankets, a dried reptile hanging from the ceiling, a bucket of piss. Nothing else. Treila stands another long few moments in the open doorway, and once, she thinks she feels something brush against her leg.

Nothing is there.

So she goes hunting.

She prowls throughout Aymar like she's looking for rats, checking every crevice. She can't get into the great hall, where the king is once more cloistered with his guests, or even see through the windows, the crowd is so thick around it. And everywhere else, she doesn't see Phosyne, or Ser Voyne. They're not in the keep, not in the yard, and Treila is ready to scream when she thinks, at last, to check the chapel.

She's not halfway there when she sees Phosyne.

The madwoman is running, weaving, staggering as her weakened muscles threaten to revoke support. She's making straight for the keep, and Treila hesitates. Racing to intercept her might draw attention, when Phosyne is, at least, alive, and likely headed back to her room. But then Phosyne pitches forward, and Treila can't stand to let her hit the ground that hard. She springs across the dusty space between them.

Treila catches Phosyne before she can fall, but can't hold her upright. She sinks slowly to her knees, laying the madwoman across her lap, cradled in her arms. Phosyne flinches away, babbles something incomprehensible.

Treila slaps her.

It doesn't help. She'll need to take a different tack.

"I need your help again," she says, even as she fumbles in her pocket for another nibble of fruit. "Listen. Are you listening?"

But Phosyne is just shaking, not saying anything, gaze darting behind Treila again and again. Back toward the chapel.

With a sinking feeling, Treila turns to look, too.

Ser Voyne is staring at them.

She's not in armor. She's not even armed. But her hands are covered in blood, and for just a moment, Treila is a girl again, staring at her father's headless corpse, staring at Ser Voyne's impassive face, splattered crimson.

She lets go of Phosyne. She barely hears her flee.

Ser Voyne crosses the dusty yard to her in long, rolling steps, proof of the muscles that lie below her arming jacket, her breeches. Her eyes are fixed on Treila, and Treila thinks, distantly, that she should be running too.

She doesn't move, not even when Ser Voyne stops right in front of her.

"Why are you on your knees, my lady?" Ser Voyne asks. Her voice is low and rough, as if she's been screaming. But her expression is kind, entreating, wholly focused on her.

Treila can't breathe.

"Come," Ser Voyne says, and places one gentle hand beneath her elbow, guides her to her feet.

This is an opportunity, Treila thinks, but the thought is distant. She should be triumphant. Here is Ser Voyne, soft and caring. But where is the guilt? The confusion, even? Just confusion would be enough, would make *sense*, where this kindness does not. This is not how their second meeting was supposed to go. Ser Voyne was supposed to find her again, and approach cautiously, ask her name, ask if it is really, truly her. And Treila would have playacted fear, flinching away from any touch, begging for mercy.

Mercy, Ser—mercy, for the price my father has already paid for his treason.

But everything is different now, and Treila can't get the words out, can't even pull away as Ser Voyne steers her toward the garden where they sat together not three days ago. All because Ser Voyne looks at her with adoration, not disbelief.

Her heart is breaking, her whole world close to shattering into a thousand pieces she will never be able to put back together. This doesn't change anything, it *can't* change anything; her father is still dead, her family still destroyed, and she still has no future beyond catching rats in dying castles. But if Ser Voyne has already suffered for it—if Ser Voyne tells her that she has thought of Treila every day, even though Treila was just a girl, just collateral damage, then Treila doesn't know who *she* is anymore.

Because Treila was betrayed by Ser Voyne, and hates Ser Voyne. And right now, she doesn't feel hate. She feels—raw. Out of control. Desperate and needy and longing.

She lets herself be seated on the same bench. Stares as Ser Voyne kneels at her feet.

All around them, impossibly green shoots push up from the earth. Young plants, plants that should have sprouted months ago, were eaten weeks ago. But here they are, incontrovertible. Food, fresh *food*, and Treila should not be so delighted, because she needs to get out, not stay. Everybody must get out, not stay. Food here is worthless if they can't break through the siege.

And yet all of her reason feels as distant as her rage. She's too giddy. She stares back at Ser Voyne, and can't stop herself from asking, desperately, "Where has your doubt gone?"

"Far away," Ser Voyne says with a small, sheepish smile. "I understand now how foolish it was, to be so surprised by your presence. To mistrust it so. Of course you're here, because . . . because I have need of you."

Treila can't stop the shocked sound that ekes out of her throat.

Focus. She never thought she would have Ser Voyne so close, with all her armor shed. Treila has a knife at her belt, a knife that would fit so perfectly in the notch between her clavicle and her ribs, right into her lungs, and it would be so *sweet* to hear her gasping, breath bubbling as she thrashed on the ground.

Wouldn't it?

And wouldn't it be even better with Ser Voyne hanging on her every word, kneeling at her feet like this? Yearning for her touch?

Because she *is* yearning. Treila can see that. Shaking, she reaches out, fits her palm to Ser Voyne's cheek. The older woman leans into it. Her eyes close in decadent pain.

"My lady," Ser Voyne breathes.

Treila's lower lip trembles. Her free hand hovers above the hilt of her knife, then falls.

She can't do it. This devotion is too much. It makes her feel powerful in a way that feigning fear never would have.

And even if it doesn't hurt Ser Voyne quite so much, Treila can still seize her original goal. Ser Voyne does not feel guilty, no, but she *adores,* and that might be stronger than shame. Treila can break her faith with it. Dismantle every belief that led to Ser Voyne so cleanly severing her father's head from his body.

"Have you ever questioned your orders? Ever hesitated to fulfill them?" she asks.

"Not yours," Ser Voyne replies.

Treila frowns, tries to think—what orders? Girlish orders, for refreshment, for lessons, for sparring in the yard. Those orders? They meant the world to her, but she'd been fourteen, spoiled, desirous for the first time in her short life. That Ser Voyne marked them is . . . she can't think of the word. She can only shudder.

"And King Cardimir's?" she presses.

And she is treated to the most beautiful sight she's ever seen: Ser Voyne's lip curling in contempt, in barely restrained *hatred*.

"You know the answer to that, my lady," Ser Voyne says.

"No, I don't think I do," Treila says, and leans closer. Her breathing has quickened so much that she is almost hyperventilating. "Do you truly hate him so? I would never have guessed." She is breathless.

"He has misused me. I know that now, thanks to you," Ser Voyne returns, and her tone now is urgent. As if she *needs* Treila to understand. "I have followed every order he has given me, even when it conflicts with what is best in me, with where my strength arises from. I thought that he knew best, but he has led me astray."

"Yes," Treila whispers, raises her second hand to cup Ser Voyne's other cheek. Her skin is so hot beneath Treila's touch, a sheen of fine sweat appearing on her brow. Treila wants to kiss it. Wants to drink it in. "This is all I've ever wanted you to know. I've wanted you to realize it for so long. For years, Ser Voyne."

"I didn't realize how long I'd been waiting for you," Ser Voyne confesses.

Treila is shaking. Tears burn at her eyes, tears she can't afford to shed. But what if she could? What if she could, for the first time in five years, lay down the burden of her rage, and rest a while, knowing she would be fed, and clothed, and loved?

Understood, at least.

But then Ser Voyne's brow crumples in that sweet confusion Treila has been waiting for, the same confusion she wore the last time they sat in this garden. The confusion of realization, of shock. Treila draws back reflexively, then realizes that Ser Voyne's attention is now fixed on something behind her. She turns and sees the Constant Lady, standing at the entrance to the garden. She holds a humming skep in Her hands, and She is looking straight at Treila with fury in Her multicolored eyes.

Treila is on her feet in an instant, ready to fight, but determined instead to kneel.

She's had too many long years where bowing her head has been the only way to save her neck. She's well-practiced.

"My Lady," Ser Voyne says, in the exact intonation she had used when asking Treila why she was on the ground, and Treila winces. The world comes back into its proper orbit, everything once more in focus. Of course. Of course Ser Voyne did not see Treila and think of little Lady de Batrolin—she thought of the Constant Lady.

Though the Lady is arrayed in layered finery, and Treila cowers in the dirt in a drab smock, missing a stocking. Aside from their blonde hair, Treila can't see the similarities.

Now that they're both in view, it's clear Ser Voyne can't, either. The confusion falls from her eyes, and she goes to the Lady, kneels at Her feet. The Lady's gaze bores into the crown of Treila's bowed head a moment longer, and then She turns, fabric whispering over Her feet. She lets go of the buzzing skep with one hand, places it atop Ser Voyne's head. She murmurs something Treila cannot hear.

Cannot hear the words of, at any rate. Treila strains to pick up the tone, hackles up, ready to flee if she must.

But whatever fury Treila thought she saw is gone, or never existed at all. She hears warm tones, soft murmurs.

She glances up in time to see the Constant Lady kissing Ser Voyne's lips.

Treila makes herself look away. She fights to control herself, shame and embarrassment burning hot in her blood. It takes long, desperate minutes for her to feel steadier in her skin again, and by then, Ser Voyne is long gone, at the heels of her new mistress.

Bewitched. Seeing nonsense. *Speaking* nonsense.

She should be grateful to have this cobwebbed veil snatched back from her eyes so swiftly. She doesn't have time for this. She needs to go find Phosyne again, and perhaps now the heretic will have calmed down enough for Treila to demand more of her.

Determined, Treila turns to go, and is surprised to see one of the saints. The Loving Saint, bent low in the dirt. He is planting seeds, working his hands into the soil out of season, but it looks beautiful

as he does it. His skin is flawless, his eyelashes long, his hair shining. She hasn't cared about the Loving Saint since she was a little
girl with the crush all little girls seemed to have on him, well before
she ever met Ser Voyne, but now she feels her heart give a little tug.
Something beautiful, in all of this mess. It's soothing just to watch.

He doesn't look up, even when she drifts a little closer. Behind
him, in the furrows he has already filled, she sees shoots breaking
through the soil. They grow so quickly she thinks she can hear them.

Her stomach aches. It's easier to understand than the quieter pain
in her chest. She's going to eat tonight, regardless of everything else.
She's too tired to resist now; for all her caution, she is not a fool, and
she is still human, at the root.

The Loving Saint hums, quietly. Plants another seed, and another.
They are all different sorts, enough to feed an army. She recognizes
only a few. One in particular is translucent, almost flat, but curved.
Its bottom edge is marked by a thin white line, its top by a pink stain.
It goes into the ground, and not a minute later, it too is sprouting, its
cotyledon pale and thin, growing fast into a spiral.

When she looks away, she finds the Loving Saint gazing up at her.
He says nothing, but he quirks a brow, smiles.

She flushes and turns to leave.

He doesn't stop her, and she's back in the keep tower when she
slows long enough to think again about that seed. It didn't look like a
seed at all, the more she thinks of it.

It looked like he was planting a fingernail.

But that can't be right.

It grew like all the rest of them.

19

HOSYNE SLAMS THE door to her tower shut and falls back against it, gasping for breath, the world spinning around her. Her throat *hurts*. Her cheek merely stings from where Treila struck her, but she feels both points of assault like brands. They're the only thing holding her together, because every time she remembers falling through the chapel wall, she thinks she might fall through the floor next.

She sinks to the floor, hugging her knees to her chest. "Ornuo?" she manages, and holds one shaking hand out for a warm, scaled flank.

She feels only air.

"Ornuo, rotten boy," she calls again. "Pneio?" she tries, when there are no rustles from the mess around the room, no skittering claws on stone. "No, no, no," she whimpers, standing and pitching herself toward her workbench, knowing what she won't find, knowing she's even more screwed than before.

They're not below the table, or behind the stinking refuse bucket, or on top of her bookshelves, or beneath the stairs. She climbs up to the loft on hands and knees, trying to think like them. She sees the hints of their existence (faint scratches where they have sprinted around the room in the middle of the night, chewed chair legs, the whisper of shed scales), but nothing indicating they're *here*.

Then again, they hid for five days straight when Ser Voyne was still in residence.

Phosyne sits down heavily in the windowsill and claws at her scalp, the necklace of bruises on her throat giving an echoing ache. There are too many disasters for her mind to fix on any one of them at length. But for now, she sees Ser Voyne, the blood on her hands, the empty, confused look in her eyes. Phosyne shouldn't care. In context, she shouldn't care about Ornuo or Pneio, either; if they burn down the smithy, so what? That will neither drive off nor help the saints in whatever they are here to do.

The weakness in her whispers that, if it's truly her fault these beings are here, and if they truly bring a feast tonight, then that is her miracle accomplished, and perhaps everything will, in the end, be okay. The work is done, though she doesn't know how. She can rest, can't she?

The sick pang in her stomach answers that.

Something bangs against the door.

It's a lot softer than when the king came calling, but more firm than her door shifting in its frame that morning. Phosyne stares. More knocking. Fear has soaked her veins clear through, and she can hardly stand, but all the same, she finds herself before her glassed pipe, peering out into the hall, not sure what she expects to see.

It's only Treila.

Only. Only? Phosyne groans and pulls away from the lens, needing a moment to sort out exactly how she feels seeing Treila again. On the one hand, her cheek still smarts, and she doesn't entirely remember what Treila asked of her out in the yard. On the other, she still seems to be herself, not so far gone as Ser Voyne is. But ultimately, she is useless; she can offer some fruit, maybe, but what then?

The door moves in its frame. Phosyne should have barricaded it.

"Stay out!" she calls.

The door opens anyway. Treila slips inside and closes it, and her skin is ashen. Her eyes are wide, her jaw set. She looks *young* like this, young and vulnerable.

Phosyne hesitates, then approaches cautiously. "I said *stay out*," she says, for lack of any better idea.

Treila glances at her, but she doesn't apologize.

"How do you untangle madness from reality?" she asks instead.

And isn't *that* right at the heart of things? "I wish I knew," Phosyne says. "What happened? You look . . ." She waves a hand, as if that will define the exact mixture of broken looking back at her.

Treila purses her lips, then shakes herself, and that vulnerability falls off like dead leaves. "You seem marginally more coherent," she says, thumbing at her upper lip, not meeting Phosyne's eyes. "I still need your help. More, really."

"Escaping."

"Exactly." Treila rolls her next thought around in her mouth. Phosyne waits, wringing the fabric of her robe between her fingers. She can't help herself; she keeps darting looks at the door. Pneio and Ornuo out on their own is *bad*, but so is everything else. Treila has the right idea. Running is the easiest, and maybe best, answer.

"Your candle worked," Treila says, drawing her attention back. "I took it down to the cave I found, it lit just fine."

So it *wasn't* her blood that did it. Good to know.

"It didn't show me anything I hadn't seen before, though."

Phosyne grimaces, then takes a step back, wrapping her arms around her waist defensively. It won't do much to protect her if Treila is angry, but Treila doesn't seem angry.

"So you need something else," Phosyne says. "I'm not sure I have anything left to give." Another step back, just in case.

"It didn't *show* me anything," Treila says, getting up off the ground and dusting off her skirts. "That doesn't mean I didn't find anything. You remember the crack I told you of? The one I wanted to widen?"

Phosyne nods.

"It spoke to me."

Oh.

Now *that* is interesting.

Phosyne cocks her head. "What did it say?"

"*I've missed you*," Treila breathes, then shudders, a whole-body thing accompanied by a look of pure disgust. "Among other things. I—it spoke the first time I went down, as well. I assumed I'd imagined it."

"You say *it*," Phosyne points out.

"Well, it can't be human."

"Can't it?"

Treila shakes her head, curls bouncing. "It sounds like a boy," she admits, "but the crack faces the cliff. Even if there are other tunnels beyond it—which the candle illuminated, actually, so there *is* space back there, thank you—they don't lead back to the Etrebian camp."

"They could lead farther down," Phosyne says. "To the base of the cliff."

"Why would anybody climb all the way up?"

"To offer rescue?" Phosyne suggests. "There are farms down in the valley. It's not impossible."

"It's not *human*," Treila snaps.

Phosyne holds up her hands, backs away again. "Why not?" she presses.

"Because what kind of human asks for a *finger* in return for safe passage?"

Phosyne's gaze drops to Treila's hands. Five fingers on each. No blood on any of them. She isn't sure whether she's relieved or disappointed.

Treila sees her looking and clenches her fingers into fists. "It only spoke while the candle was extinguished. When I relit the candle in an attempt to see its face, the gap was empty. I've left it burning down there, but I need tools. Answers, of some kind. I need to get out of here."

"And what do you think I can give you?" Phosyne asks. "I can clean water. I can light a candle. Beyond that . . ."

"How does it work?" Treila demands.

"What?"

"All of it. How does it work? You say you cleaned the water? How did you figure that out?"

"It's hard to explain. How do you untangle madness from reality?"

Treila scowls at the echo.

Phosyne tries to smile. It doesn't work. "I can show you my notes, but they won't make sense. None of it makes sense, not the way the Priory's constructions do. It's . . . intuition. Uncontrolled intuition. Hard to guide. Hard to explain. Hard to understand, even for me. You need a pick, not me."

"Horseshit," Treila says.

Phosyne frowns. "Excuse me?"

"That's all horse shit. That you don't know how it happens. You're telling me that you wander your way into miracles that *can be re-peated by others*, but you don't know how they work?"

"I can tell you instructions. I can't tell you how I know them."

"You're lying. That isn't how the world works."

"I'm Ser Leodegardis's madwoman," Phosyne reminds her. "I have never claimed to be anything else."

"Well, you *need* to be," Treila snaps. She begins to pace. "What do you need, to be able to focus? What little is left in this damned place, I can get it for you."

"It's not a matter of resources. I've already been *given* everything, don't you see? It either happens or it doesn't, with barely even *intent* behind it," Phosyne says angrily, too tired to think better of it. "I didn't *ask* for the Constant Lady to arrive!"

Treila's eyes widen. Her mouth falls open. Her brow draws together, and Phosyne realizes with a lurch that she has badly miscalculated. Offering to help solve the mystery of the saints would have been one thing, but now she has taken ownership of the whole mess. She feels a noose around her throat, or maybe Ser Voyne's fingers.

"They're here because of you?" Treila asks.

Phosyne squeezes her eyes shut and tries to fall through the floor or, failing that, a minute into the past. The world refuses to move. Time, likewise.

"You say you didn't *ask* for them, but—" Treila's voice falters. Confused. Young again.

"It's not the first time," Phosyne confesses. "Months ago, two—creatures appeared. Arrived. I don't know from where, but the gates hadn't opened, just like they didn't open yesterday. And at the time I must have known how I'd called them here, but now I can't remember, so I must be going mad." She chokes on a laugh, covers her face with her hands. "I don't know *how* I do any of it! None of it makes sense, except that it *does*, somewhere inside of me, my thoughts go every which way and then they crystalize. Today I passed through solid stone, when Ser Voyne fell upon me, and—and—" Phosyne gasps. "And this is the first time I've been rightfully *scared* of it all!"

She's shouting by the end of it, tearing at her hair.

Treila doesn't look the least bit frightened, though. She steps closer, instead. Looks at the mess that is Phosyne with *hunger*.

"Solid stone?" she asks.

Phosyne nods, head jerking on her spine, a broken puppet.

Treila grabs her wrist. "Then you're coming with me. Now. Because if we can get out, none of this is our problem anymore. Do you understand me?"

"It's *all* my problem," Phosyne whispers.

"Just because something's your fault doesn't mean you have to fix it," Treila counters, and tugs Phosyne after her.

"My research—my notes—the *creatures*, they've gone missing, somebody must have opened up this room while I was at the chapel, and oh, Treila, the prioress—"

Treila slaps her again. This time, Phosyne *feels* it, and stops talking. Stops moving. Stops thinking, just for a moment.

She just stares at the floor.

"Sometimes," Treila says, slowly, carefully, enunciating every word, "you just have to leave it all behind and start over."

Phosyne nods, and lets herself be dragged from her tower.

20

ER VOYNE KNOWS these halls.

They are as familiar to her as breathing. She has spent time here, but when she tries to remember how she has spent her days, she comes up empty. It doesn't bother her in the slightest, but it is curious, and she has had a most curious day all around.

In the great hall, the grand feast is being laid out. Something more wondrous even than the meal the saints provided the night before. She can smell the roasting meat even from where she stands inside the main keep tower. Her job, bestowed on her by her beautiful Lady, is to walk the ramparts and these towers to find anybody who lingers, anybody who has not heard of the most generous invitation to eat and be merry. She's already found a few small clusters, mostly people too weak to move. She has fed them honey and smiled upon them until they roused and staggered off toward salvation. The others she has persuaded through alternative means.

Her hands are covered in a sticky mix of red and gold.

This is the last retreat left to check. The ground floor, which smells of leather and sweat and metal, is empty. In fact, most of the keep is empty. The king, that wretched, glorious man, has been loyal and true. He has taken his household, and Ser Leodegardis's too, to the great hall. They have been there all morning, providing the hands her Lady has needed to give them all such bounty.

Most of the keep is empty. She does, however, hear scrabbling from below. The lower rooms, storehouses, workspaces.

Rats, searching for their next meal. Thieving little rats, who do not have the decency to heed her Lady's invitation.

There should be metal on her shoulders, she thinks, an errant thought that distracts her just as she reaches the steps. There should be metal, like the Warding Saint wears. Where has it gone? She doesn't rightly remember, and that, too, is curious. But then the rats shift and squeak again. Closer this time.

She descends a few steps, rounds a corner. This room is lit by thin shafts of daylight, throwing heaps and piles into shadowy relief. A perfect place for hiding.

She spots her rats, two forms huddled above . . .

A hole, at the base of one of the walls without windows, nearly hidden by a cleverly placed barrel.

Ser Voyne knows these halls, and is fairly certain that there was no hole there before. She feels cool air. Smells the damp.

Both rats are staring up at her. Rats, and not rats; they are women, too. Her eyes glance off one with blonde hair, her gaze refusing to resolve her features, and lands on the other. Gaunt, dark-haired, twitchy.

Ser Voyne's hands flex at her sides. She remembers anger. Her hands, around this woman's throat. *You are to look after me.* The words float through her mind, make her shudder.

They're talking to her. It takes effort to listen.

"—it's nothing, just a cache," the blonde one says, though Ser Voyne cannot see her at all now. "Just a hiding place. I was getting food—"

The words mean little to Voyne, as if she can't hear them. There is sound, she knows there is sound, but the words simply don't matter.

Ser Voyne stalks forward, remembering how it feels to impale one-self upon a blade and keep moving. She has given her vow, and seizes the woman she is supposed to look after by the throat.

She lost her, earlier today. She remembers that, too. She *lost* this woman. *Phosyne,* the name appears, emerges as if from fog. "You are out of your tower," she says.

Footsteps behind her. The blonde one—the Lady? No, not the Lady, she has made this mistake before, she is *not* to turn around— flees.

"Ser Voyne—" Phosyne stammers out, weak hands on her wrist, trying to break her hold. Ser Voyne will not let go of her. She hauls her closer, instead, pulls her charge against her chest. Wraps her other arm around Phosyne's waist so she can't escape again.

Keep her away from stone, memory whispers to her, and so Ser Voyne hauls her toward the stairs. There's too much stone around them, beneath them. She needs to get this creature to the yard.

"Please, you're hurting me," Phosyne protests, her legs tangling with Voyne's. When she trips, Ser Voyne keeps her upright. When she trips *again,* Ser Voyne growls and pauses, only long enough to pick her up and sling her over one shoulder.

It knocks the breath from Phosyne and keeps her silent until they are outside again.

The air is hot and sodden. Her chest feels like it is weeping. Phosyne, gone blessedly still, sweats against her. The yard smells not of shit and desperation but of spices and wine. The feast, at last, has been laid out. Bodies fill the space, and Ser Voyne picks her way between them.

The great hall cannot fit everybody, of course, and so long runners of fabric, beautiful tapestries and cut-up tents, have been laid out across the upper and lower yards, forming the shadow of tables. Every runner is heaped with food, green and red and golden, chard and apples and radishes, and every type of meat besides. Roast fowl, grilled eel, pickled eggs and salted pork. There are ewers of wine, glistening in the sunlight, and all around them is the smell of *bounty.*

All around them are hungry, desperate faces. They stare at the food, but nobody reaches for it. They are pinned below the gaze of the Lady, who waits just outside the entrance to the great hall.

Waits for her.

Ser Voyne's heart swells, beats double time, and she almost forgets Phosyne slung across her shoulder, until she moves to kneel at her Lady's feet and has to shift the weight. She pulls Phosyne from her then, and lays her out like an offering before her Lady.

Phosyne stares up in—

Not love.

Ser Voyne shivers, unbidden, suddenly afraid. Why doesn't Phosyne look upon the Lady with love? Or fear, at least? This is anger. Insult. Disgust.

Ser Voyne is reaching for her throat when the Lady intervenes.

"What a treat you have found for me, Ser Voyne," She says, and smiles beatifically down at both of them. "So much more welcome than your last discovery."

Blonde hair. Green eyes. Roughspun clothing. It's almost a memory.

So is the image of a girl without a face. Is she here? Did she follow them? Or will Voyne need to go after her, round her up?

That's an issue for later. For now, the Lady is kneeling, reaching out to brush one of the uneven, lank curls out of Phosyne's face. Her expression has changed. It isn't generosity, not anymore. Something has sharpened in Her, but it isn't anger, either.

Her Lady looks . . . excited.

"And are you the little mouse who so unsettled my knight?" She asks, voice low and rich.

Phosyne is no longer shaking. She has gone very still instead, a sighted mouse indeed. A sighted mouse with a voice, however. "What are you?" she asks, voice as steady as her hands.

"Our Constant Lady," Ser Voyne interjects. "Avert your eyes, you are not worthy to—"

"Hush, Ser Voyne," her Lady says, and she cannot speak. "What do you think I am, little mouse?"

"Something summoned," Phosyne says.

Yes, they have called to the Constant Lady for—for a long time, though again Ser Voyne can't remember the details. Or why they called. But they called, and She has come, a blessing and a salve, and—

"Oh, I was not summoned, little mouse," her Lady says. She cups Phosyne's jaw, head tilting like a curious bird's as She takes her measure. "I go nowhere I do not please. But I do wander everywhere." Her yellow lips curl. "Come, eat with me. I wonder what you think of my gifts."

"No," Phosyne says.

Ser Voyne reaches for her with a voiceless snarl, but her Lady waves her off again. "Sit with me, at least. Perhaps you can tell me of the water."

Phosyne's pallid skin goes paler still.

"I have tasted it, and it is sweet," says the Constant Lady, and at last She rises. She touches Ser Voyne's throat with one slim finger, and Voyne feels her voice return. Feels herself move once more. "Take a seat at my table, dear knight. Bring with you your little pet."

Phosyne rolls onto her belly and tries to stand, but Ser Voyne is faster, now that she is freed. She pulls Phosyne, lifts her with one arm below her knees, the other below her shoulders.

"Let me go," Phosyne begs, even as Voyne passes her Lady and plunges into the heat of the great hall.

At the head of one of the great tables is King Cardimir, Ser Leodegardis at his right hand. The picture of proper order. But Ser Voyne feels nothing, walks past him, for her destination is greater still.

Her Lady's table sits parallel to the king's, and in mirror image to him, the Lady's chair sits, empty and draped in silks to receive Her at the head. To that chair's right is the Absolving Saint, standing behind his own. He inclines his head as Ser Voyne approaches, and looks down with a silvered smile at Phosyne. Phosyne stills, frowning, staring back with intense curiosity.

Ser Voyne jolts her, breaking her concentration.

"Sit, Ser Voyne," the Absolving Saint says, and pulls the chair out.

For a moment, she is confused, but then a rush of gratitude fills her. She sits. He tucks her chair in. He looks at Phosyne while he does it, as he traps the skinny woman between Voyne and the table so that escape becomes nearly impossible.

"Our Lady would have you both as her guests tonight," the Absolving Saint says. He reaches out as if to touch Phosyne's brow, then hesitates, glances to the door. He pulls his hand smoothly back. He leaves them.

The Loving Saint and the Warding Saint, too, are out of their seats, their chairs remaining empty as they drift between the tables, touch brows, shoulders, backs. They bow to whisper in ears. They fill plates, though nobody yet dares to eat.

"Don't you see this is all wrong?" Phosyne whispers, glancing up at her, shivering. "This isn't how people act."

Before Ser Voyne can question her, or even parse what Phosyne has said, what little noise there was dies away completely.

It leaves only her Lady, speaking out in the yard to all that are gathered there.

"All this bounty, I give to you, who have suffered so terribly," the Lady says, and though She does not shout and has no criers, Ser Voyne can hear it clear as a bell from where she sits, even with a wall and a hundred bodies between them. "I would mend you where you have broken, nurture you where you have been left to wither. You are my garden, and I shall tend you until you reach your fullest bloom. Eat, and be well."

And seemingly as one beast, they all descend upon the food.

The great hall echoes not with talks or prayers or cheers, but with chewing, swallowing, gasping, sucking. Ser Voyne and Phosyne alone keep their hands still.

"Ser Voyne?"

She looks down at Phosyne, who is trembling again. Panic lights her eyes. "Let me go," Phosyne begs. "Let me go, and I swear to you, I will go back to my tower, I will do my work, I will not impose on anybody. I won't go back to the hole. But don't keep me here."

"No," Ser Voyne says. "We must remain. We must eat. The Lady said—"

"What have they done to you?" Phosyne asks, and she is shaking. "You aren't in there anymore. They've taken you."

Ser Voyne blinks, frowns.

And then the Lady enters the great hall.

She is glory made flesh. Ser Voyne watches, breathless, as her Lady approaches, observing the desperate, thankful gorgings on either side of her. Below Her yellow paint, Her cheeks are full of high color, and then Her eyes are fixed on the two of them, and She smiles. Ser Voyne ducks her head, unable to withstand the glory of Her regard.

The Lady takes Her seat at Ser Voyne's left.

Ser Voyne stares at her hands, searching for the right words to say to express how honored she is to sit at the Lady's right hand, but before she can fumble out anything at all, the Lady speaks.

To Phosyne.

"Well, little mouse," She says, filling a fine porcelain cup with water from a polished ewer. "I have tasted this water, and it is sweet, but it wasn't always so. And now it tastes of you." She lifts the cup to Her curling lips, takes a long sip. Her eyes do not leave Phosyne's.

"I can't imagine I taste sweet," Phosyne says, wariness in her voice.

"Oh, but you do." She reaches over to them and takes Voyne's wrist, guides her hand to release her captive and take the cup instead. Obediently, Voyne drinks, thinking of sweetness and Phosyne's body against hers in the chapel.

The water is not honey, but it is undeniably good. It is cool, and soothing, and Ser Voyne feels something in her unwind. But with it comes confusion, and she stares down at Phosyne as the Lady plucks the empty cup from her hand and sets it aside.

There's something wrong, here. She's not supposed to be at the Lady's right hand. She should be with her king, and Phosyne should be up in her tower. This is not the proper order of things. This is her liege's castle, they should be seated at his table, and yet he has been relegated. Set aside. She can see now that his table is smaller, that it is shadowed, and that nobody at it can see the slight.

She remembers the weight of a knife in her hand. Prioress Jacynde, kneeling. At her feet? No, at the Lady's, but also—

Also—

"Here, my dear knight," the Lady says, and offers up a morsel of meat. It is rich and unctuous on Ser Voyne's tongue, and it washes away the memory of blood. She forgets all about Cardimir.

Phosyne looks between them. Her brow pinches further. Voyne can almost see wheels turning behind her eyes. She feels a faint thrill go through her at the sight.

"And does this food taste of you?" Phosyne asks.

The Lady's smile grows. "I do provide," She concedes. "All of this and more."

"You brought no carts with you. No supplies."

"Didn't I?" the Lady replies as She serves Herself a helping of fruit and several more thin slices of meat from the vast array of riches before Her. Voyne would do it for Her, but her hands are busy keeping Phosyne in place. The Lady uses Her fingers to pull each bit of food into bite-size pieces, and then She lifts a bit of meat and offers it to Phosyne, as if Phosyne were a tame little thing.

Phosyne draws back. Ser Voyne squeezes her knee hard in censure.

"Am I not your Constant Lady?"

"Not the Lady. And even if you were, you would not be mine," Phosyne says, and for her disrespect earns Ser Voyne's other hand tangled in her hair. She leans back, bruised throat exposed, but she does not writhe or pant. "I have not taken honey in nearly a year."

The Lady looks over the length of her, presented across Ser Voyne's lap. "No," She says, "you have not. But not, I think, for lack of love."

"Love implies a presence in my thoughts. These days, there's more an absence."

"A bold confession."

"An honest one."

"I will concede you lack a longing," the Lady admits. "You will need to eat something soon, little mouse. Already I smell rot upon your breath. You will not last much longer. Do you choose to die, rather than accept help?"

Phosyne looks like she's about to argue, but instead says nothing at all.

"You are not a fool, little mouse," the Lady says. There is a hint of warning there.

Phosyne should know better. But then, deference has never been her strength, even when it would benefit her most.

The Absolving Saint returns, bearing with him a platter upon which a steaming, fragrant joint of meat rests, surrounded by split pomegranates, stewed mushrooms, verdant lettuces. Defleshed bones ornament the plate like scattered pearls, eight in all, none the same exact size or shape.

In her arms, Phosyne goes rigid, as if she's made of wood.

The Absolving Saint places the platter before the three of them.

He picks up carving fork and knife, and begins to slice petals of flesh away from the two bones that run through the center of the shank. He places two on Ser Voyne's plate, and her mouth waters.

Cinching Phosyne tight against her with one arm and leaning forward to pin her to the table's edge, Voyne reaches out and picks up a piece. It is tender and slippery between her fingers. She is mildly surprised to see her hands are still covered in blood and honey.

It wouldn't have mattered before. Before? But she has a memory of heavy iron in her hand, between her and her food, carrying it to her lips instead of her sticky fingers.

She takes a bite anyway. She chews. She swallows.

She lets the Absolving Saint take her hand when she is done and wipe it clean for her, then reaches for more.

In her lap, Phosyne sounds like she is crying. "Look. Please, look at what you're eating," she entreats.

Ser Voyne looks. The roast weeps glistening fat, rests in pools of oil that shimmer in the candlelight and sing with spices. Voyne can't help but lean in, can't help but select another glistening slice from the beautiful arrangement. Horse? Whatever beast it came from was heavily muscled, but Voyne has never seen a shank with so much meat upon the bone before.

"Don't," Phosyne begs.

Ser Voyne takes another bite half to spite her, half to model good behavior. Phosyne will need to eat, and soon; she is so fragile in Voyne's arms.

When she has eaten the last of what is on her plate, ignoring Phosyne's wheezing breaths, close to panic, Ser Voyne drinks deeply from her cup. It is water, not wine. The cool sweetness of it breaks over her, and the confusion is back.

She knows the taste that lingers in her mouth, the fat that coats her lips and the shreds of flesh stuck in her teeth. Just like she knows these halls, just like she knows that she should be wearing metal. Frowning, she takes another bite, chews slowly, closes her eyes. It comes apart easily between her teeth, slides over her tongue, and she *remembers* this, though last time she had it, it was not spiced half so well. Last time, there was smoke. Last time, there was blood.

Last time, she had been so hungry, the hungriest she had ever been, and the meat had been parceled out so carefully between her and her men, and . . .

"Ser Voyne," her Lady says, pulling her away from the memory. "Attend to your charge. She needs your firm hand, I think."

Of course. Phosyne's body struggles in her arms, and Ser Voyne clamps down harder, holding the frail woman against her chest. With one hand, she grabs up a honey-drenched fig; with the other, she presses against Phosyne's jaw, spreads her chapped lips wide. With one finger, she pushes between Phosyne's teeth.

"Eat," Voyne demands.

Phosyne bites down. Blood spills from Voyne, and she cries out, dropping the fig, loosing her hold. And then the pain is gone, and Phosyne is gone, sprinting wildly for the exit. Voyne is on her feet, but the Lady reaches out and clasps her bleeding hand. She draws it to Her own lips, and Voyne pants, torn between two duties.

"Stay, Ser Voyne. She will come back, I am sure. She must eat sometime," the Lady murmurs into her blood. But Ser Voyne cannot hear her, because she knows the taste of this meat, and Phosyne is not in her tower, and all of this is wrong, it's *wrong*, she knows these halls, she knows this anger inside of her and—

And she's supposed to be saving this castle.

She pulls her hand from her Lady's lips, and races after Phosyne.

From behind, she thinks she hears her Lady laugh.

21

OYNE'S BLOOD IS sharp and metallic in Phosyne's mouth. It's also rich and full of life, and she should be swallowing it down just from desperation, but instead she spits the moment she gets into the keep proper, even though the knight is likely just behind her.

She can't. She *can't*, not after seeing Voyne eat piece after piece of a man's arm. It's all she can do not to vomit.

Her brain is on fire, the Lady's words echoing in her head, out of order, recombining. *Oh, I was not summoned, little mouse* repeats again, and again. It brings no relief.

Phosyne didn't call these things here, and that now appears to be the worst possibility of all.

She's in the main garrison room, staring at the doors available to her, wondering if she should retreat to her tower, or down into Treila's tunnel, when she sees a shadow move against the far wall. The late-afternoon sunlight is harsh, the shadows deep. Phosyne freezes, trapped between Ser Voyne, who must be close behind, and whoever lurks ahead of her.

Treila steps out into the light.

"Where is she?" Treila whispers.

"Close," Phosyne confesses. "The tunnel—"

"Not when she can find us again so easily. She'll look there first." Treila beckons, and Phosyne comes close enough that the younger woman can seize her wrist, draw her close. "Your best bet," Treila says, "is outside."

Outside, Phosyne hears singing. Joyous cries. It's far more animate than it was when Voyne hauled her through it. She shakes her head. "If the Lady—no, that *creature*—sees me again—"

Treila doesn't question Phosyne's hasty correction; perhaps she's already drawn the same conclusion, that these strange visitors aren't what they appear to be. "She won't, there's too much going on," the girl assures her. "Our mistake before was thinking we were safe because nobody was here to see us. It just makes us easier to spot. Go, hide, I'll come to the tower tonight and we can try again."

"What about you?"

"The other servants will wonder where I am, if I don't put in an appearance soon." Treila grins, and it's manic and cocky. Phosyne remembers, then, to be afraid of this girl, too.

"Don't eat the food," she warns, glancing over her shoulder. She thinks she hears footsteps.

Treila looks, too, so she probably does. "Of course not," she agrees. "We'll be out of here by dawn. Now *go*." She releases her grip, and slips back into the shadows.

Phosyne takes a deep breath, stomach cramped with fear as much as hunger, and ducks out into the yard, back into the masses.

Most are still seated, still gorging themselves on impossible food, but some now, finally, are on their feet. They are singing and dancing, celebrating. Two nuns, their heads bare, their habits discarded, smear honey on each other's lips. Phosyne stares at them for too long before moving onward, looking for somewhere she can sit and disappear.

But if she sits, she will stand out if she does not eat, and she is *certain* she should not eat. Even before she saw that limb at the Lady's table, recognized that it could not belong to any ungulate, noted the eight wrist bones arrayed around it as decoration—

Well, the Lady had very clearly wanted her to eat, and that alone is enough to put her off.

She finds the stairs down to the lower yard, takes them with her shaking, unsteady legs. There's no sound of Ser Voyne behind her, and Phosyne lets herself slow a little, take each step with care. If Voyne is not behind her, then she's at the Lady's feet again. Broken, certainly. Twisted, undoubtedly. Whatever spell has fallen over

Aymar that makes the king not question his visitors, that makes starving people wait to eat until granted permission, rests heavily on everybody who Phosyne saw in the great hall the night before, eating the first offerings of impossible food. And it rests heaviest on Voyne.

And does this food taste of you?

I do provide.

Phosyne stops, mouthing the exchange again. The pieces rearrange themselves. The food is the method by which these minds have been ensnared, yes, but *why?*

Because the food is of the Lady—that is, because the Lady provided it. Because to sit at somebody's table, to let them feed you, is to create a bond. This is more literal, perhaps, than the usual bonds of hospitality, but she can see it clear enough: this castle, its inhabitants now belong to the Lady, because they have accepted Her gifts. Longed for them. Rejoiced in them.

And though the king welcomed the Lady into Aymar, somewhere in the mix he has lost his primacy. The Lady should be a guest, except, of course, that She is their rescuer, and beyond that, to all appearances, their deity. Even if She is not the Lady in truth, the king clearly believes Her to be so.

Aymar, Phosyne realizes, no longer belongs to the king.

It's territory. Territory and fealty and Ser Voyne's loyalty, transferred to another.

Phosyne starts pacing again, nerves afire with every connection she makes. She almost doesn't see the ripple in the crowd, so wrapped up in horrors is she. But there it is, people parting, and Ser Voyne is once more looking for her.

She cannot let Voyne take her back. Of that, she is certain. But she is too frail to fight, to run. All she can hope for is to confuse Voyne long enough to evade capture, slip back into the crowd.

She ducks behind one of the cisterns.

There are six throughout the lower yard, all rising three feet or so above the ground. They are covered now with tarps, to stop the hot air from stealing more water than it returns, but the one Phosyne hides behind has its cover rolled back. Water for the feast. Water from the rains that stopped months ago, topped up with as much as could be drawn up from the fouled well, cleansed with her invention.

Water that was not provided by the Lady.

I have tasted this water, and it is sweet, but it wasn't always so.

Now it tastes of you.

"Oh," Phosyne says. She remembers both times Voyne drank from the cup the Lady had given her. Both times, she had faltered. Grown confused. Looked at Phosyne, and Phosyne had felt she was so close to *understanding* again . . .

And then another bite of food, and it was gone.

Ser Voyne is close now; Phosyne can hear her panting breath. There's nowhere to run where Voyne will not find her. Maybe, if she had gone down to Treila's tunnel instead of out into the yard, she could have hidden. But there is water in the cistern below her, and there's a way in.

Phosyne hopes she is seeing reason, not madness.

She hauls herself over the edge of the cistern.

She lets herself fall.

The cistern is not deep, but the water level is low, not enough to form a cushion. Phosyne lands hard. There *is* water enough to cover Phosyne's nose and mouth, but she's too stunned to move, even as she feels herself choking. She has to sit up. She has to move out of the way. She has to—

Ser Voyne stares down at her.

Phosyne flinches, and is finally able to roll over, push herself up, cough out the water in her throat. She forces herself to look up. "Well?" she rasps. "Are you coming, Ser Voyne?" It's a challenge she's almost too afraid to make, but she needs to test this. Needs to get her down here.

She watches Ser Voyne pace around the rim like a dog in a cage. And then, just as Phosyne begins to worry, the knight leaps into the cistern.

Voyne is stronger, better fed, and she lands on her feet, unsteady but upright. She is trembling with barely constrained—what? Rage? Or more confusion? She prowls closer, and Phosyne flattens herself against the wall of the cistern.

It's hewn from stone. She can disappear again, if she needs to.

She thinks she can, anyway. She just doesn't know how far she can go. A wall is one thing; the bedrock of an entire castle another. There isn't a walkway on the other side. Oh, but this was a bad idea, and Ser Voyne is close now, getting closer, stinking of spices and meat and sugar, and there is murder in her eyes.

Then it's confusion again. Water beads along her brow. Sweat, surely, but the cistern is also humid, the water warm from the sun. If the air out in the yard was already thick to breathe, this is like drowning.

Slowly, Phosyne lowers herself to the ground. Into the water again. It's only a little over a foot deep, but she hunkers down into it, cups her hands beneath the surface.

Ser Voyne kneels, too. Reaches for Phosyne's throat.

Phosyne makes herself lean forward into it, and lifts her hands between them, to Ser Voyne's lips.

"Drink," Phosyne says, as Ser Voyne's fingers brush her neck.

Ser Voyne hesitates. Licks her lips.

Bows her head and sips.

Her eyelids flutter. The lingering anger in her brow goes slack. Her hand leaves Phosyne's neck and cups Phosyne's hands instead, bringing them closer to her. The water is running out Phosyne's fingers, but Voyne drinks and drinks, guides their hands down to scoop still more water, drinks *again*, mouths at Phosyne's palms even as the last of the water drains away.

Ser Voyne shivers. Shudders. Quakes. Bows over Phosyne's hands and presses them to her fevered brow.

And then she sobs.

22

HE GREAT HALL roars.

Treila sits next to Edouart's mother and gives herself over to the rush of it. Laughter trips off her tongue, sto- ries too, praises, gratitude. It's every feast day wrapped up into one, and all around her, food is torn apart, swallowed whole, pressed against others' lips.

Nobody has noticed yet that Treila is not eating.

They're all too distracted, and it's enough to serve food onto their plates, refill cups, stoke the fires of conviviality. Down deep, Treila is terrified, but on the surface, she is laughing. Her eyes gleam in the firelight as night descends.

She feels a sort of power, knowing she's still got her head. Seeing everybody else lose theirs. She knows that the meat Simmonet chews is human flesh. She also knows that he can't tell, even though the foot of whoever it belonged to was served up right alongside it. Treila has taken it upon herself to pick the scraps of meat from between the little bones, because it will get eaten either way, and it's too distracting to see people touching it without processing what they're holding.

And it feels good, to pass food to Simmonet, to Edouart, to see their hollow cheeks flush with delight as they chew and swallow. They have been so hungry, and now they weep with delight.

The flesh is oily between her fingertips. It smells divine, driving back and overwhelming the stench of unwashed, filthy bodies all around her. She only stays her own hunger by clinging to a scrap of irrational anger, that this flesh would delight where the bones she had been forced to gnaw bore only raw and frozen gristle, skin that had gone paper-thin, muscle barely more than a memory.

She keeps working at it even as her stomach cramps and lurches, because it is easier to resist a bite of flesh than the perfect apples, oozing berries, roasted courgettes.

Take it, take it all, you know better than to deprive yourself. She has earned her selfishness. It is all that protects her. But she'd be a fool to think she's any less at risk of bewitchment than Simmonet. She cannot make the gamble.

Across the hall, the Lady still sits at the head of her table, and the king at his. Treila sees no trace of Ser Voyne and hopes that means the madwoman is safe. The seats beside the Lady remain empty. Her saints instead flit around the other tables. They move seats, serve food much as Treila is doing. The Absolving Saint in particular disappears into the kitchens only to return with fresh platters. The cooks are all at Treila's table. There's nobody working the fires.

She thinks of saying something, pointing out the incongruity, but decides against it. She waits for somebody at her table to notice she has gone silent, but they hardly notice her at all. It's like she's invisible when she isn't in motion.

What she wouldn't give for this talent on a normal day.

But then she realizes somebody *is* looking back at her. Clear skin, shining white hair, long lashes brushing his cheeks as he tilts his head slightly in greeting from across the hall.

The Loving Saint crosses the room, and every body in the way shifts aside so he can pass.

Treila goes through her options: run, and invite a chase; look away, and pretend she is as starry-eyed as all the rest; take hold of her knife below the table, and wait to see if it is needed.

She chooses option three.

She even straightens where she sits on the bench, bold and counting every step he takes. At first, those he passes stare up at him, but as he nears, they don't spare him a single glance. Nobody at Treila's table reacts as he reaches it, except to shift aside as if gently nudged with an invisible hand. They clear a space across from her.

He sits.

"Are you enjoying the feast?" he asks, leaning one elbow into the masses of discarded bone and fruit skin on the table, pillowing his chin upon his fist. The silk he's draped in wicks up juices, staining fast, then blanching white again as quick as breathing. His nails are clean. No trace of dirt from the gardens.

"I am," she agrees.

"But you're not eating." His gaze flicks to the metatarsals littering her plate, the pile of meat beside it. "Just playing with your food."

He, then, is not so bewitched. And why would he be? She files that detail away. "Would you believe me if I told you I'm not hungry?" Her hand below the table shifts on the knife.

"I'd believe you more if you said this was unappetizing," he says. His voice is sweet, his tone delighted. He is fascinated. He is measuring just how lucid she is.

She wants to know what will happen if she acknowledges that lucidity. She says, "No, you've cooked it well."

And he *blossoms*.

"This isn't the first time," he says, and there is something like glee in his voice.

Treila considers the pile. Feels the ghost of tendon between her molars. It's a private memory, but she looks back up at him through her lashes. "Dark things happen in winter woods."

His smile spreads. "They do indeed. But what of the fruit? The honey?" He trails one finger along a bit of thick comb, lifts it to his lips. Suckles it off.

"I told you," she says. "I'm not hungry. But I appreciate the ambience."

"Fine words for a stitching girl." He looks her over, measuring, appraising. "But not always a stitching girl, I think. Where *did* you come from?"

There's a hint of a threat in his voice, all wrapped up in delight. Any trace of gentleness is gone from him now. He's sharp, wickedly so, and Treila is certain now that this is no Loving Saint.

"Come closer," she says, gaze raking over his body as she takes his measure in turn, "and I might tell you."

She thinks Phosyne might be able to learn something from his gutted corpse, and she thinks she can get it out of the hall without anybody noticing, if she's quick. If she's good.

He rounds the table and places one knee on the bench beside her, caging her in with his broad shoulders. The curtain of his hair falls around them both. Her smile twists into wicked glee, and she rises fast, knife flashing.

He catches her by the wrist, the point less than an inch from his gut.

"Do you know," he murmurs, voice silken and low, so quiet she shouldn't be able to hear it through the din, and yet it winds around her ear, "that is perhaps only the third knife I've seen in this entire castle?"

She's panting, adrenaline sick in her veins, and she jerks her hand. Forward, first, then back when he does not let her stab him. But he doesn't let her retreat, either. She should be frightened. She should be *terrified*, now that she's played her hand, but instead she's leaning closer, as if to kiss him.

She wonders if he'll let her.

"Ser Leodegardis ordered all iron collected a little over a fortnight ago," she tells him, voice barely above a breath. "The Priory had need. All our knives, all our tools, even the iron banding on the doors—all went to the nuns. Only the knights kept their armaments."

She shifts her grip on the knife, just a little, just enough to draw his eye down. "And I kept this," she purrs.

"Because you were afraid, or because you were hunting?" He's smiling at her, still, and if anything, his cheeks are flushed with higher color now. His thumb strokes at her pulse. Yes, he would probably let her kiss him.

"Hunting," she says.

He makes a pleased little noise that's almost swallowed up in the conversation all around them. "It makes a little more sense now. That look you wore in the garden."

Treila inhales sharply. "You were watching."

"Of course. It's not often I see such a beautiful mess of confusion. Gallant Ser Voyne was not acting as you expected, was she?"

"No," she admits. Considers. "The last time she saw me, it unsettled her. Weakened her walls."

"You wanted to bring them tumbling down, but instead found them transfigured."

"Replaced."

He hums. "Oh, you are a sharp little thing, aren't you? Eager to cut, and drink deep. She missed it."

"That's intentional," she murmurs. No, Voyne can't know at all. But then she thinks a moment, realizes he means the Lady, and she goes still.

"Intentional to all the world," he agrees. "Don't worry. I won't tell Her."

"Why not? Don't you serve Her?"

"Sheathe your knife, and perhaps I can answer some of your questions."

And he lets her go.

It would take just the slightest jerk forward to slide the knife between his ribs. But she doesn't even hesitate. She pushes the knife back into its sheath and into the folds of her skirt.

She offers him her empty hands.

Perhaps augury is not the only way to get something useful out of him.

He takes her by the wrists, and climbs off the bench, leading her away. She follows, heart hammering, wondering if she's making a terrible mistake. But this creature is a clever sort, and just like with Phosyne on the ground beneath her, she finds she likes being seen for what she is: a threat.

The doorway he tugs her through leads out into the yard, but not into the masses crowded around the tables. Instead, it's into the empty stretch of dirt that leads to a stairway, up onto the walls. He climbs backward up them, never missing a step, never letting go, and then they are up and in the wind, above the noise. In the dark.

He draws her into a shadowed corner, lets her crowd him there. She tangles a hand in his silken hair simply because he doesn't stop her.

"You promised answers?" she murmurs.

He winks. "Not promised. Offered. There's a difference. My first piece of advice to you is to keep track of which is which."

"A gift or one half of an exchange."

"Very different," he agrees. His skin is cool. So is his breath.

"You know," she says, studying his features, "I have never understood why you look like this. So unnatural. All of you saints, I suppose, but . . . you more than the rest."

"I don't have to look like this," he says, and his tongue peeks out between his lips for a moment. "This is a just a canvas. I am whoever it is you love. Or, perhaps, long to be loved by."

As she watches, his white hair turns black. It spreads from where her fingers grip it tightly, to his scalp, to his eyebrows. Eyelashes. It shortens, too, draws up through her hands and disappears like water, and then it is close cropped to his skull on one side, braided and heavy on the other. His features dance and shift as well, his narrow jaw widening, his broad shoulders slimming down the tiniest bit. Even his height changes, until she is staring up at Ser Voyne.

No, not Ser Voyne; there's too much mischief in those eyes. But the Loving Saint looks close enough to make his point, and it's enough to set her stumbling back, pupils blown wide.

Run, the animal part of her says. *Run, now. This is nothing good.*

But then he's back to his old self, the form he wears in paintings and in icons. He stretches his arms above his head, arches his back, looks at her through pleased and pleasing eyes. "Yet another tasty little detail about you," he says.

"You saw me in the garden," she points out.

"Yes, but I didn't expect you to retreat just now, when you pushed so close before." He beckons with one long-fingered hand.

She is warier this time. But she does step closer, until she can once more hear his languid breathing. "You are no saint," she ventures.

His brows lift, pleased. "I am to them," he says, nodding down to the bodies below. "But to you, no."

"Because you are what I desire?"

"Love. Desire. Either. Both. But no, you're not *quite* right. There's a truth at the core of me. Just like there is to you." He reaches out, and she's close enough that he can trail fingers up her arm, along her collarbone. "I can see it. So can the Lady. Or She could, if She were not too preoccupied with jealousy. It's not like Her, to miss the knife but block the stab." Up, up, touching her neck now, then her jaw, then her lips. He traces their outline. She thinks of biting him. "But

Ser Voyne is a prize, I'll grant you that. Something so strong, turned so brittle with mishandling."

"And so She's *jealous*?" It's laughable, but Treila remembers the fury in Her eyes in the garden.

"She thinks She is unmistakable. Entirely unique. The brightest star in all the sky. What a blow, to see Her creature mistake a grubby servant girl for her Lady. And that blow leaves Her too angry to ask *why* Her creature made the mistake at all."

He leaves the wall, drops his hands to her waist, her hips.

"Why didn't you eat? It wasn't what we were serving," he asks.

"I couldn't be sure whether it was a gift or a bargain. I like to know what something costs before I pay for it."

"And yet your body must have been screaming for it."

"I'm used to resisting what my body screams for."

He leans in, lips against the shell of her ear. Treila knows better than to give in, to luxuriate, but she can still appreciate it. Still tilt her head to the side. She doesn't let him steer her against anything that would block her escape, stands firm where she is, but she pushes her hips into his touch.

"Somebody's told you to be careful," he guesses. He rolls their hips together and he shudders just as much as she does. "You were hungry in the garden. But something happened between then and now."

"I saw what you were planting."

He pulls back, grins. "A little transubstantiation. I'm glad I had an audience. But there is something else. Trapped in these walls, you will need to eat. You know that. Unless . . ."

She waits. She runs her hands along his chest. She pulls at his hair again, and he sighs, eyes half-lidded.

"If you have a way out, I would suggest you take it," he murmurs. "Whatever the cost. You won't have the choice soon."

"And if I stay?" she asks, knowing she won't, but curious all the same. She's curious about that fury in the Lady's eyes. About what, exactly, this creature under her hands is. About how it would feel for him to don Ser Voyne's guise again, and sink to his knees, and . . .

"If you stay," he says, eyes shining in the evening light, "it is eat or be eaten. But I promise I'll make it good."

23

OYNE SHAKES IN the shadow of the cistern wall.

They need to move. That is clarion clear in her mind while little else is. They've been here for too long. The sun was still up when she followed Phosyne down this way, and now it's not. The air is thick and hot, but the water is cooling quickly. She's shaking, and not entirely from her thoughts.

But her thoughts are terrible enough to keep her pinned, huddled up into a little ball. She feels it all at once: the Lady's lips on hers, the glory of being seen, of being valued, once more. Jacynde's faithless tongue held tight in her hand while the woman sagged limp beneath her, unable or unwilling to defend herself. The cut of the knife. Sitting at the Lady's feet in the garden, pouring out her heart, only to see the Lady across the way instead. Confusion. Desperation. Apologies, begging, a gentle hand against her head. Blood and honey on her hands, people crying as she hauled them to the feast, then forgetting to cry as soon as they were placed at their seats.

Phosyne's weight across her shoulder, in her lap, the cut of her teeth into Voyne's finger. The Lady, laughing, barely caring about Voyne at all.

And the clear taste of water, the feel of Phosyne's throat beneath her hands, the sudden loss as she evaporated into stone.

Confusion.

Confusion.

Confusion.

She's crying again. She needs to stop the tears, needs to stand up, needs to get out of this cistern and take Phosyne with her. Somewhere safe. Somewhere she can think, and they can talk, and perhaps find a plan to salvage all of this.

If it can even be salvaged. Voyne isn't sure it can be. Maybe it's that uncertainty that keeps her shivering on the ground. Or maybe she's just too tired to move. Too tired to fight.

Her head hurts so badly.

And then she hears Phosyne calling for help, and she's up, and moving, and has her hand clapped over the other woman's mouth in an instant. "Quiet," she rasps, and drags Phosyne back under the shade of the tarp, away from prying eyes.

Phosyne lets her.

Voyne licks her lips, trying to find more words where the one came from. "If somebody hears you," she says, haltingly, stumbling over each syllable, "then She can hear you, too."

That Voyne feels not just panic, but *joy*, at that idea? That is reason enough that it can't be allowed to happen.

Phosyne nods, and Voyne releases her. It's hard to stay standing, but she forces herself to, forces herself to meet Phosyne's eyes as she turns to peer up at her. "Welcome back," Phosyne says.

Voyne flinches and looks away.

"I doubt anybody heard me. The feast had gotten loud," Phosyne adds, as if trying to placate her. And that makes sense. Voyne has just hauled her bodily to the Constant Lady's table, and before that nearly strangled her. Has been her minder and her jailer. Of course she fears Voyne.

Freeing her mind, however she did it with the water, is only a tactic to stop Voyne from pursuing her further. Nothing more. It is not—it is not kindness.

Voyne takes a few deep breaths, makes herself focus. Phosyne is right; the feast *has* gotten loud, with raucous singing, squeals of laughter. It sounds like they've been rescued, but Voyne knows Etrebia still waits beyond the gates. She's known that all along, but for the last day, it hasn't mattered at all.

"There's no ladder," Phosyne says, drawing her back to the cistern.

"It's kept out of the water," Voyne replies automatically. Logistics steady her. "And there's only one left. Not here."

"Then how do we get out?"

Voyne hazards a glance at her. She looks weaker than she did a day ago. Her eyes appear sunken. Her hair is dry now, but it's plastered to her forehead. "How did you intend to get out, when you jumped in?"

It's hard to tell in the dim light, but Voyne thinks she blushes. "I hadn't thought that far," she admits. "Was more focused on testing a hypothesis."

Voyne looks down at the water.

"Yes," Phosyne confirms.

"Later. Explain it to me later." She wants to know *now*, but the longer they stay here, the weaker Phosyne will get, and the greater the chance of the Lady coming to look for them. Voyne steps back, looks around. The walls are hewn stone, not even blocks that might have toeholds, but slippery, undulating, unbroken rock.

She should have suggested steps be worked into the sides, back when Etrebia first cut them off here, and they'd set about improving the cisterns. More fool her.

Water sloshes as Phosyne leaves her side and goes up to the wall itself, just outside where the tarp covers, no doubt so she can see up to the rim. She places both hands flat on the stone and stares forward, bullheaded, then looks up. Voyne watches as she touches the top of her head, slides her hand against the stone level with it. She steps back, regarding it and the empty space above.

She looks at Ser Voyne.

"Come here," she says.

Ser Voyne jerks into motion.

She has no control over herself as she stalks through the water, and it makes her breath come sharp and thin. It doesn't *feel* like prowling the keep for the Lady (though remembering how, exactly, it felt is like trying to grab hold of a dream), but she is sure it didn't feel this wrong. This uncontrollable. No, she'd thought she was in perfect control.

Right now, she *knows* she is a puppet.

She reaches Phosyne. She bares her teeth. "Don't do that again," Ser Voyne growls. It's half warning, half plea.

Phosyne stares, confused. Then she nods. "No, of course not," she says. She licks her lip, brow furrowing in thought, before finally turning and gesturing at the wall. "If I lift you, can you reach the top, do you think?"

Voyne snorts. "I don't think you can lift me." But the idea does have merit. "Reverse it. I lift you up, you go get help, get a ladder."

"And I get dragged back to the great hall again, and you're stuck here until your Lady comes to fetch you?" Phosyne's tone is not kind, but Voyne figures she earned that. She's right, after all: when they go up, Voyne needs to be first out. She needs to assess the situation, figure out the best options available. Otherwise, they'll both be lost again, and Voyne isn't sure if she can claw her way back without the madwoman at her side.

"You're right," she concedes. Best to be practical and honest, here, even if she's burning with shame, immolating from the inside out. Even if her head still hurts and her mind threatens to spin apart at the slightest breath. "The problem remains, however, that you haven't eaten in days and, even if you had, the heaviest thing you've lifted in a month is your chamber pot."

And Phosyne hasn't lifted even that since Voyne took over her care and feeding.

Phosyne won't look at her as she asks, "Do you have any better ideas?"

"No," she admits. Still scowling, she thumps her hand against the rock.

Then she looks over at Phosyne curiously. "The chapel," Ser Voyne says. She only remembers snatches. Less detail, even, than what she has done for the Lady, if only because it felt like her mind was being teased out through the fault lines of her skull. So many conflicting demands, concepts, desires. But she remembers Phosyne's hand on her cheek. Her body against the rock. And then— nothing. Just the wall.

Seeing Phosyne outside the chapel, fleeing.

Phosyne, now, swallows thickly, then grimaces. "I already tried,"

Phosyne says. "It isn't working, whatever it was I did. And in the chapel, there was a place to land on the other side. I've already thought that one through."

Voyne tries to follow the logic, what it must mean. Phosyne, inside the chapel, then outside. It's impossible, but so is her leaving Cardimir's side voluntarily.

(Was it voluntarily? She remembers a knife in her hand, and—)

The thought is gone, but it leaves her burning again. Ser Voyne splays her fingers out against the wall, slick with algae. "I am not interested in waiting here to be reclaimed," she says, as much to herself as to Phosyne.

Then she grabs Phosyne's hand and presses it to the stone in the exact same place. Phosyne is forced to stumble closer, and Ser Voyne cages her in, broad chest against her back, arms on either side of her.

"So try harder," Ser Voyne growls in her ear.

Phosyne struggles against her, and Voyne's breath gusts hot upon her neck as she stares at the madwoman's hand—

And her hand disappears into the rock.

Phosyne goes very still, and Ser Voyne gasps, staring at what is now a stump. No, not a stump, because a stump would not meet so evenly with the wall it presses into.

"Oh, *fuck*," Phosyne whispers, and then she's struggling. Hyperventilating. Her head knocks back against Voyne in her panic, and just as Voyne reaches to steady her—

Her hand emerges from the rock. It's barely there for a moment, a memory more than a real thing, and then it is flesh and blood and uninjured.

Phosyne flexes it, and every piece moves as it ought to.

Voyne takes a step back, then another. It's too much. Too much to see, too much to understand. But Phosyne looks over her shoulder at Voyne and her eyes are alight with the same fervor Voyne saw in her when she created her everburning candle, and if Voyne has any hope of untangling what has happened to her, she needs this impossible creature on her side.

Phosyne puts her hand flat on the wall again. She lifts the opposite foot up and braces her toes against the rock, too.

"Do it again," she whispers.

This time, Voyne feels the compulsion crash into her. Her shoulders rock as she tries to control her breathing, resist it. But it doesn't work, because she's too busy being confused that Phosyne *wants* this, wants her to cage her against the wall, exude all of Voyne's greater physical strength and all her intimidation.

But then she remembers Phosyne against the chapel wall, and how, at first, Voyne was certain she was enjoying being choked.

Her breath hisses out between her clenched teeth, and Phosyne shudders. Her hand and foot sink into the wall. Voyne pulls back, a fraction of an inch, and when Phosyne tugs, she can't pull out of the rock.

"This is what you wanted?" Voyne asks, feeling lightheaded.

It pulls a mad little laugh from Phosyne, and she's already pushing up, getting her free foot against the wall, her free hand extended. Without help from Voyne, she sinks in again. She starts to drop, as if the earth remembers to clutch at her, but when she's got the original hand and foot free, the stone firms up once more. She's suspended from the wall. She is *part* of the wall.

Voyne thinks she's going to be sick.

Phosyne does it again, and again, then stops halfway up the wall, looking back over her shoulder. She's grinning. Voyne can't look away.

The part of her that is all logistics and tactics, however, can still speak. She hears herself say, "This has the same problem as before. You'll be exposed up there. Alone."

But maybe that doesn't matter. Maybe all that matters is Phosyne gets out, and all the rest will fall into place.

Phosyne purses her lips. "Go up first," Phosyne says. "Use me as—as a handhold. A ladder."

And there's that compulsion. She grits her teeth. "*Don't*," she snaps. "I can't—" Because now all she can hear is *use me use me use me* and that is not useful in the slightest.

"I'm sorry," Phosyne says, but she doesn't look it.

Voyne grimaces, steps closer. She can't help it, so she tries to channel it. Tries to think. If she climbs up now, she'll just dislocate

Phosyne's shoulder. So instead, she presses her hand to Phosyne's calf. "Get in deeper," she says. "So the rock is holding more of your weight."

"You'll have to push me, or I'll just fall," Phosyne says.

"I have you," Voyne murmurs. She places her other hand on Phosyne's hip. It's warm through the clammy fabric.

She feels when the rock releases its hold on Phosyne, and in return, she heaves upward. Phosyne melts into the rock, a little bit at a time. Voyne shifts her hold, braces her feet against the floor, and tilts Phosyne forward. Forward, until her nose is just brushing the wall. It's not like pushing somebody into sand or mud or anything but air. It's hard to keep her balance.

And then the weight is gone. The rock is taking it.

"Quickly," Phosyne gasps, and maybe this time it's hurting her.

Voyne doesn't hesitate. She adjusts her hold on Phosyne and hauls herself up, feet pushing against the wall beneath them. Her arms slide around Phosyne's waist, her hands clutch at Phosyne's shoulders. Phosyne feels too delicate beneath her, and she is shaking mightily. But she holds. The wall holds.

And then Ser Voyne is climbing on top of her, booted feet against her shoulders, and Phosyne is whimpering in pain, almost screaming. Voyne's hands close around the lip of the cistern. With one last great push, Voyne lifts herself from Phosyne's body and up into the night.

Behind her, she hears a broken sob, a splash, a thud. Voyne twists and sees Phosyne sprawled out in the shadows below.

At least she has not fallen through the floor. And as Voyne watches, she twitches one hand, sits up. Voyne looks down at her face, a pale circle in the dark, and thinks of how easy it would be to leave her.

But the thought is short-lived. She goes and retrieves the ladder. It's not hard. There are people all around her, and they barely look at her. They laugh. They aren't afraid.

They should be afraid.

Later, Voyne tells herself, and slides the ladder down into the cistern.

Phosyne meets her on solid ground, then collapses to her knees.

"No," Ser Voyne says, and hauls her up, forces her to walk ahead of her. They can't stay here, can't linger. For now, they are unseen, but that could change at any moment. She keeps a hand on Phosyne's lower back, shoving her along. She's rough. "Look frightened," Ser Voyne demands.

Phosyne does it well.

They weave through the crowd, which parts for Ser Voyne. The runners that stood in for tables are no longer parallel, and food is spread across the ground, spread across the refugees and guards and servants who roll about and laugh and cry with relief. There's no way for them not to stand out, upright and moving with purpose, but Voyne does not see the saints. She does not see the Lady. If they are about, they are well-hidden, and if they see her and Phosyne, they see only their knight dragging Phosyne back to where she belongs.

She cleaves to that duty, because otherwise she would be lost, helpless not to go to the aid of Aymar, gone mad with pleasure and gratitude, heedless of the danger.

They reach the keep without issue. The halls are as empty as Voyne made them, when the sun was still out. Up, up, and they are right outside Phosyne's tower when Voyne finally lets her hand drop.

24

ER TOWER DOOR is open.

Phosyne tries to remember if she left it that way when she went down to the tunnel with Treila. Possibly. After all, the boys are gone. The memory makes her wince, but there's nothing for it. There's food for them, at least. She tries not to feel grief at the thought of losing them. Of seeing them next on the Lady's lap.

Well, she has Ser Voyne now instead.

She pokes her head in and, seeing nobody and nothing waiting for her, slips into the room. Voyne is right behind her.

Her gut gives a renewed pang now that she's back in a space that is ostensibly safe for her, and she goes to the box she keeps her rations in. All meat, of course, and her stomach twists at the sight. She can't smell the feast here, her only blessing, but the memory of it, divorced from the evidence of how wrong it is, is enough to make her ache.

Treila. She will just have to wait for Treila. Beg food off her once more, and—

There is food on her workbench.

Phosyne edges closer warily, looking for signs somebody has been here before her. Treila, perhaps? But it's not dried fruit on her workbench. It's also not the luscious offerings the Constant Lady had tried to tempt her with. It looks like . . .

"Hardtack," Ser Voyne says, staring at it. "I thought we gave out the last of it . . ."

The reminder of exactly how bad the situation is, even absent the unnatural feast below, nearly knocks Voyne off her feet. She sinks to a crouch, covering her face with her hands. That she doesn't moan is, Phosyne thinks, likely only because of her training.

Phosyne picks up the biscuit, turns it over in her hands. Most of it is dry and grainy, what she'd expect, but one corner is covered in a thin film of slime. She lifts the biscuit to her nose, breathes in.

She smells sulfur.

"Oh, you clever boys," she murmurs, then takes a bite.

Or tries to; it's so hard it nearly breaks her teeth, and she hisses in pain. No matter; her hands are wet and her robes are soaked. She wraps the brick in her skirts and presses until she feels it give a little. It's still too hard to bite, but she can scrape the top layer off with her teeth. It's too salty by far, and otherwise tastes like sawdust, except for the faint hint of sweetness on her tongue as her saliva breaks it down.

Bread. Bread, bread she can *eat*, and she, too, sinks to the floor.

She has scraped all the soft bits off and is soaking it again in the folds of her robes when Ser Voyne manages to speak again. "I don't understand what happened to me," she says.

Phosyne looks over at her. She is still hunched over, almost prostrate.

"I'm afraid I don't have many answers," Phosyne says. "I can tell you what I saw, from outside. Would that help?"

Voyne nods.

"I saw you at Her table last night, eating food that She must have conjured from nowhere. And I saw you this morning, at the chapel. I found Jacynde above you, with her tongue cut out. Your hands were covered in blood."

Voyne shudders. "She said . . . She said a faithless tongue was worth more as food than to eat food."

At first Phosyne takes that to mean Jacynde said that, but of course not, of course it is Her. The Lady. "Faithless?"

"Last night," Voyne says. "Prioress Jacynde came to make us see sense. To make us understand that the food could not be explained. But the Lady cowed her. Pulled apart her armor by articulating all of the prioress's doubts. She couldn't withstand it. She let them give her honeyed wine. And then she stopped fighting."

"But the Lady holds grudges."

"It didn't feel like that," Voyne whispers. "It didn't feel like retribution, or even lesson-giving. It felt like . . ." She frowns. Closes her eyes. "Harvest."

Phosyne pulls the softened biscuit from her robe and stares at it, stomach curdling, before she sets it gently upon her workbench for later. "Somewhere, on those tables down there . . ." She goes back over the evening. Sees the Absolving Saint presenting the roasted arm so proudly. The Lady chewing bits of flesh.

She says nothing. She can't make herself say it. Ser Voyne either understands or she doesn't. Either way, the other woman gets up and begins to pace.

Phosyne works on mastering her stomach, putting the realization aside for later. Exhaustion wins out over both, but it dampens down the horror enough that Phosyne can make herself grab the biscuit, scrape another layer off with her teeth. It goes down thick and gluey in her throat.

At length, Ser Voyne stops pacing. Her shoulders rise and fall with a deep breath, and when she exhales, she looks a little more like Phosyne remembers. Flinty-eyed. Strong. The transformation is impressive; Phosyne can almost forget how small and broken she'd looked in the cistern, and their clothes aren't even half-dry yet.

"So," Ser Voyne says, turning to Phosyne and, after assessing her appearance, approaching as if afraid one or both of them might spook. "What next?"

Phosyne bites at her lip, then looks at the door. Still no sign of Treila. "There's a way out. Maybe. We're waiting for the girl who knows the way."

Ser Voyne does not look as relieved as Phosyne had expected. In fact, she looks angry.

"No," Voyne says, voice firm. Unyielding.

Phosyne blinks up at her. "No?"

"No. We aren't leaving. We stay here. We fix this. We save them."

"*Save* them?" Phosyne asks, disbelieving.

"If what happened to me is happening to everybody in this keep," Ser Voyne says, slowly, as if trying to explain something to a very distractible child, "then we cannot leave them to suffer. Even if we delude ourselves into thinking the Lady has kind intentions."

They both know She does not.

"We don't know what they are," Phosyne says. "What they want. What the limits of their powers might be."

"Then we study them." Voyne's stern expression is turning into a scowl. "We have a duty, Phosyne."

"To martyr ourselves?" Phosyne asks. There's a part of her that doesn't want to leave, not yet, but that part is curiosity, and her curiosity has taken her nowhere good. It certainly isn't any feeling of obligation. She lost that the moment the Lady said She was not summoned.

"To serve. We have protected those people from Etrebia, and we will protect them now, as well."

"Did we? Protect them from Etrebia, I mean. Because from up here it has looked as though we have only prolonged death."

Ser Voyne's jaw clenches. Phosyne realizes she's made yet another mistake. The fragile peace between them is about to crack, and either Voyne is going to bear down on her again (and she'll probably like it again), or Phosyne's going to tug on the leash, command her to *stop*, even though she keeps promising she won't do it again, because she's scared and because she wants to see the power work once more.

But neither happens, because the tower door opens and Treila slips inside.

Ser Voyne's reaction is—confusing. She wheels toward the door, as Phosyne would expect, and Phosyne is already up off the floor to get herself between the two women before Voyne can threaten or lunge, but as soon as Voyne can see Treila she goes limp.

Treila stares up at her, eyes wide at first, then narrowing to slits. Voyne's gaze slips away.

Phosyne wants to ask, but she has more important questions. More urgent ones, at any rate, now that she has a better sense of just how powerful the food being served down below *is*. She turns to Treila.

"Did you eat the food? Any of it?"

Treila screws up her face, turning her attention to Phosyne. "No, of course not." Her voice is just the same. Her posture's a little different, more tightly wound, perhaps, but all in all, she is *Treila* in a way that Voyne was not Voyne before the cistern. "Are you ready?"

Impatient, more than before. What happened to her, down in the revels? There are lurid suck-marks on her throat that weren't there earlier.

A brush with the chaos, then. A seduction. Phosyne only hopes she's kept her head.

"I—yes, of course." She looks back at Voyne reflexively.

Voyne's brow is clouded with confusion.

At first, Phosyne thinks she's hit a wall. That the water only lasts a certain amount of time, and everything is about to change again. But then Voyne blinks once, twice, and asks:

"Who are you talking to?"

Phosyne takes a step back, as if her body could be hiding Treila from sight. Voyne watches her, of course, but then glances at the door. Doesn't react to Treila standing right there. Just like she hadn't reacted to Treila down by the tunnel.

"She can't see you," Phosyne realizes.

"What?"

"No, she *can*," Phosyne amends, because Ser Voyne is looking at Treila's edges, perfectly avoiding the substance of her. "She can't *notice* you."

"Phosyne—" Voyne tries, but Treila talks over her:

"It's the Lady's fault."

Phosyne holds up a hand, and Voyne goes silent, watching her warily now. "The Lady?" Phosyne asks.

"Yes. She saw me with Ser Voyne earlier. For some reason, Ser Voyne thought I was *Her*, though I didn't . . . realize it at first." She doesn't look pleased at the memory. "I thought the Lady would kill me, but Ser Voyne went to Her obediently, and . . ." She gestures. Pauses, looks like she is going to stay something else. She rubs at the shell of her ear and doesn't say it.

But Phosyne thinks she understands. "The Lady has made sure Voyne won't confuse you with Her again."

"Exactly." Her gaze returns to Voyne. "It's irritating, but not in-surmountable. Probably a blessing. She's docile, now?"

"Yes, and coherent. I—"

She's cut off by Voyne seizing her by the upper arm, hauling her away from the door.

"Phosyne," she murmurs, voice low and dangerous. "Tell me, right this instant, what you see. Who you're talking to about me."

"A friend," Phosyne says.

Treila quirks a brow. "She can't hear me, either?"

"Apparently not."

"*Phosyne.*" Voyne's fingers tighten.

"It's another facet of your bewitchment," Phosyne says, looking up at the knight, wishing that what she's about to say isn't going to make everything worse. "The Lady is preventing you from seeing somebody. Her name is Treila."

Voyne's face goes blank for just a second. "What?" she asks, and she's a little breathless.

Phosyne glances at Treila. Treila huffs a small laugh.

This is far more extensive than Phosyne could have imagined. Simple, in its comprehensiveness. She clears her throat, tries again. "Tell me what you hear. Are you ready?"

Voyne nods.

"Treila."

Again, blankness. Then she comes back to herself; she doesn't say anything, but Phosyne can see it as a quickening behind her eyes. A few seconds pass, then Voyne goes, "Well?"

"I said it."

"You—" Voyne chokes a little, lets go of Phosyne, backs away.

"Tell me what you've heard me say," Phosyne asks. She shouldn't feel this fascinated. She should probably be far more afraid.

Voyne concentrates. "That the Lady is preventing me from . . . something. I didn't hear the rest."

"Then I can't explain it. You will have to trust me. Do you trust me, Ser Voyne?"

No, she very clearly does not. But that doesn't mean she won't.

Her throat bobs. "Whoever you're talking to," she says, slowly, "is a friend. And is not them."

"No. I promise you that. Do you recall, I said we may have a way out?"

Voyne nods.

Treila makes a displeased sound.

"This is our way out."

"We will stay." Her gaze is blade-sharp again. The tension between them crackles, shifts, back to the way it was before Treila's arrival. But then Voyne falters. She glances toward what she cannot look at, and her eyes slide off, and it looks like it hurts. She can tell it's wrong. "Unless—unless we can return, after. Perhaps some distance will help break whatever is influencing my mind."

Phosyne looks to Treila.

"Is it one way?" she asks.

"I don't care," Treila says.

And that is a good point. Once they're out, they're out.

"No," Phosyne translates, lies to Voyne. "So we're going to take the chance."

Voyne shifts uneasily, as if she wants to argue, and Phosyne prepares herself to command, but it isn't necessary. Voyne nods, then gestures for Phosyne to precede her. "Clear the way for me?" she asks.

She sounds vulnerable when she says it.

They creep out once more into the echoing, empty keep. The distance between the tower and the tunnel seems longer this time, but then, every excursion Phosyne has made in the last week has been harder than the one before. Voyne follows at a safe distance, but Treila stays close.

"An odd situation," Treila says.

"Just another of many. The feast, how was it?"

"Wine-soaked," Treila says. "A girl could lose her head in there. Everybody else has."

"If something happens," Phosyne tells her, "if we don't get out right away—the water is safe. In the cisterns. It has some fortifying effect. Clarifying." She gestures back toward Voyne.

"And what will we have to pay for that?" Treila asks.

Phosyne frowns. "Pay?"

Treila throws her a gleaming smile in the dark. "Don't worry about it," she says.

Phosyne wonders if she should.

"You're taking this better than most," she ventures. By *most*, Phosyne mainly means herself and Voyne. They're holding it together, sure, but Treila is . . .

Treila looks energized by it all. She plunged into the belly of the beast to blend in, and has come out of it looking not disgusted, not exhausted, but exhilarated.

In answer, Treila looks back at Ser Voyne. Voyne's head turns, eyes averting. She almost stumbles on the next step, which Phosyne doesn't think she even notices. "I've already had all the rules of my life turned upside down before," Treila says, finally. "It's easier to keep your head when you know it's all you can rely on."

25

ER VOYNE WANTS to be herself again.

She'd almost managed it, in the tower. She'd almost moved past the echoes of Phosyne's commands, the blurriness of her memory. But now she can't look directly ahead of her, if directly ahead of her is Phosyne's "friend," and she can feel herself beginning to unravel again.

It's tempting to believe Phosyne is speaking to herself. She wants to haul Phosyne back up to the tower, where she *belongs*. Phosyne herself had cemented that in her mind, somehow, in the chapel.

After she—

After she—

Ser Voyne makes herself face it fully: after she carved the prioress's tongue from her mouth and gave it to the Absolving Saint to take back to the Constant Lady. To eat.

It's like reaching a fire after a day out in whipping snow. It hurts. But the pain turns to an ache turns to some measure of restored movement.

But as she passes the next window, a glint of gold in the night catches her eye. She knows she can't afford to stop, but she slows, and then she sees him: Cardimir, out in the upper yard, attended by two saints, his crown upon his head. Fires have been lit, sending everything into stark, unsettling relief. The Absolving Saint and the Warding Saint stand close by; the Warding Saint clutches one of Cardimir's servants, a woman Voyne knows. Her skirt is hiked up above one leg, baring her thigh.

The Absolving Saint kneels before her, and touches her vulnerable skin. Her head lolls back. Red blooms where the Absolving Saint touches, enough blood that Voyne can see it from here as it falls into a goblet. The same one she has sipped honeyed wine from so many times in the past. There is a ring of people around the horror show, watching, kneeling, adoring. Nobody moves to stop any of it.

The Absolving Saint stands. He draws what might be honeycomb from his sleeve, crushes it into the cup. And Cardimir, without hesitation and with an easy air, takes the goblet and begins to drink.

Disgust wells in her. Disgust, and terror, and a bright urge to race out into the yard, to lunge at the saints, to rescue her king.

Except he doesn't appear to want rescuing.

Neither did you, she reminds herself. She didn't flinch. She didn't protest. She didn't even pause to consider who she had been eating.

Her stomach lurches.

A hand seizes her elbow. She recoils, hissing, but it is only Phosyne. "Come on, we don't have much time," Phosyne says. A feeling of weighty silence follows on, and then Phosyne shakes her head. "Our friend says to tell you that he's hardly worth saving. But more importantly, they will stop you if you go to him. Or they will make you hold the cup."

Voyne flinches.

She wants to close her eyes as she resumes her descent. She doesn't want to see herself fleeing.

They reach the ground floor of the keep, and then slip down the stairs to the little room where Voyne found Phosyne earlier. She knows she was just here, can remember it, but it's all a little slantways. She hates this. She hates being unsure of herself, of feeling so unsteady. She has a *purpose,* the same one she's had for six months, and that should be enough.

But she's not wearing her armor. She doesn't even have her sword. Everything feels strange, and she's not even sure who she is, anymore. That thought isn't hers. It's more like scales being peeled up. Something slipping out from underneath. She hisses.

There's a touch on her wrist. Phosyne looks up at her.

"We're here."

Not much longer, then, until they're outside, and maybe Voyne will be able to think straight. It's the only hope she can cling to as she looks around the little room, and sees again the hole where the floor and a wall join.

Phosyne is looking up and to the right of it, and then she averts her gaze. Voyne tries to look where Phosyne had, but flinches instantly; she feels the deflection like the crackle of lightning in wool blankets.

At least she feels it, this time.

"Is that really necessary?" Phosyne says. Not to her, though. A pause. Listening. "No, I can move just fine like this." She plucks at her robes. "Ser Voyne much the same, I think."

"What?"

Phosyne flushes a little. "Our friend recommends undressing. Apparently—"

And then nothing. Silence. More than silence. Voyne grimaces, touches one ear.

Phosyne cocks her head. "Incredible," she murmurs. Voyne wishes she didn't sound so delighted.

"I will remain clothed."

"Right. Of course. Perhaps, though, I . . ."

And then she's fussing with the toggle of her robe, and then she is nude. All bones and angles, skin pallid and loose where there was flesh beneath before. Bruises, where Voyne has touched her. Voyne looks away, suddenly short of breath.

"It will make the climb easier," Phosyne says, or passes along. Voyne isn't sure which. The other woman is wrapping the worn fabric into a bundle, if the sounds are anything to go by. "Right. Well, off we go, then."

Voyne nods, hazards a glance. Phosyne is clutching the bundle to her chest. It helps. Slightly.

"Through here," Phosyne says, crouching down. Ser Voyne's head pounds. This absence with them, that she cannot hear the name of, cannot look through, cannot look at—it will drive her mad, soon enough. It makes it impossible to look at the hole. Their companion must be in front of it, or inside it.

"I can't see the way," Voyne confesses, then focuses on her breathing so she doesn't vomit.

Phosyne hums acknowledgment. After a minute or so, she clears her throat. "Try to look again?"

Voyne does, and this time, she can see the gap again.

"Go first," she tells Phosyne. That way, at least, she has half a chance of seeing where she's going.

Of course, the tunnel is entirely dark. Voyne realizes her mistake as soon as she wriggles into the tunnel (really, no more than a crevice) and finds she can't see anyway, but she is far too aware of Phosyne squirming ahead of her. It's mostly sound. Sound, and stench. She hangs back, lets Phosyne get a little farther on, and then begins to crawl.

Phosyne is a small woman, and her "friend" must be similarly built, because where they seem to slide through the stone, Voyne has to force every inch she gains. Her shoulders catch on outcroppings. Her hips need to be twisted this way and that to navigate sharp turns. She feels too large, hemmed in, crushed.

The stone, at least, is cold, blessedly cold, and Voyne takes a moment to press her burning cheek against it, eyes closed. Ahead of her, she hears Phosyne crawling, and the unsettling nothingness of their companion's movements beyond. She focuses on Phosyne to try to block out the nothing. She edges forward a few more feet.

Her head collides with rock.

She hisses, ducking, and tries to feel out the path ahead of her, but comes up with only stone. Stone and stone and more stone. No gap at all. She can hear Phosyne ahead of her, but can't reach her.

Her entire body goes hot, then freezing cold, and her headache feels like it will split her skull apart. She gasps for breath, retreats.

"Ser Voyne?" Phosyne calls.

She doesn't stop until she's back in the keep, dry heaving, curled up on herself like she'd been in the cistern. Somewhere behind her, there's movement, and then Phosyne is beside her, a hand hovering over her shoulder, unsure if she trusts Voyne enough to touch.

"What's happening?" Phosyne asks. "What are you feeling?"

"There was no tunnel," Voyne says, because she doesn't know how to describe the sickness in her now. She doesn't want to tell Phosyne that she craves honey on her lips with a fervor that scares her.

That she wants to see ringed irises, not Phosyne's flat gray eyes. She wants the Lady. She wants to run to Her, fall at Her feet, and she's almost too far gone to feel horror at the image.

"But I was ahead of you," Phosyne says, and, at last, touches Voyne's shoulder. The contact sends a jolt through Voyne. She pulls away, afraid of what she might do if she doesn't put distance between them.

"I know," Voyne snaps. She's up on her feet, pacing. "I *know* that, I could hear you, but there was just unbroken rock. There wasn't a way through. I shouldn't have been able to hear you through that, I don't—I don't *understand*—"

She doesn't understand any of this. Her brain is on fire, her limbs do not always obey her, and she wishes more than anything that she could wring the Lady's throat, the way she's killed a hundred others.

The nothingness of their companion enters the room, and Voyne snarls, turns away, slams a fist into the wall because if she doesn't, she might lash out at the woman she cannot see or at Phosyne, and that will only make everything worse.

Phosyne doesn't speak. Voyne supposes that means she's listening. Voyne hopes that means the nothing has a plan.

But then Phosyne shakes her head, says, "No, no, we'll just try again—"

"There's no point," Ser Voyne says. "There was a *wall*—"

"We'll give it some time, Ser Voyne and I can go in together, I can try to see what's stopping her—"

Nothing. Nothing fills the room. Ser Voyne breathes hard through her nose, fights the urge to flee.

And then nothing is gone again. It's just the two of them left, Phosyne looking between Voyne and the hole, the hole and Voyne.

"Well?" Voyne asks, when she can speak again.

"She's leaving without us," Phosyne says. She clutches the bundle of her robes to her, fingers tight. All of her is tight. Every muscle in her narrow body is tense.

And Voyne realizes then that if Phosyne goes back into the tunnel, Voyne will not be able to pursue her.

Time stretches. Voyne almost kneels, almost begs, because she doesn't want to be left here alone. She makes herself wait instead. Wait, and hope that perhaps Phosyne will credit duty more than survival.

It is a stupid choice to make, but Voyne hopes that she makes it.

When Phosyne unrolls her robe and drags it back on over her head, Voyne weeps.

26

ALFWAY BETWEEN THE keep and the grotto, Treila curls up against the stone and laughs.

It's not sane laughter. She knows very well it isn't. It's the laughter of the absurd, of the tragicomic, and she is shaking apart with it. Not only can Ser Voyne not see her, not hear her, not conceive of the *concept* of her, but the very earth spits her back out when Treila tries to draw her into this grotto she now thinks of as her own. There are more than a few glistening jokes in that, and she wishes she could tell the Loving Saint, because she knows he would laugh against her skin.

She should go back for Phosyne; a little more cajoling, perhaps, and the woman would likely follow her in and leave Ser Voyne behind entirely. Treila saw the bruises on her, after all. Has put together a little of their dynamic. But that might take time, and the Loving Saint's echo is still ringing in her head.

And she knows exactly the cost she has to pay to leave on her own. It's small enough.

When she can will herself to move again, she slinks through the passageway. It's easier this time, and not only because soon she can see the glow of Phosyne's candle at the other end. It's not roomier, exactly; if there were more space around her, she would fear getting lost. But it is *simpler*. She doesn't scrape herself as often. The tight pinches aren't quite as tight as she remembers them being.

At last she emerges into the grotto and sets about dressing once more. It's quiet, save for the faint trickling of the water, the susurrus of fabric over her skin. No Phosyne, no Ser Voyne, no refugees, no saints. The air of simple safety is almost strong enough to make her forget to fear the creature in the darkness.

He doesn't say anything to greet her. The candle, after all, is still burning.

Treila looks at the crack for a long time, flexing her hand at her side. The Loving Saint's words echo in her head. *If you have a way out, I would suggest you take it. Whatever the cost. You won't have the choice soon.* It could be a trap, of course; perhaps he said it knowing it would drive her down here. Perhaps whatever lurks in that crevice is a friend of his.

She knows that just because it felt genuine, the way he purred against her skin, it doesn't mean anything. He's a good liar, down to the bone. He must be.

But she doesn't think he was lying when he warned her to be careful of bargains. *One half of an exchange.* She will not get something for nothing. Any way out was always going to cost her.

Here is what Treila knows: there is no chance of survival here, and no chance of retribution, either. The Constant Lady has taken that from her, and no matter what the Loving Saint says, Treila has enough of a sense of self-preservation not to go toe-to-toe with a woman who can simply *erase* her from Ser Voyne's awareness. Treila's not happy with it, will never be happy with it, but there are other people still outside the castle who had a hand in her family's destruction. And, perhaps, it is poetic to let the king and his attack dog rot here, even if it's not Treila's doing. Even if they're barely aware of it.

There is no chance of survival *or* triumph here, and though Treila is stubborn and hungry for satisfaction, she'd rather live short one finger than die sulking and lurking in a castle gone mad.

Pity about Phosyne, but really, Treila doesn't need her anymore.

She douses the candle.

Near-darkness folds around her, cool and enticing, and she wets her lips. Tucks the wax into her pocket and approaches the crack.

"Hello, clever," it breathes. "I missed you."

Treila shivers and plants her hands against the rock, one on either side of the fissure. "And I, you," she returns, though it's not true in the slightest. The lie is sweet on her tongue.

Her creature laughs, delighted, either without guile or adoring her own. "And will you feed me this time? It's not so nice, to tease."

"Oh, yes," she says. "But first, a few questions. I want to know the shape of your teeth before they pierce my skin."

"Clever, clever," he sings. "Ask away."

"And what will I owe you for answers?"

"Somebody has been teaching you," he replies. His tone has shifted. Treila can't discern if he's irritated or afraid.

And *that* is certainly an answer, all on its own. She doesn't think her creature knows about the castle's guests.

She doesn't think it's the Loving Saint on the other side of that gap, waiting for her to flinch.

Treila rolls her gaze castle-ward. "We have visitors," she says. "Strange visitors. They say it is eat or be eaten."

The crack hisses. Seethes. It's for just a moment, but the sharp stench of iron accompanies it, lingers even when the noise is gone and Treila wonders if she really heard it.

"Your questions?" he asks, sounding normal once more.

"Your price for answers?"

A pause. "The questions will pay for the answers."

She thinks that the price may have changed, just a little, now that he knows there's competition aboveground. Another successful feint; her lungs burn with satisfied arrogance.

"Will it hurt very much?" she asks, and leans in once more. Slides her hands closer to the gap.

He makes a pleased sound now. This is far more to his liking. "Yes," he says. "Oh, yes."

She shivers again, but keeps up the slow stroke of her palms on rock. "And will I survive it?"

"It's just a finger," he says, as if that answers the question.

She waits him out. She stops where she is, hands only a few inches from the divide. She waits for him to protest, to realize this is more negotiation than interrogation. It doesn't matter that she knows his answer; it matters that he *gives* it.

"Yes," he says at last. "You will survive it."

Treila shifts her fingers closer. Strokes the stone. A faint breeze, like an exhale, ghosts across her face, and she leans into it. "And I will be out of this castle, able to make my way to wherever I wish?" she murmurs, voice low and sighing, as if she's giving in to a fantasy. "If I let you take a finger of my choosing, will I emerge from Aymar Castle onto the plain beyond, safe and sound?"

She lets one fingertip slip from the stone, hover in the space just before the darkness.

"*Yes,*" her creature sighs. "But."

"But?"

"But should you wish to return," he says, and she can *hear* his smile, "the fee will be a little higher."

He doesn't specify. She doubts she could make him if she wanted to, but—she doesn't want to. Doesn't *need* to.

Resolved, Treila extends the smallest finger of her left hand into the darkness.

At first, there is nothing. Then the brush of gentle lips against her knuckle. A tongue, laving from the web between little and ring finger up to the very tip, prodding beneath her fingernail. She thinks of the Loving Saint, planting his tainted seeds, and grips her free hand tight against the stone so that she doesn't flinch, doesn't pull away. *It's eat or be eaten*, she tells herself, and she cannot eat darkness.

But it can eat her.

Teeth close around her first knuckle, test the heft of the joint. Treila clenches her jaw and refuses to close her eyes or look away. There's nothing in the darkness that she can see, and so there is no warning when the bite comes, and there is nothing but pain. Treila cries out, falling forward, catching herself against her left shoulder on the stone.

Tears burn her eyes. She's yanked her hand back from the crevice, helpless to resist, and nothing stops her. Nothing stops her, but nothing opens for her, and she stares at the abbreviated length of her finger.

There is no blood.

"It's not so nice, to tease," her darkness whispers. "That's not enough to set you free. A little more, clever. Just a little more."

Treila's crying. She doesn't want to be, but the pain is too much, even though there's no blood, even though there are no longer teeth against her skin. For a moment, she doesn't think she can do it. Doesn't think she can complete the bargain, offer her hand once more to the creature in the crevice.

But she has suffered worse. That long winter, starving, cold, too shocked and confused to be angry yet, not angry enough to keep herself alive. And yet she is. She found her spite, at last, and rode it out of the forest.

Treila harnesses that spite again and thrusts her hand into the black.

The second bite is faster than the first, one more knuckle gone, and Treila howls. She screams. She thrashes, but she keeps her arm in the gap, and she can feel it grip the length of her arm. There aren't hands, no, though the lips and tongue still work against the skin of her palm. If anything, it's like she's enveloped in a spiral of interlocking legs, jointed and pulsing and tangling around her. She presses her forehead to the rock and pants, desperate not to move, desperate to see this through.

And then the third bite. The last one, severing her finger cleanly from her hand, and this time the pain is like scalding oil, shooting up her veins, and she is on her knees before she can stop her fall. She tumbles forward, and the stone is not there anymore, it was never there, and she is in a tunnel of flesh. She is crawling. She hears laughter all around her as the limbs of this monster convulse and slide and grasp. Treila pushes forward all the same, grips skin, grips stone, and then—

And then—

And then she emerges into sunlight and the sigh of a breeze through grass.

27

HE SOUNDS OF the feast beyond the keep walls have died away when Phosyne and Voyne leave the little room with the crack in the world. What light there is comes from a pale half dawn, gray and strained. It falls on bodies, sleeping sprawled across the stone.

Nobody has gone back to their pallets or beds, and instead slumber seemingly where they fell coming in from the feast. There is very little sound. Phosyne and Voyne step over bodies and ascend the stairs, not quite looking at each other because (at least in Phosyne's case) that would be to acknowledge just how scared they are.

Phosyne doesn't want to be here. She wants to be on the other side of that tunnel, puzzling with the thing that Treila met down there, looking for another way out. It should have been easy to leave Voyne behind. Physically, it would've been. But then Phosyne thinks of Ser Voyne compelled to obey her orders, and remembers her confusion, her terror, as she surfaced from the Lady's control instead, and she feels guilty for even considering abandoning this woman.

Besides, she can always leave on her own, if she changes her mind. Probably.

"We'll need a plan," she says when it is just them in the staircase, halfway up to the tower. "A real one. A specific one."

"Our enemy is powerful," Ser Voyne agrees, slowing.

"Study won't be enough." Phosyne crowds up against Voyne, half so she can speak softly, and half because she feels exposed. Her room would be a far better venue for this conversation, but she wants a promise now. Something more than Voyne's determination, before

Treila arrived, or her tears, after Treila left. A promise that Phosyne is not making the wrong choice.

"No." Voyne studies her face in the dim light. Mulls something over, behind her shadowed eyes. "My sword—the Lady took it from me. That is a place to start. And the water. Everyone must drink water, and soon; the day's heat will only grow."

"Unless they mean to kill us all." Phosyne smiles. It's a little hysterical. "In this heat, if they can keep the feast going—"

"They've already stopped the feast."

"For tonight. But if they don't give out water to everybody, I don't think they'll know to ask, anymore. Two days, then, at most. Right?"

"Surely thirst can punch through their intoxication."

Phosyne says nothing. Waits for Ser Voyne to understand the obvious.

Her shoulders sag a few seconds later. "We can't assume that," she says.

"No, we can't. We don't even know what they want." Except obedience, from Voyne, and—what, from Phosyne?

Attention?

The Lady had addressed her like a pet, but not exclusively (not like the king does); there was an eagerness to be seen. To be listened to. And She had allowed Phosyne to dig in her heels and refuse Ser Voyne, up until a point. It had amused Her.

She had wanted to know more about the water. What else might She like to know?

"The water is a good place to start," Phosyne says, rubbing at her brow. She leans against the curved stone wall, inches away from the breadth of Voyne's body. She feels sheltered there. Hidden. "It serves two purposes. It keeps everybody alive a little longer, and it might loosen the hold on them, like it did on you. But how can we distribute it? There are too many mouths, and the Lady will see the change, I am sure of it."

"And we do not have unlimited stores," Voyne murmurs. Her brain is engaged now. She leans in to Phosyne, conspiratorially, even curves her body slightly around Phosyne as if to hide her. "But we can hope for rain."

"It's not just water, though. It must be purified. By my hand." She considers. "Or by my powder, as it may be. Perhaps we start from the powder, not the water."

"Perhaps." Voyne gazes down at her with something very like hope, then pulls away, shaking herself. "This is no place to discuss strategy."

"No," Phosyne agrees. Thinks to say *lead on*, but stops herself shy. No more commands, no matter how innocently meant; she must be more cautious.

They begin to climb once more.

They reach the final curve of the staircase without issue, and Phosyne sways on her feet, exhausted, as she takes the last turn.

Prioress Jacynde lies motionless in front of her door.

Her skin is as red with heat as when Phosyne last saw her, her brow as paper-dry. She is alive; of that much, at least, Phosyne remains certain. But how she came to be here makes less sense. There's no sign of the young nun—or anybody, for that matter. There is only Jacynde, eyes shut, body still except for the fluttering of her pulse in her throat.

Behind her, Ser Voyne swears and takes a step back. No doubt thinking of the chapel, remembering now with a clearer mind what it was like to carve out the woman's tongue. "I—I can't—"

"Then don't," Phosyne says. She thinks. They can't just step over the body, leave the prioress here alone. And she suspects Voyne will adjust, once the shock has subsided. "She needs water. I guess we are starting from there after all."

It's probably not safe for Ser Voyne to go to the cisterns alone, but it's not that much safer if Phosyne goes with her, either. Or for Phosyne to go on her own. But it will give them more of the lay of the land, of how many sleeping bodies have fallen scattered and strange across the yard.

"Consider it reconnaissance, as well?" she adds, making sure to force her voice into a questioning lilt at the end, to make sure it isn't a command.

A glance over her shoulder shows Ser Voyne looking relieved.

"Yes," she agrees. Looks down at Jacynde a moment, swallows heavily. And then she rolls her shoulders. "I'll be back soon."

She looks like a knight again when she strides off. It's comforting. Phosyne watches until she disappears around the curve of the stairs.

Right. Jacynde, then.

Phosyne pushes open her door and drags the prioress's body inside and over to her own pallet. It is surely nothing like the bed Jacynde is used to, Phosyne is only too aware now of how it stinks, but she has no other real options. She gets a rag, dips it in the little water she still has, and lays it against the side of Jacynde's mouth. She's no doctor, but she figures that should help. At the very least, if this insensate sleep is anything but natural, it should break through it.

But the water does not, in fact, miraculously restore the woman to consciousness.

With a groan, Phosyne sinks to her knees beside the woman and mops the water over her exposed skin. There's no fresh blood around her mouth, at least. Whatever Voyne did is done.

It's strange, to wash Jacynde's exposed scalp. To have this woman, prickly and powerful and angry, limp beneath her hands. Once, Jacynde was Phosyne's entire world (though Jacynde barely noticed Phosyne until Phosyne had already begun to slip away). Her sermons and preferences and biases had shaped Phosyne's life and belief. Had guided her through her faith.

Her faith is . . .

Her faith is complicated, even without considering the form of the Lady walking the castle walls Herself, instead of being carried as a statue in a litter. She's fairly sure that her faith wasn't always so complicated. There must have been months, *years*, when it was as simple as breathing—or, at least, simple enough that she could wrestle with her doubts within its confines. But then her mind had started to turn, and her research had shifted from waterwheels and pulley systems to the basest nature of water itself, because she'd heard it *whisper*.

Not literally, of course. But she'd been helping test a new dam design, ruminating on how much she could convince a river to change its nature, and then the sun had caught on the water a certain way, and she'd been able to taste it without dipping a hand in to drink, had *heard* the quality of the light on the surface and down, lower, where she could not see.

From there, everything had fallen apart. Fallen together. She'd given up on structure. Her duties became less and less important than her theories, and she began acquiring books: fiction books, and recipe collections, and alchemical treatises that would have gotten her excommunicated.

Did get her excommunicated, eventually, along with all the rest that had gone wrong.

And where was her faith in all of that? There was no moment when it stopped, when she decided she no longer believed in the Lady or Her saints. She isn't even sure that she *doesn't* believe in them (the actual concept of them, not whatever is wearing their costumes). It just hardly seems to matter anymore.

At any rate, now Jacynde is just a woman, and a half-dead woman at that. Phosyne doesn't know what to do. If the water doesn't work, must she try something else? A way to restore vitality, or belief, or holiness?

That might be it. Jacynde's holiness, her proximity to the ineffable, has been forcibly stripped away.

That doesn't give Phosyne much hope that she can fix it.

Her musings are interrupted by a knock at her chamber door, and she forces herself up on creaking knees. Sunlight filters through the window in the loft with the character of midday, though Phosyne doesn't think it's been half so long as that.

But what does she know? She's mad, isn't she?

At any rate, Ser Voyne has returned, and it's time to get to work. She stumbles to the door and hauls it open without checking.

The Lady stands before her.

Her saints are in attendance as well. They fill the small hallway, and Phosyne hopes that Ser Voyne is far, far away, isn't already on her way back.

"Hello, little mouse," the Lady says, smiling. Her eyes are bright. Phosyne meets them for half a second, then looks away, chest burning. There's too much Phosyne wants to know, wants to ask her. Wants to believe. "May we come in?"

"No," Phosyne says.

Phosyne wishes she'd said the same to the king, when he called, because that one word actually *works*. The Lady doesn't move. She doesn't even step closer to try to force the issue.

She does, however, peer over Phosyne's shoulder. "What a beautiful little world you have for yourself," She murmurs. Her tone is gentle. Genuine. Intrigued. Not mocking, like Phosyne thinks it should be. Anybody's would be. Even Treila, who hadn't necessarily been *bothered*, hadn't actually approved of the squalor.

And the Constant Lady, by contrast, appears delighted. She is looking up, now, and Phosyne turns to see Her gazing at the corkindrill hanging from the ceiling. And then, crouching and tilting Her head, up at the bit of occluded window in the loft, which Phosyne is surprised She can even see from there.

Phosyne straightens her spine. The Lady is, if nothing else, an enemy. That much has been clear since Phosyne first set eyes on Her, cemented in the horror of the feast. That she now feels flattered and wants to preen is immaterial. "Have you come to negotiate?" she asks, doing her best to sound strong. She thinks she sounds a little like Ser Voyne. Or Treila; Treila would know how to handle this creature.

"Negotiate?" the Lady echoes curiously. "I simply wanted to speak again, now that you've had some time to marinate."

Phosyne's skin pebbles.

"This castle—we can give you nothing," Phosyne says, taking the measure of the Lady and all three of Her attendants in turn as she speaks. "We are dying. There's no way out. So why have you come here? Deliverance?"

The Lady laughs. "Of course not."

Well, at least that is settled.

"But do you really think you can give us nothing?" the Lady continues. "You have breath enough, still. Life."

"Life that you are purchasing with your feast," Phosyne tries.

The Lady smiles.

"Life, and love, and fear," She agrees. "And power. There is power here, as well. Let us in, little mouse."

The flattery makes Phosyne shiver as much as the threat. She opens her mouth to say no all the same.

"Let us in, and we will help you with your guest."

Phosyne goes stiff. She is a poor liar, down to the bone, even before she glances over her shoulder at Jacynde. "I don't need help," she tries anyway.

"I smell fever," the Warding Saint says. "Sun fever—it is dry and scorched."

The Lady smiles. "Jacynde de Montsansen?"

"Yes," the Absolving Saint says. "Yes, I can smell the propolis beneath her nails still."

"She's dying," the Loving Saint adds.

Phosyne's heart beats triple time in her chest. They have not crossed the threshold yet, not even toed the edge of it, and Phosyne could just shut the door. Could hide. Letting them in won't help Voyne return safely, and she should not risk herself for Jacynde.

But they haven't brought food with them. Phosyne has her water. Perhaps it is safe. Perhaps . . .

"No," she makes herself say.

They do not leave.

"There is so much power in you," the Lady sighs, instead, closing Her eyes and parting Her lips as if She is tasting the air. "And I do not think you even notice it, most of the time. Tell me, little mouse, how it feels to speak."

Phosyne blinks. "I . . . to speak?"

"Can you feel the urgency in your own words? The press of muscle that is not muscle, the slide of conjuration? When you purify your waters, what does it taste like, the notes that you sing into being?" The Lady's eyes are still closed as She recites this litany, lips curling, pleased and pleasing. "Do you even know what it is you do to the world?"

There is nothing for Phosyne to do but swallow thickly, mind spinning, touching lightly upon every way she has nudged the fabric of reality and felt it shift.

"You don't know what it is you do," the Warding Saint murmurs. "You've only just begun to see."

"Let us teach you, sweetling," the Absolving Saint says, or *sighs*, really, as he gazes at her with calm focus.

Phosyne shivers.

"You know?" she asks, unable, in the end, to resist. She wants context too badly. Wants to understand what it is she's reaching for. Wants to know what it means when she sinks into stone.

Voyne can't give her that.

This is how they get you, she tells herself, letting the words sound like Treila's because Treila, Phosyne knows, will not let herself be so easily tricked. Hunger is not so hard to resist. Phosyne has done it before.

"We know you've done things your kind are not meant to do," the Loving Saint says.

That causes a ripple of reaction. The Lady does not look *angry*, per se, but She does go very still, and the Warding Saint takes one step back and turns to face the white-haired one.

The Loving Saint only smiles.

"And what do you get, for teaching me?" Phosyne asks, because it can't be this easy.

"Entrance," the Lady says.

"No," Phosyne says again.

The Lady's smile, at last, turns brittle.

Teaching is ongoing. If she lets the Lady in, she doesn't want to let Her in for all time. To accept would be to form a relationship, but Phosyne only hungers for the knowledge, not the attachment. She needs to draw a boundary.

Phosyne considers a moment longer, and then steps into the hall.

The Lady regards her with something that looks like pleasure. "A novel solution," the Lady admits. "But that doesn't tell me what we will get instead in exchange for teaching you."

Phosyne turns away, puts her back to them. "Teaching me is the reward," she ventures. "For not harming me."

She thinks she hears the Absolving Saint gasp in delight.

"Very well," the Lady agrees.

Phosyne shivers with triumph.

"What do you wish to do?" the Lady asks, at her shoulder now. Her fine hands hover close to Phosyne's waist, but do not touch. "For I do believe that, should you wish to do something, anything at all, you can find the tricks to make it happen."

"Like the water," Phosyne says, uneasy.

"That, and more," the Absolving Saint says, at her other side. They're both close enough to touch her. Neither does.

"But we will only teach you one thing, in exchange for your safety this one time," the Lady purrs. "So choose carefully, little mouse."

Phosyne stares into her room.

This whole exchange hinges on the belief that these creatures *want* to teach her. Phosyne is fairly certain of that, bolstered by their response to her explanation. But she doesn't know at what point their desire to harm her will outweigh that longing to instruct. Helping Jacynde is the safe option; they have already offered it once, even knowing that she feels no great loyalty to her anymore. Asking for the correct words and actions to banish them from the castle is, almost certainly, too much. And in between?

She could ask to learn how they summoned food.

How they had bewitched Ser Voyne.

How they had enticed an entire castle to eat at their table and lose their minds.

What she wants, though, is to ask what they *are*. What they fear, what they crave, what they have come for. But that's not on offer.

So she reaches for the next step removed from *what* they are: "Teach me how you came into the castle, unnoticed."

The Lady's hands settle at her waist, and Phosyne feels teeth pressed against her throat in a smile. "Gladly," the Lady says. "Close your eyes, and taste honey on your tongue."

28

ER Voyne sees no trace of saints as she makes her way to the cisterns.

She does see the sun too high in the sky; only minutes ago, it seems, it was dawn. But now the yard is baking, and there are too many people still passed out in the dirt, baking with it. Their skin is growing red and hot.

Like Prioress Jacynde's.

She can feel Jacynde's writhing tongue inside her fist. She can feel many things that should be far away, fogged over, but it is as if the heat of the sun and the clarity of the cistern water has laid her open. She feels the tongue, and the impact of her sword hilt into an unarmored skull, and the frigid chill of a failed campaign in winter, when she and Leodegardis had been left with no choice but to carve up the dead and portion them out to the survivors.

She has seen so much suffering. She has been the instrument of it so many times: the edge of the blade, the lick of the flame. It's easier to cast it as protecting Aymar, protecting her king. But from another angle, it is only violence. If she serves the wrong master . . .

Voyne cannot allow herself to dwell on it. Not even as she feels acutely every whimper, every keen, every begging tug at the edge of her armor that has ever happened.

Nobody here is begging.

They sleep like the dead. She recognizes many of them; there is no order to who has fallen where. She tells herself that the steady rise and fall of their chests is merciful: sleep stops pain, and they are, at least, alive.

This is no Carcabonne. A battlefield strewn with dead, and a liberated castle empty of everybody she meant to save. There is still a chance here.

She draws up water, bucket by bucket, and fills what oilskins are at the ready. She fills cups, too, after she dumps out honeyed wine. She ignores the bloody remnants where the Absolving Saint bled that woman for Cardimir's thirst. There are so many people here, lying at her feet, needing to be saved. She tries to save them. She props up first one, then another, tipping water down their throats. Some swallow. Some choke. One wakes up and screams when he sees her, and Voyne remembers, too late, that she is the reason his arms are covered in half a dozen red stripes. Her nails on his flesh, hauling him to this banquet.

After that, she can't do it anymore.

It won't be enough, she reasons. Phosyne was right. She could give every person in this yard a drink of water, and wait for them to rise, and she would have no way to keep them safe from another offer of food. There are too many people here to lead. So instead she turns her strength to getting them out of the heat. The sun beats down on her as she hauls limp, helpless bodies into shade.

She hopes it will be enough.

Most that she moves are whole and healthy, save for the burning of their skin. But a few . . . a few have been ravaged. She finds strange wounds: a kitchen boy missing stripes of flesh from his legs, the furrows already healing pink and smooth. A girl with her shirt missing, exposing her belly, where a window of translucent skin covers over the pulsing of her guts. Other injuries she suspects were at her hands the day before, more immediate, some purulent.

She can do nothing for them, and the knowledge tears at her heart.

And she sees no trace of Cardimir, no trace of anybody she can rouse and scream at, beg for help or guidance or leadership.

There is only so much wreckage.

Her muscles are screaming by the time she gives up, and she feels too exposed, too raw. She stumbles to the walled garden. She needs shade herself, a little shelter, but she's not ready to go back inside. Not yet. Not yet.

The garden has grown green again. She sidesteps broad, shining leaves, sticks to the thin track of dirt that still leads to the center. She sits heavily on the bench. It's not safe here, either; she remembers the Lady coming to collect her here before the feast. She remembers . . .

Golden hair.

Golden hair, and then the thought is gone again, buried, stolen from her. There is only buzzing left, and emptiness, the same feeling she felt in Phosyne's tower, in the tunnel below the earth. The nothingness that has replaced something that once was. Voyne fists her hands in her hair, shudders. She can't even remember what she was thinking of, when the buzzing started. The garden, perhaps? She remembers the Lady. She remembers her king telling her that it was time to begin eating their own, remembers fighting it, but it all runs together. Those weren't the same day. The Lady came later. But it is the Lady she remembers sitting on this bench with her, taking her hand, shaking the foundations of her world apart.

Voyne jolts away from the bench, on her feet again, retreating. Something foul has happened here, and she cannot think about it without bile rising in her throat.

It's easier to go back out, to keep moving bodies.

She doesn't notice how she is gentler with the girls with golden hair.

29

REILA CAN BARELY see, the sunlight is so intense. It was full night when she crawled beneath the castle, but now it's midday. It's midday, and it's mid-*autumn*, the air filled with a crisp bite, the trees around her wreathed in blazing orange.

Across the river, there is mud, and rubble, and no other trace of the Etrebian camp.

She cradles her hand against her chest, fingering the abbreviated bump at the outer edge of her left hand. There's no pain now, not even a red raised spot to mark where the darkness's teeth bit in. The skin is continuous, even-toned, soft. It feels just like all the skin around it.

It's like there was never a finger there at all, and that, *that*, is what brings her to her knees.

She clutches her hand tight, gasping, sucking in desperate breath after desperate breath, unsure of where she goes next.

A quick inventory: she has her body (mostly) and her mind (likewise), clothing and boots, a small amount of food, a candle she can light, and a knife, still tucked into her remaining stocking, safe and sound. It's more than she had when her father was executed. She'd been tossed out with only the clothes on her back and fine slippers on her feet.

If she finds somebody, anybody, she can do it again. Walk away, forget about the Loving Saint and Phosyne, Edouart and Simmonet, Ser Voyne and King Cardimir, and find some new place to make her home in.

Treila makes herself stand and trace the path of the river until she finds a bridge. It's new construction. Not well-made, but more than a felled tree. It's unguarded, and she crosses over, into the churned mud of the old encircling camp.

From this distance, Aymar is a monument. There is nobody on the battlements, and she can't make out the blocks of stone from here, only the imposing whole. It towers on top of the bluff, impenetrable, unpenetrated. There's no smoke rising from it, no new banners waving at the tops of the towers, and though she cannot see it from here, she assumes the gates are closed just as tightly.

It makes no sense.

She picks her way along the riverbank, her boots drying slowly in the damp autumn air. There's no trace of the heat that had her almost senseless just days ago. It's like she fell asleep below the earth and woke up only to find the future is now the present.

But if it has been three months, then Phosyne and Ser Voyne . . .

Treila keeps walking and does her best not to think. It doesn't matter, after all. It didn't matter the moment she left them in the keep and went on ahead alone.

Eventually, she leaves the river proper and begins picking her way up the hillside. It's steep, but there are steps cut into the sod at the worst parts, and the main road runs along the ridge above her, from Aymar into the world. As she walks, she passes more remnants of buildings and fortifications. The contravallation has been broken down to rubble, and for a moment, Treila fears that far more than a few months have been stolen from her. This looks like the work of decades.

Or of engineers. She catches sight, at last, of a smaller fortification between her and the road. The camp is small, home to no more than twenty souls, and it stands out stark in the middle of what has become a field of mud. It sits where Etrebia once centralized its command, if the walls that ring it and the emblazoned crates that linger are any indication. The bones of it are hollowed out, surrounded by tents, and a fire burns at the center.

Treila makes for it as quickly as she can, desperate for the world to make sense again.

There are guards, and they bring Treila up short, but they're not primed to kill. She keeps her eyes down and smiles and uses her quietest voice, tells them a quick little story about her father wanting to know what is happening up here on the ridge, and they let her pass. Make a place for her by the fire and let her warm her chilled hands as they cook their dinner: rabbit and squash, fragrant and safe to eat.

It is all she can do not to swallow it down in feral gulps. She could eat a whole rabbit herself, and long for more. Her carefully managed hunger tries to slip its bonds.

She picks the meat from little bones until she remembers the foot upon the table, its owner nameless, forgotten. It sours her appetite enough that she must appear normal to them.

When her portion is gone, she lets herself drift over to the man she thinks is in charge. He's not trying to hide it; he didn't eat with all the rest, and has a beautiful fur-lined cloak. He's young, with a twice-broken nose, and he inclines his head in greeting when she sidles closer.

She doesn't want to play the fool, but there are too few people here for her to sell herself as some long-ignored servant. So instead she plays the farmer's daughter, gawping at the devastation around her.

The man takes pity. Of course he does. "It's not a pretty sight, is it?" he asks.

No need to ask about the siege directly; anybody close enough to walk here would know the details. But the castle gates *are* closed. "Has nobody come out?" she asks, gambling.

She wins. "Not a soul," the man confesses. "The strangest thing. We've been here two months now, keeping watch, and nothing. Not even somebody up on the walls."

"Have you tried to go up? Force your way in? Perhaps—perhaps they have all—"

Starved. It's been long enough, judging by the season around them.

"Can't get close."

Treila frowns. Now *that* is strange. As strange as the fact that it is no longer summer. "What do you mean?"

"I mean that we have tried countless times to get near, and we have never reached the door."

"Do they attack?" She sees visions of Ser Voyne manning the

walls, sending volleys of arrows out at any who dare approach—but no, all their arrowheads have been melted down.

"No," the soldier says. "Nobody is there, and we cannot get close. The Priory has been unable to explain it. If it weren't for the fact that the king is said to still be inside . . ."

They wouldn't be here at all.

Treila nods, slowly, gaze fixed on the walls. She wants to ask about Etrebia, about how close this stretch of border is to failing, but she doesn't have to. It's obvious in how well-fed this camp is, how healthy and, ultimately, relaxed this man is beneath his boredom and frustration and concern. This is not a man at war. The enemy has been driven off.

There is a world out here to return to.

THEY LET HER curl up close enough to the fire that she could sleep, especially once she's given a blanket (worn, a little rat-chewed, but not so bad) by the man with the twice-broken nose. She closes her eyes to slits obediently, lets her body be limp and vulnerable in the dirt. Nobody approaches her, and she is quickly forgotten, left to think. To argue with herself.

It is eat or be eaten, the Loving Saint purrs in her memory. She will not be eaten; she has won her freedom, paid for it with bone and flesh, and she will not give that up.

She's not that sentimental.

Ser Voyne will suffer and die inside those walls. The king will. Edouart and Simmonet may already be turned into pies, for all she knows. Phosyne has at least half a chance, Treila figures, then asks herself why she cares. What have they exchanged except a little food, a little magic?

It should be easy to walk away.

She should be delighted to have escaped victorious.

She knows better than to think herself a coward for taking the smart route to safety.

And yet she does not sleep. The autumn chill descends in force, and with it, the memory of the winter after her father's death. The memory of how the remnants of her household starved and died. Human flesh, tough and wasted, the only thing keeping her alive.

It won't be like that, she tells herself. But she trembles beneath her blanket anyway, because her body knows better: that as kind as this camp has been to her, they won't let her stay indefinitely. That she will be hungry again. And that if she walks away, she will carry with her the weight of everybody she left behind to die.

Does Ser Voyne carry that guilt, too?

Treila rolls onto her back and stares up at the stars, and she replays her conversation with the Loving Saint, looking for proof that she is making the right choice. Instead, she finds a bigger tangle. More questions. There had been so many little fractures: how he'd responded to her knife, how he'd spoken of the thing that wears the Constant Lady's face, how he'd gazed at her as if *he* was unsure whether he'd prefer to eat or be eaten.

She will never know what is at the core of her that so angers a creature who can hide an entire person from the mind of another, that so delights a creature who can grow a feast from a fingernail. And she will never know if that means she could have saved the others.

Unless she goes back.

Two versions of herself begin to take shape: One, fleeing, too weak to take anybody else with her. Too smart to stay and risk herself. Willing to brave another long, dark winter, hoping she will survive more easily this time.

And the other, clever and possibly foolish, who believes she's strong enough to fight. To get what she wants. To finally stand and refuse to be displaced.

She could die either way. But only one option provides the possibility of victory instead of just survival.

As THE SUN rises once more, Treila stands at a crevice in the rock face far below Aymar. She plants her hands on either side of the darkness and leans in, touches her lips to the black.

"Can you hear me?" she breathes into the crack. "I'd give you another finger to get back in."

The darkness smiles. "But would you give me your ear?" it asks.

And shivering, Treila turns her face to one side and leans in.

30

HOSYNE CONJURES THE taste of honey on her tongue.
The vegetal spike of it erases the stone beneath her feet, the stench from her rooms, and all she can feel now is soft grass, blades pressing into her skin, sun beating down on her. She is warm. She is *hot*. She is burning up, and she is bedding down in flowers, and she feels the hum of a thousand bees crawling along her skin. They map her, every inch of her, and she is shaking with their vibrations, coming apart into pollen on the air.

Bees travel widely for their food. They range over hill and dale, and they do wander everywhere. They bring back with them the taste of foreign fields, nectar sweet, and they make no distinction as they crawl into the frames of the Priory's hives, packing their comb, fanning it with their wings to remove the water. They leave only sweetness and the faintest hints of where they've been. Buckwheat flowers produce dark brown honey, rich and nutty on the tongue, while meadowfoam adds a soft thickness, impossible to describe and impossible not to taste. Frame by frame, the wax is filled and capped and then, at last, extracted by the nuns. The wax is peeled away, the honey runs down, and it finds its way to waiting tongues.

Phosyne tastes those tongues as they taste her, and she fractures apart again, spread between a hundred, two hundred bodies, all pressed together inside a stone husk, keeping them piled one atop the other. They are starving. They are reaching. They feel so strongly, in the midsummer air, and they . . .

They are not alone.

They have *been* alone, for so long. They've kept this sweetness at bay. Oh, they've taken honey on their tongues, but they have not taken the true nature of the wood into them in many decades. Centuries. Too much hardness around them, too much sharpness, but now all that terrible strength has melted away, gone to nothing, and the sweetness can come in once more.

This sweetness that wears the Constant Lady's face, but is made of something far less regimented. Far less venerated.

And it is hungry. *She* is hungry. With the walls of Aymar grown strangely porous, she passes through stone as if it is air, because to her, it *is* air. She has been borne upon the air, and into the stone, and now she exists in all of it. She sees the whole of the spur that Aymar rests upon, and she is inside each beating heart within (save two, and those two, who are they, why do they not taste sweetness on their lips? But no matter—) and so, when she arrives at the gate, they will be ready for her.

But they are afraid. Fear does not serve her. She wants them to know her, to love her, and so she waits at the walls, paces them, finds her equal born upon a litter. Round and round this effigy goes, until the sweetness has learned her form. She drapes herself in white, paints yellow upon her cheeks. She chooses this form because it is pleasing and it is powerful, and when she comes to their gates, they fall at her feet.

Still, there are bonds upon her. Strictures. This castle belongs to a man. He is eager enough to bow to her, but not to relinquish his command. These people are *his*, before they are hers. She is tangled in his ownership, red threads cutting tight to bleed her. She must alter the balance, earn his loyalty and obeisance and that of all the rest. She starts small but heavy, plying him with food, playing to his belief in his worthiness to be saved. He is used to fine things, and so he does not question them when they come from her hands. He also has that honey on his tongue, and that is as persuasive as a kiss.

The castle shivers. Begins to rearrange itself. By the time its inhabitants come to her table, they are bleary-eyed and hungry, and they eat all that she can give them. With each swallow of their throat, they become hers. The red threads are rearranged. Ownership passes to her.

Ownership lets her slake her own thirst at last, sip by sip. It strengthens her limbs, light as air, with the force of a gale. And as she grows in strength, she can feel the press of other bodies at the walls. Little things with sharp teeth and empty bellies, whispering, *Let us in, feed us, let us serve you.*

So many empty bellies. The whole world is starving. But she has enough to share, doesn't she? And then, like a dispersing dream, Phosyne is no longer the sweetness, is no longer the Lady. And she is sinking.

Laughter. She hears laughter and feels hands seize her shoulders and haul her from the stone that seeks to envelop her. Phosyne's eyes flutter open and she is held in the embrace of the Lady and Her saints, these buzzing creatures, honey-sweet and just as sticky. Phosyne cries out.

"You've gone a little too deep, sweetling," the Absolving Saint murmurs. "Come back to us. Open your eyes. That's it, that's it."

"What a strange creature you are," the Lady says. "I have never seen your like. What does it feel like, to walk in my skin for an evening?"

"Too much," Phosyne gasps. "It's too much."

It's not enough. She'd like to vibrate apart again, slide once more out of this castle. But the hunger. The *hunger.* It's too much to bear, and she can't let herself feel that again. Groaning, she throws herself forward.

The Absolving Saint lets her go, and she hits the floor. It is solid.

She's halfway back into her room now. Her head and shoulders extend into her cell, and if she can just summon a little more strength, she can drag herself to safety. She grasps at the scraps of knowledge her vision gave her. These creatures, they obey certain things: territory, ownership, hierarchy. They twist those things to suit their purposes, but they can't ignore them. Phosyne's room is just that— *Phosyne's.* And if she had let them in, she knows now, all would have been lost.

But she didn't.

"Stay, sweetling," the Absolving Saint says, taking a step forward to stand over her, just at the border of her territory. "You know how we did it, but not how you will. Don't you want us to teach you?"

She rolls onto her back, heaving for breath, staring up. Just behind the Absolving Saint is the Lady, but the Loving Saint is close, too, crouching at her feet.

"I am not like you," Phosyne says, jerking one leg away as the Loving Saint reaches out to grasp her ankle. "I can't—infiltrate. I can't bewitch."

"No?"

"No." She scrabbles another inch away. Another. Now her waist has passed through the invisible barrier between them.

"Then let us teach you something else."

But they have taught her enough, more than enough to satisfy their end of the agreement, and if she lingers—

The Loving Saint catches her other leg. Tugs. She feels herself slip against the stone.

She hears claws clicking on the steps.

The smell of sulfur wraps around her, and Phosyne jerks in reflex, reaches out a hand. Her fingers skim the black, scaled muscle of Pneio's—Ornuo's?—leg as he leaps over her, and behind her he skids, hissing, to a halt.

The saints are staring.

"Something summoned," the Lady says, with deep distaste. Then She hisses and jerks back as Phosyne's other brimstone creature streaks past Her and runs straight over Phosyne's belly, clawed feet digging in. It spurs her to action, and she kicks the Loving Saint in his perfect jaw and throws herself back into her room.

It is blazing hot inside. Phosyne clambers upright. At her feet, Pneio and Ornuo bristle, hissing and slithering about her ankles.

"Lesson over," Phosyne gasps.

The Lady's lip curls, and then She smiles, inclines Her head. Bows at the waist. Her saints follow suit, conceding defeat—for the moment.

They turn to leave, and that is when Phosyne, at last, registers the impossible:

More eyes peer out of the shadows behind them.

The saints are no longer alone.

31

OR EVERY BODY she moves, Ser Voyne checks every entrance to the yard. Each time, she expects to see the Lady standing there, or one of the other saints. Her arms burn and her skin beads with perspiration. Dust rises up and forms a slurry with her sweat, and by the end, she is filthy, sore, exhausted.

And alone.

It feels like a trap. It can't be an accident, that Ser Voyne is standing now in the middle of the cleared yard, worn down, barely upright, guzzling water. She's vulnerable. She knows she's vulnerable. One word from the Lady, or one strike of the Warding Saint's fist, and she'll fall. She will. She knows it.

And yet she remains alone. That, perhaps, is why when Ser Voyne at last staggers into the keep, chin up, eyes flashing, she doesn't go immediately to Phosyne's tower.

No, there is other work to be done, in this blessed, unexpected reprieve.

She has not found Cardimir, and she has abandoned hope of it. He is either with the Lady, or cowering somewhere private. But Ser Leodegardis . . . she thinks that, if he has any of his mind left to him at all, he will be eager to mount a defense. If she can give *him* water, he will be able to help her. She goes first to the great hall, but does not see his bearded, worn face anywhere. Food litters the tables, still heaped to groaning, but it is rotting already. Lettuce has turned black and slick, and flies buzz thick above the picked-clean bones of—

Ser Voyne turns away. Goes back into the keep proper. Climbs the stairs to where, not two weeks ago, she sat with her liege, Ser Leodegardis, the chamberlain, and all the rest.

This room is occupied.

Ser Leodegardis sits alone at the table. Beside him is a cup of, Voyne knows without looking, honeyed wine. She can only hope it is not blood. His gaze is fixed on a map.

His right forearm is gone, amputated neatly at the elbow.

Ser Voyne's stomach lurches, her mouth waters, and she remembers the fine round bones strewn across the platter of roasted meat like pearls.

Not pearls. Wrist bones.

When she sits down across from him, it is with her full weight. She bows her head. She wonders if he can even see her.

"Ser Voyne," he greets.

She wonders if he is himself.

That, he doesn't offer an easy answer to, but when she looks up to him, she meets eyes that seem uncommonly clear. Then again, she hasn't gotten close to anybody but Phosyne since her fever dream broke, and Phosyne is many things, but bewitched by the intruders if not one of them.

"Ser Leodegardis," she offers, wondering what he will do with his name.

Did they talk, when Voyne was in the depths of her idolatry? Or were they only puppets? She can't remember. Doesn't want to remember.

He wets his cracked lips with his tongue.

Voyne drops her gaze to the cup of wine.

"No," he says. His voice is soft. Rueful. When she looks up at him, he is smiling, but it is not happy.

He's aware. Enough, at least. He knows there is something very wrong. "I have water," Voyne says.

His shoulders quake. She sees a flash of hope in his eyes, and then he quashes it.

"It's from Phosyne," she adds.

He hesitates, then reaches out his remaining hand.

She passes him the oilskin and he takes one testing sip, then tips his head back and pours half the bag down his throat. He coughs halfway through, spit sliding down his chin. Voyne understands. She waits until he is done, and takes the skin from him gingerly, careful not to touch. A single touch could break him, now, and she needs him with her.

"Thank you," he says, when he's taken a moment to collect himself. "Sit with me?"

She lowers herself into her seat once more, though she pulls it closer to him. It's so like all those evenings before, when they sat across from each other and discussed strategy, him treating her like her experience mattered, her pretending she was his equal. Striving to *be* his equal, to learn what made him different so that one day, she could become him. It feels laughable now. Should have felt laughable the moment the siege set in, because without victory, she has no future at all.

And now . . .

"She did this to you?" Ser Voyne asks.

"You don't remember," he answers.

Her stomach drops.

"I did this," he says. He looks down at his abbreviated arm. "You were there, I am sure, though the memory is . . . hazy. I remember only why I did it, in truth."

She tries to recollect, though her mind shies away. The night she knelt for the Lady—no, the morning after, before Jacynde, before Phosyne in the chapel—Leodegardis had accepted the king's jewel-handled knife and leaned down.

Down?

"I remember differently," she says.

He gestures down, and Voyne, reluctantly, peers below the table.

His left leg is gone.

With a groan, she covers her face with her hands. Yes, that is what she remembers. The arm must have come later. Perhaps somebody else held the blade. She doesn't think she was there for that, but is too afraid to ask.

"Why?" she asks, as shivers wrack her body.

"I made the sacrifices I needed to," he assures her.

"Needed to?" she manages to ask, meeting his eyes once more, demanding.

"It is nothing less than what you would have done, in my place." He says it as if it's the simplest thing in the world. His smile is sad but indulgent nonetheless.

Cardimir's words echo through her: *My people must eat.*

But that was a dead man. Leodegardis himself had argued with her that a dead man was worth more as food than a living horse, for a living horse would keep a little longer.

"One leg can't feed a hundred."

"But if it could? If it could feed even ten families, so that they could live another week, another month, until they are safe once more? Wouldn't you give of yourself?"

Voyne hesitates. She doesn't know what she should feel. Anger that he would ask? Horror?

Shame, that she can't simply say *Yes, they could have all of me?*

It's the last, and it sweeps through her like a wildfire. "This is why he gave you Aymar," Ser Voyne says.

Leodegardis gazes back at her without response, merely swaying where he sits. He's in pain, now, where he wasn't before.

And what of Cardimir? He hadn't made this sacrifice. No, he'd fed off his own household. He was supposed to protect them. He was honor-bound to lead, not to ravage.

How long had he been so cretinous inside? So useless on his throne?

No. No, she cannot give him any more of her time. He no longer has any claim to it.

She returns her focus to Leodegardis. "Do you regret it? At all?" Voyne asks. "Now that you can think clearly again? They took this from you, like they took my loyalty. We should have—we should have fought back. Like we were trained to."

At that, Leodegardis ducks his head. His brow furrows. "I have no regrets," he says, slowly, choosing his words with care. "I have no regrets because how can I regret feeding my people? Even if . . ."

Even if they will all still die tomorrow.

How much of their minds are both still clouded, she wonders. And for how long?

Or is it that they are seeing clearly, freed from the shackles of logic and causality? When she thinks to the starving battlefields she has fought upon, she knows that, if she were offered the chance to go back, to feed her men with only pieces of her flesh, she would have ransomed every inch of herself to get them home safely.

It just wasn't feasible, so she'd fought instead.

"They deserve salvation, not merely an extension of their suffering," she makes herself argue. She must focus on the long term, not just immediate protection. Otherwise, they will be trapped here indefinitely.

"They do," he agrees. "But I'm not sure I can win that for them."

"I swear to you that I will do it," she says, reaching out one hand to grasp his.

He doesn't let her. "Always swearing the impossible, Ser Voyne," he cautions. "No, I think it is too late for all of us. Haven't you heard them? The gates are open now. They are coming."

"Etrebia?" she asks, mouth dry at the thought that the original threat does still exist, still waits for them to falter. But Leodegardis shakes his head. He looks to her left.

They aren't alone.

Ser Voyne tears her gaze away from Leodegardis to find the room has gone dark, even though she is certain the sun was at its zenith only a little while ago. The room has few windows; they are thin, tall things, designed to be defensible. But they still let in enough light to see by in midday, even in a storm.

Unless they are blocked.

Unless bodies curl against their slanted sills and press into the gaps, covering the sun and air almost completely.

Only a little light filters in, enough for Voyne to make out an arm, a leg, the curve of a hip.

The glimmer of eyes.

There are eight window niches in the room, and every single one of them is occupied. She jerks away from the table, on her feet and reaching for the sword that isn't there. Laughter erupts from every side, and she backpedals, closer to Leodegardis.

"Do you remember," she asks him, the words rasping in her throat, "where they took my blade?"

"*I* took it," he reminds her, and she does remember it, at last. Him kneeling at her feet, and her surrendering her sword, her armor, as the Lady looked on. "They would not touch it. I placed it . . . I placed it by the throne, where it belonged."

And then his brow draws down and he seizes her with his remaining hand, hauls her close. "You must swear to me two things, Ser Voyne," he gasps out against her ear.

"Name it," she says, trying desperately to give him her full attention while keeping her eyes fixed on the prowling shadows.

"Trust in Phosyne," he says. It sounds like stone grinding on stone. He is fighting everything in himself. But the words catch the tinder beneath her ribs and ignite, burning bright. She hangs on to him and to his every word. "And protect the people."

He releases her, and she falls forward. The shadows are slinking closer, the light from the windows brightening as they leave the sills and come into the room proper.

"I swear," Ser Voyne says. "I swear on my life. I am sorry—"

And then she runs.

32

HOSYNE SLAMS THE door shut with a single thought.

The bar draws down, her workbench slides over, and she is protected, bending double, gasping for breath. Nobody knocks. Nobody tries to get in. When she's got her breath back enough to retreat, it's like any other evening she's spent alone in this room.

Evening?

She stares for a long minute at the darkened glass pane up in the loft. She stares until Ornuo nips at her ankle, and she kicks him off. It's enough movement to get her started, and she prowls up the steps and begins to dismantle the haphazard pile blocking her window.

Ornuo and Pneio are here; they have returned at least twice, and may leave again. There's no sense in keeping them from an easy exit or entrance. She needs the fresh air more than she needs them to stop doing anything, and if the Lady can't cross her threshold, Phosyne suspects the sill will have much the same impact.

And once the window is free, she can see that it *is* evening, and that something *is* wrong, because she has not been in the room for that long.

She leans out through the window, into the cooling night air, and squints down at the shadowed yard. There is another feast in progress. She sees bodies writhing in the dirt below her, fires burning. The cisterns are all covered.

She does not see Ser Voyne.

"I should never have sent her away," she says as she retreats back in. Pneio hops up onto the thick sill and coils himself around her wrist. Phosyne shakes her head but rubs at the scales below his pointed jaw. "Just like I should never have let you out. Where have you been, foolish boy?"

She gets nothing in return except the heat of his throat. His golden, burning eyes are slits as he gazes up at her.

"Where did you come from?" she adds, voice softer still. "Did you come because I was lonely?"

He shows his teeth in something like a smile.

"They don't like you at all."

She runs her hands over his sinuous body, the bunching of his muscles, the quick beating of his heart. For the first time in many months, she studies him closely. He is hot, hotter than any living thing has any right to be, and of course the scent of sulfur emanates from him. He is, to all appearances, living. He is a beast, not an imagining. Once, his brother's claw caught in the wood of her desk and when he hauled off, it broke. There'd been blood everywhere, though it had steamed and evaporated.

The saints, they are something of the air. These creatures are of fire. Phosyne knows she can manipulate the flame; her candles are proof enough of that, the realization kindled by that maddening chase out to the smithy, at this thing's heels.

This is how the learning works: side-glimpsed realizations, nothing direct, but always leaning toward greater understanding. She knew how to sing the first note from "On Breath" not because of something she understood from Pneio digging into a coke pile, but *because* he had dug into the coke pile.

If Ser Voyne was here, there's no way Phosyne could explain it in a way that makes sense, but it does. It *does*. Perhaps the Lady didn't mean to teach Phosyne at all, with that strange vision of bees and honey and red threads, but Phosyne has learned all the same. Boundaries, territory, translation. This room is hers. She is certain, now, that the Lady could not enter without permission. With Pneio and Ornuo here, the dividing lines blaze a little hotter, because they are Phosyne's.

Just as the water is Phosyne's.

Her gaze drops down to the tower room's floor. Beneath it is an entire cistern. She can't reach it from here; its pipes extend to the roof's catchment area and down to the kitchen. But there is water, *here*. It is not purified yet. It is a threat. It is a resource.

Phosyne pats Pneio's head, absently, and climbs back down the stairs. She walks past Jacynde's body, still motionless save for the shallow rise and fall of her chest. Her presence barely registers; what is below her is far more important.

This is the first cistern that existed in the castle. The well preceded it, of course, but nothing else. Before them, there was only the long trudge up to the ridge from the riverside. It will not be full; there hasn't been enough rain. But because of its safety (only rainfed, none of the earth's filth within it), it is the only source the king drank from, and so fewer hands have tapped it.

She is going to tap it.

If only she had a pick; she laughs at the thought, a hiccuping thing, reminded of Treila. She hopes Treila is okay. She hopes Treila is far away from here, whatever *here* is becoming. No matter her sentiments, though, she still has no pick, and no knife, and nothing hard and pointed enough to make a dent in the mortar below her.

But just as she has learned fire, she has learned earth, as well. She presses her palms to the floor. She wriggles her fingers. She thinks of Ser Voyne against her back, and feels her hands sink, just a little.

It takes effort, but she can keep the rest of herself from falling if she tries. Her fingers dance through rock as if it is itself water, and she moves them in, then out. In, then out. She remembers water compressing, expanding, roiling when she did the same in a tub, a stream, a river.

The stones melt like butter beneath her touch.

She presses them to either side, her hand now solid and the floor now insubstantial. The hole she carves is just wide enough to admit her bucket. That bucket is, of course, filled with waste, but a little powder and a quietly sung note, and the water she dumps it into is clear once more. She hauls up one full load, sets it on the floor safely away from the gap, and retrieves the candle that she cannot fully extinguish from the cup it is submerged in.

It flares to life. She strokes the flame. It grows hotter beneath her fingertips.

She plunges it into the bucket.

The water turns hot around her hand, steaming, *scalding*, enough to peel every layer of grime and filth up from the stone where she has worn it in with six months of pacing. A year of pacing, really; this room was hardly better before the siege began. But she knows how to keep a clean space. She kept her cell spotless all her years in the Priory, and isn't sure just when she fell out of the habit.

That's not true—she knows. It became less important to her the moment she tasted magic for the first time. The Lady was right about one thing: it is intoxicating, even as it has destroyed every aspect of her life, crushed it into dust, swept it away on the breeze. She has sacrificed her body on the altar of knowledge.

But the Lady hasn't.

So it's not required.

Phosyne turns the thought this way and that as she works, scrubbing and sweeping and dumping all the accumulated detritus out of her window. She'd call it a sanctifying, but that feels pretentious, even to her. At the very least, it is a clearing of the decks. She refamiliarizes herself with every inch of her rooms, every join of stone.

She stops when she reaches Jacynde.

The woman is, at last, stirring. Perhaps it's the damp cloth still on her lips. Perhaps it's just the time, the darkness that is flooding the room because Phosyne hasn't bothered to light any lamps or candles, save the one that lives in the steaming bucket. Whatever it is, it's making her eyes move below her closed, swollen lids, making her hands curl and grasp at the thin blanket below her.

Prioress Jacynde did not drag herself to Phosyne's door. She was left there, by . . . who? It is possible, maybe even overwhelmingly so, that the nun who first called for Phosyne's aid came back for it once more. That, faced with Jacynde insensate, not healing, she hauled the woman's body to the door of the one person in the castle who might still be safe.

But.

Phosyne thinks of red lines, of territory, and wishes she could close her eyes and see again the blazing map of Aymar, and see if, perhaps, red lines tug at Jacynde's wrists, her lips. If that is what moves her now.

Is this a breach? The Lady had tried to win entry by an exchange. Is Jacynde's body a gift, too, offered with some intention of collecting on a return, later?

"This isn't a safe place for you," she tells the prioress, and earns a whimper in response. "There's no safe place for you at all."

"Please—" the woman moans, or Phosyne thinks she does. All the finer points of her letters are erased by the lack of tongue.

Ser Voyne would tell her to care for this woman. To ignore the danger, or willingly face it, for the sake of another. But Ser Voyne *isn't* here, and Phosyne needs to make this space sacrosanct if they are to have any hope of untangling the mess around them.

So Phosyne grabs hold of the pallet and drags Jacynde toward the door.

The other woman fights it, as best she can. Her eyes open to slits, her head lolls, her legs push ineffectively against the reed mat, the blankets. "No—no—" she gasps.

Phosyne lets go only to unbar the door once more, to shift her worktable out of the way. She half expects her audience to still be there, waiting, hungry, but when she opens the door, there is only pitch darkness, as if something is blocking up the window from farther down the stairs.

It is a menacing sight. Unnatural.

All the more reason to move swiftly and with purpose. She turns and grabs up the mat again. Jacynde tries to pitch herself off one side, but is far too weak.

Phosyne shoves the whole mess out into the hall.

"I'm sorry," Phosyne tells her. "I know I'm supposed to care."

Jacynde meets her gaze at last. She is frantic. She is fading. She's on the cusp—one firm push in either direction could be her life or her death.

"But I don't."

Phosyne closes the door.

33

REILA ISN'T SURE how long she lies there, in the cavern below Aymar, cradling the side of her head and hearing an endless, clear ringing. A candle burns bright beside her, but doesn't melt. It could be minutes, or hours, or days, or weeks—she no longer trusts time to make sense. All she knows is that she is alive.

Probably.

It doesn't hurt, not anymore. Like her finger, the pain subsided more quickly than it should have. But next time it will be worse. She knows it will. Her creature of the gap in the stone let her back in for a pittance, because he is confident she will need to flee through his embrace again soon. When the time comes, he might ask for a hand. A leg. Something more.

He is confident she will pay it. If she's indebted her future self, she's going to make it worth it. First, she needs to find Phosyne, tell her what she's learned about the world outside. Use that strange mind of hers to calculate their next move. See if, perhaps, they can't turn Ser Voyne into a weapon for their own ends.

She leaves her candle burning and climbs up to the tunnel.

She hesitates.

This darkness doesn't have hands or teeth within it, she knows that, but she feels a phantom pain in her bones all the same. She has been here before, oversensitized, ready for another blow. It will just take a little patience and a lot more force.

Treila strips, makes her bundle. Feels the edge of the tunnel and leans in, listening for whispers.

There are none. She flattens herself out and crawls forward.

Like before, the tunnel makes her way easy. It's definitely larger now; several times, she has to grope around unseeing to find where the path hooks around to next. The dimensions are stretched so much that it doesn't feel like the same tunnel, and her heart pounds in her chest. She wants to stop, to retreat, to flee.

She pushes forward instead.

It is nighttime once more when she emerges into her workroom, shivering uncontrollably. The ringing in her head has subsided, one small mercy. Her hands are clumsy as she dresses, sets her blade back into her boot. She keeps her gaze fixed on the doorway, taking deep breaths, trying to discern the scent of turning leaves. But instead she smells baking stone, baking skin. Vital, urgent scents. And she can hear singing.

It's still the height of summer here, and at least some of the castle's occupants are still alive.

She slips up into the keep proper, moving low, slow, quiet. The ringing creeps in once more, but she listens past it with her remaining ear, head cocked, eyes lowered. The singing continues, coming in through the windows, echoing across the stone. She recognizes hymns, but the singers keep falling into hysterical laughter that sounds half-pained.

In the main room on the ground floor, she sees guards, sitting at a table as if to play dice. As if nothing at all has changed. But they do not wear armor, and they do not play dice. They stare at nothing, fingers twitching on the tabletop.

There's no good way past them out to the yard, so she climbs higher instead.

One floor up, Treila creeps into the room she is meant to be sleeping in, expecting to find it empty as it was when she last left, but no, it is full to bursting. People litter the floor, recognizable but in different arrangements than usual. So many are curled up against one another, resting in unfamiliar embraces. Sleeping mats overlap and rumple, blankets tangle.

Simmonet is sleeping, as is Edouart. Both still alive. They look a little plumper, but that might just be the soft moonlight, and their easy stillness. Nobody is writhing or crying out in the dark. Nobody wears a visage of hunger and pain.

It is a strange, discomfiting sight. Treila leaves them behind, taking the western tower up to what has served as the throne room as long as the king has been in residence.

She doesn't make it past the first turning, because there stands the Loving Saint.

He looks surprised to see her, though that means very little. He glances at her over one shoulder from where he crouches on the steps, peering into the throne room beyond. His fine lips curl into a smile, and he turns in full, leaning back and regarding her down the length of his lithe body.

"You left," he says, by way of greeting. His voice seems to prompt a new wash of noise in her missing ear. A harsher sound, this time. A droning, coarse at the edges, familiar somehow.

"I came back," she corrects.

A bruise discolors his jaw. It's so incongruous with the rest of him and with what she knows (he can take on Ser Voyne's skin, but he can't hide an injury? What use is his metamorphosing, then?), that she's reaching out to touch him before she can stop herself.

The Loving Saint seizes her wrist before she can reach him. It's her left wrist. She's reaching with just her thumb and three fingers, and he sees it, the missing one, and he stares at it with—

Not hunger. Anger. So much anger it nearly burns her.

"You said," Treila murmurs, "whatever the cost."

She pushes her other hand into her hair, baring the smooth expanse of jaw where her ear once sat. "So I paid it twice."

That earns her an actual snarl. It's bestial, and accompanied by his fingers tightening hard around her wrist. It feels honest when he jerks her arm hard, and she sprawls down across him on the steps.

"Are you jealous?" she whispers in his ear, her heart hammering, feeling both terrified and *alive*.

And with that he shoves her off him, to the side.

Gingerly, Treila untangles their legs that last little bit and sits up on one of the steps. She's wedged between him and the wall, and can see only a sliver of the throne room, but she watches it instead of him. She gives him a moment to pull himself back together, get his breathing under control.

Just like when the creature in the dark grew angry that she'd learned the rules of the game elsewhere, the Loving Saint's knee-jerk response tells her more than any words. These two predators are territorial, and they don't like knowing they aren't alone in this little fiefdom.

She ponders her next question, turns it over like a coin across her knuckles. The humid night air has resolved around her into summer, certainly, so there's no point in mentioning that she knows it's autumn beyond the walls. But if time does not flow at the same rate here as it does in the world at large, she might have been gone for— who knows?

"What did I miss?" Treila settles on. It's just coy enough that he'll enjoy it.

He huffs something that might be a laugh. He's on his hands and knees beside her, and he prowls a step up, then glances back over his shoulder to her. "The wizard in the tower is learning how to walk the tightrope."

That can mean nothing good. But she hasn't toppled yet. That's something.

Treila wriggles onto her hip. The stairs aren't particularly wide. It's a long fall down. He's on the outside; she could push him. She wonders if he would fall, and if he did, if it would matter. "How many feasts have gone by without me?"

"It never really ends," he replies. "But don't you want to know about your knight, too?"

"She isn't mine," Treila says, too quickly. She feels exposed after.

He just grins. "She's been on the prowl," he tells her. "Looking for answers. Looking for something to fight. Looking, I think, for her sword."

His gaze drifts to the doorway, and Treila's follows. She creeps forward, enough that she can see somebody moving in the gloom. Not Ser Voyne, though. No, whoever it is has a shorn head, and is unsteady on her feet. Treila can hear her rasping, roughshod breathing.

The prioress, she realizes, weak and staggering.

And then there is a laugh, sliding through the humming of her missing ear, and a wash of sunlight. The Constant Lady steps into the throne room. Treila strains to see more.

But the Loving Saint catches hold of her arm and pulls her back. "It's not safe in there," he murmurs, body warm against her back. "Better to watch the shadow play."

"They wouldn't know I was there," Treila argues, but goes still all the same. The Loving Saint's hands stroke over her hips. His mouth falls to her neck, featherlight. She should kick him for his troubles, but it feels good. Indulgent and sweet, with a blistering edge.

She strains to hear words. There is the soft murmur of one voice only, the Lady's, and then a wet, slick sound, a wail, a thud.

Treila knows those sounds, though not in that order; by the time her father's head was parted from his shoulders, he could no longer scream. Her skin goes cold. Insensate. The buzzing in her ears turns all-consuming, obliterating.

It is the sound of bees, erupting from the hive, swarming over her, piercing her flesh.

"Where's your mind gone to?" the Loving Saint asks, taking her chin, dragging her out of the dark. "Somewhere frigid and angry."

Foolish girl, she thinks, viciously. But she's shaking now. She can't help it. Five years. Five years, and she shouldn't be so reactive. She is better than this. She has made herself better than this.

"What was done to you?" he murmurs. "What did they take from you? I can smell the scent of snow on your breath. Snow, and blood. Your winter woods." He pets her sides, and she can feel him wriggling, peeling, untangling. He is searching for that core of her, that thing that makes her dangerous, that element the Lady cannot predict. He thinks he is going to find it. "What are you remembering?"

She makes herself soften. Be easy for him. "Only bad dreams," she says. "Of when I had a tender heart."

"Is that why you run away so readily?" he asks, nuzzling at her pulse.

"You told me to go," she reminds him. Her breath catches in her throat.

"And yet you came back. Changeable thing. We're not so different, I think, you and I." She can feel his smile against her skin, and the lightest brush of teeth. She doesn't flinch. "Why did you return?"

"I wanted to." It is the truest answer, if not so simple as it sounds. She toys with options, angles she can show him. What would intrigue him? What would keep her safest? What would make him spill some new detail?

"Your knight calls to you so loudly?" he asks, and oh, she hasn't led him far enough astray at all.

"I want to *win*," she says, too quickly, too honestly, as she turns to face him, reclining across the steps. She came back to prove she was clever enough, quick enough, not only to get out alive, but to salvage something of value. Save a few other lives, even though nobody had come back for her after her father's death. But that isn't the whole of it.

If it were, the mention of Ser Voyne wouldn't gall her so deeply.

She's still clinging to girlish dreams of revenge, even now that they're pointless. Sentimental loathing, useless here. She tenses under his touch, half expecting him to grip her harder. To fall upon that show of weakness.

But he doesn't.

She tries to focus of the feel of his hands, his mouth, to divine some meaning in the patterns they map onto her skin. There is not much to see, nothing visible to analyze. But over his shoulder, there is movement.

"What is that?" Treila whispers, gaze skipping up to shadows that seem to move, to dance. Past the buzzing in her ears, she hears breathing, too many dissonant tempos to belong to just her or the beast against her.

"The rest of my kind," that beast murmurs. "Drawn to the feast."

"There are more?"

"So many more, little things that like to eat my leavings. We've made a path for them to come and play. Are you afraid?"

Bravado wins her nothing here, but honesty doesn't, either. Instead, she tries to study them.

He takes her silence as nerves all the same. "If you're afraid of other teeth, I could stake my claim on you. If you asked nicely."

"Hasn't somebody already done that?" She tilts her head to one side, bares her missing ear once more.

From the corner of her eye, she watches as his beautiful lips ripple into a snarl, then recompose into a pleasant smile. "Oh no, you didn't let them. You negotiated well." Yes, he is a jealous monster; if he wants to lay claim to her, she can use that.

It's still hard to look away from the unknown threat and focus on him instead, but she does it smoothly. She arches up so that their bodies press together. Maneuvers them onto their sides so her back is to the wall once more.

"And you think I'll negotiate poorly with you?"

"I think you have less to lose now." His eyes are heavy-lidded. He thinks he's winning.

She kisses him to help that thought along. It's light. Teasing. Barely a breath.

"You made a mistake, last time we spoke," she murmurs against his mouth. "You told me I was worth something."

"Did I?" He kisses her again. She adjusts her posture little by little, so that she maintains enough space to move, to retreat, even as she lets him tip her chin back, nurse at her lower lip.

"You'll have to promise me something more than a good time."

"What if I let Ser Voyne see you?" He nips, swallows down her small, shocked gasp.

"You can't offer that. What would your Lady say?" There is a hierarchy here, one she thinks she can exploit. And better not to think of the possibility of Voyne seeing her again. She only needs to stay here a little longer, figure out what else she can learn.

"She doesn't have to know," the Loving Saint purrs.

He presses on her shoulders, and she has no choice but to slide partway down the length of his body, until her mouth is close to his hips. He means it to be seductive, but the angle makes her bristle. He thinks she is weak.

She must put them back on equal footing.

Her hand finds her knife. She slides it from her boot as she trails her lips along the line of his hip. His hands slide into her hair, and his eyes narrow to pleased slits.

She presses the flat of the blade to the inside of his thigh.

He goes still as death.

"Surely you're not afraid of a little danger," Treila says with a coy smile, leaning back for a better view of his face. "Surely you trust me. What say we mark each other?"

She trails the point of it up his body, up his throat, until it touches the underside of his chin. Now it's him who's afraid. Cornered-animal afraid. Even though he could take another form in an instant, or even simply back away. It's like the steel of it holds him fixed upon its point.

Only the third knife he's seen since he arrived, hm? Yes, she supposes with the Priory's requisitions, there aren't many blades left. Strange, though, for him to be so frightened.

A whisper of sensation on her hand: a bee, alighting, wings shivering in the air. Treila flinches.

For one second, the blade no longer touches the Loving Saint at all.

That's all it takes, and then she's falling back, the Loving Saint rising up to his full height. His beautiful face doesn't shift, but the tension that dances between them has a different edge, now. He, like all the rest, is *hungry*, and he watches her with the eyes of a shrike, prepared to impale her on barbed thorns to keep her all to himself as he tears her to pieces.

The creature who cocks his head and scents the air is something old.

He smiles, and his teeth are sharp.

"I'd recommend you run, little girl."

And Treila does.

34

LEANING THE REST of the room is barely the work of breathing.

Pneio and Ornuo even help, their bodies drying out the stone once she's cleared it. Everything is back in its place so quickly it's as if it never left, as if she never fell apart into the frazzled shell of a woman. It should feel unfamiliar, this care and order. But she slips into this new skin of hers gently. It feels like coming home.

Phosyne prowls her entire room and, finding nothing else amiss and no sign of Ser Voyne's return, she turns to herself. She is filthy. She is skinny and weak, barely more than a particularly cantankerous corpse, refusing to succumb. And, most importantly, she can still taste honey, just a little. Can still feel the hands of saints upon her flesh.

She needs a bath.

There's no tub in this room, of course, nothing but her bucket of water, but there is the cistern below. Through the hole she created, she drops a few dried lavender sprigs, followed by another sprinkling of her clever purifying powder. They disappear into the dark pool of water below her feet. Next, she lowers in her steaming bucket; as it overflows, she sees the candle inside light up the whole cistern gold, sees the water begin to heat. And then Phosyne widens the gap in the floor and lowers herself down.

She sinks into the water, robes and all.

Two dark heads peek over the rim and stare down at her, but Pneio and Ornuo make no move to join her. She beckons, and they just sit down, sniffing the air. Only creatures of fire, then, not water. She shouldn't try to force their nature.

They're also undoubtedly *hers*, more even than she is herself. No need to purify them. But Phosyne can still feel the lingering traces of the Lady's influence on her, and she ducks under the surface of the water, letting her clothes weigh her down as she scrubs her face, her hair, her hands.

She opens her eyes and gazes up, even as the water stings her corneas.

She opens her lips, and lets the water scour away the last of the honey.

When she hauls herself up from the cistern, a minute or an hour or a day later, she is clad not in roughspun, poorly cared for robes, but in silk. Her skin glows faintly. Her body feels whole and healthy for the first time in years.

What a trick.

She glances down at the candle still burning in the cistern, then decides to leave it there. The gap, though, she closes. It only takes a few touches to pull the stone back into place, leaving a few latticed gaps to allow fragrant steam to perfume the room.

"That's nicer, isn't it? It does get so dry." She smiles at Pneio, who gazes fondly at her, then rolls onto his back, proffering his belly. She pets it. It is lightly furred, small tufts of fleece wedged below the edges of scales.

She wonders how well it would burn, and plucks a pinch of it.

35

OYNE KNOWS THE layout of Aymar very well. She knows each doorway, each yard, each wall; if she has not stepped foot in some for weeks or months, she still has the design etched inside her skull. The Lady used this aspect of her, along with all the others, to roust out each hiding place before the feast.

Now, Voyne uses it to flee.

Castles are not meant to be raced through, but she has no other option, not as the shadows descend on her and nip at her heels. They have no substance to them—not like people, not like hounds—and yet they chase her down. She can't make out details, only slashes of color, strangely flat, horribly unnatural, but she can taste their hunger.

They clot in the stairwell; she finds the only window wide enough to accept a body and slips through out onto the meager footholds that stud along the tower to another entrance one level down. She clambers, scurries, steals her way across spaces not designated as paths but designed to assist a defender. If she can get to the lower level, she can move to the other staircase. Get to Phosyne.

But outside the walls, the unnerving beasts still pursue her. Where before they were shadow, now they are air; she sees them as smears of black and red and gold and white on the boiling hot sky. Below, she can still see the insensate forms of people she dragged to safety. She almost says a prayer for no new splashes of carmine in the dust, but she is already too late.

Below her, on one of Aymar's walls, she can see Denisot, the chamberlain. He crawls like a dog, bleeding from his hands, his knees, his feet. He is naked, and on his back are those same smears of flat color. And at their edges, his blood, splashing onto the stone.

A small procession follows him, of humans this time. No—a parade. One has a horn. Voyne ducks and scrapes and claws her way around the tower, so that she can't see them anymore. The stone is not kind.

She wishes she had Phosyne's skill, to pass through rock from one side to the other. She must, instead, rely on geometry.

Inside again, and the press of bodies grows close. Laughter, dry and burning, crackles against her ears.

And yet—

It all falls away as she nears Phosyne's door.

Something is different about it. The proportions are the same, the strange repurposing of the defensive slit beside the door. There is nothing, at first, that marks it as changed. Except the torches by her door are long-since burned down, yet they flash and shine now, driving back the shadows. Even as she staggers closer, they grow, brighten. They pulse, as if with a heartbeat—one much quieter than her own.

Progress. Phosyne has made some progress. This is like her strange everburning candle, and her head swims with relief.

Phosyne is safe. Phosyne is safety.

Her hand hovers above the door, preparing to open it. Or should she knock?

(Knock? This woman is her charge. This woman is insane. This woman is—)

She doesn't open it or knock.

Behind her, there is the sound of paper rustling. Dried curls of bark, one against the other. They are waiting. Waiting for her to retreat. Waiting for her to go begging to Phosyne for some order.

But Leodegardis has given her direction, something solid, something old and familiar and true. She must take the throne room. Her sword is there. Retrieve the sword; protect the people from this new, worse threat.

She casts one last, longing look at Phosyne's door and dives back down the stairs.

Voyne's training, all her experience, is nothing against a foe that seems to be at once a single heaving organism and tens of individuals. She has no weapon but her fists, and finds herself grappling and tearing more than striking. They part like wool rovings, then coalesce once more. Long fingers pluck at her, seize her elbow, haul back on her ankle. There is nothing to parry, only jaws to kick at, and those jaws dissipate between one sunbeam and the next.

While the Lady and Her saints are so terribly close to human, these things are smoke and scent. They echo with the same salivating lust, but lack their betters' table manners. Flashes of color, flashes of light, there and gone again, flat in one moment, fulsome in the next as claws rake over her back.

She howls in outrage.

But for all the blows that land, none stay. She bleeds, but from scratches only. Not enough to even slick the floor.

If they wish to slake their hunger, there are a hundred other bodies waiting, willing, wilting in the heat outside. They are chasing her for sport.

Killing a stag for sport and trophy is the same for the beast, though. The end point is still death. They will tear her apart. She changes tack; she cannot fight back, but she can endure. Every time she tries to engage, tries to bite back as they rip at her arms, her legs, she loses time.

She drags herself the last few steps down to the throne room door.

And like sun spilling over the horizon, the Constant Lady stands just beyond it.

No—Voyne cannot allow Her that name. The name alone makes her head spin, makes her stagger up to her feet, yearning in that sunlight's direction. Toward the memory of how good it had felt to serve. How pure. How simple.

Simplicity is a lie. Service is never easy, not when done right.

Her sword is beyond that sun. But its light has driven back the biting shadows; nothing grabs at her as she steps into the throne room. No more scratches, no more testing bites. Blessed relief.

"Hello, pet," says the False Lady. "You've gone journeying." Her eyes drop to Voyne's hands a moment, then trail over her body.

Voyne longs for armor, feels exposed, too naked, in her gambeson and leggings. "Journeying, and brought me nothing home. How thoughtless."

Voyne refuses to answer. There is blood on the air, fresh, stinking. Not hers, too strong to be hers. The hungry things in the shadows only tasted small droplets. She cannot see her sword, or anything she can turn into a weapon.

Turn back. It sounds like Phosyne's voice in her head, or maybe even Leodegardis's, advising some final measure of caution. But there is no way back, and only one way forward.

She lunges.

And then the air shimmers, and she is on the ground. The monster's foot is on her shoulder, pressing lightly. Her skirts are soft, whispering over Voyne's ruddy, sweat-slick cheek. "No, I don't think so," the creature says. "You do keep a civil tongue in that head somewhere. Use it."

Voyne's heart beats double time, and her mind is swamped beneath a tidal surge, up and over. She can barely breathe.

"I will kill you," she makes herself say. "I will kill you for what you've done to this place."

The world is hazy. Her muscles burn with frustrated impetus, a hunting dog kept penned in.

"But I have made it beautiful," the False Lady says. Her foot moves. For a moment, Voyne is free, but she can't make sense of direction enough to fight. Instead, she is lifted into Her lap. A coddled creature. Mind its little fangs, its shrill bark; it thinks it is so much larger than reality.

She can hear the faint buzzing of bees. It grows and grows. A hive is gathering. She forces herself to look around. She cannot allow herself to slip away, not again.

The Absolving Saint enters, the shadows parting to admit him. From this angle, she can see their teeth, like slashes of white paint or bird shit on stone. The saint bears a platter. He brings it to his Mistress, kneeling to lay it by Her side.

The False Lady reaches out and plucks a dainty from the dish. It looks for all the world like a bloom nestled between two lips. But when she blinks again, the lips are the convolutions of a mushroom, and it is the bloom that is made of peels of flesh.

Another blink, and it is pastry and fruit.

"Will you not eat something?" She says, and holds it to Voyne's mouth.

"And was this carved from Leodegardis as well?" she whispers, stomach heaving. She thinks again of the stump of his arm, and the pearlescent wrist bones on the platter the Absolving Saint last presented her with.

He is a skilled cook. Does he seek to disguise what he has made, or to rarify it?

It would taste good, she knows. So good, so easy, so succulent. A perfect bite, and the moment she swallowed, it would wipe away all the agony of her resistance. Her tongue along lips, the pantomime of a kiss—but if they are his, those lips carry with them the vows he asked of her.

Trust in Phosyne.

Protect the people.

She keeps her mouth firmly shut.

"Not him," the Absolving Saint says, but too late to sway her; she has taken the strength she needs. She glares at him and pictures herself flaying his own lips away. His teeth are white when he speaks, too clean and perfect to be anything but fake. "I intend to savor him; he is not to be so quickly used up."

"And neither are you," the False Lady purrs.

"Your dogs don't seem to know that," Voyne spits, jerking her chin toward the door to the throne room. Those sharpened figments, those painted vicious shadows, crowd it.

"You cannot begrudge a beast its nature," the Absolving Saint replies. "Or its joys. Why should they not frolic, like the people of Aymar we have rescued for you?"

She tries to surge up, to snap her own teeth at him, but she's too weak. The False Lady's hold is too firm.

"You need your strength," the False Lady coos as She guides Voyne's attention back with a touch. She leans back and pulls at the fabric of Her robes, until Her breast is bared. Voyne can't look away.

She stares as the monster draws one fingernail across the alabaster flesh, parts it like a fleece.

Instead of blood, golden honey oozes forth. It drips down, coats what is almost, but not quite, a nipple, a strange knot of rosy, shining flesh.

"Eat," She says, softly. Her other hand cups the back of Voyne's head. "Drink. Let me nourish you."

Voyne turns away. She wants to snarl in threat, or to retch in horror, but the honey smells so good, rich and sweet, so sweet—

Was this how Phosyne felt, when Voyne pressed her to eat the comb?

"You trust in the little mouse to fetch you home again, don't you?" the False Lady murmurs. "Just drink, and allow yourself two masters. We both want to cultivate you, Ser Voyne. You have room enough in you for both."

"I know what loyalty is," Voyne bites out, because only the abstraction of duty can help her.

"You do so enjoy your suffering," the monster says. Her nails scrape over Voyne's scalp, sharp enough to make her gasp. "I thought death your art, but now I find myself reconsidering. You have learned the many gradations of pain, I think, receiving and giving, and you still search for yourself within it all. I thought to give you a life free of pain, but that was never what you wished for, was it? Even gentleness is pain for you."

Her words slide home, a misericord between the ribs. It galls her, drives her to argue, but she fights the urge. Another trick; this is another way to bring her defenses down. She would not be so focused on her if She were not frightened, if Voyne did not pose some threat.

(Or perhaps She only plays with Her food, the same way the shadows on the stairs did.)

The beast moves beneath Voyne, rolls her. A slip and blink and then Voyne is on the floor. The False Lady hauls her up to her knees, and Voyne can see now that she is within reach of the throne. Behind it must be her sword. A little farther; she has passed the test. She is so close.

"Stay here," the Lady says into her ear, hands sliding along Voyne's shoulders and then disappearing entirely. "Stay, and hope the little mouse remembers you exist. She has so many new and lovely worlds to explore—for you must know, I have shown her such wondrous sights."

And then She is gone, and Voyne can hear nothing but the waiting breath of painted faces and the buzzing hum of bees.

36

HERE IS ONLY one obvious place for Treila to run to. One person:

Phosyne.

Her creature of the tunnel may let her out again, but she refuses to squander the price she paid. Her missing ear sings with aimless noise as she races across the room she used to bed down in, making for the other staircase. But it is blocked with a clot of shadows, faces leering out of the darkness in the suggestion of cheekbones and chins. She doesn't let herself look closely. Out, instead, into the yard, then down and around toward the kitchens.

Not everybody is sleeping. In the distance, she sees three girls dancing. Their feet, she thinks, are bleeding. Shadows wait to lap at the sodden dirt.

She doesn't let herself look. Moves instead into the kitchen, because she knows there's a staircase out the back that will lead to the tower that contains Phosyne.

The main hearth has no fire in it. The tables are laden with ingredients, but nobody cuts, nobody stirs, nobody kneads. The cooks are all absent. Even the Absolving Saint is missing, and she wonders if he, too, is at her heels. She can hear laughter behind her, and smell pepper on the gust of too-close breaths. But every time she peers at shadows, they refuse to move.

Her missing ear is shrieking now. A warning, or something else?

She slips through another door and hesitates as cool air washes over her.

The Absolving Saint has been busy. Quarters of meat hang from the ceiling, the rib cages and bellies hollowed out, the spines split down the center. She has seen venison jointed out and hung to age, and this is much the same. But the proportions are all too familiar. The pelvises are round instead of flattened, the thighs long and luxuriously muscled.

She slides between and pretends they are just sides of pork. The muscle is pink enough. But there is so little fat.

It's not as easy to lose herself here as it is in a crowd of the living, but the bodies hang thick enough that she feels unseen as she creeps through the hall. Her tinnitus dulls, softens, and she can breathe again.

The sides of meat breathe with her.

No lungs to move the ribs, but something is shifting the hooks above. She glances down. No feet against the floor, but shadows. The meat begins to part.

She turns and runs.

There, the servants' stairs, and she is up them in a flash. She caught many rats here, broke their little necks, heard their shrieking just before they died. It rises in her ears, then falls, rises again. At its loudest, she nearly trips, though she can't untangle the causality. Is it responding to her stumble, or warning her of an attack?

She doesn't plummet, regardless. And then she is inside again, and going up, up, until she reaches a familiar hallway.

There are bright-burning torches outside the door that were not there before.

How much time has passed, she asks again, even as the ringing in her ear turns into a brief but deafening chorus.

The door opens.

The woman standing there is almost unrecognizable. Her black hair curls softly against her gaunt cheeks. Her embroidered robes cling to her emaciated form. She is beauty and death wrapped up into one neat little package, and Treila flinches back reflexively. But she knows the cut of that jaw, and something of the mad light in those eyes.

It's Phosyne.

INSIDE, THE SAME transformation has been worked. The room *gleams*, it is so clean. Perfumed steam seeps from a grate on the floor that Treila is certain was not there before. Every worktable and desk and scrap of furniture is organized and polished, and everything is so *hot*.

Sweat drips from her, and the air is hard to breathe. But she can't find it in herself to be afraid; she's too tired and desperate.

(*Foolish girl*, she tries to tell herself. But with only one ear, she barely hears it.)

It is hot, yes, but this is better than a frigid, starving forest.

She sinks onto a mass of cushions. They are plump and generous, with no stink of sweat on them or hint of mildew. They are better than anything she has ever slept on.

"You've come up with a miracle," she says, and her lips feel thick and slow. Unaccountably clumsy. She blinks, languid, catlike.

Phosyne has followed her, and settles on the cushions beside her.

"Your ear," Phosyne murmurs, and trails her fingertips over the smooth skin where it used to be before Treila can flinch away.

At the touch of skin to skin, the chorus erupts once more inside Treila's skull. She gasps, spine arching.

"Does it hurt?" Phosyne asks, and she sounds more curious than concerned.

Fair play, Treila concedes, when the noise softens. It's exactly how she'd felt standing over Phosyne's dying body that first night. The thought is half-hysterical. Phosyne reaches as if to stroke her brow, then hesitates.

Realizing it might hurt her.

And then she does it anyway.

Treila sags, boneless, as the noise doesn't surge. There is only the normal faint ringing that has been with her since she returned. The cushions are still so soft.

"My ear was the price of returning," she murmurs. "My finger the price to leave. I did, you know. Leave. There's nobody waiting for us outside the gates anymore. We could just walk out, I think. Maybe."

To a different world. A later world. A world where Etrebia has lost, at any rate, and that is the only thing that matters, surely? A world where Etrebia has lost and they are not being carved up into meat.

"The tunnel?" Phosyne asks. Her gaze is vague, as if she is looking down through the floor to it. But, of course, that's impossible.

(But so are miracles. Treila would do well to stop asking questions.)

"The tunnel. But it will cost us." The words come out—soft. Weak. Desperate. "It's not so great a cost," she hastens to add, in case Phosyne wouldn't offer an ear, or a finger.

(What did she offer to receive this?)

Treila knows better than to trust, but she can't do this alone. Not anymore. And Phosyne—Phosyne is not Voyne. She doesn't trust Phosyne guilelessly. Phosyne is a tool. She just needs the tool to have its own motive force, for just a moment, until she catches her breath.

"Of course," Phosyne murmurs, considering. "It makes sense, that your creature beneath the castle would charge for safe passage through its territory." Her hands haven't left Treila. They map out her boundaries, find her ankle, her missing sock.

Treila flinches but can't argue, but she also knows she's missing something, with this talk of territory. With Phosyne's new possessiveness.

"The king gave them Aymar," Phosyne attempts to explain. "They stole in via the Priory's honeybees, but he could have stopped them. He could have turned them away. Instead, he ate their food, and now Aymar is theirs."

Yes, they do act like they own the place. But she owes them no fealty.

"We can't win," Treila says. "You know that, don't you? These *things*—they're so hungry, and there are more of them now. In the shadows."

Phosyne rises from the cushions, hands washing over one another again and again. "Have you seen Ser Voyne? She can be our bulwark."

Treila looks around the room, as if seeing it anew. It is changed—and empty of any other living creature. Her heart falls at a rate she doesn't want to examine. "She's not here?"

"No," Phosyne says. "I sent her to help the people down below. To take the measure of the enemy. *You* haven't seen her?"

Treila shakes her head.

Phosyne's hands clasp tight together.

"Right. Forget her. We have other options," Treila says. None a winning move, but trying to find Voyne in the chaos of the castle will only leave her vulnerable. The Loving Saint made that clear, and she suppresses a shudder as she remembers his teeth.

She's too late for her preferred prize; she must make her peace with that. "I can take you to the tunnel again. Perhaps, if you speak to the thing beneath the castle . . ."

Her plan ends there. All she knows is she cannot leave alone again.

Phosyne isn't looking at her.

She makes herself stand. She is unsteady on her feet, too tired, but she knows better than to ask Phosyne for food; there will be none, or none that will be safe to eat. "There's no time left. Come with me," she says.

"No," Phosyne replies, calmly.

And Treila realizes that the shivering mess of a woman she found nearly starved those few nights ago is not just unrecognizable, but gone entirely.

"Stay here," Phosyne says. "Or leave. Whichever you prefer. I only ask that you decide now, because once you do, I can't let you take it back. But I am going to get back what is mine." And Phosyne looks down at her hands for just a moment. "She needs me," she murmurs, and Treila thinks she wasn't meant to hear.

Treila stares.

Phosyne glances up at her, and for a second, there is both the disjointed mess of a girl and the frightening lick of a flame.

"Will you stay?" she asks.

And Treila shakes her head, and slips past her to the door.

Phosyne does not call after her.

37

HEN THE DOOR closes behind Treila, the room settles into silence.

Phosyne gives Treila a head start. Too awkward, to meet upon the stairs. Instead, she takes a moment to breathe. Her eyes close, and she lets herself spread. Not physically, she does not sink into the stone, but she remembers how it felt to ride on a bee's wings through the meadow, and she can see, all around her, a widening circle of—not light, it is not light, but it is visible all the same. She can feel them, her little borders. They're small but strong. They embrace the room, making such a lovely garden for her. And then, beyond them: the whole of the main keep tower, spidering out from where she stands. Four shining beacons, fever sweet. One walks the walls. Another is close by, hunting, blood running hot. Another beacon is in the garden, and the last down in the great hall.

Only her bee-brought visitors. And they have nothing like Ser Voyne at their feet.

In between them, a riot of thinner color, all bleeding one into the next. She hears breathing, from below. So many bodies, piled upon one another. Giggles, too, at the barest edge of hearing.

Still no trace of Ser Voyne.

Ser Voyne won't look at all like them, Phosyne reasons. She will be a solid little stone, a pebble refusing erosion.

That pebble is—there, just below her feet. Near at hand. Down, bright and shining, in the throne room.

She is alive, Phosyne feels sure of that.

Phosyne opens the door.

Her hallway is empty. There's no trace of Jacynde, but of course, Treila would have said something if there were. And there is no trace of those hungry shadows she can sense, those hushed giggles. The twin torches she kindled from Pneio's and Ornuo's wool burn bright and hot, keeping them far away.

She thinks to take one with her, but can't risk breaking the boundary that is her tower. She may need it yet.

Into the darkness she steps instead. Down, down, until she reaches the door to the heart of the keep tower.

Ser Voyne kneels there before the empty throne.

(Not a throne, Phosyne corrects absently; it's just a chair. A chair that, when Ser Leodegardis sat in it, was still just a chair, but when King Cardimir sat in it *became* a throne. And King Cardimir is not here.)

Still, Ser Voyne kneels as if it *does* contain her liege, and Phosyne approaches obliquely so that she can get a glimpse of the knight's face. Her brow is furrowed (but when is it not?) and she looks . . . tired. The light has not gone out of her, no, but where she had looked upon Phosyne with barely concealed adoration after she chose to remain with her in Aymar, now she has retreated into herself.

This is not how this woman is meant to be. Phosyne has never seen her in her glory, in her element, but she can imagine it well enough. Astride a charger on a battlefield, armor gleaming, eyes flashing with certainty and precisely focused rage. Kneeling here, at this throne (chair), adoring and ready to serve, to turn the keen edge of her focus on any enemy that dare come.

It is a lovely picture. It is, Phosyne suspects, what the Lady sees in her as well.

She thinks to greet her, breathe her name into the midnight stillness of the room, but Voyne hasn't noticed her. Voyne hasn't noticed much of anything. It's likely, even probable, that something has happened between Phosyne's tower that morning and this room now, that she has fallen once more at the Lady's feet in the interim—and that would be Phosyne's fault, for not keeping her close at hand. Or perhaps she has wound down, her springs uncoiled, needing to be issued another directive, another command. Phosyne doesn't know the specific steps of the dance between them; maybe it's only through the continued application of will that Voyne even exists, now.

An odd thought—it's in her voice, but not her accent. It doesn't *taste* right. Taste is important. The Lady had tasted different, honey on the tongue. Phosyne doesn't taste honey with that thought, but something spiced, like a cumin seed cracked between her teeth.

Interesting.

Some change, accompanying her transformation, her room's? Some impingement of the unseen world onto her mind? Perhaps her leaps of intuition, of recognition, have taken on a new character with her broadened appreciation of the world. And what a leap it is, that maybe Voyne doesn't exist without somebody to obey. Phosyne tries to follow the taste of it. She gets nowhere.

Nowhere, that is, except the throne.

It's right in front of her now. She's watching Voyne, so she didn't notice when she got this close, but now her hand is on the armrest. She hesitates, but only briefly.

She doesn't taste cumin anymore, but the memory of it is . . . persuasive. It makes sense. Phosyne wants to test it.

Phosyne sits on the throne.

Ser Voyne's head jerks up, immediately, as if on a tether. She meets Phosyne's eyes and her lips part. She is . . . she is *beautiful*, radiant, kneeling there. She belongs there. There is purpose in her eyes, in her limbs, and if Phosyne could taste her skin, she would taste . . .

Competence. Loyalty. Devotion. What do those taste like?

Ser Voyne is going to protest. Phosyne knows her well enough now; Voyne will be angry that Phosyne is sitting where her liege should sit, where Leodegardis should sit if not. Phosyne doesn't belong here.

But Voyne isn't protesting. She's looking at Phosyne with something that looks very much like longing.

Phosyne rests her head against the back of the chair and decides to pretend. Just a little. Maybe it's the high of defending her room, carving out a little square of territory in this benighted castle; maybe it's just perversity, for she has so much of it even in just her little finger. She remembers the cistern, Voyne on her knees. She remembers the smithy, Voyne's body flush up against hers, angry, raging, but still so tightly leashed to her duty: protect Phosyne, make her produce a miracle.

"Come closer, Ser Voyne," she whispers into the thick heat enveloping the room.

And though Ser Voyne shudders, she does not resist or protest. She shuffles forward on bended knee, close enough for Phosyne to touch.

This is not the time or place. They exist in a small circle within a larger, infiltrated world. The Lady and Her saints prowl these halls, and at any moment, eyes might blink at them from out of the darkness. Out here, Phosyne has no ready defense against them. If she were a rational woman, she would tell Voyne, now, to get up. To follow her, back to her rooms. They could cross that threshold, collapse into safety, and perhaps even play this game a little longer, if this impulse hasn't fizzled out by then.

But Phosyne is not rational. She is powerful. She has cleansed her land and her body, and she sits now wearing fine silk robes where once they were roughspun wool, and she has done *all* of this herself.

Phosyne reaches out and cups Voyne's cheek.

"I have made a place for us," she murmurs.

Ser Voyne presses her cheek into Phosyne's palm and closes her eyes, tight. She shivers. She is full of barely restrained energy.

She wants to be led. Commanded. Phosyne can't taste it yet, but she knows it.

Desire is a strange, unfamiliar beast. Phosyne isn't sure when last she truly let herself feel it, but it's kindling in her now.

"Touch me," Phosyne tells her.

And Ser Voyne does.

It's not tentative, not at all. One moment, her quaking knight is nuzzling her palm, and the next Ser Voyne rises up, covers Phosyne with her body, presses her to the seat. Her knee remains bent—she still offers just the slightest capitulation, or perhaps she expects Phosyne to push her back.

Phosyne doesn't. She grins as Voyne's hand fits itself around Phosyne's throat, the way they've practiced, and she arches her spine. She lifts one foot, hooks it around Voyne's leg, wishes there was armor there.

She wishes for a lot of things.

She asks for only one: "Talk to me. I know you're in there, Ser Voyne."

Voyne answers with a moan, her hand tightening. But the bond between them compels. "You're like Her," she gasps out.

She sounds as angry as she is adoring. Ser Voyne didn't speak to the Lady that way. No, this is just for Phosyne.

"But you remember that you hate me," Phosyne says, voice reedy from the weight of Voyne's fist.

Ser Voyne grimaces, relents just a little. Just enough to draw so close to her that Phosyne could kiss her lips

"I don't hate you," Ser Voyne whispers.

"Because I haven't told you to?"

Voyne convulses, then, halfway to a seizure. Her hand tightens, then drops to Phosyne's shoulder. To the throne beneath. She is panting. "Because this isn't you. Phosyne—"

She doesn't want to hear it, and so she stoppers her knight's lips with a kiss. It's better than fighting her. Better than feeling shame, too, or hesitation, and the important thing is that Ser Voyne doesn't hate her. She's groaning into Phosyne's mouth, her hands sliding down along her body. All the world beyond the two of them is gone, and Phosyne is so eager to tip into the abyss.

And then the flavor of cumin blossoms between her teeth, fills her mouth, overwhelms the taste of Ser Voyne's skin and brings with it the certainty that they are not alone. Phosyne pulls back, looks up, and sees a waiting audience of eyes, a hundred of them, more, all watching, all set above grinning, hungry mouths.

38

HOSYNE GOES RIGID and cold beneath her hands.

Voyne tamps down the twin surges of rage and relief, jams her knee into the hard wood of the throne to still her swirling thoughts. Whatever bewitchment Phosyne is under, she is under it just as deeply, and it takes all her willpower and her anger to pant out, "Seen them at last, have you?"

"They aren't moving." Phosyne's voice has shifted tones, from thick with want to nervous curiosity. Her hand is still on Voyne's shoulder, though, stroking, possessive.

Voyne shudders. "That doesn't mean they won't. They were likely waiting for us to be—"

Distracted.

"Don't move," Phosyne says, and the compulsion is a punch to her gut. Voyne lets out a low whine. Something flickers in Phosyne's eyes, then, and she offers a small smile. "Sorry. You *can* move. I just—if we stay like this, it holds the moment. If we move apart, they may strike."

It is logical. That doesn't mean Voyne likes it.

Beneath her, Phosyne is clad in fine silk. She smells like flowers and gives off a subtle, pleasing warmth. She doesn't seem quite real. "What happened while I was gone?" Voyne asks, thinking of the flames outside Phosyne's door. "You said—you said you made a place for us?"

"The Lady came to teach me."

Voyne jerks back at that, and their audience murmurs, titters, and Voyne thinks she hears claws upon the stone.

Phosyne's hand drops from her shoulder but takes her wrist,

squeezes in warning. "It's okay," she says. "I took what I needed and no more. The room is safe, now. We need only return to it."

And get away from whatever madness has led to Voyne wanting little more than to rest her head in Phosyne's lap.

Unless that madness is coming from her, learned at the False Lady's knee.

Voyne cannot trust her. Of course she cannot trust her. There is a buzzing in her ears, growing louder, impossible to ignore. She is kneeling at this throne, and Phosyne is upon it, and—

She needs distance. She needs to think. More than anything, they both need to be gone from this place before the creatures watching them get bored and take their hesitation as a chance to lunge.

"Behind you, please—my sword. I could not reach it. You must give it to me." The throne has held her ever since the False Lady left her here as, what, an offering?

Phosyne looks as uncertain as she does, but she at last lets go, twisting and leaning over the edge of the throne, peering behind her.

Phosyne's fingers clutch tight at the back of the chair. Her knuckles turn white in the gloom. "I don't see a sword, Voyne," she whispers.

The buzzing is so loud.

"It must be there. Ser Leodegardis—he said—"

"Come, *look*," Phosyne orders, and Voyne lurches forward, angry and thankful both.

Until she looks.

On the floor, Prioress Jacynde lies dead, run through with a blade. With *Voyne's* blade. At least, Voyne is halfway certain it's her blade—whose else could it be?—but it is covered top to bottom with a lattice of comb. Honey mixes with Jacynde's blood, and the wax cascades over the corpse, binding it to the sword and to the floor both. Only her face, twisted in agony, is still recognizable.

Bees crawl along the whole tableau, a dark and shimmering mass. Their buzzing merges with the whispered breaths and laughter coming from the shadows.

How long? How long has Jacynde been there? How did she get here from Phosyne's care? She should have been safe. Shouldn't be—
skewered—

But how didn't Voyne notice this, when the False Lady taunted her? She never got close enough, she tells herself. The buzzing was already in the air. Wasn't it?

Would she even know if the monster had bridled her again, compelled her to kill?

Yes, she tells herself, but for all her bucking anger, she can't be sure.

It doesn't matter, she tells herself instead. What matters is that she needs her blade. What matters is that when she tries to reach for it, her arm refuses to obey.

She can only look.

"Free me," Voyne whispers.

"You are free," Phosyne says.

But Voyne isn't. Something has changed in the time between Phosyne letting her drink in the cistern and now. Something changed when the False Lady left Voyne kneeling. Voyne isn't free at all; she cannot act without somebody to act *for,* and she hates herself for it.

"Please, Phosyne," she begs.

Phosyne flinches. She has, at least, that much shame. "Take up your sword, Ser Voyne."

And like a hound let off a lead, Voyne lunges.

She tears into the comb with her hands. The wax is warm, molten between her fingers, but there is so much of it, and the honey that bursts forth from each ruptured cell makes her clumsy. The bees have no such problem; they rise in a dark swarm, their buzzing growing cacophonous. And then the first sting pierces her flesh. The second. The third. She tries to close her hands around the hilt and heave, but she can't grip it. It slides away every time. Pierces deeper into the body below them both.

The pain is growing. She shuts her eyes, shoves her face down between her arms, and tries to retreat, but she can't, because Phosyne's order is too thick in her veins. She hears herself pleading. Crying.

In her panic, she fears Phosyne will leave her like this. Will watch her be stung to death, subsumed into the hive that is forming too rapidly to be natural. That Voyne was wrong, that this *is* Phosyne, in truth, and always has been, merely waiting for the moment when all the rest of the world cracked away and left her unstoppable.

"No more!" Phosyne cries. "Ser Voyne, retreat!"

And, at last, Ser Voyne does.

She falls back, chest heaving, eyes rolling in her skull. She can barely see, but her face is the least-stung of her. Her hands are beginning to swell. Her scalp is a searing cap of pain. She shakes her head, forcing herself to focus.

Long-limbed *things* have crawled down from the windows, and advance in cautious waves. Eyes glint at her in the dark. Phosyne is rising from the throne, and she is beautiful and terrifying all at once. She is glowing. Voyne feels heat rolling from her. She tips her head back and sings one quaking note, and all the reed lights in the room flare to life.

The shadows, caught by the light, resolve into something not quite human. They are like paintings, frescoes, pale faces staring back in the flickering glow. They don't move when Voyne looks at them, but she can't see them all at once. At the edges of her vision they're only smears, bits of gold leaf and charcoal. They are prowling. They are getting closer.

Phosyne reaches for her.

Ser Voyne surrenders to the last order she was given and runs.

Maybe it's Phosyne's distance from the throne; maybe it's the strength of Voyne's own panic; maybe it's some whispered order she does not hear as she pounds down the stairs. But as she runs, her mind comes back to her. Full awareness returns to her, and with it, horror. She is retching as she reaches the ground floor, stumbles over the bodies sprawled below her. Some stir. Some ask questions. She ignores them, throws the door open.

The sun is blinding overhead when Voyne pitches out into the yard.

She has stopped trying to make sense of time.

Space, though, she thought she could count on. She knows the dimensions of Aymar intimately, knows how many the upper and lower baileys can hold comfortably, knows where every entrance to the towers that stud the walls are.

Nothing is where it should be.

This place has transformed since she tended to the fallen beneath the blazing sun. The walls tower above her, the ground undulates away, and the sky spins lazily. Voyne makes it only three yards at most before she stumbles, falls, vertigo swarming over her in a hazy rush. Inside. If she goes back inside, the walls and floors will join as they ought.

If she can only get up to Phosyne's tower, instead . . .

Voyne can't risk it. She must go to ground somewhere else. The cistern's depths, perhaps, if only for a little while. Long enough to think. To regain mastery of herself.

But unlike the last bright sunlit moment Voyne was outside the keep, the people in the yard are awake. They are on their feet. They are—

Well.

The Absolving Saint stands at the head of a table and slides a piece of sharp, shining glass beneath the skin of a man who lies naked beneath him. The saint flays him carefully, a beatific smile upon his silvered lips. The man sings.

Sings, not screams.

In the lower yard, down by the cisterns, a man holds aloft his daughter like an offering. Blood runs down the little girl's arms and legs. At his feet, his other children crowd and press, lapping up each drop that falls.

And around it all is the audience. Even in so much drowning sunlight, Voyne can barely make out their contours. They are light flashing off of quartz, heat haze, splashes of whitewash on stone. They are flat, where the bodies they advance toward are thick and curved and so real Voyne can't stand to look at them.

But they do have weight to them. Dust scatters in their wake. And when one bends to the flayed man's chest and bites—

Well, their teeth rend flesh as well as any beast's.

Voyne keeps her head down through all of it, shaking, shivering, cold in the hot noon sun. She feels like she is drowning. She feels like she is dying. But that's hardly new. What is new is only the intensity of the feeling. She takes solace in the fact that she doesn't feel hunger when she sees these horrors, unlike everybody else around her.

But it is her lack of hunger, of course, that marks her.

She's in the shadow of the south wall when it happens. When the first set of eyes settles on her, sees through the thin veil of her act. Voyne only knows because she stumbles as she walks, has to put out a hand to support herself, and as she tips forward, she sees the whites of two eyes replaced with piercing gold, pupils dotting the center, widening as they take her in. They measure her weakness. They see her falter.

Voyne is running before she has time to rationalize any of it.

The nearest open door leads into the smithy. It's fifty yards away, if that. She has a clear shot, or as close to it as she's going to get; the nearest tableau, a woman carving pieces of her flesh and placing those bloody scraps into her own mouth, isn't close enough to reach her.

Her muscles burn. Her head pounds. The world keeps trying to fall away, to pitch and yaw, but she closes her eyes and sprints.

Behind her, she hears paws, hooves, feet in the dirt. Her pursuers snarl. They call to her, desperate for her aid. They laugh.

The wall of the smithy is as solid as it was when she slammed Phosyne up against it, and she collides hard, wrenching her shoulder. She gasps, eyes open, spun around to face what is coming for her. Everything tilts. She sees a flash of movement, feels pain in her leg, kicks out. Punches. Scratches. Fights, like she has not fought in years.

She gains a moment's freedom. It's enough.

She throws herself into the smithy, expecting only more chaos, more horror, more blood—

But the building is dim, and warm, and all but empty.

There is only one man inside. Theophrane, the head blacksmith. He sits surrounded by his tools, as if he's built a nest of them. They're in no fit state to be used, all jumbled up, but he does clutch a punch chisel like a dagger. It would do some damage, if he lunged.

"Get out," the blacksmith says.

She ignores him but keeps her distance, gasping for breath as she shoves the door closed and leans her whole weight against it. She locks gazes with the blacksmith, daring him to argue as the beasts outside hurl themselves against the wood.

He doesn't, but he doesn't lower the chisel, either. Soon, sooner than Voyne would have expected, the thuds slow, then cease.

Easier prey outside, perhaps.

He waits until she's eased up against the door to demand, once again, "Get out, Ser Voyne."

He knows who she is. He knows to be afraid. He's hiding, trying to defend himself, and—

And that means that he's not under their sway.

She lifts her hands, hoping to gentle him. "You're safe here?" she asks.

His throat works. He lifts the chisel up a little higher. "Not if you're in here with me."

She sinks down to one knee, hands still up. "I just need space to think. I will not harm you." She scans the room. It's steady. Nothing spins. The world has reasserted itself, and she lets out a low, helpless moan, fisting her hand against the floor. "Out there, I—"

"You're one of them," Theophrane says.

And there is the memory: the lead-up to the feast, before Voyne found Phosyne huddled below the keep. There were so many who needed to be brought to the table. She had honey for so many of them.

Her beestings itch. They throb. There is blood beneath her nails, too. Jacynde's blood.

Theophrane's blood, before.

When she looks back up at him, she can see them, the purpling bruises on his face, his throat. She dragged him out of this building, threw him down, ordered him to eat. His fellows had held him, then, when she left to resume her patrol.

"I wasn't myself," she protests, half apology.

He doesn't care. She can't blame him.

"And you won't be yourself again soon enough," he mutters. He is so thin. He is starving. He doesn't look at all like the people out in the yard.

"Did you eat?" she asks.

He grimaces. It bares all his teeth. "They tried to make me."

"But?"

"But it all came right back up. It turned to ash in my mouth."
Theophrane hesitates. His beard has gone patchy over the last
six months. "Maybe—maybe it would've been better if it hadn't. I
wouldn't know, then, would I? What's happening out there?"

"No," Voyne says. "No, you wouldn't."

And wouldn't it have been easier if she didn't know, either?

But she does. He does.

Silence stretches between them, broken only by the occasional ecstatic cry from without.

"They hate iron," Theophrane says at last. "At least, I think it's
the iron. It's the only thing I can figure that saved me." He displays
one muscle-corded forearm. His skin is flecked all over with what
looks like soot, until Voyne realizes it's not on the surface of his
flesh, but underneath. The blurred edges come not from particulate
but from the lens of skin.

"It gets in you," Theophrane says with a bitter twitch of his lips.
"Iron filings, all the rest, in with the burns. Unavoidable. But when
one of those things tried to take a bite of me, it slagged its jaw. I built
the ring after. They haven't gotten close since."

"Iron," Voyne repeats. She thinks of her sword, skewering Jacynde. All the iron that they gave to the Priory, that was melted
down and turned into ammunition. So much lost armor. So many
lost weapons. Even the few iron nails in this place, stripped from
their moorings, given to Theophrane to melt down and repurpose.

All gone, now, gone over the walls.

And the false saints came in its absence. The False Lady and the
bees that have gone mad with Her arrival kept Voyne from her sword.
It makes sense, now.

She can use this.

"One piece," she says, rising to her feet. "Give me one piece from
your ring. Anything. I can use it. I will fight them." It's as good as a
sword, if what Theophrane says is true. If it isn't, he loses nothing,
not really. "Whatever you can spare. Please."

He glares. He does not move.

"I can take it," Voyne adds, voice softening, "or you can give it."

She is stronger than he is. She's been kept better fed, even before the saints arrived. Not, she understands now, so that she could protect her liege, but because she was a prized possession, and it would not do to let her waste away. So honeyed wine and the last of the cheeses were for her. She feels guilty, so guilty, but not enough to surrender her strength for it.

In another life, Theophrane might have looked on her as his salvation. The hope of rescue. But instead, even as he pulls something from the pile, he glares at her with hatred.

He tosses his offering at her feet. It's a hammer. Small. The head is rough iron, the handle worn wood. It's well-loved, but useless now, if only because the metal makes up such a small portion of it.

She doesn't look away from him as she crouches and picks it up. Her fingers are thick and swollen, stingers still embedded; the joints almost don't close around the handle. But she doesn't look away, even as she straightens, retreats to the door.

"Your little witch did this, didn't she?" he asks. "You should have killed her that day she nearly lit my shop on fire."

"It was already too late," Voyne tells him.

His expression shutters. He draws tight within himself.

Voyne opens the smithy door and steps back into the blistering sun.

The Warding Saint is waiting for her. At his heels are the shifting, refracting shapes of a hundred observers.

"Come," he says. "My Lady has need of you."

Voyne grips the hammer harder. She feels something ooze from the punctures. Blood, honey, something else? "I have no need of your Lady."

He considers this, taking her measure. Can he see Phosyne's touch still on her?

He holds in one hand a piece of ripe fruit. It glistens with juice. Her stomach roars in answer to it.

The Warding Saint extends his hand to her. "Eat," he says. "You will feel better if you eat. The little mouse won't hold your lead anymore. She is a far crueler mistress, isn't she? No art to it, no kindness. She doesn't care what you want, does she?"

It's a transparent ploy, and yet Voyne is still tempted. She is, in her heart, tired. What can one hammer do against the writhing mass of hunger before her? And what can one madwoman, sitting on a throne and ordering Voyne to kiss her when they both remain in danger, really offer for protection?

But Voyne is sick to death of following orders. Any orders.

The hammer cracks into the Warding Saint's head like his skull is only as thick as an eggshell.

He falls at her feet, howling, writhing, the crater smoking with a bitter stench. Honey spills out of him like blood. She falls to her knees and brings the hammer down again, again, into his cheek, his orbit, his jaw. He splinters and falls to pieces. She slams the iron down into every chink in his armor, pulps every exposed inch. He howls until the last. He spasms. He sobs.

His armor is not as heavy as it should be, and is not made of steel. The buckles do not work well; they are poorly made, poorly balanced. The straps don't feed smoothly through them. She knew this from the start. She saw this the first day they arrived.

She didn't know to be afraid of it.

Still, she strips it off his body, belts it all in place on hers. It's just pageantry, but it makes her spine a little straighter, a little stronger. She hefts the hammer in her hand, dripping as it is with honey, and looks out in challenge at the prowling host before her. She sees a face, two faces, three. They are gone as quickly as they appeared.

They are not the only things moving. The tableaus have broken apart. People, people she is sworn to protect, are edging closer. She wants to open her arms to them. Take charge. Tell them she is here to right these wrongs.

But behind her, the door to the smithy hangs open. She hears Theophrane shouting her name. Begging.

She stands, head spinning. At her back, her audience is prowling closer; she can feel it in the hot pepper breath that gusts around her. She can hear the crack of bone as they devour the offering she has made for them. They feast upon their own; they make no distinction.

Her world is shaking at the seams. She has done something wrong. Her gut twists.

In front of her, she sees bodies. A mass of bodies. Farmers and trappers and cartwrights and shop clerks, unwashed and half-starved and piling into the smithy. They rush through the door like a wave.

She can make out every hair on their heads, smell the stink of their bodies, and when she looks at them she doesn't feel drunk or drifting.

They are human, only human, but they tear Theophrane apart all the same.

39

T's DAYLIGHT OUTSIDE the keep, but Treila barely no-tices until she sees that the mortal inhabitants of Aymar are awake once more, and it is easier to find her way.

Easier, but far more exposed. She wants shadows. She wants darkness. She doesn't want this target painted on her back. It is so much worse to flee from monsters in the light of day.

If the Loving Saint is still seeking her, though, there is no sign. She doesn't risk looking back as she plunges into the press of bodies before her. There are so many. They are all distracted, all with juice- and blood-stained lips, all clamoring for sustenance. For salvation. Who they turn to changes. In one knot of humanity, it is a child, counting out beans in the dirt, offering one out of every ten to the ravenous crowd around his feet. In another, it's a tangle of three men, mouths open with pleasure, flesh sticking and sliding in a mess of blood and sweat. As long as Treila presses toward the center, and then allows herself to be pushed back out on the other side, nobody notices. Nobody cares.

But that doesn't mean she's safe. One moment she can see half again as many bodies, though they are thin and insubstantial, and in the next, they are gone completely. Her head spins. The whole world tries to spin with it, but at the wrong rate, blurring and doubling.

Unacceptable. She jerks her head once, lips curling in a snarl, and forces herself to look. The seasons refuse to progress, time continues to unspool, but she is *here* and she will make sense of it, the way she has made sense of all the rest.

The world rights itself between one blink and the next.

She is, of course, not alone.

The rest of the Loving Saint's kind are scattered throughout the yards. They look like paintings, unearthly and flat. They should be incapable of movement, but they aren't. Their limbs, when they have limbs, slide and jerk and reconfigure as they prowl across the yard. Most ignore her, but a few look up at her attention. With hunger. Without her saint's mark on her, they will hunt her down and eat her. She knows that, better than she knows anything.

And he will not be far behind them. She can practically feel his hot breath on her neck already.

So she ignores the damned arrayed before her and dives, instead, into the walled garden. It will lead her back inside, through the kitchen door. Inside is safer. Inside is less exposed.

But the garden is not as she knew it.

It is less a garden and more a jungle now. Plants grow verdant and high, blotting out the sun. The air is thick with pollen and sap and greenery, and Treila has to force her way into the thicket, into the dark. It folds around her, welcoming. The dark of the forest, waiting for her still.

Heaving for breath, Treila squirms between the glass needle-covered vines of what looks like an enormous squash plant. At this scale, the needles drag across her skin, not piercing, not sticking. Still, she is covered in scratches on the other side. Her blood clings to the vine. She is shaking as she presses deeper, inside a yarrow plant ten times the size of any natural thing, and huddles as its perfume clogs her nose, makes her shiver.

It will hide her scent, though. It will hide her from sight. It will give her a minute, just a minute, to catch her breath and think.

The knife in her hand will protect her, if she uses it well. If she can get behind her Loving Saint, she can plunge it into his back, and even if his fear was only mortal nerves, she can kill him all the same. But she will have to be careful. He can take whatever form he pleases. She will need to derive some test, some way of knowing.

He is sentimental. He is jealous. He won't trust her, not one bit, but if she offers him something he would like . . .

Perhaps the gap, below the castle? Perhaps that would be enough to snare his attention. Then, down in the dark, she can offer him for her freedom instead of another piece of herself. A way out, when she has won the rest of the day.

Yes. Yes, that is the best option here, and she just needs to be strong enough to take it. She just needs her confidence back. Needs to remember that she isn't prey.

She hears footsteps.

She is no longer alone.

Instinct makes her cower. It's five years ago, and she's huddled in the roots of a tree, a hollow that might have been an animal's burrow, once, but is too shallow to truly conceal her. She's being hauled out by her hair, desperate hands pawing at her, testing the meat left on her bones. No, no, she is in Aymar castle, she is hiding in the garden, and just like five years ago, she will not give in so easily.

Treila adjusts her grip on the knife. Shifts inside her hiding spot, peers through the gloom. She looks for flat white faces, those hideous paintings come to life with sharp teeth, and sees nothing. No flashes of light, no jerking limbs.

But she does see blood.

Blood on cloth and metal and skin. The other presence in the garden is keeping low to the ground, is stalking through the shadows. On the hunt. Treila shifts and makes out something gleaming and heavy in one of the hunter's hands.

Then nothing. Rustling. Stems bending, snapping. The hunter is not coming straight toward Treila, but they are coming close enough. Treila debates staying still and quiet, or pushing farther into the green.

She is so tired of being still and quiet. Her blood is boiling in her veins. If it is another human, she can overpower them—if they're actually a threat at all.

If it is a saint, she won't hesitate to strike this time.

She takes the measure of the land around her, listens carefully to judge her hunter's path. She turns to her left, eases herself from the tangle of yarrow and between stalks of some flower that looms over-head. Petals and thorns caress her cheeks as she edges forward and left and right, weaving through the forest. The shadows are a gift. A mantle. Something to strengthen her limbs and her heart.

But when, at last, Treila reaches a small clearing, it is around a familiar stone bench.

And Ser Voyne stands across from her, bloody and beautiful in gleaming armor.

Treila's breath seizes in her throat, and she retreats a few feet back into the shadows.

The slick sound of death in the throne room, the buzzing of bees echoing around the Loving Saint's words, both have primed her poorly. Ser Voyne, in armor, bloody and disheveled, pitches her straight into the painful vice grip of memory. Of nightmare. Her father, out in the yard, upon a platform. On his knees. Begging, as Ser Voyne raised her blade. The audience: her family, the king, every servant of her house. She'd looked away, when the sword fell. When her father's humiliatingly desperate noises ceased, and there was only the wet *thunk*, the roll of his head.

You have no time for this. She forces herself to look at Ser Voyne and remember her, weak and so reliant on Phosyne.

But is it even her? The armor she wears is all wrong, sitting strangely. This might be instead the Loving Saint, wearing the guise best suited to hurt her. To spur her to foolish decisions. To run and fall at this woman's feet and beg for her protection.

Beg, because Ser Voyne owes her this much, doesn't she?

Five years. It's been *five years*, and she is being a child, wanting to still play out this drama. Wanting some apology for what is done and gone.

The Loving Saint is hunting her. And this, she is certain, is a trap. It is time to cut out her weakness, once and for all. She adjusts her grip on the knife, this time for keeps, and begins to edge around the clearing.

Treila's halfway to her target when her foot lands on the curved shell of a snail. It cracks open before she can pull her weight back.

Ser Voyne's head jerks up at the sound, turns in her direction.

Treila freezes. She's in the weeds, but not so far back as to be invisible—to anybody else. She waits for Voyne's gaze to skip over her. Because the real Ser Voyne cannot notice her, she reminds herself. Cannot even conceive of her.

But she is seen.

Voyne's eyes widen. Her jaw goes slack for a moment, then tenses. There's a flicker in her eyes, like there was after her confession, when she'd turned to see Treila for the first time in so many years: pain, and confusion, and the smallest hint of submission. There's none of the bewitched adoration.

It is a cunning mask.

Her flesh is blotched red and her hair, where it is not shorn off, is plastered to her scalp with sweat. It's not the form the Loving Saint took upon the battlements, but he's capable of many others. He's advancing on her now like she is a skittish colt, one hand out low, placating.

She wishes he would just lunge and take her.

Shaking, Treila brings her knife up between them.

The saint stops. Holds up his hands. There's a hammer in one of them. Not even a large one, made for war: it's small, for small work. Treila wants to laugh, it's so ridiculous. A hammer might do as much damage as a sword, but Voyne would never wield one. Whatever he is, cannot get the details right of being human. "I won't hurt you," he says. It sounds so much like Ser Voyne, but voices must be as easy to ape as faces for him.

"You're lying, even now?" Treila can't help herself. Can't keep her mouth shut. She edges farther into the clearing, circles around one side to get the bench out from in between them.

She wonders if he has a heart, and if it lives in the same place it does in her own chest.

"I have never lied to you." Voyne's eyes turn wary. The bafflement is gone.

"You've always only been playing with your food."

Saint Voyne cocks his head at that.

"From the first time you saw me, I could tell what you were," Treila says, grinning. "So hungry and desperate for personalized attention. Nobody else could really see you, could they? Just me."

"Calm down. Please. Just for a moment. Think clearly, Treila," the Loving Saint says with Ser Voyne's mouth. *I'm older than you, stronger than you, hungrier than you,* he does not add.

There's something wrong with this, but Treila doesn't have time to sort it. One of Voyne's ears is red and swollen. And the fingers—

No time.

"I am thinking clearly," she returns, grinning. "I know the rules of this game as least as well as you do by now."

That makes the beast in knight's clothing hesitate. About to argue that Treila can't fully comprehend, or afraid that she might?

"I'm not here to hurt you," he says, and casts the hammer into the nearby brush. She gets a better look for just a moment; his fingers are swollen and red as if stung by bees. They look like hers did, five years ago. Why? Why would he do that?

To boast that he is no holy thing, either?

There's a flicker of doubt in his eyes. He's a better liar than that, though. Something's wrong.

She makes another snap judgment. Should she soften under his words, his vulgar apparition, so that he'll get closer, or stand her ground? She has so much practice pretending to be what she is not.

But she's tired of it, and the one good thing he has given her— that this whole mess has given her—is the freedom to shrug off her disguise.

Treila takes another step closer, blade shining in the dappled light of their little world.

"Funny," she says. "Because I'm here to hurt you."

She throws herself at Saint Voyne, lips peeled back in a snarl, and catches him around the waist. In Voyne's guise, the saint is far more solid, heavier and more thoroughly muscled, and if not for Treila's dagger, could no doubt just absorb the blow. But the blade glints in the garden's filtered, shaking light, and Saint Voyne dances back, sidesteps before Treila can strike home.

Treila falls forward, spins, rights herself. Gets her footing.

Voyne's mouth is hard now, and it's harder to see the Loving Saint in her. Her eyes glint. She is menace and power and skill.

Treila darts forward again.

This time, she is lucky; her blade catches Voyne's armor, and it should glance right off, but instead it sinks in, slides home. It's just Voyne's arm beneath, but it draws a cry all the same. Draws blood. Voyne roars and swings her fist; her knuckles slam into Treila's side, send her sprawling.

Treila tumbles in the dirt. Rolls to her feet. Gets back up, grinning even as she gasps for breath.

It's just like their old sparring matches, except that back then, they both had swords, and Treila obeyed the forms drilled into her. Now she is a wild thing, scrapping for survival. She slashes out with her blade again and when that strike is dodged, she grabs at hair, at clothing, at flesh. If Saint Voyne gets close enough, Treila will tear her throat out with her teeth.

She doesn't get a chance. Voyne sends her crashing to the ground again, this time with a knee to the gut. Treila loses her grip and the blade goes flying, hitting the dirt and skidding into the undergrowth.

"Don't fight me," Voyne spits, all her weight on top of Treila now. "Don't be afraid."

"Does it make the meat sour?" Treila hisses back.

Voyne flinches.

It's enough. It's enough that Treila can squirm out from under her, can pitch forward, toward the knife, and—

And then she is struck in the back, borne down hard against the bench. Voyne's fist is around her throat. Treila thrashes, manages to get onto her back but no farther. Voyne is between her legs, and Treila can't help but laugh at that. Even now, this is the Loving Saint's nature. He is lust and hunger and temptation.

She has, perhaps, three heartbeats left until the saint begins his feast. Voyne's form is strong and heavy, and Treila can only writhe between him and the bench.

The only mercy is that the ringing in her head has, finally, gone silent.

"How will you have me, then?" she snarls. "Now that you've got me here at last?"

That drags a wicked laugh from him, and he leans down closer, so that their lips are almost touching. He looks into her eyes, and still, there's some shred of desperation there. Some question. He didn't want it to pan out this way.

Voyne didn't want it to pan out this way.

It doesn't matter who she's talking to, not now. It's both of them together. If the Loving Saint wants to devour her in Voyne's skin, then he will take the brunt of all her combined rage, all her spite and vitriol.

"You never knew me. You will never know me. That core of me you were so keen to take the measure of, you'll choke on it before you get the smallest part of me. You're weak, pathetic, hungry, clawing after scraps, too afraid to rule yourself." When Treila grins, she knows there's blood coating her teeth. "What you wouldn't give to be in charge, but you'll never have the strength. Too busy aching in the shadows. We're the same, the two of us. You're just desperate to be seen. So desperate you'll kill for it. Die for it."

The Loving Saint falters, finally. Stares down at her, brows drawn together, fist loosening around her throat.

It's an opening. It's the last opening she'll ever get. It's action or death and, above all else, Treila refuses to die.

So she arches up and kisses Voyne's split and bloodied lips.

40

REILA DE BATROLIN, fierce and broken, kisses like she is dying.

Voyne returns her fervor before she can think better of it, blood high in her ears, body trembling. This is who she could not see. This is the hole in the world. The iron she'd gripped so tightly must have pulled the scales from her eyes, and revealed Phosyne's co-conspirator, her way out. Treila de Batrolin.

She is the living embodiment of the moment Voyne began to doubt, before she was King Cardimir's decorative defender, before she was reduced to ornamentation, stolen from the field. When Lord de Batrolin plotted against her liege, Voyne had turned without hesitation on an old friend, a mentor, and slaughtered him in front of an audience.

In front of this girl, trusting and so full of promise.

She'd meant to keep track of her, after. To keep her safe somehow. She'd failed, and Treila had been lost, thought dead. The winter had been hard. The winter had been more than hard. Later, Voyne had read reports of what was found when the ice thawed: bodies reduced to gnawed and pot-polished bone, the refugees of de Batrolin's household reduced to nothing.

But Treila hadn't died. No, she'd lived, and she is wild now in Voyne's arms. They fall from the bench, to the ground, tangled in each other. This is not the compulsion to throw herself on Phosyne's mercy; this is older, darker. This is five years of desperation, knowing that Treila had trusted her, *wanted* her in her adolescent fervor, awkward and so sure despite it.

It's good that Treila is so red in tooth and claw; when Voyne saw her, meek and vulnerable in the garden for that brief moment before she fled, it had galled her to her very core. Treila de Batrolin, broken by what Voyne had done to her—if she'd been left with her mind for much longer, if the monsters had not arrived, it would have been Treila who destroyed Voyne from the inside out.

She still might.

"I'm sorry," she gasps. "I'm sorry, I'm sorry, I didn't know—"

Treila doesn't let her speak. She rolls them over, straddles Voyne, and she is so small, so light.

"Did you make me want you?" Treila asks, pulling back just far enough to see how her eyes flash. "Did you know from the start? Was it always your intention to break me?"

"Never," Voyne says, aching, clumsy hands fisting in Treila's soft clothing. She needs armor. She needs to be protected.

Treila surges back down for another kiss, arches, stretches against her. One of her hands leaves Voyne's side, but Voyne is drowning, too confused, too overwhelmed. This is not how she wanted this to go, but somehow it is perfect. Treila was right, of course; she has spent too long aching in the shadows.

But there's no way for Voyne to come before her still serving a king. No way to make amends if the False Lady once again hides Treila from her sight. No way to hold her if she is too tightly tangled in Phosyne's spiraling web.

She can't serve Treila, but she can protect her.

Treila returns to her fully, and Voyne reaches up to cradle her jaw. She kisses her tenderly, now, trying to tell her everything. Trying to make things right.

Pain blossoms in her throat.

Voyne looks down to see Treila's fist forced against her neck. In that fist is the hilt of her dagger. The blade is buried deep. It has cut through her esophagus, her trachea, her veins and arteries and everything that she needs to live.

Strange.

She never thought she'd die like this.

41

HOSYNE IS STILL sitting on the throne when she feels something snap inside her.

The pain emanates from her throat, just below her jaw. It is sharp, stabbing, nowhere close to her heart, but the meaning is undeniable enough. Either she is dying or—

Or something has happened to Ser Voyne.

All she needs to do to check is close her eyes, but she doesn't want to look away from her audience for even a second. They ring the throne and Jacynde behind it, staying at a polite distance for the time being. She can't quite make out where one figure ends and the other begins. In the gloom of the throne room, they are little more than smudges of flashing pigment, glittering gold where their lips part and they show their teeth.

They aren't talking. Aren't making any sound at all now, save for their breathing.

They are waiting.

Phosyne isn't sure if they're waiting for her to show weakness or to show strength. She's still a little intoxicated, still fixed on the memory of Ser Voyne's skin under her hands, Voyne's obedience under her voice. She'd been beautiful even in her agony, and the memory makes her shudder. She's not supposed to think that.

What is she becoming?

42

ER VOYNE LIES dead in the garden.

Her hair remains dark. Her face is slack and unchanging, no sharp teeth revealed by her parted lips. Beestings pock her scalp, gnarl her hands. Nothing at all marks her as anything but a mortal woman.

And Treila has killed her.

"I didn't mean to," she says to nobody. Her voice wavers. Her eyes pulse with unshed, unbidden tears.

Didn't you? her own thoughts whisper back.

She did mean to. Of course she meant to. But Voyne being dead was never the point; the point was to see her suffer. To *cause* her suffering. And instead, Treila didn't even know who it was she was killing until it was too late.

That's it. That's why she's crying now, finally, unable to stop herself.

It's not because it felt so good, kissing her, that she'd almost forgotten the knife entirely.

She's still huddled by the body when, minutes or hours later, she hears movement from the other side of the thicket surrounding them. Not footsteps, not quite. It sounds more like plants being pulled over one another, a sort of cyclical shushing almost like waves on a shoreline. For a moment, Treila is frozen. She doesn't want to leave Voyne's side, doesn't want to lurch back into motion again.

By the time she remembers to panic, it's too late to grab the knife, even if she could bring herself to touch it. She slides back into the shadow of the greenery and watches, empty-handed, as the saints emerge on the other side of the clearing.

The Loving Saint is first. He's not bothering with any mask of civility; he's still the hungry thing from the stairwell. His head moves from side to side as if he's scenting the air. Scenting her, scenting shame. But if he is, the whole clearing is dripping with it; there's no way he'll be able to pinpoint her.

She thinks.

At any rate, Voyne's corpse catches his attention in the next instant. His lips part. His brows draw down.

"Well," he says, "that answers a few questions."

"It raises a few more," his companion says, his voice shivering through several notes at once. Treila's head throbs, the ringing that had faded as she grappled for her life kicking up once more.

The Absolving Saint comes to stand over Ser Voyne's body, disgust twisting his silvered lips. His attention fixes upon the handle of the knife where it protrudes, unmoving, from her throat. There's so much blood, spilling out beneath her, painting the dirt.

The Loving Saint recognizes the dagger. It's the only explanation for the way his lips twist, for just a moment, into a feral grin. But he doesn't say anything. Only looks up and scans the closest shadows—for her, no doubt.

Treila does not breathe.

He's proud of her, she thinks. Or proud of himself. What a tangle he's made of her (or has she made it of herself?).

"I'll tell the Lady Her pet is dead," he says.

And then the Loving Saint flits out of existence. A blink, and he is gone.

Assumptively alone, the Absolving Saint crouches beside Voyne. He does not touch. Not her skin, not her armor, not the blade itself. That disgust is louder, now. He looks almost ill. "What a waste," he murmurs. Treila doesn't think he's referring to the death.

After that, he is silent, and she is hollow. The quiet wraps around them both. It is strangling. It leaves no room for her panic or her sorrow, only dull attention. It's too risky to leave, but she doesn't want to leave. She doesn't want to be parted from Voyne, not any more than she's already managed. She knows she should go to Phosyne, tell her what has happened. Tell her they still have a way out. Tell her about

how afraid the Loving Saint is of iron, of how much its mere appearance disgusts the Absolving Saint. There are so many threads to tug
on that might lead the way to victory or, at least, safety.

They all feel so limp in her hands. She's not quite sure who she
is now.

She feels unmoored.

A part of her hopes that when the Loving Saint returns, he appears
just behind her. Close enough to bite the shell of her ear, whisper a
greeting, and then tear her own throat out. But when, at last, he does
rejoin them, he comes on foot once more, from the direction he came
before. This time, the plants part and stay parted. They form a path.

And once more, he is not alone.

With him are, of all people, Edouart and Simmonet. They're
too small to lift Voyne's weight alone, of course, so there are others
too—but Treila can't look away from them. She watches as they take
Voyne's shoulders, indifferent to the gore, indifferent even to who
they are dragging away. She remembers a night that feels like a lifetime ago, when she played dice with them and listened to them wax
poetic about Ser Voyne's strength. Her glory.

They don't care, now. It's all been washed out of their brains. Ser
Voyne is just an object in their hands.

No better than meat.

43

HOSYNE, STILL HEARTSORE and vertiginous, is spared the need to choose her next action when the door to the hall swings open. Behind it is the Constant Lady, in Her full raiment, alone. No saints in attendance, no human followers, just Her in all Her terrible loveliness. Some details have shifted, though, truth shining through the mask She wears. The yellow paint upon Her cheeks and lips is stained a deeper orange. The blooms woven into Her gown have grown wild with thorns.

When She walks, Her steps ring as if She is shod in metal shoes.

The ring of watchers parts to let Her through. She stops only a few feet away, languidly surveying Phosyne and her throne.

"It suits you well," She says, brow quirked, lips pursed. "My lesson helped you, then? You've shed your paupers' guise and found a place of power."

Phosyne's mouth curls in a snarl. She isn't in the mood for this. She needs to go to Voyne, find out what has happened. Her hand falls away from her throat, curls around the armrest of the throne once more. "Your creatures trap me here."

"Do they?" She glances over Her shoulder at them, lifts a hand.

They fall back, respectful of Her power. They remind Phosyne of how Aymar used to defer to Cardimir, how the nuns responded to Jacynde. There is a hierarchy, something more than a master to Her beasts.

They climb back into the window slits, block them up until there's no light at all except for the flickering flames of the reeds. They're burning low. How long has she been here?

"You can leave at any time," the Lady says. She strokes one of Her thick braids. Her nails are long and sharp; were they always this way?

Or is the time for disguises long past?

Slowly, cautiously, Phosyne stands. Her robes cling to her thighs, sweat-stuck to the skin below, but a twitch of her hand sets them right. She doesn't know if she actually touches the silk to do it.

"An improvement, to be sure," the Lady says with a smile. "Look at you. So imperious. I expected it would take you far longer to find a throne, little mouse."

I only took it because—

The protest dies in her throat. Because why? Because Voyne needed her to? No. Because Phosyne wanted to see what would happen? Closer, and she feels horrible for it.

She says nothing, tamping down the swirl of questions. She can't afford weakness, not in front of the Lady.

"Are you going to flee back to your room?" the Lady asks. "I saw your work. Very nicely done. Your beautiful little world has strong walls of its own now."

She is leading up to something. Phosyne knows it, but can't divine what it is. "I am not fleeing," she says, meeting the Lady's gaze. Her eyes remain those unnerving rings upon rings of color. "But I am leaving." Phosyne steels herself, goes to step past Her.

The Lady reaches out and touches her wrist.

It's a light touch, not enough to stop her, but it makes Phosyne falter all the same.

"Stay a moment," the Lady says, voice quiet, for her ears only. "You and I, we have much to discuss."

"I want no more lessons."

The Lady makes a small, doubting sound, but doesn't push. "Are you afraid, little mouse?"

"Of course." She sees no point in lying. The windows are full of shifting impossibilities. Her stomach remains all but empty. She thinks she hears screaming from the yard, though it's hard to tell; it might be singing. "I've seen your hunger."

"I sup on flesh and bone, petal and root, the same as you, but more rarified things besides: lust and longing, fear and ecstasy."

The madness in the yard below. The dancing of the people of Aymar, their hedonistic dissolution. All of it to feed Her and Her creatures.

"You play with your food," Phosyne says.

"I season my meat, and keep it occupied. I give it fertile fields to fat itself. You will see soon, little mouse. You will come to understand the satisfaction of having everything available to your teeth. I can see your hunger, too."

And Phosyne *is* hungry. But it's not the hunger of an empty stomach. It's the need to taste. To chew. To consume. She wants to indulge.

She tamps down on the urge. That is what led her to that throne, what led her to command Voyne, to take what she wanted with no thought to their surroundings, the danger they were in.

Phosyne realizes she is trembling.

She stays perfectly still as the Lady slides Her hand up Phosyne's wrists to the sleeves of her robe, fingering the fabric. She makes herself watch the progression of those pollen-stained fingertips, and as she does, she realizes these robes are familiar. They are very much like Jacynde's. They are very much like the Lady's.

When did she do that? *Did* she do that, or did they change when she wasn't looking, the way the painted faces watching them move whenever her gaze slips off them?

Phosyne doesn't remember. The trembling is getting worse. She must be stronger than this, if she is going to walk out of here in one piece.

"Do you fancy yourself Jacynde's replacement?" the Lady asks.

She flinches. She can't help it. "No."

"And yet she is dead behind this throne you've taken for your own, with Ser Voyne's sword straight through her."

"I didn't place her there."

"But you had taken her into your care. Did you abandon her, little mouse, to fend for herself? That is a cruel thing to do. You surprise me."

"I needed to build my walls," Phosyne whispers.

"And you did not want to take on an obligation to somebody else."

Quiet, a moment. Even the bees seem to go still. The Lady touches Phosyne's jaw, still featherlight, and applies just a little pressure. An indication, a request.

Phosyne looks at her once more. They are of a height.

"Tell me, little mouse—would you go into your room, that pretty, sheltered world of yours, and leave all of this behind, if you knew it would sustain you?"

A night ago, she would have said yes.

Now, though, the world has gotten a little bigger. Her desires have grown teeth. "No," she says. "No, I want freedom."

"An understandable want. I can fulfill it."

Phosyne bares her teeth in something that is not a smile. "And what would you require in return?"

"There are many things you could give me," the Lady says. Her hand has not moved. "The exchange, I think, could benefit us both. We are not so different."

Phosyne closes her eyes for just a moment, for just long enough to see that the Lady blazes before her, but that she burns with nearly the same intensity.

She reaches out, touches the Lady's cheek, mirroring perfectly. Her eyes are open again. Her mind is racing.

"Were you like me once?" she asks.

The Lady cants Her head. Considers. Drops Her hand and steps back so that She can regard the full length of Phosyne.

"Do you mean, was I earthbound? Was I born of a womb, and did I drink milk as a babe? No." Her gaze flicks up. "But could you be like me, one day? I think that is the far more interesting question, little mouse, and I think it is the one you mean to ask."

Phosyne's throat is very dry. She is thinking of sinking into stone. Of lighting candles with blood. Of bewitching a whole castle into feasting upon its own.

She has never questioned where her power comes from—only where the knowledge does.

The Lady smiles. It is gentle. She holds out both hands.

Phosyne struggles not to take them.

"Give me your name, little mouse," She murmurs, "and I will give you your answer."

And for one blistering, parched moment, Phosyne wants to.

But then she thinks of how the Lady says Ser Voyne's name: with ownership. She would do the same with Phosyne's. There's a power in it, a worth, or else She would not be asking for it.

The Lady notes her hesitation. Steps closer. Their audience holds its breath, waiting to see what Phosyne will do.

"Give me your name, and the nightmare will end."

Phosyne lifts her chin. Pulls her hands into fists at her sides.

"What do you have to gain from this?" she asks. "You have every soul in this castle as it stands. Surely you have everything you desire."

"Not everything. And not every soul."

"So you want mine."

The Lady doesn't deny it.

This does not match her understanding of the situation. Phosyne is not important—or, at least, she *was* not important. The Lady and Her saints have come to devour this castle, and Phosyne is only a curiosity, an unexpected snare in their plan. But then she thinks of the feast, of being laid like an offering at the Lady's feet, and how delighted the Lady had been to see her. How quickly She'd become fascinated.

Her world is getting smaller. Her breathing is growing faster, shallower, panic threatening to pull her under completely. She staggers away from the Lady, mind racing, eyes darting around the room. She is surrounded on all sides. They shift and spark in her periphery, flat white faces getting closer, and they have teeth, they have so many *teeth*, and she has teeth too, she could tear them all to pieces—

No. No, she has to get out.

She will go to Ser Voyne, wherever she is, and throw herself on her mercy. Beg understanding. Ask for a plan, any plan, because they are running out of time and have no more room for games.

She is in the doorway when the Lady's next words strike.

"You will not find your knight out there, little mouse."

Phosyne halts. The skin along her spine crawls. Her throat aches. "What have you done with her?" she asks, fighting to keep her tone even.

"Nothing at all. But your Ser Voyne is dead."

The pain in her throat intensifies. It is like a blade cutting through flesh and gristle. Phosyne sways on her feet from it, from the horror in her gut and the answering anger that flares to life beneath it.

Treila is gone. Voyne is gone.

Phosyne is here, alone among the wolves.

"No," she whispers. "No, I refuse."

The Lady draws even with her once more. Holds out a hand.

"Come and look upon her yourself," the Lady says.

Phosyne, lost, takes it.

44

HEY TAKE SER Voyne to the chapel. Treila follows, head down, ducking out of sight when she is able. When she realizes where they are headed, she takes another route, and finds herself unseen, as if when Voyne at last looked upon her and saw her once more, Treila disappeared to all the rest of the world.

Or maybe she is so grief-stricken that she doesn't notice when others are close, as long as they don't reach for her.

Either way, she approaches the chapel alone. But just outside, she stops. The space, usually bright and open, is crowded and shadowed. Everything, every hive box and pew and abandoned icon of the saints is covered in honeycomb. What was once so meticulously maintained is now all but buried, encrusted and sealed shut with wax. In the gloom, flames dance atop what Treila realizes with a lurch are timekeeping candles—but made tall and monstrous, winding and uneven. No wonder night and day seem to blur together, if that is how each hour is being measured.

The room hums with the beating of a thousand wings, the air darkened by a roiling swarm of bees.

She has arrived before Voyne's body, but not by much. She sees them approaching, the bearers with their shuffling feet and unseeing eyes. For all their bewitched sleepwalking, though, they look strong. Well-fed. Cheeks are flushed with life, and nobody trembles or stumbles beneath the weight they carry.

The knife in Voyne's throat is barely noticeable, past the bright gleam of her strange armor.

And then she is gone, inside the chapel, down a walkway that Treila cannot see from her current vantage. She circles around to another entrance.

She hesitates, flinches as a bee circles her and makes as if to land. Feels again that desperate winter, her body swollen and stung, cast out. They could do it again. Descend upon her, drive her away. Are they not the Lady's? No. The Lady is not the Priory's Lady. She is something else, something worse; the Loving Saint made that very clear.

She forces herself to edge into the chapel. There is nowhere Treila can step that will not break and spill a surge of honey, and so she doesn't try to be careful. With each step, she waits for the bees to come to her. But they don't. They mass in great undulations farther in, or crawl upon the fresh comb, but none come close to her.

She finds herself a little gap, a cradle of wax that guards her on three sides, with barely an opening wide enough for her to enter. From within, she can see most angles, with a little stretching. She is careful, as she settles in, not to step on any bees.

Her heart slowing, she notices, finally, that the sharp-toothed watchers of the yard are all but absent.

The only creatures in this chapel, aside from the bees, are human. The pallbearers kneel before the plinth where Ser Voyne has been laid out, as if for a funeral.

Her father, Treila thinks with a pang, had no funeral. So many of her father's servants were buried in a poorly marked grave in a winter wood. But perhaps she should take joy that Voyne's funeral will be more perverse by far.

The knife still protrudes from Voyne's neck. Treila doesn't know why. It's garish, gleaming in the harsh sun that filters in, almost as bright as the shine of her breastplate.

No, not hers. The Warding Saint's.

Treila finally realizes that she hasn't seen him anywhere.

It's only the Absolving and the Loving Saints who appear at the chapel's entrance. They take up posts by the doorway, but aside from their positioning, they look quite at their leisure. The Loving Saint sips from a chalice. It is gold. It is likely the king's.

When he lowers it, his lips are red. He is drinking blood like it is wine.

It is eat or be eaten.

Treila clenches her fist, feels the absence where her little finger should be.

And then the Lady enters. It is the first time Treila has seen Her since the feast. She still wears Her holy raiment, her garlands of flowers, and here, in this chapel, She is horrifyingly at home. She should be sitting on a dais. She should be accepting prayers.

She does not enter alone.

Phosyne is with Her. Nothing has dimmed her newfound cleanliness, the perfection of her robes, her skin. The squalor of the world cannot touch her, and she seems to accumulate light, illuminated out of keeping with the darkened chapel. Treila's mouth goes dry at the sight; she looks like she has been carved out of marble. She looks like she belongs here.

It takes a moment for Treila to realize who is missing: the king. Cardimir should be in attendance at Ser Voyne's funeral, to mourn the passing of his pet. Should be, but his regency is hollow: ever since the Lady first stepped foot inside of Aymar, he has abdicated all responsibility. Wherever he is, Treila doubts he'd care to know his prized knight is lost.

Useless. So useless.

As the Lady and Phosyne near the plinth, Phosyne slows, then stops. Her shoulders grow tense. Her chin lifts with the sort of brittle sharpness that Treila recognizes all too well.

"And where is your Warding Saint?" she asks. This is clearly the continuation of some other conversation, started far away from here.

"Dead as well," the Lady replies.

"The armor?"

"I imagine she took it before her own death. It was her hand that killed him."

"And who killed her?"

"I do not know."

At the door, the Loving Saint shifts, but says nothing. Treila shrinks deeper into the shadows.

Phosyne finally moves once more. She drifts up to the plinth and lays both hands upon it, not touching Voyne's body. Her shoulders sag. She looks very tired.

"Dead," she says, softly. "And neither of us there to see it."

The Lady hums, and approaches as well. She is watching Phosyne, though, not the body. Her eyes glitter in the warm half-light.

"You knew, the whole time we spoke?"

"I did. Does it change your decision?"

What decision? Treila leans closer, eyes fixed. What has Phosyne agreed to?

"It depends. Do you know of a way to reverse death?" Phosyne's voice is acid.

Treila thinks the Lady is smiling. It's hard to tell from here.

"I might," She says. "Give her to me."

Phosyne's inhale is audible. Sharp. "No."

"Give her to me," the Lady says, "and you may ask for anything in return."

Anything.

Buried in that promise is a hint of hope. *Anything* might include Voyne's resurrection. But it might not. The Lady has promised everything and nothing all at once. She has not guaranteed She will even grant a request, only that Phosyne can make it.

She'd be foolish to say yes. Treila wishes she could go to her, show Phosyne her hand again, the side of her head. Make her understand that bargains are all tricks. That she must be careful what she is giving up.

And Phosyne looks like she's about to say yes.

It is all Treila can do not to cry out, to rush to the plinth and throw herself across the body there. *You did this,* she reminds herself. Ser Voyne is now nothing but flesh. On that day, back in the garden before it was twisted and warped into what it has become, she had told Ser Voyne that she understood what hunger demanded.

Phosyne settles one hand on the gleaming armor that covers Voyne's chest. Her head is bowed. Treila can't see her face. Can't judge what she is thinking.

Treila holds her breath.

"You can't touch her, can you?" Phosyne says, breaking her long silence. She reaches out as she says it, trails one finger along the hilt of Treila's blade. It's simple. Utilitarian. "Not while this is here. Otherwise, you'd just take her. You wouldn't need to ask."

The Lady's jaw tightens. "Always clever, little mouse. Always so perceptive."

"And they can't touch her, either." A glance to the saints.

"No. None of my kind."

"But mortal hands may." Phosyne indicates Edouart and Simmonet with a flick of her gaze.

"They may." The Lady does not look happy, to give these concessions, but She does give them. Her generosity makes Treila nervous.

"And yet you did not have them pull the blade out." There's a hint of childlike wonder in Phosyne's voice that does not match the fierce pride in her eyes as she looks back up at the Lady. "Because they can't either, can they?"

The Lady does not respond.

"But you think I can. So rephrase your offer. You will give me anything I ask for, if . . ."

She has reworded it herself. The Lady knows it, too. She tenses. She says nothing.

Phosyne huffs a small laugh.

"Send your scavengers away," Phosyne murmurs, barely loud enough for Treila to hear, "and leave me to think. And then the two of us can speak again."

Treila half expects the Lady to strike out at Phosyne. To physically haul her from Voyne's body, to threaten, to assault. But instead, She inclines Her head. "Always clever, little mouse," She repeats.

She lifts a hand.

In the next moment, the chapel is empty, save for Phosyne, Treila, and the pallbearers, who are as still as statues, heedless of anything outside their skulls.

And Voyne, of course.

Without the audience, the chapel feels larger. Outside, the sun is near the horizon somewhere out of sight; Treila can't tell if it's dawn or dusk, if either has any meaning anymore. Whichever it is, it's made the bees quiescent.

Phosyne returns to the plinth. Her fingers hover over the dagger, then over the gleaming plate covering Voyne's chest. Her gaze is fixed on Voyne's face, as if she is waiting for an answer.

"I know you're there," Phosyne says. It's not aimed at Voyne.

Treila flinches.

"Come out, please," she adds, voice softening. "Don't make me do this alone."

Treila rises from her sticky nest, but takes only two steps, just enough to be visible around the pillar. The pallbearers do not look up.

Phosyne finally looks away from Voyne, taking Treila's measure.

Treila's clothing is stiff with blood.

"It was me," she says, before Phosyne can accuse. Easier, to take the blame directly, than to wait for Phosyne to put the pieces together.

More dangerous, though; Phosyne's expression twists into a livid snarl. Treila braces, in case she lunges.

But they are different creatures. Phosyne's weapon is not her body. And that does nothing to dull the edge of her voice as she murmurs, "You took what was mine, Treila."

If anything, it makes Treila more afraid.

"Yours?" Treila breathes. *No, mine,* she thinks.

And at that, the dark cloud on Phosyne's brow breaks. It doesn't disperse, though, merely fractures. Pain flashes through. Cautiously, Treila comes closer. Holds out a hand.

"Yours?" she repeats, a question now instead of an argument.

And slowly, Phosyne kneels before her. Covers her face with her hands. Her shoulders spasm.

Treila rests one blood-stained hand on top of her head.

"Before," Phosyne confesses. "I found her in the throne room. She was trapped."

Trapped, where Treila knows the Lady found Jacynde. Where the sound of a blade parting flesh had rung out. Had Voyne been there, too? No, the Loving Saint would have used that if he could have.

"I took the throne," Phosyne says, voice muffled by her palms.

"And she came to me on bended knee. No. I *made* her come to me on bended knee. And I didn't feel bad about it for a second. You . . . I think you should have left me to die on the floor."

Treila lets out a jagged little laugh at that. Her fingers tighten, tangle in Phosyne's hair. "And I should have let the Loving Saint eat me."

Phosyne's surprised inhale is rough. It catches in her throat like a blade has pierced there, too. But she lifts her head. Treila lets her hand fall back to her side. They stare at each other, at their failures, their weaknesses.

"It's all a mess," Treila whispers, when she can hold it in no longer. "Every bit of it. We should leave. For real, this time. It will cost us, though."

"It will cost us either way," Phosyne says. She scowls and wipes at her mouth, climbs back up to her feet. She looks at Voyne. "There are things the Lady wants. That She finds valuable. If I can find the right combination, strike the right bargain—I could still fix this."

"Could you?" Treila asks. She's not so certain.

"I could," Phosyne says.

Treila does not ask how she knows.

Phosyne stares down at the knight for a long, silent moment, then shakes her head, plucks at her robes. Steps back. "Take her," she says. "Take her, down to the tunnels. Hide her there. But don't leave."

"Can we even hide, now?" Treila asks. "There are so many of them."

Phosyne holds up a hand, closes her eyes. A faint note thrums upon the air. It sets the bees back to buzzing. Treila shivers, falls back a step instinctively.

Then Phosyne opens her eyes once more, and all is as it was. "It's safe, there. The same force that kept Voyne from following us in will keep the Lady and Her creatures out."

"And the distance from here to there?"

"Will not be easily crossed. But I think I can distract them. They want me at least as much as they want her. I will use that."

"What has happened to you?" Treila asks, even as she edges closer to Voyne's body. "What *are* you?"

Phosyne's smile is hollow. She does not answer.

Instead, she goes to stand before the pallbearers. She is every inch the saint now, in this aspect, in this place. She has the clothing, the bearing, the command. She could be carried about the wall on a litter, and not look out of place.

"I know you have drunk of my water," Phosyne tells them. They lift their heads at that. "I know that you reside, the smallest fraction, in my domain. You will help Treila bear this body a little farther, and then you will find a quiet, shady place to rest."

Treila covers her mouth, then turns away. She does not want to see this.

But she can still hear it. The rustle of clothing, the creak of joints. There is no answering speech. No acknowledgment, or gratitude, or hatred. Only bodies, coming to lift Voyne up once more.

And the sound of Phosyne leaving.

Treila stands motionless for a long time. Too long, she is certain, but she is so tired. She hurts so much, and there is still work to be done.

But she has been here before. She has dragged herself out through the dark of the forest.

She grits her teeth and leads the way to the tunnel below the keep.

WHATEVER IT IS that Phosyne does to draw the attention of the Lady's creatures, it works; Treila sees no trace of the many-limbed flat things, though she sees the wreckage of their hunger. Blood stains on the stone. Bits of scalp and hair. Bones in the windowsills. The saints were gentle, by comparison.

There is not much time left.

When they reach the workshop, Treila bids Edouart and Simmonet and all the rest to leave Voyne there. They obey. They do not recognize her, or even mark her, save to follow her command.

She gives the two boys a shred of dried fruit all the same. She makes them eat it, and then she releases them.

Alone, she regards Voyne. She regards herself. She regards the gap in the rock. It will be hard to drag Voyne through in her armor. It will be hard to pull with Treila's skirts tangled around her legs. But she can't bring herself to change a single thing about them, not yet, not even for pragmatism's sake.

So when she backs into the hole and grabs Voyne's shoulders to haul after her, she does it stumbling and falling and cursing.

The tunnels are wide enough now, at least, that Treila can pull Voyne's corpse alongside her as she descends. It is not easy, and in the dark, she feels too dearly how Voyne's skin is only the temperature of the air, how strange and slack her limbs are. She will stiffen soon enough in the rigor of death, and she will be even harder to move, so Treila does not allow herself to falter. She gives herself no breaks. She pulls and tugs and when Voyne's armor catches on the rock, Treila squirms between the body and the stone to get to the blockage, to maneuver them both to safety.

Safety. Treila wants to laugh. Treila *is* laughing by the time she reaches the cavern.

It's still lit by Phosyne's candle, flickering bravely against the black, and it gives her enough light to find a good spot to lay out Voyne's body. It's a flat stretch just beside the glowing little creek, far from the crack in the wall at the other end. Between the golden light of the candle and the blue cast of the stream, Voyne's face is a sculpted death mask.

She looks peaceful, somehow. Even where the stone has scraped her forehead raw.

Treila settles a hand on Voyne's chest. Her fingertips can just reach the blood-sticky skin of her throat, and after a moment's resistance, Treila gives in. Feels her skin simply to feel it, instead of to perform a task. She is so very solid. So very real. Not a ghost, not a fragment of Treila's past.

When Treila bows her head, she feels a surge of longing. It is clear, and piercing, and it cuts through everything else inside of her.

This is not how Voyne was meant to die. This is not how Treila wanted to be reunited with her.

Treila wanted Voyne in her glory days, after she had liberated Carcabonne and come to Treila's home to recover. She wanted the woman, strong and beautiful and noble, who had indulged Treila's desires to learn swordplay, who had allowed Treila to fawn and flirt. A kindness to Voyne's host; generosity to his daughter. Treila has always wanted that Voyne precisely for her impossibility. To find her would have been to go back before that long winter. Back before Voyne had sliced Treila's father's head off.

Before Treila had learned what suffering was.

She curls her fingers around the hilt and wishes she had Phosyne's power to remove the blade. She longs for the safety of the knife in her hand once more.

But no, that's not right. She doesn't want to hold it; she wants it gone.

It's insulting, sticking out of Voyne's throat. Wrong. She wants, so badly, to give Voyne a shred of dignity, to have the blade removed, to let her *rest*, and suddenly it seems like the most important thing in all the world. Down here, there's only one hungry mouth, and it waits for the candle to be extinguished. Down here, the Lady cannot reach Voyne, and so Voyne can lie in gentle repose until Phosyne finds an answer.

Phosyne is not going to find an answer. Treila saw the hunger in her eyes. Phosyne is a moment's weakness from becoming like the Lady.

There's no point in staying. Treila eyes the gap, and the pain of losing her finger, her ear, echoes through her. She glances down at Voyne, at her hand on the knife. If she could only pull the knife out, she could offer Voyne in place of her.

She could.

She wouldn't.

What she wants, what she truly wants, is to unspool time. Go back to when Voyne was alive and they were curled together in the garden. If Treila hadn't grabbed for the knife—if she had listened, actually listened, and realized that they were playing out, in terrible irony, the opposite of when Voyne had knelt at her feet and thought her the Lady—

Well. Things could have been very different, couldn't they?

Treila's hand shifts on the knife, loosens, almost falls away. A sob hitches in her chest. "You taught me how to fight," she tells Voyne. "It's not fair that this one time, I wasn't supposed to." Her fingers tighten. Stubbornly, petulantly, childishly, she tugs on the blade.

It slides free.

45

ESURRECTION IS NOT so different from coming back to herself in the cistern.

There is the tectonic shift, a fundamental reordering of her mind, her body, her very being. There is the chill, settling deep into her bones. And above it all there is the disorientation, the sudden realization that there are holes in her memories, that she does not know where she is, that something has gone very wrong.

But there are fewer tears this time.

Instead of crying, she convulses. She gasps for breath. She clutches her throat and writhes on what feels like stone, but is uneven, uncarved, far more natural. She doesn't know where she is, but she knows she is cold, and that breathing is hard.

It becomes less hard with every breath, though. That's not usually how this goes.

And it's not Phosyne beside her, but—

Golden hair. Wide, evaluating eyes. Treila de Batrolin crouches, curled in on herself, across a small, glowing creek. She's clutching her dagger tight. In the low light, Voyne can still see the metal is dark with her blood.

Old blood. There is no fresh blood beneath her hands, and no incision in the skin below. Her fingers flex and bend without issue, all the swelling of her beestings gone. Her trembling slows. Voyne realizes, with a strange buoyancy, that she is *alive*.

And that just a few moments ago, she was in a garden. She was kissing a figment of her past. That figment had murdered her. That figment is watching her now, with an expression that Voyne has no idea how to read, knife at the ready.

On the battlefield, she is trained to be a snarling, vicious beast. And in captivity, in Aymar, she has strained at her leash and burned to transmute frustrated rage into furious action. But death, she finds, is not so galling as *dying*. And her memory of dying is oddly pleasant. A relief, a surprise, a final lack of struggle. Perhaps that is why she's not angry. Why she isn't primed to rip and tear and *fight*.

Or maybe it's that when the spasms pass, Voyne is too exhausted to sit up. Too exhausted to defend herself.

"Will you kill me again?" she asks, finally, when she thinks she can speak. It comes out in a hoarse croak.

Treila grimaces, and Voyne notices that it's not only the glow of the water that is illuminating them, but a candle, somewhere behind her. "I might," she says. There's no conviction behind her words. No real threat, Voyne thinks. Whatever drove her in the garden is gone. Transformed into what looks like agony.

She must be as intimately familiar with suffering as that perversion in the throne room had accused Voyne of being, by now. Starvation, frostbite, the loneliness of wandering the land shut out of everything that was once due to her.

It wasn't kind, what Voyne did to her. Perhaps they are evenly matched, now.

"How long have you been here? In Aymar?" she asks. "How long did I not recognize you?"

A coughing fit sweeps her up, cracking at her ribs. Her world goes hazy, then clears again. Treila is a little closer now.

"As long as you've been here," she says. Her whole body is tense. Coiled. She may not be driven to attack, but she may still snap, like a startled dog. The longer she is polite, the tighter she will be wound. Voyne is intimately familiar with the process.

"I killed your father, Treila de Batrolin, and I have no regrets," she says. It is kinder, she thinks, to be honest.

Treila bares her teeth, lunges. But the knife hits the stone between them, and it is just the girl on her, hands trembling even as she fists her hands tight in Voyne's matted braid. Her breath is hot on Voyne's face. Bare inches separate them as Treila's chest heaves, as she struggles to get control over herself.

"No regrets?" Treila whispers. "None at all? So loyal to your master?"

Voyne doesn't look away. "He deserved it," Voyne she says. "After Carcabonne."

Treila's brow creases. Some of the tension bleeds out of her hands. "Carcabonne?" she asks, confused. "What are you talking about? What does Carcabonne have to do with *anything*?"

"Your father died because of Carcabonne."

"My father died so Cardimir would look strong," Treila spits. But her hands have slipped entirely from Voyne now. She gets up, backing away. Something is strange about her hands. One finger, Voyne realizes, is gone. Frostbite, from that winter?

Or something else?

Where *are* they?

"My *father*," Treila says, "was trying to save our people from starving."

Voyne takes the measure of her infirmity. Makes her fingers twitch. Her calves tense. It's not enough. "And what did your father do, to buy the grain he smuggled in?" she asks. Didactic, the way she remembers talking to Treila in those golden months between when she had paid in horrors to win back Carcabonne and when she again spilled blood.

"Salt. He shorted Cardimir his salt. Sent the rest to—to Etrebia."

She is so certain.

"No, he didn't," Voyne says, and shoves herself upright. She gets as far as sitting, then has to sag against the nearby wall.

Across from her, Treila is quivering, taut as a bowstring. "He said we'd sent them salt," she repeats.

"He gave them Carcabonne."

For a long time, Treila doesn't move. Her eyes go unfocused. Voyne wonders what she's thinking about. What she remembers. Carcabonne had been only three months before they'd met. Voyne had been fresh off the field of battle, not newly made a hero but certainly newly shined, when she'd arrived at Treila's father's house. She'd spent much of her recuperation there. And then the king had come to visit, and brought with him the findings of his spymasters, and everything had gone to shit.

Voyne thinks, mostly, of Carcabonne itself. Of the blood. The fire. Etrebia had already held the fort by the time Voyne and her soldiers arrived to take it back; all of Carcabonne's knights had been slain, all its people slaughtered or hauled over the border and sold into slavery. They had come very close to all-out war that winter. But they'd been lucky, heard the first whispers of treason early enough to stop Etrebia from stealing anything else.

It had just taken a while to discover who had sold them out.

"You're lying," Treila whispers, finally.

"No," Voyne tells her.

"Nobody said anything about Carcabonne. When you killed him. When you cut his head off, you said—you said it was the *salt*—"

"I said nothing," Voyne murmurs. She waits for Treila's hands to close around her throat again; they are spasming hard enough at her sides, and Voyne is helpless. Voyne is destroying her world all over again. "But yes, that was the reason Cardimir gave to everybody who asked. Treason, but of a lesser sort. Because we judged it would be better for the king to appear cruel than to appear weak. We cleaned house quietly, after that."

Treila doesn't grab her throat. She covers her own eyes instead, moans into her hands. She sits back on her heels.

She laughs.

The laughter turns to sobs, eventually, and then to silence, and then it is just the two of them, breathing in the semi-dark.

"Five years of my life," Treila says at last. "Five years of my life, trying to defend a massacre. If I had known—"

"If you had known, would you have enjoyed your suffering?"

Treila does not answer.

"I had no other choice but to cast you out," Voyne said. "But that does not make it less terrible. I have no regrets, because I protected my country, but if I could have done it differently . . ."

She trails off, unsure of what she means to say. In the end, all she can string together is, "I am glad you're alive, Treila."

The words ring in the silence of the little grotto they're in. Voyne looks away from the girl, finally, to regard where she is, and what she has left. She is alive; they are underground. She feels like herself. She'd forgotten what that was like. It's like her veins are filled with cool water, steady, strong.

She has been reordered. The Priory would likely have something to say about it. Phosyne, too, surely. Some transmutation. Some alchemy. Death as a transforming fire.

"Help me stand," she commands, half expecting Treila to laugh in her face.

"No," Treila says instead.

"Then tell me where we are."

"Below the keep."

"And the rest of Aymar? The—fiends that have walked its halls?" She realizes, then, how miraculous it is that Treila is here at all. That she isn't up with the horrible throngs, gorging herself on flesh and bewitched fruits. In the strangeness of her resurrection, they had seemed to be in a world all their own. But they haven't left it. "Your mind is clear?"

"Unfortunately," Treila says. "When I killed you, I thought it was the Loving Saint, wearing your face. But that's a more mundane sort of madness, I think."

And finally, it clicks. "Phosyne's way out. You were the one I couldn't see."

Golden hair. Yes, she remembers now, so many of their meetings in the garden.

"We can go," Treila says. "We *should* go. I have food, we have this exit. I've left before. We can do it."

Freedom should be tempting, but there's no cowardice left in her, either; Treila's blade cut that away, along with the fog inside her skull. "No." She tries to rise again, and again her limbs are not quite strong enough. But they are getting stronger.

Treila stares down at her. "You can't mean to die for your king still. Not—not after all of this."

"I don't mean to die at all. I mean to fight. There are too many people still alive up there to abandon. And Phosyne—"

"Phosyne is changing. And not into anything good."

Voyne licks her lips, remembers how Phosyne had looked on the throne. She can't help her shudder. "Then all the more reason to end this. Treila—the knife."

Treila goes to it, eyeing it mistrustfully. As if she does not want to touch it again.

"These creatures can be killed by iron," Voyne says.

"Maybe, but—there are so many. Too many."

"Take the knife," Voyne says again. "Get it to Phosyne. Give it to her. It cut through whatever enchantment had hold of me, it might do the same again." She might not even need to die for it to work; when Voyne had clutched the hammer in her hand, she had been able, at last, to see Treila. "No matter what, she will know what to do with it."

Of that much, Voyne is certain, down to her bones.

Treila is clearly struggling, though, even as she picks up the knife. She has seen something Voyne has not. She is wary. She is clever.

"Brave girl," Voyne murmurs, and Treila looks up at her, stricken, like the blade is in her belly and not her hand. "I trust in the both of you. And I will follow as soon as I am able."

"You're certain?" Treila asks. "You don't think I'll fail?"

"I think you haven't let yourself die so far," Voyne says.

Treila hesitates one last time, then jerks her chin toward the candle. Voyne can see it now, glowing boldly against the dark. It's one of Phosyne's; there's no melted wax around its base.

"If I don't come back," Treila says, "if it's been too long, don't come after me. Don't let them have you again, don't even risk it. Promise me."

"And where would I go?"

"There is a creature, here. In the crack in the wall." She motions with her chin to a line of deeper darkness that splits the dimly lit wall. "While Phosyne's candle burns, it can't hear you. But douse it, go to it, ask to leave. The thing that lives in it can get you outside the walls, just—just negotiate carefully. And don't come back. Only one of us needs to be a fool."

Voyne nods. "I understand. Now, go."

"I'll come back," Treila promises. She hesitates. Voyne wants to touch her, wants to press a kiss to her brow, wants to hold her. But she doesn't need it. What Voyne and Cardimir and the world have made her—what she has made herself—is strong enough on its own.

One last breath, and then Treila pushes herself into the earth and, in another moment, is gone.

Voyne sits, unmoving, for a long time after. She counts her breaths. She tenses and relaxes each of her muscles in turn. When she is ready, she pushes herself forward onto her hands and knees. She crawls to the candle.

She douses it in the creek, then sits back and regards the gash in the world.

"Hello," she says. "Let's have a chat."

46

HE KEEP IS empty when Treila emerges from the tunnel. She expects to see hungry, pale faces as she creeps up the stairs, but there are none. There are no tangles of limbs in the windows. There are not even any sleeping, sated bodies on the floor. The whole edifice is silent, and the pained chaos of Treila's heart quiets with it, knowing that she has no room for feeling, only for caution.

If it is silent, then something has changed. Something has gone wrong.

She must get to Phosyne as quickly as possible. Carcabonne and Ser Voyne and her father can wait a little while longer; they have, after all, waited for five years.

Treila steals out into the courtyard. It is night, and the upper and lower baileys are both empty, though the dirt is stained in too many places. Still, there are no scraps, no bones or torn flesh, no abandoned tents. There is only soil, dusty and dry and barren.

But the great hall's windows blaze with light, and a soft murmuration drifts from them as well.

Treila takes the long way to it, clinging to shadows, back against the stone. She clutches the knife in her hand, watching for any sign of saints or beasts. Ready to fight. Ready to carve a path.

There's no need. She reaches the great hall without seeing so much as a flicker of a shadow that is not hers, and she peers inside.

The room is full of bodies. There is laughter, a hundred voices raised one atop the other, singing at the far margins. There is delight. There is happiness. It shreds at her nerves, discordant, and Treila retreats until she finds an empty window into the corridor that leads into the great hall itself. She tucks her blade in the folds of her skirt and prowls forward, the way she had the night of the feast.

And it is so like the night of the feast, when she enters the great warm room. It feels like the whole of the castle is concentrated here, though Treila knows that to be impossible. The walls could not contain them all. But the crush of bodies is so much tighter and hotter than it was the night of the feast, and the yard outside so empty.

Treila, shivering, pushes her way in. Every brush of skin against skin makes her flinch. She waits for one of the faces to turn, to see her with the Loving Saint's piercing eyes, or the golden blank hunger of the beasts, but there is only mindless rapture. Nobody cares that she steps on their feet, that she crushes them into their neighbor. Nobody reacts at all, except to let her pass.

And then the bodies begin to thin. Each step becomes a little easier. Treila stops just short of falling out of the press of bodies entirely, held up by a flash of yellow—the Lady's face, turned away from her, gazing out to the center of the clearing.

Phosyne stands before Her.

Before them both, the king hangs upside down. He is naked, pale, just a man.

Less than a man; Phosyne has opened his belly, and his organs lie at her feet on golden platters. They have been carefully sorted. His kidneys gleam. His liver glistens. His heart still seems to beat, though Treila is sure that is only a trick of the light, or of her own rising gorge.

In Phosyne's hand is a knife not made of iron but of bone. It is sharp, though; she is flensing the skin from Cardimir's corpse with casual flicks of her wrist. She is focused, wholly, on her work, reducing a great man to nothing more than a hanging side of meat.

She is *fascinated*. Treila can see it in her eyes, when at last she wises up and focuses on the butcher instead of the butchered. It's easier.

And it means she's looking when Phosyne at last realizes that Treila is there.

It's a subtle shift. It's shocking that it happens at all, Phosyne is so clearly enamored with her newest project, her newest investigation.

She doesn't stop, of course, but she moves through the rest of the flaying knowing that Treila is there. She joints the meat knowing that Treila is there. She presents each lovingly sectioned cut of flesh to the Absolving Saint knowing that Treila is there.

She speaks to the Lady, words swallowed up by the heat of the room, knowing that Treila is there.

It's a fine dance, from that point forward. Phosyne is clearly in no position to simply slip out of the room as the party only grows once the king's cuts have been carted off to the kitchens to be cooked up. Treila lets herself be swept up in it, if only to obliterate herself a little longer, so that no prying eyes might find her. It's a sick echo of the first feast, with Treila playing the bewitched guest once more. Her knife burns in her fist.

She should be pleased that the king is dead. What Voyne said is, in the end, true: what was done to her *was* monstrous. Thrown out into an already starving countryside at the tail end of a brutal winter, with not even an understanding of why. Perhaps her father earned Voyne's blade through his neck. Perhaps her father even earned his family's disinheritance. But there were gentler ways. Kinder ways. Cardimir did not choose them.

And yet she can't bring herself to feel vindication. He probably didn't even notice when he was strung up.

She wishes she could have feasted on him five years ago, though.

The tide of the room has pushed her nearly to the door to the yard when Phosyne, at last, finds her. They see each other across a scrum of bodies, much the same way the Loving Saint had first caught Treila's eye. Maybe that's what makes her blood run cold, or maybe it is just rational fear of how much like them Phosyne has become. Her robes are finer than the last time Treila saw her. They are heavier with embroidery. They are dyed in soft and shifting colors. And Phosyne is clean, so very clean, no blood on her at all.

Treila turns and runs, throws herself back into the tide, lets herself be swept away, danced across the hall. She wants to lose herself, but she is tripping, staggering, something catching at her feet. She's felt like this once before, near Phosyne's rooms: it must be some manifestation of her power. Treila hisses a curse as she is steered back to the door, but when she looks up, Phosyne is not there. When she looks down, there are darting shadows. Not the flat painted things, but something else, something substantial but elusive.

And then she's outside. Alone.

There's heat around her legs, burning hot, and then it's gone, too.

"You shouldn't be here," Phosyne murmurs from the shadows.

Treila jerks and whirls, body tightly strung. Her eyes dance around the courtyard. Nobody watches.

Treila hides the blade behind her back and hopes Phosyne hasn't seen it.

"Stay back," Treila whispers.

Phosyne, to her credit, does. She holds up both hands, empty. "Were you able to hide her?"

Her jaw clenches. "Yes."

Phosyne's shoulders dip the slightest bit. "Good. Good. I—negotiations are ongoing."

"I can see that," Treila says, eyes flicking to the hall.

"The distraction," Phosyne says, wincing. "I told you I would distract them, so that you could move undisturbed—a feast was called for."

"And the king?"

It takes a moment for Phosyne to remember to look guilty. "He rules nothing here, not anymore. It has . . . cemented our status as equals."

"You and the Lady?"

"Me and the Lady."

Treila shakes her head. Takes a step back.

"Treila," Phosyne says, voice threaded through with command. It makes Treila want to run. No—to snarl, to strike. Her hand flexes on the knife.

"And now you negotiate the distribution of the spoils?" Treila spits.

The guilt is quicker this time. "No, no," Phosyne says, bowing her head, exposing her slender neck for just a moment. "I am discerning what it is She wants. What can be safely given. I am going to fix this, I just need time."

Time.

Time, or . . .

Or iron.

Treila wonders if it will burn her, should she touch it. Surely, if Phosyne is turning into one of *them*, it will be anathema to her.

She takes a deep breath. Holds it. Lets it hiss from between her teeth.

Lets herself trust in Voyne.

"Here," Treila says, pulling the blade from behind her back and proffering the hilt. Phosyne stares at it. Looks up at Treila's face, searching. *How*, it asks. *How did you—*

And Treila doesn't know how to answer.

Phosyne closes her fingers around the hilt without a flinch. But she doesn't pull, and Treila doesn't release it. She swallows, throat bobbing, and feels suddenly, unaccountably *young*.

She doesn't know what the right move is, here. She doesn't know if it's smart or foolish to tell Phosyne about Voyne, or about the power of the iron. She doesn't know if she trusts Phosyne to do the right thing, and, more than that, doesn't know if it even matters that Phosyne knows if it's right or wrong.

"Take it," Treila says, at last, unable to make any decision except the one she's already made. She uncurls her fingers, leaves the blade flat on her palm. "It will kill a saint, if it comes to it. The Lady, too. But you'll have to move quickly."

Phosyne looks into her eyes for too long, silent and motionless, and then she takes the knife and tucks it into one of her voluminous sleeves.

"Do it for her," Treila says.

"For her," Phosyne agrees. There's still that question in her eyes. That suspicion. That hope.

Treila just jerks her chin at the great hall. "You don't want them missing you," she says. "Get back."

Phosyne nods, but still doesn't move. She reaches out her other hand, touches Treila's cheek—gently. "You can trust me," she says.

"I'm leaving," Treila tells her.

"Good," Phosyne agrees. "But you can trust me."

It sounds less like a promise and more like a plea.

They regard each other for one last moment, and then Treila turns and, behind her, Phosyne walks away, back into the castle. The door closes, and Treila breathes. The air out here is cooler now, and damp. A storm is on the way. She must return to the cavern below the keep, and quickly now. She must let Voyne know how far Phosyne has fallen.

Or she can stay, and watch the disaster she can feel in her bones is coming. But without a knife . . .

Without a knife, she is in danger.

The feast will only last so long, and is no guarantee of safety even as it rages. Treila leans hard against the stone wall, centering herself, preparing for one last dash.

And then she feels a tickle. The slightest brush of eyes over her shadowed form.

She turns.

The Loving Saint leans in the doorway.

He is not trying to hide his monstrousness anymore. His long white hair is stained red where it has trailed through blood, and beneath his nails is filth. His clothing is in tatters. His muscles lie wrong for him to be anything but unnatural.

"Where has your knife got to?" he murmurs. "Your closest companion, your dearest love."

"You saw it," she says, taking a step back along the wall, only to hear a rustling, a hissing. It's not only him that's found her. A glance over her shoulder reveals flat, white faces. The shift of limbs in the dark. She is surrounded by the saints' creatures. Her mouth is dry, her throat sandpaper. But she lifts her chin up, meets the Loving Saint's eyes once more. "It's in Ser Voyne's throat."

"But Ser Voyne isn't in the chapel anymore."

"Only Phosyne could remove the blade. Your Lady said so."

His eyes spark. He's pleased she was there—or pleased that he *knew* she was there, without seeing her. "No, no," he purrs, taking a step closer, and this time she falls back. She will not meet him now. She knows better. "Not only Phosyne. Don't you remember, foolish girl, that there is something in the core of you that the Lady did not predict? I think you could take the blade from Ser Voyne's flesh as easy as breathing. But where did you leave it, I wonder?"

His nostrils flare, even as they change in shape, melting into Voyne's.

"Did you think you were killing me, when you slaughtered her?" he asks with her voice. "How long, until you realized you were wrong?"

"Don't," she bites out. "Don't wear that face."

"She died very prettily," he continues. "Her lips were kiss-swollen. Was it from you? Did she know that you were there, or did she think the sun was merely shining upon her face?"

She vibrates with disgust, thinking of the real Voyne, loyal and strong. Thinking of the Voyne this creature could have offered her, wicked and cruel and vulnerable, too. Everything Treila had imagined her to be.

Treila cannot stop from licking her lips.

The Loving Saint laughs softly. Treila wants to hear Voyne laugh like that.

"Without that knife of yours," he murmurs with Voyne's lips, "we can have so much fun." He is close enough to kiss her now. Treila has forgotten to retreat. She doesn't know when she became incapable of striking Voyne again, even in effigy.

"But as sweet as it would be to eat you with your dead knight's face," he sighs, and Voyne's colors begin to bleed from him, his hair begins to lengthen, "I find I'm sick of playing to your fancies." His teeth sharpen. His eyes gleam in the dark, catching the moonlight.

Treila reaches for his throat, but he's faster. He catches her wrist, hauls her close. His mouth descends, and she snarls, slamming the heel of her other hand into his jaw. His head snaps back and then isn't there at all, and she's falling through him. His hair whispers over her skin as she slams into the wall, bounces off it, falls sprawling in front of a hundred dripping jaws. The first one snaps, and Treila staggers to her feet and runs.

She knows Aymar better than possibly anybody else alive, but they are faster than she, and they do not obey the same laws. They sprint along the walls, prowl the sky above as if it is a ceiling, drop down in front of her and reach for her ankles. Her screams break upon the stone and fracture, and she goes down once, twice—

But they let her up each time.

They play with her, letting her gain a few desperate feet of lead only to cut her off and send her down the stairs into the lower yard, hound her around the rims of the cisterns, close to falling. They carve gashes in her arms, tear at her skirts, knock her down, but only far enough that she is rattled, not that she is broken. The detritus of Aymar, shredded tents and abandoned clothing, tangle beneath her feet. The monsters' laughter is everywhere.

And behind them, riding the wave of their bloodlust, is the Loving Saint, grinning, scenting the air, drinking in her terror. Her missing ear surges with the roaring buzz of a thousand bees, loud enough to deafen.

Without a knife, she has no way to fight back. But there are other sources of iron. The chapel—the chapel must contain something, some astronomical measure that has a steel pin at its core. Or the garden, where Voyne's hammer lies somewhere in the botanical riot. But they have hounded her to the other end of the keep, close to the gates, and she can see no clear path around them. Her muscles burn. Her bones ache. She stumbles as she scrambles up one of the staircases to the walls, then goes down hard as fingers close around her ankle and tug her back.

She is so close. She is so close to the edge of the wall. To the long drop on the other side. To some kind of freedom, if only—if only—

If only it were not the Loving Saint who falls upon her now, his hair shrouding them like a curtain.

She twists to face him, teeth bared, but there are tears in her eyes, helpless tears.

"I told you I would make it good," he murmurs, prowling up her body. She jerks her knee up into his gut, but her leg passes right through him. He is at her side, then, hauling her up. His hands are in her hair. She screams.

He laughs and throws her down onto her stomach.

She crawls.

"You never give up, do you?" he asks. "I was going to kill you gently, eat you sweetly, but that wouldn't do you justice. You wretched, vicious little thing." His boot comes down on her lower spine and she can feel her vertebrae screaming. Creaking.

The pressure disappears. Reappears on her neck. Her leg. Her arm. He is everywhere. She flails, meets nothing but air, and only barely manages to roll onto her back.

He looms above her.

"Scared little girl, always hiding in the dark. Do you think that makes your teeth as sharp as mine?"

He flickers in and out of place, half-real, half-insubstantial. He is a hundred different people, exchanging faces like paper masks. But he sounds the same in each aspect: a pure vibration, rattling around in her skull, ramifying.

It has a source. Like Phosyne touching her brow and making choruses erupt, his existence creates the rise and fall inside of her. She focuses in on it. She can hear the core of him, static, unchanging.

The noise rearranges itself, harmonizes, settles.

Treila stands upright. She fixes her gaze on him and refuses to fall into the ambiguity, the impossibility. She *sees*.

The flickering stops, leaving behind just a smudge of white on the world in the vague shape of a man. The world is still around them. In his chest is a snarled thicket of a stomach, hungry, aching, desperate. And inside of her is a prism, a flashing diamond: heavy and unmoving, the result of every time she refused to abandon herself, no matter the guise she chose to wear.

In the center of it, a bee's stinger. A gift from the true Constant Lady? A fragment of her suffering? Something vicious and pure, either way.

Treila blinks, and the vision is gone. The Loving Saint stands before her, no longer changing, no longer moving. Panting, he stares at her, brows drawing down in belated wariness.

"You—" he whispers.

And Treila lunges.

Her teeth pierce the pale, lovely column of his throat. They crack through his windpipe even as blood surges into her mouth, coats her tongue, drowns her in sticky sweetness. *Sweet.* Like honey. There's no trace of iron, and she laughs, fierce and jagged, because of course there is no iron in his veins.

He is screaming. The noise gurgles, shrill against her tongue. She bites again, and again, chews and swallows, even as he thrashes beneath her. Her nails pierce his clothing, his skin. She claws him until his flesh is ribbons, until she is painting them both with his blood. They are on the floor; she doesn't remember their collapse. All she knows is the feel of him, the *fight* of him. She is the dark thing in the forest, feral and fierce, feeding herself in his misery.

Ser Voyne and Cardimir and her father and the whole world sharpened her teeth, taught her to use them.

And it is glorious.

When at last the Loving Saint lies still beneath her hands, when she has drunk her fill of his hot and heady blood, when the buzzing in her missing ear has quieted to a light and diffuse din, she lifts her head and regards their audience. A hundred hungry faces look back at her. She can see them all, the margins where one differentiates from another. They cannot hide from her anymore, just as he could not hide from her.

She isn't here to play their games. She is here to win them.

Treila rises to her feet, licking her lips. Her stomach feels full for the first time in many months. She scrubs one fist against her mouth, smearing the honey-thick blood across her flesh like war paint.

She takes a step back, holds out a hand.

"It's eat or be eaten," she tells her audience. "And I have made it good. Eat up, pets."

They fall upon the Loving Saint, ravenous, and let her walk free.

She makes her way back to the keep.

47

HE KING'S BODY is apportioned among his people. To his household staff go the muscles of his back. To the garrison, his thighs and calves. To the refugees, the tender meat of his arms, soft and succulent from the years of idleness after he last lifted a sword.

Ser Leodegardis is given fine slivers of heart, presented by the Absolving Saint on milky porcelain. He flinches, though his red-rimmed eyes are empty of tears. All cried out before, Phosyne thinks, as she comes to sit across from him. She holds Treila's knife in the folds of her robes. It is heavy against her thigh.

He is aware. Aware enough to recognize her, and what he has been served. But he's still bewitched enough to feed himself. His shoulders tremble as he chews. His head bows as he swallows.

He's not the only one in the hall who retains a small piece of himself. Ser Voyne had been busy, on her trip to the cistern. Her water has slaked the thirst of many, binding them subtly to Phosyne with every sip. But Leodegardis has had the lion's share. He burns with twined loyalties, to the Lady and to Phosyne, so much like Voyne herself.

"Aren't you going to eat?" he asks when he has clamped his hand against the wood of the table, as if to still it.

The Absolving Saint has disappeared back into the kitchen, and the Lady is missing. Phosyne has a moment. Below the table, she presses the knife into her lap.

"Not yet," Phosyne says.

"Did you call them? These invaders. These jailers of ours." He plainly has grasped that the thing wearing the Constant Lady's form is something else, if only by Her actions.

"No." Her lips twitch into an apologetic smile. "If I had, this would have turned out much differently."

She thinks.

"When I took you in . . ." Leodegardis grimaces in pain, as if he has to fight to remember. She's not sure if he's fighting against the haze the Lady creates inside his mind, or his own guilt for everything that has transpired. "I didn't mean to use you. Maybe I should have."

"It would certainly have given me structure. Putting me in that room, giving me no purpose except to learn . . . things got out of hand, I think," Phosyne says, and feels a pang of fondness for this man. He will not survive the night, she thinks. His other leg has been cut away. He is balanced in a nest of cushions, provided by the Absolving Saint. She oversaw the process, the negotiations. Leodegardis did not fight. In fact, he begged for them to do it, perhaps because he thought it would spare his king.

"But I do not think I can be used, not the way you would have liked," she adds, more softly now. "My knowledge does not proceed linearly. It cannot be forced. It arises as some echo of another layer of reality, like a room adjoining this one without a door. I think . . ."

I think it would have been better if I had never been kept. If she had never been sequestered away from the real world, allowed to bend her mind to the impossible. If she had not been indulged.

Or maybe it wouldn't have mattered either way. What she wants, though, is to give Leodegardis some absolution of her own.

She touches his wrist. "You did well by me," she tells him. "You did well by all of us." That was his obligation, his duty: in return for the fealty of his household, he gave them as much care and protection as he could. And now they are no longer his to lead.

"At least we did not starve to death," he says. He closes his eyes in grim humor.

No, they did not starve to death at all.

"Promise me something, my madwoman," Leodegardis says after a moment's quivering.

"Name it."

"Do not forget my kindness. Do not let this have been in vain."

It's not what she expected, but she nods, curls their fingers together for a brief moment. "I will never forget," she assures him. A part of her wishes he had made her promise to end this, but she has already promised that to Treila, to Voyne.

Remembrance is probably just as important.

"I should have let Ser Voyne leave," Leodegardis whispers as Phosyne stands once more. His eyes close in pain. He reaches for another piece of meat. "She asked to go, to get help. I told her she was a coward."

Phosyne's heart twists, a flare of anger, and she leaves him there before she does something drastic for the memory of a dead woman.

Her hands are tight upon the hilt of Treila's dagger.

She slips out of the great hall unnoticed, taking the path she did the night she fled from Ser Voyne, through the halls, up the stairs. She is not alone; the split-second images of the Lady's lesser beasts pace her as she walks, but they keep their distance. Phosyne cannot feel them the way she feels the people in the hall below, but she can see them, glittering and flat, teeth sharp and waiting.

There's blood on them. The scent of honey. Something has changed, and Phosyne hesitates on the stairs. If she ascends, her little tower room waits. She doesn't want to go there, she wants to *end* this, but for just a moment, the urge to flee rises up in her. The old urge, to hide, to become unremarkable once more.

She pushes it aside. She steps instead into the throne room.

The Lady sits upon the throne. The honeycomb has spread from Jacynde's corpse and now crawls up the wall behind the Lady, up into the rafters. Brilliant sunlight shines warm through panes of wax that now stopper the windows. The whole room is warm and humming with the movement of a thousand bees. They move in and out of the mass of the Lady's hair, Her braids coming undone. They sip at the nectar of the living blooms that wreathe Her.

The bees are not to blame; their nature has been played with as much as anybody's, their life cycle accelerated, their hive fattened on unnatural nectar. But if Phosyne drives the blade between the Lady's ribs, the comb will remain. The honey, too. The magic in it. The infiltration, the corridors filled with the Lady's creatures. It's too late to unmake what the bees have wrought.

There is little point in stabbing Her. There are a hundred more like Her within the castle walls, and Phosyne does not have the strength or skill to hunt them down one by one.

Voyne would argue with her, surely, but Voyne is not here to stop her. Voyne is dead.

Phosyne lifts her hand and shows the Lady the knife.

Her ringed eyes widen. Her golden lips part. She does not look at Phosyne's face at all, just the glint of metal. There is a flicker of fear across Her brow, but it is slight, considering how much of a danger Treila has said it is to Her kind. More than that is curiosity. Wonder. Expectation.

"From Ser Voyne's throat," Phosyne says. "You asked me for her body, but you have many already. Forgive me if I do not believe that was, in the end, your aim."

To have the body, though, the knife had to be removed.

The knife is what matters.

The Lady inclines Her head in acknowledgment. "What a wonder you are, little mouse. And so you would offer me the knife instead?"

"The knife," Phosyne agrees. "And in exchange, you will give me the castle and all the lives inside it that you hold dominion over."

Her gaze sharpens at that. Her lips curl. "Not freedom? Not knowledge?"

"Those can come later," Phosyne says, helpless but to smile back.

The knife, of course, is not just a knife. Phosyne knows that, even if she doesn't know what, exactly, it represents. It is heavy in her hand, too heavy just for the metal it is made of. She lifts it an inch higher, takes a step closer.

From the outside, it is a lopsided bargain. A knife for the castle? A knife for victory? The Lady should rightfully push for more, but She doesn't. Instead the air between them thrums with anticipation. With hunger.

Phosyne breathes shallowly, as if afraid to disturb the air between them. Her mind works. She wants to ask what the knife means, but isn't so foolish as to tip her hand.

I go nowhere I do not please, the Lady had told her, upon their first meeting. *But I do wander everywhere.*

Except—not everywhere. Nearly, but not everywhere. Something changed, to allow Her to enter Aymar. It wasn't just chance. Phosyne feels the castle spread out around her, feels its comparative lightness. Before, it was heavy. Before, the bees could come and go from the chapel, but could not carry the Lady's touch. Alone, this castle was alone, set apart, so *heavy*—

The knife is heavy in the same way.

The knife is made of iron. A castle should be full of it. Aymar no longer is.

"Wait—"

"I accept," the Lady says, rising from Her throne. She crosses the few feet between them, fine-boned hand extended. Her fingers glide across the back of Phosyne's hands, gentling her grip until the Lady bears the weight of the blade.

The iron does not burn Her, does not hurt Her, does not *stop* Her from gripping the hilt and bringing the edge to Her lips.

The tangled snarl of Phosyne's thoughts fall slack, revealing a larger tapestry. Iron, collected and melted down, forged into a one-time weapon, launched over their walls in a fruitless bid for freedom. It bought them time against their mortal enemies, but also time enough for bees to return from far-off fields. They brought something with them that tainted the honey. Something from the unseen world, something of the creature who came in the guise of the Lady, spreading a thin sheen of ownership across every person who knelt to take the blessing on their tongues. The False Lady arrived soon after, into a world all but free of iron, iron that girds towns and castles everywhere, protecting, enfolding, hiding.

Without iron, She is free to come and go as She pleases.

Without iron, there is nothing to stop Her hunger.

The Lady holds in Her hand a blade of iron, one of just a few left in Aymar, and it does not hurt Her.

"Oh," Phosyne whispers.

The Lady smiles.

It is a kindly smile. An indulgent one. She draws close to Phosyne, close enough to lean in, to press Her lips to Phosyne's forehead. "The castle," She murmurs against Phosyne's quivering brow, "and all the lives within it I hold dominion over."

Her world goes white.

Awareness staggers after, pinpoints of color resolving behind her eyelids. A hundred lives, a thousand, so many creatures and not all of them mortal, not all of them finite. Dominion is not just control; it is power over, it is power *within*. She can hear them all, feel them all. They clamor at her, screaming, shouting, and she wants to touch each and every one of them.

The refugees, ecstatic in their feasting. The lesser beasts that came to the Lady's table, now sated on honeyed flesh, waiting for command. The Absolving Saint, standing in the heat of the kitchen, watching Phosyne through layer and layer of stone, eyes cool and assessing. Ser Leodegardis set like a trophy at his side, heedless of what has happened but knowing, instinctively, to be afraid.

The Lady, too, for She holds dominion over Herself as well as everything else within Her world. Phosyne grabs on to that realization, clings to it, desperate, because it means that She cannot leave. She cannot leave so long as Phosyne remembers to hold Her leash, and so She cannot go out into the world and pass through its bonds of iron as if they mean nothing.

That is important. Phosyne must remember that. *Hold tight to the leash,* she tells herself again and again, even as the sound of her voice warps, twists, becomes unfamiliar.

She can see light refracting off water, and feel the dawning of revelation inside of her.

The taste of all these lives has opened a yawning pit inside of her. They all hold hunger in their bellies, and it is amplified, sharpened within the crucible of her skull.

What is falling through the stone as if it were water before *this*? What is seeing the boundaries of her little room compared with the whole world stretched out before her?

She wants to know all of it. She wants to touch it all, grasp it, bend it before her. The world is *vast*, and suddenly she is at the pinnacle of it, and she knows so little.

Tears streak down her cheeks, and she shudders at the cutting, burning reminder that she *has* cheeks, she has a body, she is just a woman and she is spinning out to pieces.

"Your hunger is so sharp," the Lady says. Phosyne can barely hear Her. The world is so loud, so large, and she is drowning in it. She is ever-expanding. Something inside her has come loose, and she doesn't know that she could tamp it down again, even if she wanted to.

And she does not want to.

No, no, she does want to, she *does* want to.

"You'd take everything if you could," the Lady murmurs. "And you *can.* You are a black hole, little mouse. Endlessly hungry, *endlessly,* and all you had to do was notice it. How does it feel? Is it good?"

Phosyne sobs, and rain crashes against the stone. The sky itself is breaking. She can *feel* it breaking, even if she cannot see it—but she can see it, can't she? If she shivers out of the boundaries of her skin, if she unleashes herself.

No. No. No, she must hold on, she must—she must remember what she is.

"You need a teacher, little mouse," the Lady says, and She is on Her knees before Phosyne, and isn't She so pretty like this? Her face upturned, mouth and nose golden and shining, Her eyes concentric rings of endless color. She knows something of eternity.

Phosyne shudders, reaching out to touch Her. She pushes her fingers into the Lady's golden hair. Feels every strand of it like molten fire.

"Tell me your name," the Lady entreats, so sweetly, "and I will be your firm hand. I will steer you through this awakening. Only your name, little mouse, it is such a small thing, but without it you will collapse in on yourself, snuff out the blazing light of you."

She can feel it. Can feel the impending collapse. A bright flare, and then nothing, and Aymar will be gone. Treila will be gone. Ser Leodegardis will be gone and, somewhere in the bowels of this rock, the body of Ser Voyne will be gone.

Wouldn't that be for the best? All of them, gone together.

But Phosyne made a promise to remember, and she cannot remember if she disintegrates.

"Phosyne," she gasps. "My name is Phosyne."

48

ELLO, SHIELD BEARER," the darkness whispers.

Ser Voyne's lips quirk for just a moment. "Shield bearer?" she asks. "Is that what I am?"

"It's one thing you are."

The voice flits between childish and gravelly, thin and deep, as if it doesn't know what it wants to be. Voyne can see nothing, no hint of face or form. Only the crack in the stone, and the shine of the water below. She half expects a surge of vertigo, but the world is still and steady.

"It is," she agrees.

She has the odd sensation of the darkness smiling at her. "Are you here to ask for safe passage, like the girl?"

"No."

What she wants is the lay of the land, and what Treila has told her about this thing intrigues her.

Worries her.

She does not like that something lives beneath Aymar that makes deals. It feels too much like the creatures that have torn her world to pieces.

"Come closer," the darkness whispers. "Let me see you."

It takes more energy than Voyne really has to rise to her feet, but she does it. She takes the five careful steps to close the distance between her and the crack in the stone. There is nothing within it, no point of light to suggest an eye peering out at her, no touch of warmth in the cool air to denote breath. There is simply an absence, a descent that she cannot make. The crack is too narrow to do more than slip a finger through, and she does not try even that.

"What did you take from—the girl?" Voyne asks, remembering at the last moment that they have not been using names. That this thing does not know Treila's name. Voyne guards it jealously by reflex.

"A finger," the darkness says, "to leave. An ear to come back."

"And if she wants to leave again?"

"Something more, certainly, since I don't think she'll ask to come back a second time. But she is a good negotiator."

Voyne smiles despite herself. "She is. Could you hear us, while the candle was lit?"

It is an obliging darkness. "No," it says, and she doesn't think it's lying. It sounds too frustrated. "The light belongs to somebody else. Somebody who knows how to assert a claim. When it burns, this place is not mine anymore."

Phosyne.

They are interrupted by a noise—a howling shriek, distant but echoing down the tunnel that connects this limited space to the world beyond. Voyne turns, posture shifting to something far more defensive than it has been.

The noise does not repeat, but there comes a closer crashing surge, and Voyne glances down to see the water below her rising.

"Rain," the darkness says. "Falling fast and heavy."

"Will this cavern flood?"

"No," it says, and there is a creaking rumble.

Across the cavern, the stone slides, a shifting shadow, and the water slows first to a bare trickle, and then nothing at all.

The glow persists, but is thinner now, lingering in the puddles that are left. Voyne stares at it, processing this show of force, this mastery of the environment. Heart hammering in her throat, she looks up, to the side, to where Treila left her.

The tunnel remains.

It may not always.

Her head swims. She should leave, and yet she is still not wholly herself, still not strong enough to navigate a tunnel she does not know the lay of. She needs Treila, or the darkness, if she is to leave.

"Sit," the darkness murmurs. "You are tired."

Trembling, Voyne sinks to her knees, leaning back against the stone. The crack cradles the base of her skull. She is too exhausted to move any farther.

If it takes her, it takes her, but she does not think it will.

"You're not like the—" She hesitates. She will not call them saints, not anymore, but has no other name for them. *Guests* is too euphemistic. *Enemies* too crude, too broad. "Like the invaders above," she settles on.

The darkness does not respond immediately. She wonders if it is considering how to respond, or if it is *looking*, somehow, up through the yards of rock above them.

"Tell me about them," it says. "I have smelled them on the girl, and I can feel them walk above me, but I can't hear them."

"They are hungry," Voyne murmurs.

"I am hungry," the darkness says.

"They toy with us. They strike bargains."

"In this we are alike."

She inclines her head at the darkness's honesty. "They taste like honey. They look like I do, and the girl, in the broadest sense. They ask for loyalty, devotion, adoration."

The darkness hums. "What else?"

"They abhor iron."

"Then they are not like me at all." The darkness laughs, and the ground trembles. "They are my enemy, then, as well."

"You do not fear iron? It does not strike you dead?"

"Oh, no. No, I am made of it. I could not reside below the earth and shy from any scrap of ore, any vein of metal, now could I?"

Voyne adjusts the map that has been forming in her mind since she awoke down here, weak but clearer-headed. She moves pieces about the board, not to wholly new terrain but to where she thought they might go, where she hoped they could be placed.

"You are very old, aren't you?" Her hand caresses the stone below her, stone that has sat here for centuries, millennia, the bedrock that Aymar was built upon. She wonders how long this cavern has existed for. If it's always been here, or if the water by her side has carved it more recently. Still, she knows she is thinking not in mortal years, but something larger, more expansive. "You were here before I arrived. Before my people arrived. Before the first hands laid the first cut stones aboveground."

"Not quite. I came when those first stones were cut."

Her heart quickens. "Why?"

"Because I was called for. I was bargained with. I was fed."

She thinks, then, of Carcabonne. Of blood in the snow, sinking down to the stone beneath. These castles have certainly been fatted upon death.

"What for?" she asks.

"Protection."

There is love in its voice, or at least a heady fondness. "And would you say you protect us now?" Voyne whispers.

"The castle has not yet fallen to ruin, has it? The stone it sits upon has not collapsed? I am limited in what I can do. Just as you are limited."

Just as she has been paid in blood for her protection, as well.

"There is iron in your spine," it says. Fingers trail up her back, along her shoulders, across her neck. She shudders but does not pull away, holding herself stiff and wary, wondering, wanting to know where they will go. They tangle in her hair, then come to rest atop her scalp. There are too many of them to belong to only two hands, though of course the hands they belong to (if they belong to any hands at all) need not be the same as hers.

But there are enough, regardless, to encircle her brow. To rest as a crown of sorts, and for a moment, they are a circlet not of flesh or shadow but of stone. Heavy, solid.

"The clever girl's knife, the tip snapped off within you. Can you feel it?"

Her throat is whole now, unnaturally whole, but if she swallows— yes, she feels it, a sharp little pebble, lodged behind her windpipe, her esophagus. If she strains her head from side to side, she thinks she will feel it scrape.

"Yes," she whispers.

"It is that which has cut you free from a tangle of air and fire. And now you are what you always were before—clad in iron, strong and steady. Can you feel it?" Hands press into the armor along her back, the shimmering metal that Voyne now realizes is no metal at all, but a glittering latticework. The idea of armor, not the substance of it. But where the darkness touches, it solidifies, gains the heft of steel.

She gasps at the weight.

"You are made of me," it murmurs in her ear.

"What do you want?" she asks. "And what can you give me in return?"

"They are one and the same. Destroy them. Let their blood soak into the stone. Restore order and solidity."

A tongue curls around her earlobe. She shudders, panic flaring in her breast, sharp and bright. She listens to it as carefully as she can. "Feed you once more," she supplies.

The tongue disappears, replaced with nibbling teeth. They do not pierce flesh. They are gentle. Controlled. A dog biting fleas from its mates' fur. "That frightens you."

"I won't exchange one master for another."

Cardimir and the False Lady and Phosyne—but the darkness doesn't laugh at how much practice she has at shifting her loyalties recently. It doesn't needle her, doesn't mock her.

"I do not ask for a bargain. I do not ask for submission," it says instead. "We are already one and the same."

She quakes at the thought. "But you are hungry," she whispers, wary.

"Hunger is inescapable, shield bearer," it says, and the hands at last leave her scalp, disappear back into the darkness. The teeth go with them a moment later. "You cannot gain any distance on it. It will follow you to the ends of the earth. But the hunger that I am holds this castle up. The hunger that they are would tear it away from you. The hunger that you feel would lead you to victory."

Another shudder rocks her. "If you speak the truth. If this is not another ploy."

"You doused the candle. You asked to speak to me. You never intended to ask for freedom."

"I wanted only information, not a mandate."

"You have always had the mandate."

Voyne closes her eyes. Thinks of Carcabonne, and Treila's father, headless at her feet, and Phosyne given over into her care. None of it has been easy, or simple, or even clear at the time. It is only after that she can feel the rightness of it. It is not obedience, not even loyalty, but one single note above all else:

Protect them.

She has the strength to do it. She has the iron in her spine. She has the stone beneath her feet.

"I have always had the mandate," she agrees.

The darkness bows behind her.

49

REILA IS JUST outside the keep when the sky breaks open and the deluge begins.

The clouds that have boiled out of empty air bring with them a flash and shudder of light. Not lightning, not thunder, but the sun itself roiling, spinning, careening between noon and dusk and dawn, stars springing to life and then winking out again. Treila stares up at the riot even as water falls on her with the force of an avalanche, churning the dirt below her feet to sludge. The rain plunges down her throat, chokes her, and it's only that spasming that tears her away from the sight, bends her double so she can cough and gasp for breath.

It washes some of the honeyed sharpness of the Loving Saint's blood out of her mouth and, selfishly, she clamps her lips shut, not quite ready to lose the rest of it.

She pulls herself inside a doorway.

The stones themselves begin to dance.

That's the only word for it, the way they rock and slide against one another. Gravity and mortar seem forgotten. The world is lurching off its axis; no matter how hard Treila glares, it all refuses to still.

And above it all, she hears Phosyne, screaming.

It echoes down the stairwells, piercing and pained, and Treila freezes, clinging to a tapestry that has yet to melt. It's pained, but also ecstatic, and she reaches reflexively for the knife that is not there.

You can trust me, Phosyne had promised her. And she'd known better, known not to, but—

But does the loss of a blade really matter? This would have happened either way.

There's no time for regret. Treila throws herself down toward her workshop, praying the tunnel has not shimmied closed.

It hasn't. It yawns black and beckoning in her lonely little room, with its needles and awls and waxed thread, the fragments of a life that doesn't feel like hers. Treila, the glover, the rat catcher, doesn't exist anymore. She has been washed away by the blood and flesh in her teeth.

Which is good. That Treila wouldn't have survived this long, no matter the armor she'd built for herself.

This Treila slides back down into the earth like she was made for it.

She is maybe halfway through the winding passage, the sounds dying away, the world falling back to order as she moves, when she notices the next ill omen:

Voyne has doused the candle.

The absence of its flickering glow is subtle, barely noticeable until Treila hauls herself around a bend in the tunnel, and then there is nothing but darkness and blue light. The earth itself seems to tighten around her, the tunnel constricting until rock brushes against her sleeves. Her clothes are heavy, blood-soaked and sodden, and she kicks and snarls, fighting her way through.

She tries not to think of what she will find—or won't find. Perhaps Voyne will be gone, following her direction, yes, but leaving Treila alone, and Treila does not want to be alone. Even if she knows she can kill a saint. Even if she knows she can survive this next negotiation.

But when she crawls at last to the final lip of the tunnel, she hears voices, murmurs. She plunges forward, legs tangling in her skirts, skin scraping as she tumbles from the mouth of the tunnel and back into her little cavern, secret from all the world.

Voyne sits with her back against the crack, watching her.

It's almost impossible to see her, the cavern is so dark. Even the glow of the creek is fading. But Voyne is alive, and Voyne is smiling.

Treila swallows down her panic and straightens up.

"You came back," Voyne says and, as Treila watches, plants her hands against the stone behind her and shoves herself to her feet. Her armor looks different, but maybe it's the light.

"Were you going to leave?" Treila asks, nodding at the gap behind her.

"No," Voyne says.

The darkness says nothing.

"Does Phosyne have the knife?" Voyne asks, taking one lurching step toward her. Her mouth twists with pain, but she stays upright.

Treila fights back the urge to go to her. "You were wrong, to trust her," she snaps instead. Lets Voyne take another step, then slips around her, goes to the crack herself. "We need to leave, and quickly. This whole castle is going to come down soon."

Voyne turns. Her armor is loud in the small space, clanking against itself. It sounds different now, too. Less tinkling. More martial.

Treila ignores it, shoves her hand into the crack. "Come on, beastie," she says, smile fierce on her lips. "Take a nibble, let me through."

The darkness does not answer.

There are no lips against her hand. No teeth. No curling limbs. There is nothing for Treila to bite into, nothing for her to grab hold of. She slams her other fist against the rock, pushes farther in. "Name your price!" she demands.

The only response is Voyne's hand, clapped hard onto her shoulder, but urging her back gently.

Only because of the weakness still in her limbs, surely. It is not tenderness.

"We fight," Voyne tells her, voice quiet in her ear. "That is the deal I have made."

Treila shivers, then turns, staring up into the other woman's eyes. They are calm, cool, everything Treila is not. They *incense* her.

But Voyne just reaches out and cups her jaw, strokes her gloved fingers over the dried and flaking gore Treila only now remembers. "You *fought*," Voyne reminds her.

"We have no weapons," Treila says, and her voice sounds choked and frightened.

That won't do. She firms her shoulders. Leans into Voyne's touch, a challenge.

"Get me to the throne room," Voyne says, "and I will take up my blade again."

"You're not going to like what you find up there," Treila cautions her. "The world is breaking. Phosyne is breaking it. It may not be the Lady we need to stop, now."

For all Treila knows, the Lady is dead, and Phosyne has eaten Her.

Voyne inclines her head in understanding. "Nevertheless."

Treila licks at her bloody, bruised lips. Voyne stands ready to fight. And she . . . she realizes she does not actually want to run. For all the impossibility that Phosyne has brought upon the world, Treila has tasted victory, and she is ready for more. A struggle with an endpoint beyond simple survival, beyond bitterness.

No more fleeing. No more hiding in the shadows.

She grins.

"Then follow me, Ser Voyne. Let me show you what you couldn't see before."

The earth accepts the both of them, and if the armor Voyne wears slows her down, she compensates for it well. They squirm together through the tunnel, hand over hand, the only sound the movement of clothing, the rattle of metal, and their shared breaths. So different, from the desperate attempt she made with Phosyne. So different, too, from all the times she has passed this way alone.

And then they are back in the keep, for the last time, and Voyne stands beside her in the dim light of day.

Outside, the wind is still howling. The rain has stopped, but the clouds still hang low and heavy. Below her feet, the stone shivers, but it has ceased its dance for now.

A moment's calm. She doesn't know how long they'll have it for.

Treila rolls her shoulders, loosens her jaw, and starts to climb, Voyne close at her heels.

At ground level, they are met with a fine corpse, disassembled and organized neatly in the time it took for her to retrieve Voyne. There are splashes of black and gold and red on the ground, remnants of the lesser beasts of the saints. They have made her an offering.

Behind her, Voyne growls, low and soft. "I knew him," she says. And then Treila recognizes the face, peeled carefully from the skull and draped over an upturned bowl.

"Ser Galleren," Voyne says, and stoops to touch his brow.

One of Ser Leodegardis's cousins, Treila thinks. Not a bad man, not at all. She thinks, perhaps, she met him once as a girl. But he never recognized her.

"We have to keep moving," she says, sidestepping a tidy coil of intestine that doesn't even have the decency to stink of shit. Voyne nods and rises to her feet, then leads the way.

Some of the steps are missing. Voyne and Treila negotiate the gaps carefully, trusting that what remains is as stable as it looks.

The throne room is only wreckage. The stones are blasted black with soot, and that any of the walls remain upright beggars belief. But like the rest of the keep, it is stable. For the moment.

And silent, save for the endless hum of bees.

They issue from a mass of sticky comb, not golden but rust red, that curls around the throne itself. The seat remains bare, but only just, and the bees are industrious, connecting the mountain of wax to the walls behind it in thin projections. They roil and shift, clumping together into what looks, for just a moment, like the form of a woman.

And then it looks like the form of the prioress, if the shape of a headdress is anything to go by.

Voyne steps forward.

"Jacynde," she says.

The mass of bees does not respond in words, but it lifts the silhouette of a hand. The insects compact until Treila can make out individual fingers. Another mass rises from the hive and shapes out the long straight edge of a blade, comes to rest in the figure's hand.

Treila bares her teeth, but Voyne shakes her head. "Wait," she cautions.

The bees do not approach. They do not brandish their makeshift weapon. The buzzing grows louder as the figure shifts, wavers as if drunk or dying, and then tilts the blade at its own belly. There is a sharp spike of noise, a thousand wings snapping down at once, as it pierces itself and then scatters.

Treila remembers this. The sound of it, the slick noise, the thud of Jacynde's collapse. The Lady had been there, and the Prioress . . .

The Prioress had killed herself, because the Lady could not have held Voyne's sword. Why had Jacynde done it? At the Lady's behest? Or in opposition? The bees belong to the Priory, and they have clustered over her corpse, keeping her safe.

Keeping the sword safe.

"They have filled their comb with her blood," Voyne says, almost dreamily. "And my flesh, upon a substrate of steel. They rejected me because I still held part of the False Lady inside of me. Their hives and honey have been perverted, but they never meant us harm."

Treila stares.

"I hope, anyway," Voyne mutters, sounding more herself, and picks her way across the room to the throne.

She does not hesitate, reaching into the sticky mass of wax and blood and rot. Bees rise around her, a roaring swarm, but they do not touch her. None alight, none sting, as she plunges her arm deep, to the shoulder.

She pulls her arm back and brings with it a sword, glittering and sharp in the fractured light. Maybe Voyne was right, Treila thinks.

"I thought," Voyne confesses, quietly, "that I had killed her without knowing. Or that Phosyne had done something to her, for Jacynde was in her care the last I saw her. It's . . . good to know that this was her choice, even if it was a terrible, forced choice."

"Better than what happened to the king," Treila mutters.

Voyne stills. Turns on her heel. "The king," she repeats.

Treila grimaces, ducks her head. She hadn't meant to—but Voyne will find out soon enough, if they survive this. "Dead," she says. "Eaten."

She does not mention Phosyne's hand in it.

But as if summoned by the omission, Phosyne's voice rings out through the halls. It is overloud, too loud to come from mortal lungs, but it is one clear note: the first note of "On Breath," the one Treila has used to light her candles. She shivers with it, and Voyne's head snaps up, to the stairwell that leads to Phosyne's tower room.

Eyes stare back at them.

Too many eyes, Treila notes, sliding in between that shadowed doorway and Voyne, head tilted to one side. Painted, flat faces. Frescoes in the dark. They crowd the stairwell, their teeth bared, sharp and stinking of rot. Shreds of pale flesh still linger in some of their maws. Traces of the Loving Saint. Of her generosity.

She takes a step toward them.

"Treila—"

"Ignore them," Treila says. She lifts her chin a fraction of an inch, grins. "They know who feeds them."

And as she takes another step, they part like hunting hounds, spilling out of the doorway in two ranks, creating a path.

Voyne joins her, but stops short of the door, looking back at the shifting lines. At how they strain. The tip of her blade lifts from where it is pointed to the door.

"I made a promise," Voyne says. "To paint the earth with their blood."

And Treila sees again Voyne with her back to the darkness, to the crack in the stone. Considers, then places a gentle hand on her elbow, urging Voyne back another step, until they are out from between the beasts.

"Let me," she says, in Voyne's ear, and Voyne lowers her blade once more.

Treila looks out at the creatures, so hungry and ready to rend and tear. They so enjoyed the blood of their own. And they trust her. She has given them food; she has taken ownership, of a sort. The only sort these beasts seem to understand.

She tongues the stain still on her teeth and says, "Slake your thirsts, loves, on each other's flesh."

They lunge in an instant, and then there is only red and white and gold, paint slashed across the stone, and Treila shuts the door.

Voyne regards her with something between fear and admiration. It looks good on her.

And then she turns and climbs.

At the top of the stairs, the door to Phosyne's tower room hangs open, and inside are two figures, both draped in silks, both glowing in the dim light. The Lady is wreathed in flowers, in full icon regalia, and Phosyne stands before her, rigid, face tilted up, eyes wide as she clutches at a candle. The light that dances upon the wick is every color imaginable, and those colors are echoed in Phosyne's irises.

Treila backs away.

But Voyne is right behind her, and the knight clasps her tense shoulder as she, too, takes in the scene. The Lady has not seen them, is even now murmuring to Phosyne in a low and teasing tone.

Phosyne flinches, as if in pain. She releases her grip on the candle, and it stays fixed in the air, hanging motionless. Her hands tremble as she splays her fingers. She is focused wholly on the pillar of wax.

The world remains steady. Voyne shifts her grip on her blade and steps forward.

The Lady still does not see them, but the movement catches Phosyne's attention, and her head turns, lips parting. Her brow creases.

She wails, and the world shudders.

50

ER VOYNE STANDS in the doorway, and Phosyne shakes apart, desperate for a miracle.

She is glorious in steel, *true* steel and not the Warding Saint's weightless imitation, sword flashing, the way she looked down in the yard the day of the food riot, the day Phosyne was given to her.

And she is *alive*, alive and quicksilver. Even as Phosyne spasms and the air within the room collapses into the flame of the candle, then bursts out once more, taking the fire with it in a shower of sparks—even then, Voyne is moving.

Her blade plunges into the Lady.

It skewers Her right through. Phosyne sees it burst from Her belly, shining and clean. Sees the Lady look down at it in fascination. There is no pain upon Her perfect brow.

The blade withdraws, and Voyne, too, can tell something is wrong as the Lady turns.

"Run—" Phosyne gasps, and then, with all her might, she thunders, "*Run.*" The walls shake with it. Treila is there, too, and she, at least, will flee; she is smart enough, but—

But neither of them moves.

The Lady turns to face them both, and Phosyne cannot see Her expression. Cannot see if She is pleased or furious. Phosyne has to know.

She must know.

That hunger crashes into her, steals away all her senses. Without the Lady's attention, without the candle between them, Phosyne's grasp on all the world slips through her fingers. One thing. She must focus on one thing above all the rest, because she can feel the wind gusting outside, can feel the heat ratcheting up, a boiling sun, a broiling sky.

She fixes herself on the flash of Voyne's armor. Iron that will not help her now. Iron that comes too late.

And even though Voyne must understand at least a little, she cuts into the Lady's belly once more.

It changes nothing.

The Lady walks forward along the length of the steel. It slides through Her easily. No blood drips from the wound as She at last reaches Voyne, cups her jaw in both Her hands. Phosyne sees it all in the reflection of Voyne's breastplate.

"Welcome back to the world, Ser Voyne," the Lady says. "Though it was supposed to be you on this blade, if I recall."

Voyne snarls. "It was to be Etrebia's sword," she says, "but you took that from me, too, along with all the rest."

The Lady smiles, delighted. "Vicious thing, I will take my time in savoring you."

"Voyne!" It is Treila's voice, cutting through the roar. She is close at hand, and she is streaked with blood. Hers? No, it does not smell like hers, and Phosyne is falling down a long, dark tunnel as she tries to place it. "You don't need a sword!"

They must have some other weapon. But Voyne isn't moving, and Treila isn't either.

She is trying to, but Phosyne is holding her tight.

Phosyne doesn't remember moving, but she has the woman in her arms now, and Treila is staring at her, confused, as Phosyne leans in, catches a flake of blood between her teeth.

It tastes like honey.

Blood of a saint, then. Which one?

From behind her, she hears the Lady murmuring to Voyne, trusting that Phosyne's distraction will keep Her safe. "But what is this crown about your head? You are built to obey, Ser Voyne. It is written in your bones."

That gets some response, some jerking movement that Phosyne

cannot see the whole of, because she's too busy staring into Treila's eyes.

"They can die?" Phosyne whispers. But she knew this. She has not seen the Warding Saint since Voyne's body was presented, wearing his armor.

No, the important thing is—there need be no iron to do it, because when Treila left her, she was unarmed.

Phosyne staggers back, far enough that she can see all three of them. Treila stepping forward as if to come after her, murderous and betrayed, and Voyne, her hands around the Lady's throat. The Lady in the center of it all, unflappable, serene.

There is the flash of steel, but it's not Voyne's sword. It's the knife, the Lady clutches it in one perfect hand, and before Phosyne can cry out, Treila has thrown herself into Voyne, knocked her away from the Lady, and taken the dagger in her place.

Phosyne cannot see where the blow lands, but she can hear Treila gasp, can hear Voyne snarl as the Lady steps back. The sword slides from Her belly, falls to the floor. It leaves no hole behind. A thicket of thorns grows across the Lady's robes instead, fresh armor, ready to cut.

And Treila is bleeding. She tries to move and can't, a pained and ragged cry issuing from her throat. Voyne has her in her arms, is positioned over her as if to protect.

"It would have been better if you'd never seen her again," the Lady says to Voyne. "It could be only nothingness that was bleeding out. Nothing worth saving, nothing worth staying your hand against me. What a pity that you had to return to her. I gave you a gift, glory and certainty and righteousness, and you squandered it."

Treila spasms against the floor, blood flowing from her gut despite Voyne's hands frantically applying pressure, and that reverses Phosyne's retreat, unsticks her limbs. She throws herself at them, collapses to her knees at Treila's side, fits her hands with Voyne's over the wound.

"I can fix this," she whispers. "I can fix this, I can *fix* this." She understands viscera and flesh, now, and knows healing, received it from this girl's mouth while she lay dying, rotting from the inside from lack of food. Food, food, she needs *food*. She will give Treila food and that will staunch the flow.

The Lady holds out a hand, and in it is an apple.

"Give it to her," the Lady says.

It is golden and perfect.

"No," Treila whispers. "No, I will not eat."

But the juice of it is fragrant and sweet. Phosyne wants it, and can see how it will knit Treila's flesh together again. It will obscure her mind, yes, but it will preserve her body, and what good is a clear mind beyond death?

She is panting, hyperventilating, feeling the pulse of Treila's blood beneath her fingers, when Voyne collides with the Lady in a crash of steel. The apple falls from Her hand, bruising rapidly as it rolls to a stop against Phosyne's thigh.

And the Lady is gone, and in another breath, the memory of Her as well. Phosyne blinks against a blank space, an absence, there and then gone as suddenly as it arose. Cumin coats her tongue, sharp and insistent. *Pay attention*, it says, but she is angry, she is *terrified*, and she can't heed it. The room is getting hotter, is roasting them alive, and it is her fault. She is making the floor below them tremble and see-ing colors she has no names for blossoming into being all around her.

Except no, there's something else, something tangled in the flash of light on metal as Voyne convulses, grapples with the air.

Then Treila cries out, "Down!" and both Phosyne and Voyne obey without question.

Phosyne stares at her. At the blood dried on her chin, and wet on her belly. She can see something shining, buried in the meat of her. A solid, ringing core. Something Phosyne lacks, Voyne lacks, they all are missing.

Something beyond the heaviness of iron, and even more immu-table.

While Treila stares at empty air, perfectly focused, the thing inside her glows more brightly. Phosyne tries to look where Treila looks, to the left of Voyne, but her vision drifts. Slides. This has hap-pened before, Phosyne realizes. In this very room, Voyne had tried to look at Treila, and her gaze had slid. "Go right!" Treila cries. Fresh blood streaks her lips. She is losing too much blood.

The apple still rests against Phosyne's thigh. She can't remember where it came from, but it is also important, *very* important. She must give it to Treila, must chew it fine and pass it tongue to tongue; it is meant to heal, to stop that flow of blood.

She takes a bite, juice exploding in her mouth. Her teeth crush its delicate flesh.

But no. No, if Treila eats this, it will paper over the core of her. Dim the glow. Phosyne can see that now. It will bind her.

Bind. To what? To her? Yes, to her. Feasts of flesh and food grown from nothing, feasts that bewitch the mind and heart and soul. She who provides the feast earns the fealty. But she doesn't want that. She holds too many lives in her chest as it is.

How did they get there? What is she forgetting, so momentous, so horrible?

"Left, left!" Treila cries, voice breaking. Growing weaker. Voyne pivots left and slams her sword into the blur that Phosyne can barely see, can barely remember they are fighting. The weapon does no damage, but the target must still be solid; the force of the blow throws it into the wall, and for just a moment, the Lady is visible again, golden and terrifying. For just a moment, She wears no familiar yellow paint, no beautiful raiment, but is a thing made of air and vine itself, thorn and blood, around a tangled, pulsating stomach.

And then She is gone, and Phosyne's head spins and Voyne staggers, tossing her head like a stallion.

Beneath Phosyne, Treila sags against the floor, and does not look at her. Phosyne wonders briefly, hysterically, if Treila trusts her, or if she simply cannot afford to look away.

Another crack. The thud of a body hitting the floor. Phosyne twists and looks behind her.

Voyne convulses like she's been struck, gasping for breath, barely up on one knee. There is something attacking her, Phosyne remembers. Something old and dangerous and hungry, but Phosyne cannot feel it, except for a sick sense of absence, a lurching slide when she tries to focus.

Voyne will die like this if Treila cannot be her eyes, and Treila cannot be her eyes if she loses much more blood than this or if she is entranced by a swallow of healing food.

So Phosyne dips her head and presses her lips to the bleeding slit in Treila's side, and slides her tongue, thick with chewed fruit, against the wound.

Treila shudders, her head falling back against the stone, and Phosyne can't tell if she moans from pain or pleasure.

All she knows is that the skin heals, and when Phosyne spits out blood and pulp, when she kisses Treila's side one last time, there is only a white mark to show where the blade had pierced her.

Treila shoves her aside.

Phosyne falls back, just in time to hear the crack of Voyne's skull against the floor. The Lady once more exists, standing above the three of them, regarding each in turn.

None move.

Treila is too weak to rise. Voyne has been beaten down one time too many. And the knife is back in the Lady's hands as She stands over Phosyne, surveying the destruction.

"You toy with your food," Phosyne pants. "You could have killed them five times over, couldn't you?"

The Lady doesn't answer, but the slight tightening around Her mouth suggests—no. No, She is struggling, just as they are. She is just as liable to fall.

"You can't kill them, can you?" Phosyne murmurs, frowning. "You can do nothing to them I do not allow. I hold dominion."

But that's not quite right. She did not want Treila run through. Does not want Voyne insensate on the ground, eyelids fluttering as she tries to find one last store of strength within her.

"No, little mouse. I am your minder," the Lady murmurs. "Power flows both ways."

And yet the Lady does not move to cut either Treila's or Voyne's throats.

Phosyne struggles up to her knees, claws her hands into the aether around her, feels the rumble of the heavens outside, but can find not one thing to craft into a weapon. Her mind is blank and too full all at once.

She sways. "What do you want of us?" she asks, because there are no answers at hand.

The Lady smiles. "Only free me, Phosyne, and they might still live."

Another bargain.

Phosyne begins to laugh. She is supposed to be beyond bargains, now. She is supposed to have made the right one. But there is always one more ahead of her, one more dangled morsel that she feels she would die without.

She wants them to live. She is desperate for them to live. But she will not give up this, her last shred of control, for a *might*.

With a howl of rage, Phosyne grasps whatever she can reach. The gnarled, dried husk of the corkindrill, hanging from the ceiling; its teeth are blunt but there is something unseen tangled in them. A star, burning in a vast emptiness. A glittering fragment of mica embedded in enamel. In life, it must have tried to bite the heavens. That tooth sings against her palm. She lunges.

The Lady does not step aside.

"Phosyne," the Lady says, and it is like a brand, like a muzzle. Hearing her name doesn't *stop* her, not quite, but it makes her falter. She goes crashing to her knees, losing her grip on the bit of ephemera that now makes little sense, like every other epiphany that has lingered just out of her reach for the last year. Her thoughts grow dim and fuzzy, the way they had as she had focused on the candle flame. Phosyne doesn't want this anymore, doesn't *need* this anymore.

But there is no taking it back. The Lady has her name. Phosyne gave it to her.

Except—

Phosyne is only one name she has borne.

It is the name of a woman, once a nun, who has abandoned her faith, a desperate mind reaching too far beyond its ken, a woman rotting alone in a tower, protected but not cultivated. Before that was Sefridis, believing and orderly. And before that, another name she barely remembers, a child's name. She has been through so many. She has abandoned two of them. What strains against the Lady's touch is none of them. She is, instead, clothed in fine robes, made of hunger, dancing upon the fretwork of the universe. It is only the bounds of this castle, this web of tight red string, that contains her. She is not Phosyne, not at all.

The name does not apply.

The nameless thing at the Lady's feet looks up. She grins. She fists her hands into the Lady's skirts and hauls Her down.

"Phosyne," the Lady says, eyes shining, as the nameless woman prowls up her body. As she bares her teeth, but does not bite. "Free me. Free us both."

The order slides off her like water.

Water.

Her eyes close to slits, and she sees beneath them a great pool of water, lit with burning flames. The water is hers and hers alone.

"No," the nameless woman says.

They sink into the stone. The Lady thrashes, and the nameless woman feels the bite of the knife into her ribs.

She does not care as they plunge into the cistern, into the light. They strike the water. They roll. They are separated, and the woman's lips part, inhaling, drinking deep. It pours down her throat and in through the wound in her side.

It slakes the hunger in her just a little. Just enough for her to rise up over the Lady, and to grin down in triumph.

"I hold dominion," the woman says, "over more than just you."

And she clicks her tongue.

Two sinuous black forms slip through the grate overhead, and for just a moment, the tufts of wool between their slick scales ignite, and then they crash into the water with great plumes of steam.

The water flares hot, so hot, scalding, *boiling*, and soon the cistern is filled with heady fumes purified and sanctified, and none of this is from this False Lady's hand. No piece of this power flows from the transfer of Her dominion. It comes instead from the nameless woman's past, when she did have a name, a self, a boundary.

Her skin burns.

She screams. Feels herself scalded from within and without, feels the wound close, melting shut. Her blood boils with the Lady's. She is dying.

But arms plunge down from the gap above, through the lattice-work of stone that she left in another life to vent the steam, and they're not enough, they will not bring her up, there's not enough space. They grasp her all the same. They pull, and she is light, and she is planting her feet on the Lady's spasming back, shoving her down, pushing her head below the water as she cooks, cooks, cooks.

She is lifted to the ceiling. She touches the stone and sees beyond it Ser Voyne and Treila, faces red and contorted and desperate. They are trying to save her.

She should not let them, except that she does not think she can die down here. She does not know if the Lady can, either. She doesn't know enough, can never know enough.

Panic splits her, and the rock is like air, and they haul her up into the tower room.

"Phosyne," Ser Voyne entreats. "Phosyne, please—"

She fights.

The name is like lead, heavy and stifling and she does not want to go back into that box, does not want to be trapped once more inside the body that is thrashing, snarling, biting. The stone is solid beneath her back, but only for now. The False Lady's screams are in her ears. She wants nothing more than to open her mouth, unhinge her jaw, swallow it all down and sort it out later.

"*Phosyne*," Treila says, and there comes the sting of a slap. Treila seizes her shoulders, drags her up, and the nameless woman remembers bruises on her throat, chewed fruit between her lips, a day when Treila held her in the sun and tried to calm her fraying, splitting nerves. The day she'd first sunk through the stone.

That is important. She is supposed to remember that. She is supposed to remember . . .

Kindness.

That's it. She is supposed to remember kindness. And what she is now is not kind, is not deserving of kindness, is beyond . . . all of that.

"Phosyne," she mumbles, like a spell. Like an anchor.

She feels a little smaller.

She feels a little steadier.

She doesn't want either of those things except that she *does*. This is unsustainable. She wants to have her room, her little world. She wants control. There is no control in this.

Phosyne has control, though. Little scraps, but enough. Enough to build a little world.

Groaning, she pulls away from Treila's and Voyne's hands, onto her belly. The stone below her holds, the steam rising, heating the sodden silk against her chest even as it plasters against her back, cooling quick. She stares down at the Lady, bounded by Phosyne's scraps. Boiling in her flames, in her water, restrained by the stone that lets Phosyne come and go as she pleases. The Lady is screaming. The Lady is snarling.

The Lady will be soup soon enough.

Phosyne smooths the stone back into place, sealing Her away. It goes readily.

The rest of the keep slides with it.

Because the problem remains that Phosyne still holds dominion over the whole of the castle, and all the lives within it. The knowledge still tears at her. A name gives her an anchor, something to hold on to, but it does not stop the hunger.

And it does not make the world any smaller.

She doesn't know how to set things back to rights. She does not *want* to set things back to rights. The death of the Lady feels like enough, though she knows it isn't. She wants to stay this way, but she *can't* stay this way. Outside her windows, the world is breaking; she can see stone floating in the air. She can see the moon nestled in the sun's embrace. Strange, cold twilight has enveloped the world, and for a moment, all she can feel is delight. Delight, to experience this new working of the heavens.

This can't continue.

Phosyne looks up at Ser Voyne, blade shining in her hand. She looks at Treila, blood-soaked, murderous, as certain as she's ever been.

And then she plunges her hands into the stone and lets it solidify there, chaining her. Stilling things for just a moment, just long enough. "Kill me," she begs, and bows her head to expose her throat. "Kill me, please."

The sound of metal over metal; Voyne comes close, kneels before her. Fits one hand around Phosyne's throat, as if it is meant to be there. Phosyne gasps, shudders, pushes into it.

But Voyne does not tighten her fingers, only urges Phosyne to look up at her.

"No."

51

OYNE'S DENIAL STRIKES Phosyne hard. It drags a sob from her, and the world sobs too. Aymar shudders, and outside the rain begins again.

"Why?" she begs. "Look at me. *Look.*"

Voyne looks.

She sees, through the haze of a ringing skull and burning adrenaline, a frightened, desperate woman, whose skin is red and scalded, whose robes are stained crimson with blood over her ribs, whose eyes are the same cloudy gray they were the day they met. She sees a woman she has sworn to protect, though the king she gave the oath to no longer lives, and wouldn't merit obedience if he did. She sees the woman who, in her own way, has ushered Aymar through a great and terrible transition.

The False Lady is dead, or at least locked away. If her words are to be trusted, Phosyne holds dominion over every life in Aymar, with possibly only the exclusion of Treila and Voyne.

Voyne doesn't feel excluded, not really.

"I am your minder," Voyne says, with more patience than she feels. Her certainty doesn't remove her fear, not even close. But the world is spinning apart around them, and Voyne cannot fix that herself. She can't fix any of this herself. Treila holds the leash of the beasts that wait to devour them, and Phosyne holds the keys to the world. "I will bring you back to yourself. Do you trust me?"

Phosyne bares her teeth, shakes her head.

"She will kill you if she has to," Treila says softly, from just over Voyne's shoulder. Voyne fancies she can hear a strained smile in her voice. "Do not doubt that. That she hasn't says there is still hope."

Phosyne laughs, weakly. She weeps. She folds down, held up only by Voyne's hand around her throat.

Voyne tightens her fingers just a little, a reminder of the chapel, of the cistern, of everything between them.

Phosyne's breath catches.

"Let me take you from this place," Voyne says. Her head is foggy, but she knows they cannot remain here. Sweat rolls from her skin, even now that the boiling stew below them is closed off. "Relax. Trust me, Phosyne."

She tightens her fingers, and, like in the cistern, it lets Phosyne's hands slide from the stone. Voyne pulls her up to her feet, her aching muscles protesting every inch.

And when they are both upright, together, Voyne slides her other arm behind Phosyne's knees and lifts.

She takes a moment to make sure she has her footing, and looks up to see Treila evaluating the two of them, standing as well, Voyne's sword clutched in her arms. Alive and whole. It is more than Voyne had hoped for.

Phosyne saved her, too.

Voyne could not have borne her loss. She knows that, as much as she knows she cannot abandon the woman in her arms.

Together, they leave the tower and make their way down the stairs, breathing ragged in the close space.

Outside, the wind echoes the heaving of their lungs, bursting against the face of the keep. The stairs rock and yaw beneath them, like nothing so much as a ship adrift. They are all adrift, here in the eye of Phosyne's power, raw and terrible and tasting, unavoidably, of *her*.

A snap. A cry. Something else torn loose, tossed into the swirling abyss Voyne can see whenever she passes by an arrow slit.

Phosyne is far too light, and far from pliant. She isn't trying to fight, Voyne reminds herself, but that doesn't stop the paroxysms of pain and power from twisting her frail body, pitching her this way and that, making her spine bend and nearly crack as she howls.

Treila keeps casting wary looks back at them, and Voyne keeps her expression closed off.

She hopes they will reach the throne room. She has a suspicion this will only work in that space.

Voyne has learned a thing or two about negotiations, about oaths, about intent. Everything within these walls is an exchange; their horrible guests had only made it more literal. Power bargained for sustenance. Obligations forming the warp and weft of the world, reciprocal and definitional. She was, perhaps, the first to feel the truth of it, eating at the False Lady's table, falling at Her feet. She'd come very close, she knows now, to freeing them all that first night. If she'd only kept her head, struck the False Lady instead of the Warding Saint, they could all still be slowly starving, waiting for the end.

That—that is all that waits for them on the other end, though. Voyne stops on the stairs, mere feet from the closed door to the throne room. Treila makes it a few more steps, then pauses with her hand on the wood. Glances over her shoulder.

"If I do this," Voyne says, "if I break the siege, then what next?"

Treila quirks a brow. "Then we walk out of here."

"Etrebia—"

"Is gone. I have seen it. We exist, in here, in a bubble. Beyond the gates is freedom, Voyne."

Her mouth goes dry.

"The refugees," she murmurs.

"Those that live," Treila agrees, slowly, with a fine smile, so very much like a pleased cat's, "have survived the worst siege in history, and will walk out with us. A fine trick, hm?"

A few nights' horrors for salvation.

Voyne only prays they will not remember.

"Come," Treila says. "Whatever you have planned, let's do it quick. There's one saint left in the keep, and while I am eager to tear his throat out too, I'm a little woozy."

Voyne nods, and cradles Phosyne a little closer.

Phosyne whimpers, and presses her face to Voyne's throat. Outside, lightning splits the sky, and one of the guard posts spins lazily in the air, shedding tables and chairs and, Voyne imagines, playing cards. A whole keep, rent apart.

They don't have much time to save the rest.

Treila pushes open the door, and Voyne carries Phosyne over the red and white and yellow paint that has dried tacky on the stone. The hive behind the throne has collapsed in upon itself, black now, blighted, bloated from too much weight, too unnatural an energy. There is no hum of bees as Voyne kneels and deposits Phosyne, gently, on the floor. Rises and steps over her, goes to the throne.

Sits.

Feels the echo of hands upon her scalp, a circlet of iron, a promise fulfilled.

Treila looks at her above Phosyne's shivering form, then skirts around her, comes to the side of the throne. Behind it. Her feet crush foulness, break it open, spill Jacynde's defiance back out into the world.

When Treila settles one hand on Voyne's shoulder, leaning the rest of her weight against the back of the throne, it feels right and good. Voyne tips her head back. Smiles.

Treila's lips quirk in response.

"You had better know what you're doing," she warns.

She is magnificent. Tested and honed and entirely herself. That the False Lady ever stole her from Voyne's eyes is a travesty that can only be rectified by another decade's fond appraisals.

"Do you trust me?" Voyne asks, voice catching, hopeful. "Because I trust you, to the ends of the earth."

"You killed my father," Treila reminds her. "Sentenced me to starve. And taught me how to fight, and made me hope for better things. Yes, I trust you."

Voyne nods. Looks back at Phosyne.

Watches as her spine arches against the stone.

"Come here," Voyne says. "Please, Phosyne. Just a little more."

"It's too much," Phosyne gasps, convulsing.

"I know," Ser Voyne murmurs. "But I can bear it. Give yourself back into my care, Phosyne, and I will bear the weight for you."

Phosyne must come these last few inches on her own, but Voyne believes in her.

She holds out a hand.

Phosyne stares at it, shivering half out of her skin.

"I'd like that," Phosyne whispers.

"Then come. Kneel before me."

"Swear—fealty?" Her lips twist, and then her eyes close again and she shudders, her whole body quaking. She flickers in and out of nothingness, transparent for just a moment, and then distorted, elbows tugged unnaturally far from her body, limbs attenuated.

"And in return receive protection," Voyne affirms. "A give-and-take. Not just once, but ongoing. A relationship we can negotiate."

Treila makes a considering, pleased noise behind her. "That could work," she agrees. "A reordering. Back to how it should be."

And in those words are the weight of Carcabonne, and her father's house. Treila understands as well as she does.

She, too, reaches out a hand.

"A little farther," Treila murmurs. "I don't think you are fresh out of miracles, not yet. One last one, and then you can rest."

Phosyne shivers, then pushes up. Plants her hands beneath her and lifts her weight. As Voyne looks on, she drags herself the last few inches closer and sags against the throne.

She lets her head fall against Voyne's knee, and lifts one hand.

"A miracle?" she whispers.

"A miracle," Voyne agrees. "From the depths of you. I know you know the way."

Phosyne nods and settles her hand in Voyne's. Her eyes close. She focuses, and outside the keep, the winds still to a bare hush. The floor ceases its rocking. Everything is still, a held breath.

"To you, Ser Voyne, I give the mastery of me," Phosyne whispers. "For I hold within me dominion over every life within this castle, and relinquish them to your care. And any strength that yet lives in my bones, I give also to you, so that you may direct it to where it is most needed."

A smile twists her lips.

"I could use the help," she adds, opening her eyes.

Voyne smiles down at her. "I accept," she murmurs.

And slowly, gently, the world rights itself.

It starts with an exhale; the throne room gasps, and the burning heat of summer flees, replaced with the calm coolness of an autumn day. Through the windows, no longer blocked by hungry beasts, Voyne can see the guard tower settling once more into its moorings. The world rushes to right itself. Or perhaps it is her: her knowledge of how Aymar is meant to be, its defenses, its weaknesses. Her rigid certainty that, for better or worse, the world endures human suffering. That it is worth it, to restore order, instead of breaking and beginning anew.

Carcabonne, after all, was rebuilt. The lives were lost, the suffering cannot be erased, but Carcabonne continues. Aymar will as well.

Phosyne's eyes close, and her head grows heavy against Voyne's lap, but a quick touch proves her heart beats still. Treila's throat clicks behind her as she swallows. Rests her cheek against Voyne's head, in place of any iron crown. Outside, the sun shines down clear upon the yard, and Voyne can hear the soft sounds of other lives. Not of feasting, or of terror, but of instinct. Bodies moving to the light. To water, of their own accord. To each other.

They will have so many questions. They have lost so much.

Voyne closes her eyes and lets her head fall back against the throne with a sigh. One of her hands curls into Phosyne's hair. The other lifts to touch Treila's arm.

"Is it real?" she asks them both. "Or am I dreaming again?"

"It's real," says a fourth voice.

In an instant, Voyne is on her feet. Her blade is in her hand, put there by Treila, who stands beside her, lips curling in a snarl. Even Phosyne stirs, braced against the throne, bleary eyes taking in their visitor.

The Absolving Saint gazes back at them.

Or rather it is the creature they have called the Absolving Saint; but he no longer clings as strongly to his stolen iconography. He does retain most of his mortal appearance, the right number of limbs, the correct proportions. He does not flicker in and out of view the way the lesser beasts once did. He even keeps his silvered lips.

But his eyes are glittering black, multifaceted, like an insect's. His skin is glossy gold. His hair has been replaced with one sleek, shining piece of carapace.

"Peace," he murmurs. He holds his hands apart, and they are empty. He still wears an apron draped over his front, pristine as always. Voyne remembers the platters he has born, the offerings he has made.

"Peace?" she asks him.

"Yes, ser knight," he says. "I would beg of you an exchange, if you would let me."

"You will forgive me," Voyne says, "if I am not so quick to bargain."

"An entreaty, then," he says. He lowers his head in supplication. "A favor that I shall beg of you, except that I have something to offer as well."

Treila steps forward. "And if I tear your throat out instead?"

He regards her, inclines his head again. "Then I would accept it, though I wouldn't have much choice."

"Let him speak," Phosyne says. Her words slur slightly, but her head is up when Voyne glances back at her. "He has always been a thoughtful one."

"Observant," Treila adds.

Voyne looks about them. It is three against one, and they have bested the False Lady already. She does not want to be too arrogant, but . . . perhaps. Perhaps she can take the role of leader, not warlord.

She steps back and lowers herself onto the throne once more. She keeps her sword across her knees but lifts up one hand in invitation.

He approaches.

He goes down on his knees.

He offers up—

A knife.

Treila's knife, if her sharp inhale is any indication. But the knife went down with the False Lady, into the cistern.

"How?" Voyne asks, sharp and harsh.

He spreads his palms below the blade once more, more deference.

"The kitchen," he says.

Behind her, Treila lets out a startled laugh. "The cistern."

"Just so. It was nearly too large for the pipe."

"And now you bring it here," Voyne says. Later, she will wonder at the image, turn it this way and that and hold it up in the light. A creature of terrible power, still in the kitchens, trying once more to prepare a meal. He is, she will realize, built for service as much as she once was.

"In return for this knife, Phosyne was granted dominion over this castle and all the lives inside it that my Lady held. That dominion now resides in you." He cants his head, considers his next words carefully. Perhaps he did not think to make it this far into his speech. "You want us gone, I am sure, those of us who remain. Though, to be fair, we are not many."

Treila laughs, darkly.

"But we cannot leave without your releasing us," he says. "And in exchange for returning this blade, I would have our release, if you were to be so merciful."

Voyne is not inclined to mercy. "You have destroyed us," she says, simply. "Turned us against one another, fogged our minds, induced us to indulge in horrors. You have feasted upon us. You have fed our own to us."

"You had already done it yourselves," the Absolving Saint counters. "Unknowing in both cases, I am sure."

She regards him cooly.

He quails, eventually. "It is not the same," he admits.

"No. You made us delight in it. Gave us false hope, and devoured us to your benefit."

"Yes."

"And why should I not keep you here to starve?"

The Absolving Saint hums, and gives every appearance of consideration. But it is not he who speaks, in the end, to argue for clemency.

It is Phosyne, pillowing her cheek once more against Voyne's thigh.

"The blade," Phosyne murmurs. "It lets his kind ignore the bonds of iron that have kept him at bay. That keep his kind out of towns and palaces, from doing there what they have done here."

Voyne shudders at the thought.

And to his credit, the Absolving Saint inclines his head. "Yes. And if you will take it in exchange for our freedom, we will once again be hurt by it."

"We go back to the way things were," Treila translates.

"A fair trade," the Absolving Saint suggests. "More than fair."

"And are there more of you?" Voyne asks. "More than yourself and what creatures Treila did not set upon one another? Or is this your entire world?"

Phosyne, at her hip, is alert. Judging. Treila, too, at her shoulder.

"There are," he says. "And when I leave here, the bonds we have made will transfer to all of them."

"Lying?" Voyne asks.

"No," Phosyne says. Treila does not reply.

Voyne looks up to her.

"Does it matter?" Treila asks. "There are dark things in the forest always. Something will eat regardless. Better not to risk making their teeth any sharper."

Voyne considers, then nods. She gestures. "Lay down your knife, then, hungry thing. But before you go—"

He hesitates, half-bowed.

"Phosyne," Voyne continues, "please word this for me. I want everybody in this castle who has unknowingly suffered to remain unknowing. They are stirring, even now. I would not visit this horror upon them, if it is within my power."

"Horror," Treila offers, "shapes character. And it did happen." She would know; those dark things in the forest found her years ago. But whatever she found there is not the same as what happened within these walls.

"They had no control over themselves during it," Voyne counters. "It's not the same, dear heart."

Treila blushes. Says nothing more.

Voyne looks at Phosyne.

"In exchange for the return of the knife and all the meaning therein," Phosyne murmurs, "and in exchange for gifting those in this castle that are not us, and that are not you, a gentle evening's slumber from which they shall wake fed and unknowing of anything beyond your arrival at the gates of Aymar, you are free to go and take your creatures with you, never to return to this plateau, may we never look upon you again."

The words hang in the air, heavy with meaning and intent.

The Absolving Saint nods and lays down his knife.

It makes a faint ringing sound against the stone.

When he stands, he looks thinner, less lustrous. He offers them a small, silvered smile, and leaves the throne room.

Voyne lets free a deep and exhausted sigh.

"Treila," Voyne murmurs, "tell me more about what waits outside those gates."

"I confess I know very little," the woman says, but she circles around to the front, holds out her hands. "Except that it is autumn, and there is a small band of soldiers waiting for us. Ours, not Etrebian. The world beyond is safe, for now, and waiting for us. But they will ask where the king is."

Phosyne goes very pale, even as Voyne rises and reaches down to bring her along with them.

"The king," Phosyne says, "is dead."

"He is," Voyne murmurs. Slowly, they make their way to the door. Down to the yard. Out into a crisp autumn day, the sun shining down from its right place against the blue of the sky. "But in all likelihood, one of the princes took up his mantle months ago. There was, after all, no relief force."

In scattered tents, far fewer than there should have been, they see people sleeping. Dreaming, in the shade. The dirt no longer bears any trace of blood or silty storm. Everything is still and quiet.

"The world goes on without us," Voyne adds, softly. She leans heavily against Treila, against Phosyne, as they approach the gate.

There is nobody there to man it, but it stands open.

"The way I worded it," Phosyne says, after a moment, "they will think there was a miracle here. The Constant Lady and Her saints, in truth. A visitation. An intercession."

She's right, of course. And their role in it will be lost: three starving women who struggled for mastery of themselves in the face of a spiraling world.

"Can we leave here?" Treila asks, softly, sounding unaccountably young for the gore that stains her to the bone.

"Only one way to find out," Phosyne says, and her eyes flash with an eager hunger. "And we must hope we can. For there is no food in Aymar Castle."

Voyne pulls them both close and, together, they take the next step.

Acknowledgments

The Starving Saints is a strange book from a strange time. I wrote the first draft at the tail end of 2020, after my first miscarriage (of what would be many), living largely in lockdown—I was, to put it simply, a mess. I wrote this book out of order, sometimes down to the sentence level, in an attempt to get around my anxiety. Was the book too ambitious? Too strange? Too ridiculous? I'd never tried writing a book with three POVs, or in a medieval-inspired setting, and I'd only ever written present tense in fanfiction.

So, first, to the people who got me through that wild first draft:

David, you knew from the word go that my weird cannibalism book was going to be a big one. You dove headfirst into research and theorycrafting with me, helped me figure out how obligation and fealty were going to play a crucial role in the plot, and cheered me on the whole way. This book would not exist without you.

Alex and Integra, my first readers, my rubber ducks, my dearest friends: you know what happened to Ser Leodegardis in the end, even if nobody else can. Treasure that.

Once that initial draft was wrestled into submission, it went to Art, ST Gibson, and Emma Mieko Candon, who promptly lost their shit in the most supportive and wonderful ways. Thank you all for reading this book in its larval form.

To Caitlin McDonald and Cameron McClure: you found *The Starving Saints* a home, something we knew would happen eventually, but I despaired over happening anytime soon. And, Caitlin—you were right, Ser Voyne *does* have two hands.

To the Harper Voyager team: I'm so glad to be back! Nate Lanman, you're a fantastic editor, and your focus and delight in this project was unparalleled. Owen Corrigan, that is one hell of a cover design. Lara Báez, Andrew DiCecco, Shelby Peak, Patrick Barry, and so many other members of the Voyager team that I haven't yet had a chance to meet, you've worked so hard to make this book the total package and helped it reach readers. Thank you.

Jason Stevan Hill, I first came up with the idea for a disillusioned knight, a mad mage, and a pissed-off rat catcher as a Choice of Games concept, which we ultimately didn't pursue. It took a few extra years, but those bones remain in this book. Thank you.

Cherith, Blushie, and my other Dragon Age fandom friends, I hope you enjoy my Ser Voyne as much as you did my Ser Cauthrien.

Lynn, this was the first book that I wrote in your living room. Thank you, as always, for your space, support, and hospitality. And thank you for letting me take over the entire apartment for my manic weekend banging out the last quarter of this book in wild-eyed isolation.

And finally, to my son, James: you weren't here for the start of this book, but you sure are here for its grand debut. You're going to have to steal it off my shelf if you want to read it before you're fourteen. At least.